EVE OF MAN

Anne Ferretti

A special thanks to Kay for her help and never-ending support.
A very special thanks to my husband for supporting my dreams and for never growing tired of seeing me bent over my computer.

Copyright 2014 © By Anne Ferretti

All rights reserved

No part of this book may be reproduced, or stored in retrieval form, or transmitted in any form by any means electronic, mechanical, photocopying, recording or otherwise without express permission from the author.

The characters and events portrayed in this book are fictitious. Any similarity to real persons, living or dead, is coincidental and not intended by this author.

In nature, competition to survive guarantees only the strongest species will prevail, thus eliminating the unfit. It is the evolutionary theory known as survival of the fittest.

अग्र

Table of Contents

Eve of Man
The Harvest
1 The Spread
2 US Embassy
3 The Adita
4 The Gift
5 Hulk
6 Departure
7 Crossing the Strait
8 Reunion
8 Fur Elise
9 Christmas & Planes
10 Eve
11 Flying Under the Radar
12 Unlikely Ally
13 Best Western
14 Unknowns
15 Christmas
16 Life for Death
17 Chance Meeting
18 The Greatest Odds
19 The Harvest
20 Blood Typing
21 Saving Ryan
22 Nowhere to Hide
23 Brothers
24 Germany
25 Point of No Return
26 After
27 Eve of Man
28 Proposal
29 Guarantees
30 Change
31 Final Departure
32 Paru
Excerpt from LIGHT OF EVE (Part III)

Anne Ferretti

THE HARVEST

In the aftermath of a brutal alien invasion and a winter storm that left several feet of snow blanketing the landscape, Earth's temperatures plummeted to the single digits. Veiled in the falling snow, corpses of the missing were dropped from the sky. Within forty-eight hours, other than a few desperate survivors, all signs of life had vanished from the face of the Earth. For one such desperate soul, Captain Austin Reynolds, a slow nightmare had begun as he set out on a quest across the frozen tundra that was now the United States.

He traveled under the guide and protection of a mysterious being called Eve, hoping she would take him to his pregnant wife. Eve had protected him since childhood, saving his life many times throughout his twenty-seven years and he had placed all his trust in her.

Austin journeyed to Section Seven, a top-secret facility hidden under Cheyenne Mountain. The Section was where he expected to find General Roth and answers about his missing wife. As Austin worked his way toward Colorado, he crossed paths with other survivors; Luke, a college football star; Madison, a Tampa Bay police officer; Edward, the last tax attorney standing; and Zack, a genius who made millions selling marijuana. They were drawn to Austin and he'd willingly accepted the responsibility for their safety. This was as much for his sense of duty as for his redemption.

Upon reaching Cheyenne, Austin discovered General Roth had taken a one-way trip down the rabbit hole and believed himself to be chosen by God to carry out divine orders. Roth tried to lure Austin into his web of deceit with promises of finding his wife and son. For Austin, the general's promises presented a conflict between duty and personal pursuits, which forced him to choose his own agenda over that he'd sworn to protect at all costs. The consequences of this decision led him to the planet Bliss, a newly discovered planet only a few knew existed. On Bliss, a place of untold truths and unending lies, he met Eve's people and discovered what they'd been hiding from him since Eve first came into his life.

Eve of Man picks up where **The Harvest** left off. I hope you enjoy.

1 THE SPREAD

COLOGNE, GERMANY
12:00 am
Military Counterintelligence Service (MCS)

In a room buzzing with computers and high-tech gear, a young baby-faced soldier sat at one of the many terminals, a bored look holding his face captive. He glanced up at the large screen on the wall with indifference. The live streaming video gave a bird's eye view of the United States or at least where the country should be located. He'd been assigned this duty two months ago. A shit detail as far as he was concerned. Every day the same old thing, watching the screen, watching nothing happen. He set his chin into his hand, the pressure scrunched his lips together and pushed his fleshy cheeks up into his eyes. His eyelids drooped, threatening to close down at any second. He fought the sleepiness by tapping his fingers.

Tap-tap-tap… Tap-tap…. Tap.

His eyelids fell, darkness fell, the battle over sleep was lost…

He jerked awake, sitting up with a start and taking a quick check over his shoulder, hoping his superiors hadn't noticed his lapse. With a relieved sigh, he turned back to the screen, rubbing his eyes in the process. His vision refocused on the same white mass that had covered the United States and Canada for over a year. As he watched, his eyes widened, he leaned forward and then stood up, waving his arm behind his head to catch someone's attention. An officer noticed the soldier waving and walked over to him. About to say something about his conduct, the officer stopped in his tracks, his eyes riveted to the screen. The white mass was moving, spreading down toward South America.

"It's moving," Baby Face said, stating the obvious for lack of knowing what else to say.

The others in the room gathered behind the soldier. After a year of waiting and watching, and no activity, their initial reaction was to stare, mouths agape. The mass rolled over the top of Mexico, moving slowly at first and then picking up momentum. Within a matter of seconds, South America disappeared. Only then did the ranking officer, Major Gaynor, consider sending a warning. The point of acting had come and gone, if it ever was a point at all and Gaynor just stared at the screen.

"Get Agent Bosch on the phone," Gaynor instructed the soldier standing next to him, the uptick in his voice giving away his uneasiness. The soldier nodded, his eyes still glued to the screen, expecting, or wanting, something more to take place. Gaynor cleared his throat motivating the young man to pick up the phone.

A buzz of nervous excitement flowed through the room. Although no closer to having answers than from when the cloud formation initially dropped, they welcomed and feared any sign of change. Any sign at this point held meaning over the nothingness they'd been dealing with, and also worth a rise in heartbeats per minute. Every mission or attempt to gain access into the cloud failed to provide insight or a clue to what happened. One drone after another flew into the mass, never to return. The computer systems tracking the drones proved useless, returning blank screens as soon as the drones disappeared into the white nothing. Mighty warships and submarines simply vanished from radar screens never to be heard from again. Pilots stopped volunteering after the list of missing grew to over one hundred. The nations remaining, those left to make the big decisions, gave up trying to enter the United States or Canada. *Watch and wait* became the standard approach. Watch and wait, while hoping for the best and assuming the worst.

Six months after the last drone disappeared, hope waned to a whisper and the mood darkened. In a last-ditched effort to gain access, the Russians offered their only remaining drone to fly one more mission. The drone flew in low, and they'd all held their breath, hoping data would be sent back. As with all flights before, this one failed and hopes crumbled, coming near to falling into the dark pit of despair. With all communications from the West dead, they'd no way of knowing that their concept of the worst didn't scratch the surface of the situation overseas. They'd no way of knowing how well off they'd been while the mass was stationary. Major Gaynor realized many unknowns existed still, but wasn't ready to give up. He thought maybe the time to take another shot was upon them. The prospect of going in excited and unnerved him. Traditional methods proved useless, leaving only one alternative to consider. He didn't have to wonder who would be suicidal enough to volunteer.

"Agent Bosch sir." The soldier handed Gaynor the phone.

"Bosch. You guys seeing this?" Gaynor asked the obvious first.

"You know we are."

"What do you think?"

"I think maybe it's time you cleared me to go in."

"I still think you're crazy. No maybe about it."

"Maybe I am. Maybe I'm not," Bosch said, "but your opinion of my mental capacity doesn't change anything."

Gaynor grunted in response. Despite the agent being thirty years his junior, they'd become good friends. Over the past year, he and his wife Ada had welcomed the American into their home and treated him like family, an understatement in his wife's regard. She thought of Kyle as her own son.

"Ada will never speak to me again," Gaynor added, hoping guilt would hold sway in his decision.

"I have to try," Bosch replied, desperation clung to the edge of his voice. "Or I'll never have peace."

"I know," Gaynor answered. "Can you at least wait for us to send in another drone?"

"How long?" Bosch asked.

Gaynor heard the underlying frustration in the young man's tone. "We'll have to contact the Italians. I think they're the only country with a drone. A week, maybe two." The call would take minutes to make, but Gaynor wanted to delay the agent's departure for as long as possible. The delay was as much to avoid Ada's wrath, as to allow more time to pass, to allow for, by some miracle, contact with someone, anyone, overseas.

"I'll give you one week. Then I'm going in," Bosch said. "Even if it's without permission."

"That won't be necessary," Gaynor replied. "I should know more in a couple of days."

"Thanks, Will."

"For sending you to your death? You're not welcome. And you will come by the house tomorrow for dinner."

"Need back up?" Bosch asked.

"Damn right."

"See you then."

Gaynor handed the phone back to the soldier and sat down in a nearby chair. In his thirty years working for MCS, he'd never experienced anything like this. WWII had been written into the history books by the time he was born. His grandmother had taken great pains in providing him with a full understanding of what took place during that war. As a special bedtime treat, she would tell the story of how the Royal Air Force dropped fifteen hundred tons of explosives on top of their heads. She'd go into great detail of how his grandfather dug them out of the rubble with his bare hands, only to find their home no longer standing. He wondered what his grandfather might have thought of the world's current state of affairs, of this war with an invisible enemy.

Many discussions occurred amongst Will and friends, as well as with his colleagues over the sad state of affairs. Surviving the disappearance of North America was always the common thread of these talks. The words *'minor miracle'* were thought and mentioned often, and with good reason. In the first few months, the chaos ensued like nothing Major Gaynor or anyone had ever experienced. He imagined the dark ages to have been similar. His grandmother would have blamed God; everything bad fell into God's lap as far as she was concerned. Gaynor would have argued she was wrong. God didn't own this one and though Will didn't believe in the devil as a physical entity, he believed in evil.

Throughout the turmoil, people somehow managed to persevere, to muster up a resilience they hadn't known they possessed. The surviving countries settled down into a relative calm. Markets stabilized, panic was squashed, and people moved on in the best way they knew how. A minor miracle? In Gaynor's opinion, their survival constituted a major miracle and represented only the tip of the iceberg. Sustaining in the aftermath had been the real test of their true grit. Society and its many rules persisted. New rules were instated, replacing or changing the old in order to suit the current state of affairs.

One such order, issued within hours after the event by the collective governmental powers, brought all air traffic to a grinding halt. This order was enforced for several months after the event, stranding millions of travelers, business and vacationing alike. Some resigned themselves to becoming temporary and sometimes permanent residents of wherever they happened to be stuck. For the most part, the transients were treated with kindness and hospitality. For the most part meant not for all the part, as unscrupulous predators who thrived on such situations came alive. End of days scams, money scams, you name it scams, attacked from all directions. Looters slithered out from under their rocks to take advantage of this situation that was favorable to their particular lifestyle. They broke windows, stole TVs, set cars on fire, all because the conditions were ripe. Eventually, the law dealt with the dregs of society and they crawled back into their slimy holes of existence waiting for the next opportunity, comforted in knowing there would be another. Although considered the scum of society, these parasites understood human nature better than many of those considered educated in such matters.

A few months after the event, people stopped asking questions. They stopped asking about the happenings overseas or the cloud mass. Not because they no longer cared, but quite simply because no one had the answers, so they stopped asking. At least to any government official, who many believed was either hiding the truth or didn't know what the hell happened. When an opinion formed on the latter belief, which happened often, the officials were viewed as incompetent, idiots and worse. Although the general populous gave up asking the government for an explanation, plenty of speculation went on behind closed doors and in dark corners of local pubs. All of this chatter a wasted effort. The answers weren't theirs to know.

Life continued under a constant state of unease. The weather became a topic of conversation for what might be considered obvious reasons. However, the only obvious reason was the white mass of clouds might move in their direction at any given moment. In the early days, sirens blasted the airwaves whenever a cloud mass appeared on the radar. People hid in storm shelters, and cities and towns went into lockdown. After several months of repeating this activity, resulting in nothing more than normal weather occurrences, the government ceased sounding the sirens. But unease had embedded itself into people's lives as a habit and, despite the sirens being silent, whenever the clouds rolled in people went inside not to emerge until the sun rose high in a clear blue sky.

2 US EMBASSY

The offices of the United States Embassy occupied the top floor of an unassuming ten-story brick building situated on the Rhine River. The US shared the building with Armenia, Spain, Bosnia, Italy, Australia, Russia, and Argentina to name a few. Within the building, close to five hundred people worked at the various consulates and embassies, carrying on the world's affairs in twenty or more different languages. On a normal day, the building hummed with activity; people went about their daily duties, phones rang, copy machines copied. A well-organized hive. On the day the white mass moved the bees shifted into high gear and the hum turned into a manic buzz.

In a corner office on the top floor, Agent Kyle Bosch paced in front of a wall-sized picture window, the swarming bees around him only a small beep on his internal radar. From his vantage point, the view of Cologne and the Rhine was five stars. The view was the single notable attribute of the office. A laptop and a mug of stale coffee kept company on an oversized walnut desk. An office chair and an old leather couch kept company with the desk. The walls were bare of personal effects, giving the impression the office was used on a temporary basis, if at all.

For Kyle, the office had served dual purposes over the past year. During the long days after the cloud's appearance, a place to pace, to ponder, to wonder what the hell was going to happen next and when. At night, after a few too many beverages, he'd pass out on the couch. The couch resulted in a stiff back and neck but was still his preferred place to catch the sun rising, a seldom occurrence in Cologne. If not the office, he was waking up in some woman's bed. This usually resulted in him creeping away like a thief in the night and going through great pains to not awaken whatever nameless female he'd met the night before. He made it a point to not know or remember their names. Cologne was temporary. A reminder he repeated to himself anytime his emotions tried to override his determination.

On rare occasions, he'd accepted Ada's invitation to spend the night in their guest room. Those evenings spent with Ada and Will were the closest he'd come to feeling sane, to feeling like the world had not spun out of control and they all weren't hanging on by a thread. The normalness kept him from becoming a permanent guest in the Gaynor household. Normal dulled his senses and diminished his memories to whispers in his mind. He didn't want whispers, he wanted and needed those memories to stay loud, to continue reminding him of what was at stake if he became complacent. Although he'd attempted to numb his mind and body with Kölsch on a regular basis, Kyle remained in a constant state of alertness. A curse he sometimes thought.

Curse or blessing, he was going to need every advantage at his disposal if he had any hope of surviving the unknown enemy overseas. His plan had been conceived months prior, but Will had refused to even entertain the possibility of sending him into the white mass. Kyle was confident in his success and had already decided to act upon his plan before Will called. Now, with Will's help, preparing to leave would be easier on all involved. Kyle knew that to send in a drone was a stall tactic, but he'd allow his friend that time, which was more for Ada, his surrogate mother, than Will. For Ada, who reminded him of his own mother and put up with way too much of his shit, he would wait a few more days. He owed her that much.

It was fate or dumb luck that Kyle met the Gaynors at all. Shortly before the Western part of the world disappeared. He'd been an active duty member of the United States Army for exactly three weeks. A twenty-one-year-old cocky know it all, who specialized in trouble, getting in it and causing it. Not handsome in a GQ kind of way, but in a way that women were drawn to him like moths to a flame and much of the reason why he found himself with a bleeding nose or knuckles or both by the end of a night out. Could he be blamed for the fact another guy's girlfriend wandered over to talk to him or that another guy's wife slipped her private cell phone number into his pocket? He didn't think so.

On the night they met, Major Gaynor happened to be witness to a particular brouhaha involving Kyle, fists up, in the middle of five very stout German soldiers. The offense had something to do with a fiancée of one of the soldiers. At the last possible second the Major intervened, saving Kyle from being pulverized. When Kyle later asked why he bothered, Gaynor said it was because he saw no fear in Kyle's eyes and figured he wouldn't give up until he was either dead or in a coma. The major was close to right. Fear for his own well-being wasn't an emotion that governed Kyle's life.

Kyle had accepted the major's offer for a ride home, although at the time he felt it was more of an order than a request. Gaynor hadn't lectured for too long but made it clear he didn't approve. Kyle wasn't so young and dumb to not know when to keep his mouth shut. The major could have taken Kyle to his commanding officer, who happened to be a good friend of Gaynor's. But he hadn't. He believed in the good in people and he'd sensed Kyle was good people. In the end, it worked out for the best, as it was later on that night the world went dark. When the lights came on forty-eight hours later the Western side of the globe was covered by a white mass of nothing.

In the mêlée that followed, Kyle found himself guarding the front entrance gates to the brick building where he now worked. Unable to reach their home, Major and Ada Gaynor arrived at the embassy, tired, scared and seeking shelter. Against orders, Kyle opened the gates. A bond of friendship formed between the trio and soon after Ada unofficially adopted him (officially in her mind). The couple had no children and only one nephew, who visited every few months. Ada, a retired school teacher, never lost her enthusiasm for taking care of young people in need and, if anyone needed taking care of, Kyle fit the bill.

After many tense weeks, military leaders on all sides managed to work together to restore order. During a time when the expectation was for people to behave like savages, an expectation instilled by the endless books and movies on the world's demise, they rose above their gnawing fears and trusted in one another. This trust was the one and only thing to save humanity from succumbing to primal survival instincts and reversing a millennium of progress.

In the aftermath, Kyle was recruited into a newly formed joint military intelligence agency. He was the youngest agent, but soon earned the respect of the older more experienced agents. On the German side, he had newfound friends once the news spread on how he'd helped Major Gaynor and his wife. The Gaynors were a fixture in the community, well-liked by military and civilian alike. Many parents owed a debt of gratitude to Ada, for it was her undying devotion to all children, especially those hard to reach kids that had saved some from jail and others from worse.

Now, a year later, despite having earned a reputation of being slightly unhinged and mostly unconventional, Kyle was well respected. While many men would be envious of his mission, most of the female population would mourn over the news of his pending departure, and both men and women would agree that the mission a death sentence. None of this mattered to him. All he cared about was executing his plan. A plan he'd thought through and over almost every day for the past year.

Kyle walked to the window. Outside snow fell onto the city. He gazed out across the Rhine River at the Cologne Cathedral, its many lights twinkling on the water's surface. The past year had flown by and if he had to spend those days anywhere, Germany's oldest city seemed to be the right place for him. The city was both beautiful and magical, with its famous Romanesque churches, rebuilt after WWII, along with its numerous museums and galleries. Once upon a time, before the cloud mass, it had been a popular destination for cultural enthusiasts. If the citizens of Cologne had a renewed appreciation for what the city held, he wasn't sure, but he liked to believe this to be true.

The snow reminded him Christmas was around the corner. Once upon a magical time in Cologne; a time when the Christmas markets decorated the city's center and people filled the streets. The colorful tents and the strings of lights would be absent this year. The mayor and the deputy mayors had made the decision to forgo festivities. No one grumbled over or protested the decision. Christmas spirit, or any spirit, wasn't in abundance these days. Reaching into his pocket, Kyle pulled out a small picture. He stared at the images for a long time before carefully placing the photo back in his pocket. Torturing himself served no point, not without a keg of Kölsch in hand. A knock on the half-open door turned him away from the masked serenity outside and his melancholy mood.

"Come on in Will."

The door opened and Will, somewhat shamefaced, walked in.

"Did you think I wouldn't show?" Kyle walked over and shook Will's hand.

"I was in the neighborhood." Will shrugged. "Thought I'd, you know stop by—"

"And try to talk me out of going?"

"Hell yeah. It's madness. No one's been able to get in. No one."

"I know the failure rate, but we've only tried flying into the mass. I'm going a different route."

"Right. Right. You're going across the Bering Strait. Brilliant plan. You know the men working the outpost on the Russian side disappeared into that mass?"

"They went by boat," Kyle reminded him. "I'm not."

"What makes you so sure it will matter?"

"Nothing makes me sure. But I have to try."

Will shook his head over Kyle's stubbornness. "Is there anything I can say to stop you?"

"Is there anything I can say to make you understand? What if it was Ada?"

Will pursed his lips and scowled. "Not a fair question."

"Absolutely fair. And I know what you'd do. So stop with the guilt trip and help me figure out the best way to tell her I'm leaving."

Will cracked a tiny smile and sniffed. "Hell. I've no idea, but best to get it out in the open before someone decides to call her." Will pushed the door open.

Kyle grabbed his jacket, taking one last look out the window before leaving. Night had fallen.

3 THE ADITA

The humans had christened the planet Bliss, but the Adita knew it as Paru. Paru existed long before man, with many species have come and gone before the Adita arrived thousands of years ago. To the human eye, the scenery appeared breathtaking, a paradise. In Agra's eyes, he saw a cesspool of vegetation, felt a climate of stifling heat made bearable only by the ocean's breeze. A breeze carrying a stench that never left him. In his opinion, nothing blissful existed on Paru. He was anxious to leave the planet behind and begin preparing for their future on Earth, to return to the frozen oasis that had once been his home, the Adita's home.

The memories of Earth never faded, despite the unnumbered centuries having disappeared into the vacuum of time. The Adita had once been great rulers of universes far and wide, revered as gods by many species, including man. A sour taste rose in Agra's mouth. Humans, he thought, disgusted by the mere name. A race of beings unlike any they'd ever encountered. Weak in most aspects, yet possessing a strength that defied logic. Governed by unpredictable emotions, making them dangerous and a danger to themselves. For these precise reasons, they needed to be protected from self-destructing. For a species like man to have the life's blood the Adita required for survival was an egregious insult, but one dictating the necessity of their captivity. Right or wrong. Moral or not. Such things were not the Adita's concern and certainly never crossed Agra's mind.

Many details about their future were left to be decided, but Agra's patience wore thin. He knew the Elders could not be rushed, and the Saciva's opinions would not be voiced before the final plans determined. The ninth moon fast approached. The inevitable date when the secret meetings ended and private discussions amongst the Elders ceased. The time to set their future in motion neared and, in Agra's mind as in that of many Adita, was long overdue.

A crease formed in Agra's forehead, smoothing out as he turned from the window to acknowledge Eve. Not a sound or whisper was made to alert him of her approach. He'd not heard her until she'd been close, too close, something no one else was capable of doing and had they tried wouldn't have lived to tell about it.

"You wished to see me," Eve stated as she entered, ignoring etiquette by not waiting for him to speak first.

Hiding his displeasure behind a cool smile, Agra looked upon her for a long moment, deciding upon which direction to proceed. "You disobeyed me."

Eve feigned surprise. "I beg your pardon father, but of what order did you give that I did not adhere to?"

"Do not be coy Eve," he hissed. "I'm going to assume you don't deny having bit the human, like a feral beast? Having shared with him the gift of eternal life?"

"I cannot deny that which I was unaware of being wrong or forbidden. And I only shared enough to make him stronger. He will not turn."

Agra held up his hand. "Do not test my patience with your twist on the word of the Adita. You knew it was my desire for the human to remain here. There is much we don't know about the child. Yet you not only allowed the father to leave, but you did the unthinkable."

"We don't need the human. Caleb will be grown by the ninth moon. He is strong--"

"Letting him go was not your decision to make," he interrupted, increasing anger building behind his calm demeanor. "Rules are important my dear and because you are my relation does not exempt you from following that which is written or from being punished for doing that which is forbidden. Rules aside, you have not the knowledge or experience required to transform a human in the proper manner. And, as I recall, the few attempts you made in the past, were failures. Those were overlooked, for you knew not the rules." Agra paused, holding his temper in check. "You know them now."

Eve considered her father's words but remained silent. The undertones of his mood revealed more than his words or demeanor. That something bothered him, something greater than the loss of one human, even if the human happened to be unique, was evident and unsettling.

"This matter will be brought to the council," Agra announced. "Come." He waved his hand, taking them both through time and space.

Within seconds they arrived in the judging chambers, where not-long-ago Austin had discovered the truth about his son and wife. However, a major renovation had taken place. Sophistication had replaced medieval. The crude stone floors and walls were now smooth black granite. The center, where Zack and Luke had been chained to the floor, was filled with metal benches that gleamed despite the lackluster lighting. The circle's floor, now a flawless gray stone, similar to polished marble. On the metal benches sat the council. Thirty-four pale beings, male and female, alike in appearance, having been stamped from a parent organism few knew existed and fewer knew the origins. The Saciva, giving as much the appearance of being ominous sculptures as living breathing beings, sat to the left and right of the great altar. An altar, once a crude stone fixture now shined of polished white stone.

The council stood as Agra took his place behind the altar, while Eve stood over to the side of the circle. Eve looked about. These were members of her family. Where she'd once walked the Earth as a solitary being, she now walked amongst her own. The odd thing about it was, although she'd been alone on Earth, she'd never known the true meaning of loneliness until coming home. The very presence of the Adita felt like walls closing her in, overwhelming her with a tremendous sense of isolation. The chamber's memories flooded her mind. Flashes of trials held long ago came and went, many of which ended in death sentences or worse. Many faces, many unknowns. These unknowns bothered her. A great deal of the Adita's history remained a mystery, and meanwhile, the clock was spinning out of control. To what end the clock tumbled toward, continued to elude her.

"You may be seated," Agra announced.

In a motion synchronized without flaw or sound, the council took their seats. On the altar appeared an impressive book bound in thick parchment, perhaps of an animal, perhaps of a human. The name Adita was seared into the cover. The pages of the book were also made of parchment, and symbols written in blood represented the written word. The origins of both were uncertain to most all present. The book a written declaration of all things Adita, served as an emblem of law during formal proceedings. All Adita knew the contents of the book.

As Agra turned each page the symbols appeared and disappeared. He stopped turning a third of the way into the book and looked up. "The laws of the Adita are precise and without corruption." Agra's voice filled the room. It wasn't a booming sound, like a preacher at the pulpit throwing down fire and brimstone, yet it held an authority demanding attention and respect. The congregation nodded in unison, one nod up and down. Eve watched and listened to the words spoken, to the thoughts unspoken.

"The laws of creation are precise and without corruption," Agra continued. "It is written, it will be upheld, no member of the Adita shall give that which is sacred, the gift of eternal life, to another species, human or other."

Again, his statements received a single nod from all except Eve. She knew the book front to back and realized the direction Agra was taking the council. Her demeanor suggested defiance, but her mind was void. No thoughts churned, no opinions formed. That Agra was speaking did not concern her, that he was listening mattered greatly.

"Eve, daughter of the house of Adita, how do you plead?" Agra asked.

Eve stepped forward, approaching the altar as was customary for the accused. "I broke no laws intentionally and therefore have no plead to bring forth."

A collective gasp, albeit soft, rose from the council. Eve's response was unheard of within the judging chamber. Arati, who had been documenting the accounts of the meeting, stopped writing, his hand hung suspended above the parchment.

Agra leaned forward. "Do not test the council with your insolent attitude. State your plea and remedy."

"No plea or remedy is necessary," Eve replied in an unchallenging, but confident tone. "I did not share eternal life with the human. I merely improved his DNA."

Agra slammed the book shut with a wave of his hand. The sound reverberated off the walls seeming to shake the temple down to its foundation. "The remedy shall be his death. He will be harvested. You will bring him to this chamber, so that justice can be meted out, as appropriate for the act of corrupting our laws."

Eve stepped forward. "With all due respect father, I disagree with the sentence. It is I who broke the laws, although unknowingly. The human should not suffer for my mistakes and I won't have harm come upon him."

The Saciva, who as was custom had kept a straight face and eyes forward, dared turned their heads in Eve's direction. Whispers arose, and aghast murmurs were muttered amongst the council.

"Silence," Agra's voice bellowed across the room. "All Adita are forbidden to turn another species, especially a human. Our species is designed to survive above all others. Preservation of the Adita relies on our genetics never being tainted, our blood never being shared. We have the purest blood. Flawless DNA. We do not create our kind by changing a human. An inferior being."

"And what of my son? Was he not created with that very inferior being you wish me to destroy?" Eve countered, undeterred by Agra's rising anger, or his indignation over her defiance. His words, their rules, they meant little to her.

"The creation of the boy was an experiment, a desperate measure taken in order to save our people. A last resort, one such that has never been attempted with a female Adita." He looked out over the council and back to Eve "The results of the experiment, of your son, must be examined before any decision is determined. However, if necessary the experiment will be terminated without prejudice."

"Terminated?" Eve stood a bit taller. A movement so subtle that, if it had been captured on film, the viewer would still have been hard-pressed to notice even in slow motion. Had he been alive General Roth would have attested to the impossibility.

"Terminated," Agra repeated, a note of satisfaction in his voice. He'd seen Eve's reaction, detected the twitch in her muscles the same as if she'd jumped up and down flailing her arms. "Now, please state your remedy." In this request, it was clear he expected nothing less than complete agreement and submission from Eve.

"I will collect the human," Eve replied, nodding to Agra, to the Saciva, and last to the members sitting in the circle.

A long heavy pause fell over the chamber. Eve felt her father probing into her mind, digging for truths in her words, looking for ammunition to use against her. After long last Agra picked up the book of laws, a satisfied purse of the lips graced his mouth. "In time you will come to understand the full implications of the measures we take to ensure our survival."

Eve stared unblinkingly at her father. She allowed him to continue prying, validating she spoke in earnest. Once this was found she blocked him from going further, redirecting his push to safe thoughts. If he knew she was doing so, he didn't acknowledge, leading her to surmise he didn't. In her private opinion, Agra didn't know a lot of things, that his powers were diminishing each day, each hour. She had nothing to substantiate this feeling or assumption, except her unfailing intuition.

"Your plea and remedy are noted in the journals of court for all to witness," Agra announced, satisfied Eve could be brought into the fold, could be controlled and act in the way expected of an Adita. With his statement hanging in the air, Agra vanished from the room.

Eve turned to leave. Beneath her calm demeanor, buried where Agra could not see, a force was building that she did not yet fully understand. A presence within her, unlike any she'd ever experienced. While on Earth the voice had guided her every move. She'd never known for certain if the voice was real or imagined until coming home. Knowing now the voice had been Agra's, she no longer listened like a blind fool and only allowed him access on those occasions demanding entry to avoid his suspicions. However, this new presence was not a voice at all, but a thought, a force within, that grew stronger each day. Caleb would not be terminated, she thought as she exited the judging chambers. Behind her, the walls of the chamber expanded outward before contracting inward as if alive as if they were breathing. The council stirred as a nervous vibe ebbed through the room.

* * *

Eve traveled down the halls of the great temple, preferring to walk, to see and smell all that surrounded her. The temple was a peaceful sanctuary, the planet an oasis. She did not understand or share her father's disdain for Paru. Earth was dying, saved only by the Elder's intervention. The current frozen state would be necessary for centuries to come if they wanted to salvage the planet. To begin the unthawing process now would risk overheating the core and destroying Earth forever. But Agra could not be deterred. This blind pursuit was all too familiar, having witnessed similar behavior in General Roth. The glaring difference, one of many, between the two was Roth's inferior mind could not cope with the unending failures experienced during his quest to achieve his goal. Agra would have no such failures. The Adita did not *try again*, for they did not know the meaning of fail.

At the end of a narrow passage, Eve came to stop in front of a closed door, where she waited. Soon the door flung inward. A boy of seven, whose blond hair and blue eyes were in stark contrast to everything around him, greeted her with a winning smile.

"I heard you coming," he announced and moved aside for her to enter. "I heard you all the way from the judging chambers."

"What else did you hear?" Eve paused.

"Just you." A cherub's face, the smile of an angel, the mischievous yet keen eyes gazed up at her.

She looked down into her son's sweet face but did not smile back. She knew what was hidden behind the smile. "Caleb, you know not to eavesdrop on grandfather. You know what would happen if he caught you?"

"He would harvest me."

Eve shook her head. "What do you know about harvesting?"

"Absolutely nothing." He hugged her "I don't know a thing mother. I promise."

"The harvest is not of your concern. Do you understand?" She attempted to smooth the curls out of his hair, already too long and needing a trim. In a few years that would change, everything about him would change.

Caleb nodded. "Why are you sad?"

"I'm not," Eve replied, not knowing what it meant to be sad, or to love, or to be loved for that matter. She only knew as a mother, her desire to protect her young was fierce.

"Can we eat now? I'm hungry." Caleb pulled her by the hand back toward the door.

"What do you crave today?"

"Meat. And lots of it!" he replied, sounding more like the child he appeared to be.

Eve smiled, pleased to hear these words from her son. Caleb had yet to develop an appetite for blood of any kind, turning his nose up at the various samples she'd presented to him. While this pleased her, it annoyed Agra to no end, even angered him at times. The Adita warrior's strength came from the blood he drank, not from eating meat like a barbaric carnivore. His aversion to Caleb's food choices seemed to contradict the child's overall purpose. But regardless of why, Eve made certain Agra was not around during meals. Of late she was of the opinion her father's attitude came not from Caleb's food choices, but an annoyance less perspicuous.

This, coupled with her father's insistence over Austin being brought back for harvest, gnawed at her more insistently each passing day. In the chambers, during her hearing, an essence of uncertainty hung in the air. A subtle scent, which alone would not have caught her attention had her father not attempted to hide the council's feelings from her. Having so few memories of life before her solitary journey began on Earth, she'd no idea if Agra's behavior normal. Recollections of father-daughter moments to call upon as guides were nil, a single word about her mother was never spoken. Eve squeezed Caleb's hand and vowed he would never know a life without her.

4 THE GIFT

Although his military career had been cut short, ample opportunities to witness the unexplainable had come Austin's way. Accepting that which could not be explained became the norm. Making difficult choices were also an integral component of his life. Some made were good, others not as good, but never bad. This choice, however, was singular in that no other choice he'd ever made could possibly compare. Being human was not a state most people questioned or gave much thought and Austin wasn't the exception. At least not until now, not until Eve provided an alternative in the form of a gift.

Standing in his bathroom, staring at his reflection in the mirror, staring at his eyes, he wondered if being human was a choice he could still make. His eyes, once a striking blue, were now darkened by black flecks in the pupil. He tried, but could not blink or rub away the defect. Adding to this, a less obvious change, his thoughts were moving like someone had hit the nitrous button, putting his neurons in hyper mode. All the bunker's sounds, whispers, and conversations happened in his bathroom, in his bedroom, wherever he went they were in his head, his constant companions.

What had Eve's bite done to him? The possibilities were limited, each one sounding like voodoo or the meanderings of the superstitious or insane. The most viable choice was vampirism. The validity of this conclusion not based on any scientific facts. Vampires were fantasies born out of make-believe. However, the current facts facing him, or at least the ones he knew, told another tale, a story of unbelievable myths becoming truths. The facts were saying Eve and her people, the Adita, were in some points similar to vampires if postulation was based on the mythical creature. Although, they were unlike the popular sense imagined in modern day movies and books. They were beings that existed since the beginning of time. Built into a tale of evil and superstition that was passed along from generation to generation, the words changing in accordance with the beliefs of the time or region.

Austin turned from the mirror. He didn't want to look at his reflection or think about Eve. Thoughts of Eve became thoughts of his son. A month had gone by since they'd returned from Bliss. What was the time differential from Earth to Bliss? How could they know? Zack thought the ratio to be two days on Bliss equaled twenty-eight days on Earth, but Austin wasn't convinced. Applying logic to that which was not logical, couldn't be relied upon and he suspected Bliss moved at whatever pace the Adita thought necessary. The passage of time wasn't controlled by scientific measurement or any measurement known to man. That pace, for whatever reason or lack of, was now moving faster than time on Earth. Of this latter assumption, Austin knew he was right, but couldn't have explained how he arrived at this conclusion.

All of this was meaningless conjecture and soon wouldn't matter. In less than twenty-four hours he would return to Bliss. He'd spent three weeks too long in the bunker, but Ed and Luke's lack of survival skills required attention. Not to mention the stacks of journals he'd asked Madison to plow through and, despite her speed reading capabilities, had taken two weeks to complete. The task proved a waste of precious time. After reading every single page, every word, every unfinished thought written in the margins, they'd garnered little information of solid worth, and befuddlement reigned.

Madison took notes throughout the process, ending up with one page of information that one could easily argue over its usefulness or lack thereof. Roth had been in contact with someone named Za, but no mention of Agra was noted. The purpose of keeping humans alive was commented on in vague convoluted phrases and incomplete thoughts. The harvest that Agra had alluded to was not mentioned anywhere. The journals proved an unexpected disappointment, filled mostly with Roth's obsessive rants about Eve and eternal life. The only fact of use, if to be believed, was the name Roth gave to Eve's people. He referred to them as the Adita, which meant nothing other than giving them a specific term to use versus applying those to which were familiar.

Austin didn't care about any of this. If he had to go in on a wing and a prayer, then he would do so. Nothing could deter him from going back for his son, not Agra and not Eve. Simply thinking her name brought on a whole slew of questions without answers, and an array of tumultuous feelings that bounced around the spectrum never landing on one end or the other. Coming to grips with his feelings for her left him confused and anxious. Gratitude often gave way to betrayal and anger. She'd shown him the truth about Roxanne, but something deep inside wouldn't allow him to release Roxi, to accept her existence was never real. He didn't know what he was holding on to and maybe he was as delusional as Roth. Still, he couldn't get out from under the ominous cloud, the feeling he was missing the obvious.

A noise from outside his quarters and down the hall drew his attention from the mirror, away from his problems. Footsteps approached, slowing as they came to his door. He grabbed a pair of sunglasses and walked to the front of his apartment to wait for the knock. He stepped aside for Madison to enter. Following close behind was German, the last remaining canine. Austin avoided looking directly at Madison, turning his attention on the dog.

"Did you know I was coming?" Madison asked, surprised he'd opened the door so quick.

"I was about to leave," he lied. Something he was doing more and more of lately. A habit he wasn't comfortable with, but without knowing the truth, telling it was near impossible.

"Oh. I won't keep you then."

"It's ok. I was going to check on Luke. See if he was ready to go."

Madison sat on the couch, folding her hands in her lap to avoid fidgeting. From the moment Austin had returned from Bliss, she'd made a point of avoiding him. An act he'd most likely noticed, but true to his nature never questioned, only observed. She took a deep breath and looked up at him.

"Why are you wearing sunglasses?" she asked.

"It's nothing. A migraine is all. The lights, you know." Austin took a quick step back from her. The scent of her perfume or shampoo caused his mind to swim in and out of focus. The smell was sweet, sickening in its stench, reminding him of ripened fruit at the point before it turned rotten.

"I didn't know you got migraines." She crossed her arms. "You never mentioned that before."

"Did you come here to talk about my health?" he asked, using a sarcastic tone, knowing it would set her off, wanting to derail her train of thought before it picked up steam.

Madison ground her teeth, refusing to allow his sarcasm to bait her into a terse response. She'd promised herself she wouldn't argue with him and damn it if she wasn't going to hold to that promise. Taking a deep breath, she refocused on why she was there to see him.

"I wanted to say goodbye," she said evenly, holding onto her composure.

"We're not leaving till morning."

"I'm not going to be there when you go." She perched on the edge of the cushion, her shoulders sagged a bit. "I can't do it. I can't watch Luke and Ed go." Or you. She closed her eyes, pushing her emotions away. Despite having broken down several times over the past couple of weeks, she would continue to argue she wasn't the crying type and didn't want to disprove her claim by shedding more tears in front of Austin.

Austin stared at the top of Madison's head. He heard what she was saying, mingled with what she was thinking, and tried to keep the two separated. Her scent complicated his efforts, having woven its way into his head, saturating his mind. A yearning settled deep in his stomach and his mouth began to salivate. A powerful hunger, similar to what Eve had shared with him in Section Seven at Cheyenne, overcame him. Austin fought against the rising wave, suppressing the urges asking him to do unspeakable things. Against sane reasoning or an ounce of good judgment, he sat down next to Madison, keeping a good distance between them. He had this under control, he repeated as he sat. He would never harm her.

"Luke and Ed are going to be ok," he said, using a soothing tone as much for her benefit as his own.

"You can't say that. You don't know they'll be ok." She glanced at his profile. "Luke's a kid. He barely survived Cheyenne before you took him off to far away planets where God knows what happened to him. To you."

Austin reached out and took her hand. "Maddie, I'm gonna take care of Luke and Ed." Although the words came out of his mouth, he wasn't able to control the direction his mind went. He felt as if two people existed within him, dueling for possession. A bead of sweat slid down the side of his face.

"What about you?" Madison demanded. "Who's gonna take care of you?" She no longer cared about making a fool of herself.

"Eve," Austin responded before thinking.

Madison laughed a short bitter snicker. She turned to face him. "Eve? Are you serious Austin? What is she? A vampire? A cannibal? A what? And what about her people? Or the Sundogs or Svan or whatever the hell they are? You're no match for them. How are you going to--?"

Austin stared at the wall, losing focus as Madison continued to ask unanswerable questions. The longing returned, subtle at first, growing more intense by the second. He should put some distance between them, but couldn't bring himself to stand. Madison's voice, her scent, they were like heavy weights holding him down, magnets drawing him to her. He saw her lips moving, but could no longer hear her above the humming in his ears.

"Austin? Are you ok?"

Austin grabbed Madison to him, holding her tight in his arms. Burying his face into her neck, he breathed in deep her scent. "Maddie," he mumbled against her skin. Raising his head, he mashed his lips to hers, kissing her hard, tasting her mouth with his tongue. She struggled to back away from him, making his desire even stronger, but it wasn't desire for the flesh, not in the traditional sense. He squeezed her arms, pulling her body close to him. In the distance, he heard growling. The growls grew louder. Then German barked, short and loud. The realization of what Austin wanted to do to her struck him like an ice-cold splash of water. He shoved her away, springing from the couch at the same time.

"You better leave," he said, unable to say more, unable to warn her of the monster raging inside of him.

Moving as if in slow motion, Madison wiped her mouth with her hand and stood up. "Austin what's wrong?" She took a step closer, but German came to stand between them not allowing her passage.

"Just get out. Now." Austin's voice came out as an angry snarl.

"I'm going. Damn if you don't have to snap at me about it. Have a good trip." The door slammed on her last word.

Like a hot air balloon losing all its heat, Austin crumbled to the ground. He buried his face in his hands. The sound of his heart pounding inside his chest echoed in his head and in the room, bouncing from wall to wall. A gift Eve had called this maddening state. A gift that was turning him into something less than human. Each day he'd felt an invisible force taking over his body, while a second more crucial battle ensued for his mind. The power to stop the transformation did not reside within him if it resided within anyone at all. Primal instincts fought against logic and Austin wasn't confident in the outcome. He could no longer pretend this wasn't a problem. He could no longer fight this on his own.

Picking himself up from the floor, Austin took a deep breath and held it for several seconds. He closed his eyes, focusing his thoughts, clearing all images from his mind save one, that of his son Caleb. At what point in time he chose this name and began to think of his son by such was unclear. That it was Roxanne's idea to name him this only mattered if he allowed himself to ponder over the why, which he didn't. She was gone, never to have existed he reminded himself for the number of times beyond counting. Feeling as if the beast within was subdued, for the time being, Austin opened his eyes. Standing at his feet, German waited and watched.

"What's wrong with me?" He squatted down, rubbing the dog's ears. German responded with a few wags of his tail and a short bark. "Yeah. I don't know either," Austin replied.

5 HULK

The sun rising and setting. Garbage day. Dogs barking. Kids riding bikes. Everyday common occurrence taken for granted and now gone. Replaced by others, those once thought unusual, now accepted as the norm. Over the past months the events, even those once perceived as phenomenal, had become routine. Three suns rising, no moon, no stars, no life. Each morning arrived without circumstance. Each day held a static appearance and had become routine for the few people left to care or notice such things.

Zack sat in one of the leather recliners facing the wall-sized screen in the command center. As his mind churned, speculating, pondering, and analyzing their situation, the three suns materialized in the sky. The winds subsided and the black sky lightened to a dismal gray. One cataclysmic event had changed their world forever, creating a perpetual hell where nothing changed. The view of the exterior materialized, appearing as a still painting of a vast frozen wasteland. Other than a few scraggly pines hanging on, the trees were barren. The fields were empty, having been covered in snow ever since the aliens arrived, ever since all signs of life vanished into thin air.

Except for the bodies.

Those who were dropped from the sky, emptied of anything remotely human. Those who were left behind, barely recognizable after being torn, shredded and drained of all life. Annihilated by the sharp talons of the alien predator, the elusive Sundogs, the monsters seen only by the select few remaining. The gruesome image of the truck driver he and Colin found flashed before him. He wouldn't exactly classify a corpse as a sign of life. So, aside from the departed, there had been zip. No birds, no cats, no wild beasts roaming the land, not even an ant. For all of his knowledge, Zack couldn't fathom how the Sundogs had wiped out every existing species known to man. Well almost every species, German had survived, and that they'd found him alive constituted a major miracle in Zack's mind, but to what avail? If no other canines were found, he would be the last of his kind. Thousands of species vanished from the Earth every day before the Sundogs invited themselves to the party, but Zack never witnessed those lives being extinguished or gave them any thought. If German had good health, he might live fifteen or more years. Would Zack be around when his life passed? Would any of them be around to witness this tragedy? Zack shook his head to these questions and a million others he asked over and over.

He couldn't lay all the blame on the Sundogs. It was Eve's people who were the masterminds, who controlled the Sundogs, the planet. Vampires, Luke called them. Adita, Roth named them. As far as Zack was concerned names meant little. Giving the aliens a specific name, such as vampire, would deceive the mind into thinking of them in that capacity, which could be dangerous. The Adita could not be destroyed by holy water or garlic. A stake to the heart was up for debate, seeing as how he didn't know if they had hearts. The Sundogs had internal organs, including a heart, but their skin was able to absorb the kinetic energy from the most intense of impacts with amazing effectiveness. He knew this for a fact, having tested its strength with various high-powered military hardware. Reason might dictate the Adita's skin would withstand the same level of assault, and reason also suggested they did have a heart, but reasoning wasn't exactly reliable in the current environment.

Research in the bunker's vast database on the name Adita delivered ambiguity in providing answers or hope. He'd found similar names existing in ancient script, and even stories of blood-sucking demons, gods, and angels depending on the date or region of reference. A few vague descriptions of ghost-like beings having soulless eyes peppered history, but the names Agra and Arati never surfaced. A few sightings of a waif-like being, that may or may not have been Eve, were cited. One passage referred to the waif as a witch, others called her a dark angel. One Russian tale told of a pale goddess, who delivered a group of starving settlers from the depths of hell to a heaven of abundance. The accounts were never in great detail or conclusive. The tellers often referred to as people too far 'in the cup' or too crazy to be relied upon.

When pressed, Austin had shared little information about Eve or her people. Based on what Zack overheard in the Adita death chamber, he knew she was somehow connected to Roxanne's death. But Austin had been a closed book on the subject of his wife. His reaction, and subsequent behavior belied the captain's previous obsession with finding her, but the topic was better left alone until such time Austin felt like sharing. Zack highly doubted they'd ever have the 'what happened to Roxanne' conversation.

Climate control, gargoyle looking beasts with computer chips, vampire-like aliens, all these oddities could be rationalized, maybe even explained by modern science or some sort of science. However, making sense of the Captain's attitude was beyond sense, common or otherwise. Zack sighed as if in doing so the weight of his thoughts might dissipate into the air. He knew in a few hours it wouldn't matter. The captain would be gone, Luke and Ed tagging along like dutiful soldiers. Gone on a mission to save Austin's son, to save the people in the warehouses, to stop the Adita and to most likely die before doing any of those things. Yet another anomaly Zack didn't quite understand. The paternity of the boy was unquestionable, he was Austin's son, but who was the mother? Eve or Roxanne? If Eve was the mother, the boy would not be fully human and that in itself raised many more questions without answers.

"Watching the suns?"

Zack bolted out of his chair like a startled jackrabbit. "Holy shit man. You scared the crap outta me."

"Sorry," Austin offered halfheartedly.

"Forget it." Zack leaned on the chair for support, trying to calm his nerves. "What's with the sunglasses?"

Austin rubbed his shaved head, pausing before he spoke. "Can I trust you?"

"Uh, I think we've figured that one out months ago."

"This is different."

"From what?" Zack laughed. It came out sounding maniacal rather than humorous. What could possibly be different from anything they'd experienced thus far? "Serious dude. You can trust me."

Austin reached up and took off his sunglasses. He lifted his head and looked straight at Zack.

Zack's jaw dropped. "What the fu..."

"Told you it was different."

"Different? Different is dying your hair pink or having a tattoo of Justin Bieber on your thigh." Zack stepped closer to Austin. "Man, that's not different, that's fucked up."

Austin held up his hand stopping Zack from getting closer. "I need you to run some blood tests."

"What happened?" Zack couldn't stop staring at Austin's eyes. Once blue, now blue and black. The black appeared to be spreading in the pupil like someone had spilled ink in his eyes. If it continued, his eyes would soon look like an Adita's, solid black.

"Eve bit me."

"Whhhaaat?"

Pulling up his sleeve, Austin turned over his arm exposing the purplish marks on his wrist. "Right before we left Bliss. She said it was a gift."

"Gifts come in boxes wrapped in shiny paper."

"Do you have the equipment to test my blood?"

"Yeah, but what am I looking for?"

Austin shrugged. "I don't know."

"Good place to start. You want to do it now?"

Austin put his glasses back on and turned for the door. Luke and Ed wouldn't be ready to leave for about another hour, which would allow time to draw a few blood samples, but that was all. Zack would have to figure the rest out after Austin left and by then the answers might not matter. Austin wiped a bead of sweat from his brow. The bunker's temperature seemed higher than usual, though that didn't make sense. The system Zack built always kept the climate at perfect temperatures, so maybe it was he that was running hotter than normal.

Once in the lab, Zack filled three vials with Austin's blood. The color was a combination of red and blue, the consistency thick, like cold motor oil. With the vials stored in the refrigerator, Zack pulled out the microscope. He put a drop on a slide, smeared it and placed it on the stage, not bothering with staining. The lab had a more sophisticated scope, but it took a while to set up and he had the feeling Austin wanted answers fast.

"Wanna look?"

"You do it." Austin stood to the side, sunglasses in place.

Zack peered into the eyepiece not expecting to see much without stain but was shocked when the cells appeared to jump up at him like he was watching an old 3-D video game. Large bluish-black cells were consuming the red. The foreign cells were shaped similar to red but contained a nucleus that was rapidly absorbing the normal cells. Thoughts of gamma radiation and the Hulk surfaced.

"Well?" Austin asked, growing impatient.

Zack sat back from the scope. "I don't know. I mean, I'm no scientist."

"I don't have time Zack," Austin snapped. "Just tell me what you think," he finished, using a less harsh tone.

"I think," Zack spun around to face Austin, "whatever Eve of the dead injected into your bloodstream is taking over, eating your cells like a giant piranha. Like cancer, like what gamma radiation did to Bruce Banner. And based on the rate of consumption you'll be fully vamped out within a couple of weeks."

"They aren't vampires," Austin responded in a dry tone. He expected more from Zack than to believe in fantasies.

"What does it matter what you call them? From my limited account, they're superior beings and, based on this sample, they have superior kick your ass DNA. So, vampire, bloodsucker, Adita, it doesn't mean shit. Not in stopping them anyway."

A wave of dizziness washed over Austin. "Am I becoming one? Is it changing my DNA?"

Zack breathed a heavy sigh. "Man, I don't know. I don't have enough to go on or the equipment to test that kind of thing. I could go to the hospital in Colorado

Springs, run a few more tests, but they'd take time. You could postpone your trip until I know more."

"Not an option." Another wave hit him, this one stronger.

"Then I don't know what to tell you." Zack clicked the scope light off. "Maybe you can ask Eve."

Austin shook his head. "I know this much, and I think you know it as well, once this thing is complete, it's not something that can be reversed." He removed his sunglasses.

Zack stared into Austin's eyes and repressed the urge to shudder. He didn't have to say out loud that he agreed. "What are you going to tell Ed and Luke?"

"The truth. They need to know in case…in case I become dangerous." Austin looked away, images of Madison flashed through his head.

"Dangerous how? Something happen?"

"No," Austin replied. "I gotta get…I gotta get my gear." The room wobbled out of focus. Austin grabbed for the table, catching the edge before collapsing to the ground.

Zack rushed to him. "Austin. Austin, you ok?" He turned him over. His eyes were closed, his skin pale and clammy. Zack checked for a pulse, still strong. "Shit."

Zack called Ed, catching him right as he was leaving for the barn. "I need you in the infirmary right now, bring Luke."

Ed and Luke arrived in less than two minutes, bursting into the room.

"What's wrong?" What happened?" Luke ran to Austin's side.

"I don't know. One minute we're talking, the next he collapsed."

Ed looked past Zack to the microscope and empty vials on the counter. "What were you doing?"

"It's complicated," Zack replied, knowing it was that and a few other things. The three men carried Austin into the next room and laid him on the bed. Zack checked his pulse again and it was still beating strong. This comforted and unnerved him all the same.

"What the hell happened?" Luke asked.

Various lies ran through Zack's mind, none were believable, but telling the truth wasn't an option. *You can't tell what you don't know*, Zacky boy. Another popular phrase dear old dad was fond of saying. A good philosophy to live by when you ran with the mob. Zack looked away from Austin to answer Luke. "Honestly man, I don't know. He said something about being hot and the next thing I know he's on the floor. If I had to guess, maybe some kind of flu."

"Is he gonna be ok?" Luke glanced down at his friend, noticing his pale skin.

Zack shook his head. "I wish I knew. His heartbeat is regular. So is his blood pressure." Zack sighed. "We'll have to wait and see." Not complete bullshit, but the best he had to offer and the most he wanted to share. Without having to think it over, he knew Austin wouldn't want anyone knowing about his condition.

6 DEPARTURE

A week after Austin sank into a deep sleep, Eve was wandering the temple making her plans. Sometimes Caleb followed at her heels, asking his millionth question for the day and other times he gave his mother peace and went off exploring every dark corner. Always he caught up to her for she did not wait or pause to ensure he was safe. Although her mind was void she was deep in thought, thoughts that would cause Agra much concern if he were to hear them.

Eve deposited Caleb back in his room with instructions to stay out of trouble and Agra's way. He smiled and promised to be on his best behavior. An impossibility Eve knew, for, although only seven, Caleb's abilities had advanced beyond most mature Adita. He heard many thoughts, sensed many feelings, and none more so than Agra's. The true meaning of this she had not yet come to understand, but she knew Caleb was aware of the lurking danger and of the need for caution. For this Eve was grateful, hoping her son would always be more than cautious where Agra was concerned.

Outside the temple, Eve wandered down the path through the tangled undergrowth of the jungle. The vines and limbs parted, allowing her to pass unhindered. Soon she came to the clearing near the warehouses, seven rows of buildings, thirty-five in total. She walked to the front of the first building in the last row. The massive doors slid open at her silent command. She walked past the tables of specimens hooked up to a multitude of tubes, not seeing or caring about them as a living being. They were a means to avoid an end. The Adita needed the humans if they were to continue on, to not turn into savages controlled by instinct alone. The fact that her people were already driven by a strong desire to survive, one that eliminated compassion or any such feeling beyond that of basic instinct, never occurred to Eve. Had this fact been pointed out to her, that the Adita behaved much like animals, it would not have altered her view. If asked, she would give her opinion that humans were not so far advanced from the beast. Given the choice to live or to perish, they would survive by whatever means necessary. The nature of the beast cannot be altered or changed.

Eve was almost to the end of the row when she paused at the foot of a female specimen. The sound of the woman's beating heart was clear and a quicker pace than any other. She examined the woman lying on the table. Behind the blank stare of her brilliant green eyes, Eve felt her strength radiating outward. Laying her hand on the woman's forehead, Eve explored inside. Images of a familiar face flashed before her as the woman's memories played out. Eve focused on the future and the woman's place in it. Life and death, death and life, both were associated with the woman. An overpowering emotion filled Eve's mind and body. A feeling she'd experienced when Agra spoke of Caleb's future, his purpose. The one she'd felt when he'd spoke of termination; so intense at times it liked to crush her. The same fierceness she sensed coming from the woman.

Eve made a snap decision, she would take this woman to Earth when she returned. The stranger would help Eve gain the trust of the humans and would be needed in the future. Reasons yes, but not considerable enough to ask permission to again break Adita law. An action that if taken was against all the rules and meant death for even allowing the thought to occur, but this woman was important. Making the humans accept her was in part true, but not the only motivating factor in play. Other events were going to happen in the future and this woman would play a role in those occasions. Eve's self-preservation instincts were strong, stronger than loyalty to her people and of this admission, she felt no guilt. Maybe the cause being she'd spent too much time alone or perhaps she'd taken on more human traits than she'd realized. The reasons did not matter, only Caleb mattered.

The process to revitalize the woman was complicated and not without great risk, but Eve had other preparations to attend first. She moved on from the woman, down to the last table in the row.

"Good morning Captain Chase. How does your blood taste today?" She smiled down at the putrid blob of flesh lying on the table. "Don't fret. This will be the last time."

Chase didn't stir, but Eve could hear his muddled thoughts. "Still cursing me?" She traced her finger down his arm. "Soon you can rest forever." Eve pulled his wrist to her mouth and drained the remainder of his blood. She was sorry to lose him. His blood was sweeter than any she'd ever tasted, except for maybe her first kill. He too had been a worthless despicable man she'd taken great pleasure in killing. Chase's arm fell limp to the side of the table. His heart pushed out two more beats before giving up; his rancid thoughts churned no longer. Despite her disdain, Eve appreciated his efforts. He fought all the way to the end, never believing he would die. To her surprise, his last lucid thought had been filled with regret. Not for being a despicable man, but for lost opportunities, for Charlie.

Charlie. Eve repeated the girl's name in her mind and brought forth an image of her face. She looked forward to seeing the girl again and felt perhaps their relationship might be different this time. After all, no glass prison or General Roth would be watching. And no voice of her father telling her what to do or not do. She was her own master now. Charlie would be her friend and maybe she would be more. With this thought in mind, Eve whisked herself back to the temple where she proceeded directly to Agra's chambers. She stood outside his door and waited. Rules didn't mean a great deal to her, but she knew to enter Agra's chamber without an invitation had irritated and angered him. She needed him to be calm, his mind was easier to follow when not stirred into a frenzy.

"Enter." The word, his voice, echoed in and around the hallway.

Eve pushed open the door and stepped inside, careful to keep her head down until he acknowledged her.

"Eve. A pleasant surprise. I did not hear you coming."

Eve looked up into her father's face. They both knew this a lie. Eve had made certain he heard her, for had she not taken this precaution he would have grown suspicious; he would have given her additional consideration, which Eve hoped to avoid. Let him continue to trust in his assessment of her intellect as an inferior being, one who continued to stumble about in her new way of life. As in any pack, only one alpha was allowed and that one alpha, if threatened, would attempt to eliminate any and all threats. She would not challenge his position, not now, not yet.

"I'm sorry to arrive unannounced, but I wish to discuss..."

"I agree you should leave as soon as possible. However, the matter of taking the boy will have to be approved by the Elders." He walked over to Eve. "However, I expect they will see the benefits of sending him to Earth."

"Yes, father. I think only then will we know his full immunity to the human's blood." Eve replied.

"And you are willing to take this risk?"

"I'm confident his genetics are everything the Elders expected and possibly more."

Agra paused to listen. His suspicions were always heightened when it came to Eve. He checked thoroughly but found nothing to justify his doubts. "While on Earth, you will collect the boy's father and bring him back as was decried by the council."

"Yes, of course, father." Eve nodded. "I think that task will be made easier by having his son as an enticement." Eve waited, patient and quiet, while her father looked into the future. A future guided indiscriminately by Eve. A future of certainty to sooth Agra's underlying fears and anxiety, his insecurities that she wasn't able to grasp onto.

Agra relaxed his shoulders, satisfied with what he saw. "I will speak with the Elders."

"Thank you, father."

Agra placed his arm around Eve's shoulders. "I know coming here has been difficult for you, but do you see how pleased I am with your progress of late? The discovery of the human, your return and most of all the boy. All these things have given the Elders, the Adita, great hope for survival."

Eve laid her hand on top of his, suppressing the urge to reach out and snap his neck. "Yes father, and thank you. It has been a great comfort knowing I belong here, that I have a family. One I will do anything to protect." These words couldn't ring truer, but not in the context Agra understood them to be.

"Your loyalty will comfort me in the months to come as we proceed with the harvest." He walked her toward the door. "The Svan have begun to move into the southern regions to gather more humans."

Eve hid her surprise. "Do we not have enough for the harvest?"

"For the Elders and the Saciva, yes, but we need more and especially the young. The first children the Svan tested were filled with defects. We must find as many of the purest of their species if we are to be ready by the ninth moon."

Eve chose her words carefully. "I thought we had time, several moons," she said, controlling the suspicion, keeping any concern out of her voice and mind.

"We do. We do." He smiled at her. "Don't you worry. I have everything under control. Now go prepare for your journey, while I explain to the Elders and the Saciva what their best interests are in this matter."

Eve returned her father's smile. "Thank you, father." She bowed her head to him and exited his chambers.

Once the door closed, Eve made haste to her room and found Caleb anxiously waiting. Upon seeing her, he sprung from the bed and ran to her. "Is it true?"

Eve grabbed him by the arm, her nails digging into his skin. "Silence," she said and released him. The nail marks quickly vanished. Eve knew he'd felt no pain or fear for that matter and sometimes wished he did, for safety's sake if nothing else.

"Sorry mother," Caleb chirped, undeterred by her anger, which he'd felt plenty of and was accustomed to. "I can't help it. I try not to, but the voices come and I can't stop them and then I've listened without meaning to."

"You'll learn to control them," she replied automatically.

Caleb was unconcerned. He had more important things to tell her, but caution demanded attention first and foremost. Caleb hummed a tune and listened. Agra talking with the Elders and not paying attention to him at the moment. He proceeded, choosing his words with great care. "I saw a man in my dream last night," he announced. "He'd fallen down and is sleeping."

"Is that right dear," she replied as if she could care less about Celeb's silly dreams. "We don't have time to talk about dreams and make-believe. We leave soon." She patted him on the head. "We can talk about your dreams later, right now you must prepare."

"Ok, but the man has been sleeping for many days. His friends couldn't wake him up."

"Maybe he was very tired. I'm sure he's fine." She shook her head at him. "Now go to your room. I will come for you soon."

"Where are you going?"

"To the warehouses."

"I want to come."

"No. And if you don't do as I ask, you will not travel with me to Earth," she threatened.

This propelled Caleb out of the room and took his mind off the warehouses, a subject she was constantly trying to protect him from knowing too much about. A task she was failing at, but could not worry over. This time Eve didn't walk, but used Agra's preferred method of travel and arrived at the warehouses in a split second.

Back inside the warehouse, the woman was as she'd left her. Her heart beating steady and strong. Eve laid her hands on the woman's chest and closed her eyes. From the tips of her fingers energy flowed into the woman's body, through her veins, organs and finally into her brain. Eve proceeded in a precise order, knowing even the slightest misstep would kill the woman. Death was a matter of fact Eve wasn't concerned over, but the loss of this human would be more than an inconvenience. Eve withdrew her hands and waited. After the first few minutes, noticeable signs of improvement were evident. Color returned to her skin, making the corpse-like appearance less prominent. Another few minutes passed, and Eve removed the multitude of tubes inserted into the woman. She was now breathing on her own. The danger had passed. Eve's plans were clicking along without interruption.

Long before he made a sound, Eve knew Caleb was nearby. Suppressing her anger at being disobeyed, Eve continued to listen to the woman's progress. Satisfied the process was proceeding as she expected and needed, Eve went to find her wayward son. Outside the warehouse, she searched for Caleb. Not in the manner a human mother searched for a child by shouting out his name, rather Eve closed her eyes and searched the sounds and smells. When this turned up only the faintest hint of her child, she searched using her mind. Her brow furrowed upon finding him back in his room, sitting cherub-like on the floor doing his lessons. Having a new appreciation for the human mothers she'd observed, Eve was not fooled, nor angered by Caleb's act of innocence. To a certain level, she respected the humans and was thankful for having witnessed their lives, their relationships, and interactions. All of which had been her only preparation for motherhood.

No longer in a hurry, Eve decided to walk back to the temple. The woman would not be ready to leave for a few hours, giving her time to rethink her plans. Halfway up the path she stopped. An image of a man appeared. He stood facing away from her at the edge of a large body of water. The surface consisted of choppy waves frozen in place. The man turned from the water's edge and walked toward her, passing through her and continuing down the path. Eve watched him go until his image vanished. Her brow creased in thought. How had she missed him? Tempted to follow, Eve shook her head, another time, another place, she thought and continued up the path.

7 CROSSING THE STRAIT

The Bering Strait was over fifty miles wide at the narrowest point between Russian Cape Dezhnev and the US Cape Prince of Wales. Land temperatures remained below zero and the wind was relentless in trying to penetrate through the thickest layers of clothing in an effort to reach your bones.

Kyle stood on the Russian side staring out across the sea, where the treacherous waters were a mass of frozen choppy waves, disappearing into a vast cloud of nothing. Despite not having a single clue or fact indicating land existed on the other side, his resolve had not weakened. Ada's pleading and tears, although tough to bear, couldn't change his mind either. Leaving behind his friends and adopted family was tough, but that was all in the past now. The task ahead was all that mattered. He walked back to the Mercedes, which sat idling with the heater on full blast. Inside he pulled out a wetsuit and began to undress, stopping to scan the landscape. His eyes came to rest on a single guard post, ready to give up its few remaining boards to the elements and topple over. "No one is out there," he assured himself in a whisper and then smiled, thinking he had the right to feel a little paranoid.

With a bit of effort, Kyle maneuvered into the wetsuit. The material was designed for use by the military elite and capable of withstanding the coldest of conditions through the suit's unique ability to generate heat from body movement. Kyle assumed those conditions included swimming in the Bering Strait. Records indicated the water temperature at this time of year should be in the thirty-degree range. Based on the sheer magnitude of ice, Kyle surmised those numbers were far lower.

The plan had been to swim to Big Diomede Island where a Russian weather station and border guard had been based. After months of no communications from the personnel stationed on the island, Kyle didn't expect to find anyone hanging around to answer questions. From the station, he would swim to Cape Prince of Wales, and again search for survivors. A small fishing village called Deadbear sat near the cape where he hoped to acquire transportation to take him to Colorado. If luck graced him this day, he might be able to walk to the other side.

Grabbing the keys from the ignition, Kyle hid them under the floor mat, paused in his task, thinking the chances of the vehicle being stolen were remote. Overshadowing this fact was the expectation that he wouldn't be returning and if someone did take the truck, they probably needed the vehicle more than he. With this in mind, he placed the keys on the seat and jumped out, not bothering to lock the doors.

At the water's edge, Kyle took one last glance across the ice-bound sea before rechecking that his compass was functioning, and his backpack was secure. Taking a deep breath, he pulled his headgear into place. "You got this man," he said out loud and nodded in response to himself before stepping out onto the frozen Strait. True to the military's boasts, the suit performed as intended, keeping the frigid temperatures from penetrating through to his body. If Kyle had had the luxury of observation, he would have thought to commend the military for a job well done. However, he was focused on putting one foot in front of the other. Despite what others called a lax lifestyle, he was in excellent shape. The benefits of good genes and youth, but this was no jog around the flat track. His full concentration was required.

After two hours of walking and climbing, Kyle's agility was being put to the test by the strong winds and by having to navigate the uneven terrain. Although thankful for not having to swim, the ice was no cakewalk. Every so often the ice shifted, threatening to throw him off balance. At one point it succeeded in doing just that and Kyle had to grab for the edge of an ice sheet to keep from falling into a hole. He hung there for several seconds before clawing his way up onto a flatter section. Every few feet he'd spot another opening in the ice, a hole into the abyss below. If he fell into one of those it wouldn't be a 'showstopper', it would be a 'game over'. Keeping this in mind, he picked his way over the ice using extreme caution.

When he worried the rough terrain would never end, the surface changed from jagged to flat, with no transition to forewarn him. Flat ground was a gift horse whose mouth he would not look into. Kyle walked on, concentrating hard on the task at hand. After another thirty minutes, realizing he'd walked into a thick gray-white mist, he stopped to find his bearings. He was surrounded. Fog so thick he could barely see his feet, giving the allusion of walking on a cloud. He pushed on. A half an hour later he heard the sound of splashing waves ahead. He proceeded slow and easy. Soon he arrived at the edge, where ice turned to water. A wave splashed up in his face startling him. The time had come, the true test of his endurance was about to commence. Kyle removed his regular boots, replacing them with split toe flippers made of the same material as his body suit. He walked to the edge, took a deep breath and slid into the water.

Knowing the international relay team took six days to swim the entire Strait gnawed at him a bit before he'd set out on this quest, but when doubt threatened to unravel his will, he only had to think about doing nothing. This thought alone vanquished the most daunting of his fears. The plan was to go, or no other option. A 'no-go' wasn't on the table. He couldn't explain this to Ada or Will or the many others who tried to talk him out of going. Sometimes a man had to man-up and do the necessary thing, right or wrong.

As he swam his solitary swim, being tossed about like a rag doll at times, Kyle thought back to before the great white mass devoured the United States, back to the last time he had contact with his family. Lost in thought he hardly noticed the moment when the water ceased pulling him in every direction. Pausing to take in his surroundings, he looked around at the thick fog that enveloped him. The waters had turned calm and silent. An eerie calm that sent a shiver went down his spine. In his short time on Earth, he'd lived a rather charmed life. Even after the mass cloud appeared his world had continued to be filled with good people who took care of him, even loved him like their own. He'd crossed paths with a few assholes, but never met anyone he considered evil. He'd often wondered if he would recognize evil were he to come face to face with the beast. He wondered no longer.

Kyle was cognizant of the quiet, of how each stroke seemed to bounce off the white wall of mist and reverberate across the sea. Would they hear him coming? Who were *they*? He kept moving, swimming faster, harder, cutting through the still waters like a torpedo. The only thing on Kyle's mind was reaching that island. Every stroke he thought would be his last. When another four hours had passed, his foot hit a rock beneath the water's surface causing him to almost jump out of the water. He stopped to catch his breath and calm his nerves. It was nothing, only a rock. A rock! Land was close. He waved his fist in the air with measured excitement and continued swimming, albeit at a slower pace, taking close to an hour before finding a spot to climb ashore.

With wobbly arms Kyle hauled his fatigued body onto the rocky shore, his muscles protesting the further demand to perform. He crawled far enough to be clear of the water, before collapsing on the rocky beach, exhausted to the state of being numb. After several minutes, Kyle rolled over and opened his eyes. Up above the sky was a dull gray, to his right, sitting above the horizon, were three suns. Shading his eyes, he squinted and blinked several times, but the suns didn't falter or change in number.

Kyle struggled to a sitting position and then to his knees and finally to his feet. He faltered a bit, almost falling backward, and leaned forward to gain momentum to walk. Not far from the shore was a crowd of buildings and one room shacks huddled together, some sat only feet from the water, while others were nestled into the steep embankment. No one came running to see who he was or if he was ok. The island, with its close to vertical slopes covered in snow and ice, reminded him of a ship floating out at sea. A ghost ship perhaps, commanded by a captain and crew from the netherworld.

When he reached the first building, Kyle leaned on the door unable to lift his hand to knock. The door gave way, spilling Kyle into a small reception room of sorts. Plastic chairs, a desk, and a picture on the wall made up the modest room. He collapsed into the nearest chair. After several minutes, he raised his head and looked about; his eyes came to rest on the picture.

Painted on the canvas was a small unmanned fishing boat being tossed about on an angry sea. He stared at the picture not seeing the boat or the waves or wondering where the fisherman might be. Soon, though, his mind caught up and he noticed something odd about the picture, something that didn't quite belong. The artist had splattered dark paint across the canvas. As his gaze traveled upward, he saw that the paint had been splattered on the wall and ceiling as well. Not able to find the logic in this, his numb mind worked hard to resolve what he was seeing. Several minutes passed before a complete thawing and his thoughts processed with more clarity. His mind suggested to him that maybe it wasn't paint. He dropped his gaze to the floor beneath his feet where more paint…more-paint-on-the-floor. Not paint. Not paint at all.

"Oh shit." Kyle sprung from the chair and stumbled back out the door, yanking off his headgear and taking deep, deep breaths of the cold air. Blood. He checked the steps where he stood, but they were clean. He sank down. Blood splatter, everywhere. Blood. The word repeated in his head, like a broken record not to be ignored. Kyle smacked his hands together and stood up. Bracing himself for the worst, he went around to the other buildings, only to find the same sights awaiting him. He searched a few of the closest shacks, this time finding bodies to associate with the blood. The bodies were twisted and frozen, some having the appearance of being ripped open and gutted. After checking inside three houses he quit opening doors. These were no longer homes, they were tombs. At the fourth house, he sat outside on the steps and hung his head. Dead. They were all dead. God damn it, he swore and pounded his fist on his leg.

Although his hopes had been dealt a huge blow, Kyle wasn't giving up, not now, not ever. All he could think about was getting to Alaska. Besides, what else was he going to do? Swim back to Russia? No way. He would rest here, on this island of death, and head out in the morning. If the waters were calm all the way across he could reach land by nightfall.

Having strengthened his resolve, Kyle put his mind on deciding where he should sleep. The houses were out of the question. After a quick inspection of all the buildings, Kyle decided on the first one he'd entered. Once he moved passed the reception area no signs of blood, and more importantly, no gruesome remains were found. In the back, behind the reception room, he found a small kitchen and an even smaller room with a twin bed. He turned on the water, letting it run while he inspected the pantry. When he returned with food in hand, to his amazement and gratitude, hot water flowed from the tap. After further inspection, he found the hot water tank under the sink ran on propane and discovered the range was propane-fueled as well. A hot shower and hot meal made up for the cold bed.

Later when the dark settled in outside, Kyle, dry and full of soup, settled under several layers of thick blankets. The quiet was eerie and disturbing, but being past the point of exhaustion Kyle fell asleep before he could overthink each and every sound. Sometime in the night he stirred in his sleep and almost awoke when a piercing screech broke the silence of the night. The sound was primal in every sense of the word, but sleep reclaimed him before his mind's sensors had time to process. He later dreamt of flying demons screeching through the night.

The next morning Kyle woke up later than planned and found moving an arduous task when every muscle protested his slightest efforts. He lay back thinking maybe he would wait to leave until the following morning, giving his body time to recover. Spending another night in the ghost town wasn't an appealing prospect, but failing out at sea was even less desirable. Kyle lay his head back down and closed his eyes. Soon his breathing became deep and rhythmic. Dreams of flying demons did not return. The next time he opened his eyes was in the middle of the afternoon. He was still aching but felt better having rested. He showered and headed for the kitchen where he heated two cans of chicken and dumplings soup. He added two tins of sardines and a box of crackers. The crackers weren't the crispiest, but hauling food across the Bering Strait was not part of the plan, and he was grateful to find anything edible. He didn't expect conditions in Alaska to improve, but hoped at least he could scrounge up enough to eat until, until...

"Until what?" he asked the empty room.

Based on what he'd seen thus far, the chances of finding survivors seemed improbable. Kyle cleaned up the kitchen, putting everything back the way he found it. A search through one of the closets provided a parka, ski mask, and gloves. In the kitchen, he found galoshes. They were a size too big, but an extra thick pair of socks fixed the problem. Once dressed, he ventured outside to investigate the island. Again, the first thing he noticed was the three suns. He checked his watch, then the suns, and back to his watch. It didn't make sense, but with no one to discuss the why and what of the suns, Kyle walked on toward the shore.

He gazed out across the sea, back the way he came. Despite the frigidness, the water remained free of icebergs. Several hundred yards offshore, the white mist hung over the water like a thick curtain. However, on the island, visibility was clear and the temperature, according to his watch, was five degrees. He walked along the shore. The wind blew gustily and at times pushed him sideways. He glanced over at the suns, which at three o'clock in the afternoon should have been on the other side of the island. Nothing about any of this made sense.

Behind him, a door slammed. The sound was carried by the wind to where he stood. Kyle whipped around, hands up ready to fight. Realizing no threat was imminent, his hands drifted down to his side, not relaxed, but poised to spring forward at any sign of movement. A door slammed again. His fists clenched and then eased open as he recognized the culprit. The wind was playing tricks on his weary mind, poking fun at his imagination. No one was here. No humans, he added. This came as an afterthought, a connection to the sounds he dreamt of during the night.

After he'd lost contact with his family, Kyle thought he had experienced loneliness in the truest sense. But now, here on the island, with its crushing arms wrapping around him, squeezing his breath away, he felt a sense of isolation that threatened to upend his sanity. This feeling, coupled with the dead bodies, invited panic to join the party. Standing with his back to the shore, Kyle felt removed from his body and mind. Logic fought against the darkness of solitude, against the unknown, but was losing ground fast. A voice whispered his name. His head snapped up, turning in all directions. "Who's there?" he yelled out, but the wind grabbed his voice and carried it away. A powerful gust of wind rolled off the sea, up the rocky beach and pushed Kyle from behind. Stumbling forward, he reached out for balance, but couldn't catch himself before falling onto the rocks. The jolt was enough to tilt the fight in favor of logic. As if someone had slapped him or threw cold water in his face, Kyle snapped out of his trance, squashing his fears by refocusing on his mission. Another night on the island now seemed like a bad idea, but it was too late to start the second leg of his journey. He knew he could make Small Diomede Island by dusk, but the effort outweighed the purpose. Squaring his shoulders and taking in a deep breath, he steeled his resolve.

"One night won't be the death of me." He laughed out loud, amused by his choice of words. "Better not be," he replied out loud, finding the sound of his voice helped drown out his nagging fears. An understanding of why crazy people talked to themselves dawned on him. Chuckling, Kyle walked back to the building where he'd slept the previous night. As he approached, the door slammed against the railing and despite his resolve, he jumped back. His reaction was followed by a string of curse words. Anger served as good a weapon against fear as anything. Once back inside, he went into the kitchen and closed the door. If he was going to be stuck here for the next sixteen hours he was at least going to be warm. The room was small enough to make cozy with a few minor improvisations.

Rolled towels were placed at the base of the door to block the draft. A search through the pantry and drawers turned up heavy duty aluminum foil. Using this, he covered the small window with a double layer. Duct tape helped hold the foil in place. Next, perhaps to have something to do, Kyle foiled the doorway as well, covering every inch so that not a shard of light could be seen. Once this was complete, he took a quick shower and dressed in some of the clothes he'd found, trying to not think about the previous owner as he put them on. With his gear stored in the corner of the kitchen and the mattress laid out in the middle, he felt ready for the night. Night time by his watch was approaching soon and with this trepidation tagged along. He didn't know why the dark should disturb him, other than maybe human nature dictated to fear that which makes us feel vulnerable.

Looking around at his handy work, Kyle crossed his arms over his chest and smiled with satisfaction. Silly he knew, but it was all a ruse to occupy his mind, the same way a parent distracted an upset child with candy or a toy. Kyle's eyes came to settle on the aluminum foil box and he was reminded of the movie, *Signs*.

"What the hell," he said and got busy making a hat out of aluminum foil.

With the foil hat in place, Kyle turned his attention to the issue of heat. The oven was powered by propane, safe to use indoors, and if he kept the temperature on low might get him through the night. He turned the knob to one hundred. When the temperature hit the mark, he opened the door halfway allowing the heat to flow out. He frowned. Of course, the heat was going to rise. Foil came to the rescue once again as he fashioned a hood above the oven door to direct the heat downwards. The only thing missing now was a TV to fall asleep to.

Remembering he'd seen a stack of books being used as a makeshift nightstand, Kyle returned to the bedroom and retrieved the entire collection. Sitting on the mattress he sorted through the books. All were in Russian, a language he only knew enough to get in trouble. On the bottom of the pile, he found the only book written in English. He laughed out loud.

"War and Peace. Go figure." He flipped the pages to the first chapter. "I've always wanted to read you," he told the book. "But you're so wordy. Not that wordy is a bad thing and you're pretty good at the words," he explained to the pages crammed with description. "But my attention span is short and usually preoccupied with things that don't involve many words at all. If ya know what I mean." He winked at the book. "Short sentences worked best for me. Like, 'Of course I love you' or "I've never met anyone like you," that one was popular." He chuckled at his wit and began reading. Two chapters in and the book slipped from Kyle's hands.

Sometime later Kyle awoke with a start. The warmth in the room let him know the tank still had gas. Outside the wind was silent. He listened to the nothingness. A floorboard creaked on the other side of the kitchen door, causing every single hair to rise on his body. Each and every nerve wound up tight ready to spring, but not a muscle twitched. Holding his breath, Kyle waited for verification that he was still alone.

A loud scuffling sound verified he was not. Grunting confirmed the visitor was a living thing. He imagined maybe a wild animal had entered the building, perhaps smelling the food he'd cooked earlier. From his recollection he hadn't seen any signs of animals on the island, but what else could be making those noises? A human wouldn't make that sort of noise. A thud against the door almost shocked a curse word from his mouth. Kyle slithered off the mattress over to a drawer where the knives were kept. Very easy he inched the drawer open and pulled out a knife. With his back against the cupboards, he sat directly across from the door, waiting. He absently reached up and straightened the aluminum hat from sitting crooked on his head.

On the other side of the door, his visitor continued to cause a ruckus. Chairs were shoved across the floor, followed by a loud crash and glass breaking. Kyle imagined the boat picture was no longer on the wall or in one piece. Then movement ceased, save for the sound of toenails clicking across the tile and stopping in front of the kitchen door. Kyle's eyes grew wide. His hand gripped the knife until his knuckles turned white. An incredible screech from outside the building rattled the window. Kyle braced for attack. The visitor outside his door answered back with an equally deafening screech, all the more so because it was only a few feet away. Several seconds went by before a second screech from outside responded and Kyle heard his visitor leave the building.

An hour elapsed before Kyle dared to move and only then out of absolute necessity. The screeching had shattered the window and a shard of glass now penetrated the foil. Frigid air flowed freely into the kitchen. He removed the glass shard and quickly patched the hole before climbing under the mound of quilts. Sleep came in spurts the remainder of the night with every little sound shocking him back to consciousness. When his watch alarm alerted him that it was morning Kyle couldn't move fast enough.

Inspection of the outer room revealed what he already knew. The picture lay shattered and broken on the ground; chairs were overturned and misplaced. The front door had been torn from its hinges. On the floor, left behind in the frozen blood stains was the imprint of a large claw-like foot. From this, he gathered the maker of the print was some sort of animal. A big heavy animal. Kyle stared at that print for a long time having only an inkling of an idea of how lucky he was to be alive.

Madison and Zack could have told him.

Kyle wasted no more time wondering about his visitor. He had a long swim ahead and was anxious to get going. This feeling of urgency stayed with him the entire day, which mercifully turned out to be uneventful. The sea remained calm during the crossing, allowing him to make excellent time. Once ashore he didn't wait for the welcoming committee or take in the sights. Having no idea if those things from the island would come after him, he decided to follow the exact steps he took the night before. Entering the first building with an open door, Kyle quickly looked around. A Terry's Wilderness Room sign perched above the fireplace in what turned out to be a diner or restaurant of sorts. They would have foil and foil was a must have. He went into the kitchen, snooped about for provisions before his eyes came to rest on the open freezer door. What little light remained reflected off the aluminum clad door of the freezer. As the reflection of light grew dimmer an idea grew brighter in his mind. "I'll sleep in the freezer," Kyle announced to the room, nodding his head and thinking this made complete sense. An hour later, camped out in the freezer wearing an aluminum hat, Kyle finished eating cold chili from a can. He was beyond worrying about looking or feeling stupid. In the matter of survival, he would put on a pink tutu and dance in the street if it meant saving his life; if by doing so meant the things from the island couldn't find him.

The night went without interruption, allowing Kyle much needed rest. The next day he set out to search the town of Deadbear, population one hundred fifteen. A number he knew would be closer to zero if not zero.

8 REUNION

Luke sat at the side of Austin's bed staring at the man who was his savior and friend. Three weeks had gone by and the feeling of helplessness was devastating. Austin had given and done so much for Luke, yet here he sat doing nothing, except sitting; even the chair holding him up served more of a purpose. Luke glanced at the heart monitor, still going strong. The captain would survive this. He had to survive. "Don't die man. We need you," Luke said. "I need you," he added, his voice a mere whisper. He wasn't ashamed of how he felt about Austin. How do you repay someone who saves your life on multiple occasions? Luke knew of one way, of one thing he would do should Austin not wake up. He was going to hunt Eve down and when he found her he would kill her.

How he would do this hadn't presented itself to him, but Zack could figure that part out. It didn't cross Luke's mind that Zack might not be as hell-bent on revenge. When it came to matters concerning the captain, Luke's opinions were one-sided. An enemy of Austin's was his as well. Could be the Pope, could be the devil; Luke would side against them all the same if they were not on Austin's side.

Austin's body twitched, and a moan escaped his lips. Every so often he mumbled something unintelligible. Luke thought he'd said Roxanne on more than one occasion, but could never be certain. Austin still wore his wedding ring. He'd never spoken of what had happened to his wife. Not to him or Ed, and Luke didn't think he would have shared this with anyone else, if not them. Although, he suspected Zack knew a few things that maybe no one else did. Things Austin confided in him for reasons that didn't matter to Luke. All that mattered right now was Zack figuring out what was wrong.

The door to Austin's room opened and German bounded in ahead of Madison. The dog had taken up a post outside Austin's room and left only when nature called. Colin had taken to feeding him there as well since he refused to go to the diner where his dog dish was usually kept.

"Any change?" Madison walked over to Luke.

"No. Same today as yesterday." Luke swallowed hard, choking back the lump in his throat.

"Zack's doing more tests today. Maybe he'll find something." Madison rubbed Luke's shoulders. They'd been through so much together, she thought of Luke as her family. Him, Ed and, and darn it to hell anyway, Austin as well.

"We need a real doctor."

"Zack's pretty smart. He'll figure it out. I know he will," Madison said this with more conviction than she believed. And her doubt wasn't because she didn't have confidence in Zack, he was a genius for heaven's sakes, but they had no idea what they were dealing with. She wondered more than once if maybe they shouldn't be near Austin at all if maybe he was contagious and should be quarantined. This suggestion wasn't well received when she broached the topic with Luke, so she stopped asking, but didn't stop wondering. Madison pulled a chair next to Luke's and sat down. She wanted to tell Luke about what'd happened when she went to see Austin, but no matter how she worded the scene over in her head everything sounded like craziness. Luke wouldn't want to hear that she thought Austin had changed, that something was seriously wrong.

"Tell me about Bliss," Madison said, deciding it best to keep her doubts to herself for now.

"It was beautiful," Luke replied. "Like a tropical island."

"Warm and sunny?"

"Very."

Madison sighed. She missed the sun, the beach, her mom. She missed hearing her mom nagging at her. For the longest time, she had been able to conjure up her mother's voice. After the initial drop, when Madison had feared she was the only human left alive, her mother's voice kept her going, kept her from losing her mind. She hadn't heard much from her of late.

"Memories fade," Madison said out loud not meaning to do so.

"What?"

"Nothing. Um…never mind. So tropical and what else?" she asked.

"Weird creatures, like dinosaurs, and giant birds with huge colorful feathers. It was crazy, like Alice in Wonderland crazy."

"What about the temple? And the Adita? What were they like?"

Luke glanced at Madison, his lips pressed tightly together. "Have you ever watched a lion stalk its prey?"

Madison nodded. "Not up close, but you know on TV."

"My dad took me to Africa when I was ten. Most kids go to Disney World, I went to Africa. Anyway, we were riding across this open plain when the guide stopped and pointed. Fifty feet from where we'd stopped a pride was lying in the shade under a tree. It was the lions and their cubs. My dad let me use his binoculars and I remember looking into the lion's eyes. I knew she was looking right at me and was going to eat me. My dad thought it was hilarious, but I had nightmares for months."

Luke turned from Austin and lowered his voice. "The Adita remind me of the lions."

"Like animals?"

"Yeah, kind of, but highly intelligent," Luke replied. "And I don't think we've seen the last of 'em. I think they're getting ready for something bigger and probably a whole lot worse for us."

"What makes you think that?"

Before Luke could answer the overhead lights began to flash. Madison and Luke shared a look of trepidation. Who could be approaching the bunker? Other survivors seemed unlikely and, even more so, that they would know how to find the bunker. Luke and Madison rushed out of the room. They were joined along the way by Colin and Charlie. By the time they reached the command center twelve of the fourteen bunker occupants had crowded into the room.

"Where's Zack?" Ed asked.

Zack burst into the room. "I'm here."

The group parted allowing him to reach the computer controlling the cameras. On the screen they watched a vehicle turn off the highway onto the road leading to the ranch house. They held their breath when the vehicle drove on to the barn and parked outside the big door. Inside the cab were two people. Zack closed in on the driver, but a ski mask was in place making recognition or identification impossible.

The driver's door opened; the driver stepped out.

"A woman," Madison noted.

"How do you know?" Ed stared at the person, wrapped head to toe in winter gear, revealing nothing.

"The feet." Madison pointed. "Too small for a man."

Ed followed her finger to the figure's boot-clad feet and nodded, although he couldn't say one way or the other if the feet were too small for a man, he knew Madison had good instincts about people, so her assessment was good enough for him.

The woman walked up to the door and pounded on it with a gloved fist. After a moment she looked up at the hidden camera and waved. A wave saying come out, not hello or is anyone in there. This person knew people were waiting inside and knew those people were watching.

"What the..." Ed muttered.

"Is everyone here?" Zack asked.

"Everyone," Madison replied after a quick count.

"Then who the hell is that?" Zack asked, but was gone from the room before anyone had time to think, let alone answer.

The group watched in silence. Finding survivors was as exhilarating as it was frightening. As the current status of the group stood, they had peace and harmony, but harmony among men was a precarious state. One bad seed could turn their haven upside down. And though no one would say so out loud, Austin's illness weighed heavy on everyone's sense of security.

Outside the woman waited. She no longer waved at the camera which Madison thought seemed odd as if the person knew Zack was on his way. Madison watched her, but she stood so absolutely still that she appeared frozen in place. The passenger chose that precise moment to exit the vehicle drawing everyone's attention in that direction. By the size, Madison guessed it was another woman. Following behind her, a smaller figure jumped out, one they hadn't been able to see.

"Oh shit. That's a kid," Ed said.

"I didn't think any were left," Luke commented and instantly regretted saying it out loud. "Sorry, Ed. I didn't...I'm sorry."

"It's ok," Ed replied, although Luke's words stung like hell, he knew the intention wasn't malicious. Besides, Ed was a bit in shock himself. No children survivors had been found, not that they were aware, and other than the nightmare in Lamar, they hadn't seen bodies of children dropped from the sky or found elsewhere. Having one show up now was pretty astounding.

* * *

The barn door slid open and Zack stepped out holding a rifle. "Can I help you?" Zack chose his words carefully, all the while scanning the horizon for an ambush. No one came out of the woods.

"I'm looking for Austin Reynolds," the woman responded in a soft voice he almost couldn't hear. In the bunker's infirmary, Austin stirred and German's hair rose on his back.

The woman's response caught Zack's full attention, as well as those listening inside. "I don't know any Austin Reynolds."

"Please Mr. Londergan."

Zack lowered his rifle. "How do you know my name?"

"Eve told me I could find my husband here. Here in your bunker."

"Your husband?"

"Yes. I'm Roxanne, his wife."

"His wife. I thought you were...he said you were..."

"Dead. Yes, I know. Eve had no choice. Her father made her lie to him."

"Can I see your face?" Zack was beyond baffled but hadn't completely lost his senses.

The woman removed her headgear to reveal her face.

"Oh shit," Zack said upon seeing it was Roxanne or at least she looked like the woman in Roth's pictures.

Inside the command center everyone, especially Madison who was intimately familiar with Roxanne's face, watched in awe. The entire Roxanne business had been off limits. No one dared ask or even talk about her amongst themselves. Yet here she was at the bunker in the flesh. Focused on her being alive, they'd all forgotten about the other woman and the child who were still standing by the vehicle.

Zack ushered the women and child into the barn. Roxanne waited for the child to come before she followed Zack inside. The doors slid closed.

Inside the command center, they all turned their attention to the screens showing the inside of the barn. They watched as the group descended into the floor.

"I thought she was dead," Colin commented.

"I guess we'll find out soon enough," Ed replied.

Luke shrugged his shoulders in confusion. He'd been in the temple and heard Agra say Roxanne was dead. Austin had said she was dead. Luke didn't like this. Those blood sucking aliens couldn't be trusted. He didn't trust them. They had no way of knowing what their agenda might be, but Luke was certain their plans wouldn't favor the human race. The bloodsuckers needed Austin and what better way to do so than by using his wife as bait. If she was his wife at all.

Within a few minutes, Zack called on the radio asking everyone to meet him in the recreation room. That he didn't bring the visitors to the command center told Luke Zack had doubts as well. This comforted Luke to some extent knowing he wasn't the only one suspicious. A glimpse of Madison's furrowed brow told him she wasn't convinced either.

Inside the recreation room, Zack helped the second woman remove her coat while Roxanne knelt at the child's side doing the same. She did not look up when the bunker's residents piled into the room. Charlie and Colin were the first through the door. Jeremy helped Anne, who was ready to give birth to twins any day now. Grace, the other pregnant girl from Roth's program, followed them in. Zoe, the youngest at thirteen, came in with sisters Sue and Jane. Luke followed behind with Barbara. They stood back allowing the newcomers space, trying not to stare and make them uncomfortable. Roxanne seemed very much at ease, as did the boy. Madison entered, followed by Ed, and at that precise moment, Roxanne turned the boy around.

Madison's jaw dropped open. She'd know those eyes anywhere. "His son," she whispered, but how was that possible? Roxanne looked up, meeting Madison's astounded gaze with one that was slightly less than cool. Madison dropped her eyes to Roxanne's neck. Her mole was there as it should be.

Ed had stopped behind everyone and couldn't see the two women or the boy. The group moved forward to introduce themselves and Ed moved with the flow. When Luke stepped aside, allowing Ed passage, the world suddenly floated away from him. All sounds ceased; he felt himself falling. From far away a familiar voice called his name. Time slowed to a halt and then, like a speeding train, rushed back crashing into him at full speed.

The second woman, a pretty blond with bright green eyes, walked toward him. "Edward?"

Ed found his voice. "Jenny? Jenny. It's you. It's really you." And with that Ed's legs faltered beneath him. Luke was standing close enough to catch him before he hit the floor.

8 FUR ELISE

As the bunker residents were having their happy and strange reunions, Kyle was recuperating in Deadbear, Alaska. Two days of rest and he was back to feeling like himself. The aches had diminished for the most part. Better than that, no midnight visitors or dreams of screeching monsters. If not for seeing the footprint, he might have convinced himself it was all imagined.

Although the town gave every indication of being uninhabited, Kyle planned to look around before leaving. He would need supplies for the trip, but had reservations on what he might be able to find. First thing had to be clothing. Still, in his special suit, Kyle walked down the vacant ice-covered street to Kwiki Pete's gas station. A sign above the door read, 'Get it now, cuz tomorrow it'll be gone.' Another sign announced, 'All your camo needs are right inside'. Camo was good enough for Kyle.

He grabbed the handle of the door and paused. Someone had taped an obituary clipping to the inside of the window. The newspaper was yellow and cracked and the writing difficult to read. However, someone had used red ink to scrawl R.I.P. D. Reynolds across the bottom in big letters. All around this were the faded names and initials of the bereaved. The date of Mr. Reynolds death was some eighteen years ago. Old D. Reynolds must have been a popular man here in Deadbear, Kyle mused. Or Kwiki Pete was too lazy to remove the newspaper.

Inside the gas station, Kyle found the promised camo wear. Pants, shirts, socks, boxers, and more were available in medium, large and extra, extra-large. A few children sized garments hung on the rack, but not many. Kyle couldn't imagine living in Deadbear as an adult, let alone growing up there as a child. What a nightmare, he thought with a shudder.

After grabbing two pairs of everything in size large, Kyle added four pairs of socks and a pair of boots one size too big. He threw in a bright green and red striped scarf and hat set. This was better than the tablecloth he currently wore, which smelled like old bacon fat and cigarette smoke. Beggars had to take what was left behind, and he wasn't complaining. He laid these items on the counter and went back through the station scavenging for anything else deemed useful.

In the end, he had a small grocery cart containing the clothing, two bags of canned food, a bag with Tylenol, aspirin and various other medications, as well as a bag filled with several frozen bottles of water and Gatorade. Satisfied these provisions would get him through the next couple of days, Kyle returned to the diner with his goods.

Once back inside Terry's Wilderness Room, Kyle heated a can of soup on the stove and spread out a map on the counter. He ate the soup straight from the can while looking over the map. The plan was to go across the Norton Sound to Emmonak, a one hundred twenty-mile trek and then head to Anchorage, another five hundred miles as the crow flies. He fished a marker from the grocery cart and traced his route to Anchorage and then on down to Colorado. The task provided him comfort and something to do but wasn't necessary. He'd studied the maps so many times over the past year, the route was imprinted in his memory.

Wearing his new camo over his wetsuit, Kyle needed to find heavier clothing. The wetsuit wasn't made for permanent wear. His stomach tightened at what he must do, but he had no other choice for now. The town didn't offer a shopping strip where you could get your nails done, cash for the title of your car, grab a foot-long sandwich and shop at the Big & Tall. The gas station was it, and the only parka available had been two sizes too small. He hoped his search would turn up what he needed and fast.

Bundled to the best of his ability, with the hat and scarf secured tightly around his head, Kyle headed back up the street to the residential part of town. He found a handful of small homes that were more like shacks, and he marveled they'd survived this long in an upright position. The first in the row seemed the ideal place to start his search.

Two broken wooden steps led to a worn front door. The numbers eight zero hung lopsided from rusted nails. Kyle knocked on the door. He waited a few seconds before trying the handle. At first, it stuck, and he couldn't help feeling relieved. He gave another hard twist and the latch retracted. Pushing the door open, Kyle stood at the bottom of the broken steps staring into the house. The door opened into a small living room where he could see an old brown and blue plaid recliner and a metal TV stand. Past the chair was a doorway leading to what he assumed was the kitchen. No sounds came from the house. No bodies were visible from where he stood.

Taking a deep breath Kyle pulled himself up over the steps and into the house. He looked around hoping to get lucky but knowing he wasn't going to find what he needed right inside the doorway, in the safe zone. Not going to be that easy junior. He walked through the stranger's house, eyeballing their personal belongings. On the other side of the kitchen, he found a bathroom and beyond that two small bedrooms.

On the wall of the first bedroom was a poster-sized picture of Thor above a twin bed. The comforter matched the poster. The bed was empty. Kyle moved on to the next room where a queen bed took up most of the space. On the bed was a mangled pile of quilts and sheets. Above the bed's headboard someone had splattered dark paint. Kyle stared at the splatter, similar to that in the boat picture.

Not paint, you idiot.

Kyle's eyes drifted back to the pile of blankets. The room was poorly lit but provided enough illumination for him to see blood stains on the bed and floor. Not knowing why he felt compelled to walk into the room when his body was screaming for him to turn around, to leave, to not look any closer, he stepped closer to the bed.

Yeah, there's a body under all those blankets you fool, but you don't need to see it. He tried to reason himself out of the room but was held in place by the magnetic draw of the gruesome. The appeal of the morbid that took control of a person's will, making them want to see things they knew deep down they'd regret seeing. Things that stuck with you for a long time and, after having had time to fester, they came back to you in much grander fashion than when seeing those things for the first time. Reason never stood a chance against the lure of the fascinating, no matter how evil. He had to see if this was as bad as the people on the island or if maybe those gory details had been conjured up by his exhausted overworked brain. Yes, he had to know, had to see, for sanity's sake, that was all.

Kyle reached out grasping the edge of the blanket and pulled it back slow. The quilt caught and held. Kyle gave it a quick yank, but it wouldn't come free. He swore under his breath and tugged again, this time with more force. The quilt, along with the corpse attached to it flew off the bed knocking a startled Kyle backward onto the floor.

"Oh shit. Oh shit." He pushed the body off his legs and scooted back against the wall.

The deceased lay partially exposed with the pile of bedding tangled around its lower body. The face was mangled beyond recognition, but Kyle gathered by the hair and clothing it was a woman. Or had been before someone or something decided to shred her face and gut her like a pig. Through blood-matted hair, an empty eye socket looked out at him. Why would someone take her eyes?

"Yes Kyle, why on God's Earth would someone take my eyes." the corpse asked. "Have you seen my bedroom slippers, dear?"

Kyle scrambled over to the doorway, keeping an eye on Mrs. Mangled, waiting for her to rise up, to lunge after him, but she didn't. He paused in the doorway, his heart beating like an eight o eight drum. He wondered about a Mr.

Mangled and where Mangled Junior might be. Were they going to want to chat with him as well?

Kyle stumbled from the house, tripping down the steps and out into the middle of the street. What on earth had he been thinking when he decided to do this? Forget navigating the unforgiving wilderness of Alaska, he couldn't even navigate this small deserted town. He leaned over at the waist and stared at the boots on his feet. Not his boots, but the gas station's boots. Not his clothes, not even his boxers. All around him silence and death screamed at him, gnawed at his confidence, wore down his will.

Above the noise in his head, an unexpected sound floated along in the brisk wind. Kyle straightened up and listened. Again he heard it. The distinct sound of music. He pulled back the scarf, exposing his ear, and cocked his head in the direction of the noise. Soon he heard it again, loud and clear, the plinking of a piano. Kyle walked down the street toward the plinks. The closer he drew, the clearer the sounds became. Whoever was playing, was pretty good. He recognized the tune as something classical, but beyond that observation hadn't a clue. Beethoven was never his thing.

Kyle paused in front of a small blue house with white lace curtains, a red door and steps all in one piece. The music was definitely coming from inside. A piano player could be a psychotic killer, he supposed, after walking up to the door and knocking. The player, or psycho killer, stopped playing. The last note hung in the air as if it too listened. Kyle waited, but no one came. He knocked again.

"Hello."

The piano player killer did not answer.

He tried the handle. Locked.

"Hello," he repeated a bit louder and knocked on the door again. Determined to find the source of the music, Kyle twisted harder on the door handle and banged on the door. "Come on I know you're in there."

"Hands in the air mister," a girl's voice demanded from behind him.

Kyle started, stumbled and fell off the stoop landing on his hip. He groaned and rolled over. "Oh shit," he said to the end of a double barrel shotgun. Behind the gun, with her finger on the trigger, was a young girl. She wore a purple dress over green tights. Her feet were tucked into florescent purple galoshes and her hair was in two long braids under a pink knitted wool cap. Despite the weapon, he thought she appeared harmless and, at least for now, he felt certain she was not a psycho killer.

"Hands up," she demanded.

Kyle held his hands in the air. "Now what?"

"You one of them?"

"One of them what?"

"One of them aliens?"

"No, not an alien. I'm an American. My name's Kyle Bosch." Kyle lowered one hand.

"I said hands up mister. I'll shoot you. I swear I will," she said, making her point by shoving the gun closer to Kyle's face.

"Please don't do that. I'm already having a bad day."

The girl stood her ground, but Kyle could see she was thinking things over, sizing him up, weighing her options, or chances. She lowered the gun.

"I'm gonna lower my hands ok?" He moved slowly keeping an eye on her trigger finger.

The girl nodded, taking a step back and raising the gun barrel a couple of inches. Her eyes remained cagey, her posture on edge. The weapon was almost as tall as she, but she handled the weight with ease.

"What's your name?" he asked.

"McKenna."

"Just McKenna?"

She nodded.

"Were you playing the piano?"

She nodded again. "It'll be dark soon." And with that, she turned and disappeared around the side of the house.

Kyle jumped up and followed, but when he rounded the corner she was nowhere in sight. "McKenna."

Her head popped out from a hole in the siding. "This way." She pushed the siding over revealing a passageway.

Kyle knelt down eyeing the diameter with skepticism.

"You'll fit," she said with confidence and moved back.

About to stick his head into the hole, Kyle paused. What if she wasn't alone and this was a trap? A real live psycho killer adult might be waiting inside. The word cannibal surfaced in his mind, and further fueled his doubts. He glanced up at the gray sky. The light was fading fast. He walked back out to the street. Was there enough time to make it to the diner, he wondered and doubted at the same time. The two crescent suns had faded away and the main sun was losing what little luster it had. Even running at full speed Kyle knew he wouldn't beat the night. Dark, he found, arrived in a blink, falling like an iron curtain and, though not fully convinced of what he'd heard on the island was real, confirmation wasn't desired either. With only seconds remaining Kyle went back to the hole and squeezed himself through.

Once inside, McKenna pulled the siding back in place. Using a rope, she lowered a large piece of plywood over the hole. Kyle looked around surprised to find himself in what had the appearance of a bedroom. The furniture had been shoved to one side of the room. A dresser held several planks of wood up against the wall. Kyle assumed a window was behind the crude barricade.

"Come on." She tugged on his sleeve. "We have to get to into the back room."

Kyle allowed her to lead him down a narrow hallway to another bedroom only slightly bigger than the first. Once inside McKenna shut the door, slid three bolts into place and pulled on a curtain rope which released an aluminum clad blanket that covered the door. From the corner a battery powered lantern cast a dim circle of light. The single window was covered over in layers of aluminum foil and the walls were also covered with aluminum. Kyle stared at the foil, suppressing the tremor traveling up his spine.

"Here, put this on." McKenna handed him a hat made of foil. "So they can't see inside your head," she responded to his gaping stare.

Kyle removed his scarf and hat, replacing them with the aluminum hat. McKenna, serious as a heart attack, put her hat on as well. "Are you hungry?"

"Yeah. Sure." After meeting the Mangled family, he hadn't thought much about eating, but now realized he was quite hungry.

In the corner, on a small nightstand, was a loaf of white bread and a jar of peanut butter. Water bottles, paper plates, and plastic utensils were stored on the shelf below. McKenna busied herself fixing dinner. From a small cooler, she pulled out a jar of red jelly.

"I hope you like P.B. and J." She glanced over her shoulder, eyebrows raised.

"My favorite," Kyle proclaimed, although he hadn't had one in years. Not since he was a kid and mom packed his lunch. Kyle's hand absently went to his chest, where hidden underneath the layers of camo was the picture of his mom.

McKenna handed Kyle a plate with two sandwiches and some potato chips. He accepted the plate from her. "Looks delicious. Thank you." He fully expected the chips to be stale.

From a closet, she pulled out two regular sized folding chairs and a metal T.V. stand. She set the table up, placing a chair on each side. On the table, she placed napkins and two bottles of water.

"You can sit." She gestured to the chair.

Kyle sat holding his plate in his lap.

"I don't usually have company." McKenna sat in her chair also holding her plate in her lap. She bit into her sandwich and watched Kyle while she chewed.

Kyle took a bite and was surprised to find the food tasted fresh. He ate a potato chip which still held quite a bit of crunch. They ate in silence, the crunching of chips the only sound in the room. After they finished McKenna promptly cleaned up. The chairs and tray were returned to the closet. The plates were rolled up and placed in a garbage bag. The empty bottles were added to another bag that was already full of plastic bottles.

Kyle watched from the corner, staying out of her way. He got the impression she followed this routine every night and surmised it was similar to the routine her family had followed, minus certain aspects. He wanted to ask about her family but didn't know how to broach the subject. Although accustomed to dealing with crying ladies, a distressed little girl was not territory he felt prepared to tackle.

McKenna walked over to him. "If you need to use the bathroom, you have to go through the closet. I made a tunnel"

"I'm good."

"Ok."

"Now what?"

"I usually read until I get tired, but we can talk if you like," she offered and then turned red as if embarrassed.

Sensing she wanted to talk, Kyle smiled and replied, "Talking. Yeah, I like that idea." And he did. She might be able to shed some light on what happened when the cloud dropped.

"You go first," she said. "Oh, wait, I almost forgot." She vanished into the closet, returning shortly with a propane powered heater. "I couldn't get the cap off."

Kyle nodded and took the heater from her. With a little encouragement, he was able to twist the cap off and attached the propane canister. He set the heater on the nightstand and turned it on low. Within minutes the room was toasty warm. McKenna shed her parka and boots revealing a scrawny frame.

"That's wonderful," she sighed, beaming. "I haven't had heat in months. My first heater ran out and this was the only one I could find over at V&G's Feed store." She pulled two sleeping bags from off the bed and handed one to Kyle. "We can sit on these."

Guessing by her height Kyle thought her to be ten or eleven years old, which meant she'd been eight or nine when the white mass moved in. And she'd survived all this time. Kyle was floored and somewhat embarrassed at his previous behavior. Once situated, McKenna waited for Kyle to speak.

"Um. Well...so what was it you were playing on the piano?" he asked.

"Bagatelle in A Minor," she replied with a wave of her hand. "Fur Elise. Beethoven." She went on to Kyle's blank expression.

"Ah, Beethoven." Kyle recognized this. "You're pretty good."

"I practice every day."

"Did your mom teach you?"

"No. I taught me."

"You did?"

"Yep. Mom didn't like the piano. She wanted me to play the guitar and become a country music singer. I like the piano."

Kyle was impressed. "Are you…is anyone else…"

"I'm the only child the aliens didn't take," she jumped in. "They took most of the adults. Except for old crusty Trooper Riggs. They killed him in the street later. I was glad. I mean, not that he was killed, but you know, he was kinda crazy and he didn't know I was still alive."

"I understand. Have you seen them? The aliens?"

"Yep. They are big and ugly like a fierce gargoyle, but uglier than that and bigger. They are as tall as my house and have long pointy nails on their hands and feet. And their teeth are long and sharp. When they killed Trooper Riggs they opened him up like a book. From the middle" She demonstrated. "He was old and mean anyway."

Kyle didn't know if she was making this up as she went or she'd really seen such things. They'd speculated about aliens having arrived on the planet, but no one wanted to believe it.

"How come they didn't take you?" she asked, stretching out on her sleeping bag.

"I was in Germany."

"The aliens didn't go to Germany?"

"No."

McKenna yawned. "Do you think they will?"

"I don't know."

"Why did you come here?" Her eyes fell. "Why didn't you stay in Germany?"

"I need to find my mom and sister."

McKenna didn't respond, Kyle was sure she'd fallen asleep. He turned the light down low. As easy as he was able, he picked her up and laid her on the bed, covering her with the quilt.

"Mr. Kyle," McKenna mumbled, laying her hand on his arm.

"Yes."

"Don't leave me here."

"I…" Kyle fumbled. "I won't." And he wouldn't. What kind of shithead would he be if he left her here all alone?

"Promise?"

"I promise." He laid his hand over hers, only moving after certain she'd fallen asleep.

Outside an object, thrown by the wind, hit the side of the house. Kyle jumped a little, but being in the presence of this brave little girl made his former doubts subside. If he couldn't be brave on his own, he could and certainly would be brave for her. Reaching to turn down the lamp, he noticed the calendar on the night table. Half of the days of October were crossed off. Kyle flipped to November, where Thanksgiving Day was circled. He flipped to December. Christmas was circled in red with a big black X marking out the day. It was the saddest thing he'd ever seen.

9 CHRISTMAS & PLANES

Madison sat alone at the diner counter. The rest of the bunker residents were still sleeping. She sipped on her coffee, savoring the aroma and rich taste. It was a Hawaiian blend Zack had brought back from town. He didn't say where he'd found it and she didn't ask, preferring to believe it came from a store rather than someone's pantry. Happy for the time alone, she used it to think, to meditate, and to mull over all those things she'd pushed to the back of her mind for one reason or another.

So much had happened in the past few days it was difficult to grasp onto anything that made sense. Since arriving, Roxanne had not left Austin's bedside. The boy, Austin's son, remained with his mother never venturing out on his own. As far as Madison could tell, he was not allowed to speak much either. Madison had tried to reach out to Roxanne, but had been greeted with a coolness that should have come with a frost warning. The subject of Austin's wife and son seemed to be on everyone's taboo list. A frustrating obstacle for Madison, who had questions, a multitude of questions.

Ed and Jenny had not come out of Ed's living quarters and she wondered how Jenny might be taking the news about everything that had happened. How do you take something like that on top of everything else? As hard as the past year had been for Ed, Madison thought Jenny was going to have a more difficult time adapting.

Pouring another cup of coffee, Madison went and sat in one of the booths. She slid to the end of the bench, leaned against the wall and stretched her legs out so only her feet hung over the outside edge. As she sipped her mind wandered. She revisited Section Seven, the Dodge City Diner, down to Tampa and circled back to the bunker. Anne's babies were due at the end of December. Grace was due only a week later. Christmas babies and a New Year's baby, Madison thought. The word Christmas played around in Madison's mind wanting to be noticed. Christmas.

"Christmas," she said out loud.

"Did you say Christmas?" Zack grabbed her foot making her jump. "Sorry didn't mean to startle you."

"You didn't. I mean you did, but..." Madison swung her legs around under the table. "My mind was elsewhere."

"On Christmas?" Zack sat down across from her. Ever since she'd made it clear he wasn't the guy for her, keeping his distance was constantly on his mind and harder to do each day.

"I was thinking about Anne having her twins in December and how they might be Christmas babies. I hadn't realized it was coming up. You know Christmas"

"Should we have some kind of celebration?"

"I don't know if 'celebration' is the right word considering our circumstances."

"What are our circumstances?"

"Whatta ya mean?"

"I was wondering what you thought of everything. Of life. The future. You know, our circumstances. "

Madison stared at him for a long moment. She'd given plenty of thought to many things, but not to those things. Not to their situation or their circumstances. She lived in the moment, never thinking too far ahead. "I don't know. I haven't given it much thought. Have you?"

"I have," Zack replied, his tone uncharacteristically somber.

"And?"

"And I think celebrating Christmas might be a good thing. Especially for the younger crew. One last hurrah before the ship sinks."

Madison thought this over. "You think they're coming back? The Adita?"

"Yep."

"What more do they want? They've already taken everyone." Madison's voice went up an octave. "Except us. Except for a few survivors. We're no threat to them. Why would they want...?" The answer smacked her in the head. "They want Austin don't they?"

Zack nodded, glad she was quick to pick up on things. He needed to confide in someone, someone he could trust to be level-headed. He had reservations about Madison remaining neutral in regard to Austin but knew she could be trusted.

Madison's cop side took over as she watched Zack's facial expressions change. "Do you know something?"

"I do, but you can't tell anyone. No one. Not Luke or Ed or anyone," he emphasized.

"I won't. I promise."

Zack pondered for a moment, considering what he was about to say. "Did you see Austin before he went into the coma?

Madison nodded.

"So you saw his eyes?"

"No. He had sunglasses on. Inside his apartment. When I asked about it, he, he flipped out. Why? What's wrong with his eyes?"

"Well," Zack started, clearing his throat, "it seems Eve injected him with some sort of something into his veins and his blood…"

"What do you mean injected?"

"Ah, not injected. Bit. She bit him."

"What! Are you kidding me? Bit him? Come on Zack," Madison argued, but with little force because what he said didn't seem all that preposterous.

"Not kidding. Came straight from the horse's mouth."

"Austin told you that." She rubbed her forehead. "Ok, so she bit him."

"So, I've been taking blood samples since he passed out. At first, the foreign cells, or Eve's cells, were consuming his, but then yesterday I noticed his cells were fighting back. They were eating or consuming, the new cells."

"Sounds very sci-fyish. What does it mean?"

"Not sure yet, but it's like when your body fights a virus or bacteria. Except Eve's cells are the Hulk of viruses."

"Sounds more like cancer," she said with not a little note of sarcasm.

"Cancer? Ah. Hmm." Zack pondered for a few minutes. He hadn't thought of this as a disease to be treated.

"What's the aha look for?"

"You, my dear, may have come up with a possible solution." Zack flashed her one of his 'melt your heart' smiles.

Madison's heart did more than melt, it jumped in her chest and her cheeks felt flushed. Don't make a fool of yourself Mad, her mom chided, choosing that precise moment to chime in after being silent for weeks.

"Is this a private party?" Luke plopped down next to Madison, saving her further embarrassment.

"Not at all," Zack answered. "We were discussing celebrating Christmas."

"Christmas? Really?" Luke scowled. "What's to celebrate?"

Madison and Zack exchanged a worried glance. Both had noticed Luke's demeanor changing, his attitude growing worse by the day.

"Hey man, lighten up. It's not the end of the world," Zack said and then chuckled at his choice of words.

"Glad you think this is such a joke. Do you have to be such a smartass about everything?"

"Hey, what's your problem?" Madison turned to look at him.

"I don't have a problem. We have a problem." He slid out of the booth. "You all act like living down here is gonna go on forever. We eat and drink like we have a never-ending supply. No one talks about the future and what happens when all the shit runs out. We keep taking people in. Two of the girls are going to have babies. How are we supposed to support everyone?"

"What would you have us do? Turn them away?" Madison asked.

"No. That's not what I'm saying at all." Luke ran his hand through his hair, searching for the right words. "What I'm saying is we can't live like being down here is only temporary and one-day things are gonna return to normal. That's never gonna happen. The vampires…the Adita, the whatever, made damn sure of that."

Madison refrained from telling Luke everything was going to be ok. A stupid thing people say when they don't know what else to say. Besides, Luke wasn't a kid anymore. He was twenty-one, old enough to be treated like an adult.

"Come on Luke. Sit down. Talk to us."

Luke looked at Madison for a long moment, his expression hard, and his body tense like he was ready to fight.

"Please," she implored.

Luke's shoulders relaxed as he took the seat next to her. "Sorry for the outburst."

"Don't apologize dude. You're right. We haven't given the future much thought," Zack admitted. "But it's hard to think about something you don't expect to happen. You know?"

The diner's door opened and closed. Zack waved Ed over.

"Morning all." He slid into the empty space next to Zack. His face was pale and dark rings circled his eyes.

"Hey Ed," Madison replied. "You doin' ok?"

"Ah, not really."

Madison reached out and held Ed's hand, stopping herself from saying everything would be ok. Damn it if there wasn't a less meaningless phrase. "How's Jenny?" she asked instead.

"She's strong." He swallowed hard. "Stronger than I am."

"Has she told you anything about the Adita?" Luke asked.

"Not really. She doesn't remember being taken or anything that happened that day. She only remembers waking up and Eve being with her. She said the warehouses were full of people. Perhaps hundreds of them, but she couldn't remember seeing any children."

"Does she remember what happened to Ryan?" Madison asked.

Ed shook his head. "I don't think so. All she could tell me about that day was walking into the kitchen holding the tray of hot cocoa. She doesn't even remember seeing the Sundogs. I mean the Svan. She said she had a faint recollection of traveling at a tremendous speed and feeling like her body was being ripped apart.

I guess they took her through the portal. Anyway, we'll be ok. If Ryan's still alive, and I believe he is, I'm going to find him."

"How are you going to do that? Luke asked.

"I've been looking at that map Maddie took from Roth's office. All the circled areas are in remote parts of the country. The roads aren't even noted on the map. If the Adita have warehouses on Earth what better place to hide them. I'll search every single one. I'll save as many people as I can. If Ryan's in one, I'll find him. I have to find him."

"But there are thirteen circles spread out from Canada to Florida. That'll take a long time." Madison replied.

"What else do I have to do?" Ed snapped.

"I'm going with you," Luke announced.

"Thanks, man. I could use the help." Ed gave him a wry smile.

"Do you know how to fly a plane?" Zack questioned, but didn't wait for an answer. "Well I do and finding these...what are we looking for again?"

"Camps. Warehouses. I'm not sure." Ed shrugged.

"Well, finding these camps or warehouses will be easier and faster from the air."

"You have a plane?"

"Had a plane. I sold it before the Sundogs arrived, but I bet there're a few at the airport not being used."

Ed couldn't believe what Zack was telling them. "Why haven't you tried flying over the country looking for survivors?"

"Colin's afraid to fly. Like deathly afraid. I wasn't going to leave him here alone." Zack shrugged. "And since you guys arrived a few months ago things have been kinda crazy."

They all nodded. Madison, who was keeping a journal, could have told them hardly a day went by that she didn't have some new astounding event to write down. "How big is the plane?"

Zack thought he knew where Madison was going with this question. "I think it best to use a small plane and make short jumps from one city to the next, trading out planes in each. Probably a four-seater if I can find one that'll run." Zack's mind worked fast and plans for this excursion were rapidly unfolding.

Madison looked directly at Zack "You can't leave until after the babies are born."

Zack relaxed. She said you, not we, meaning she wouldn't fight to go with them. He needed her here, but it wasn't fair for him to ask this of her. She hadn't signed up to play den mother. "I'll stay to deliver."

"That's four weeks," Ed protested. "What if the Adita return before then? What if the harvest, or whatever they have planned, happens before then?"

"Chill man. We can check out a couple during that time. I think at least two are within an hour's flight of here," Zack responded.

Ed relaxed upon hearing this. He had to take action and now. They had no idea what the harvest meant, but he felt once this event took place, saving Ryan or the human race wasn't going be a possibility any longer.

"We'll go to the airport and shop for a plane. I do believe they are having a get one free sale today and today only."

Everyone smiled, allowing their tension to ease away. Any reason to smile was welcomed.

Ed looked around the table. "So what were you all in deep conversation about before I came in?"

Madison sighed, "Christmas. We were thinking about celebrating Christmas." It seemed silly now to think of Christmas. An ordinary thing, from an ordinary way of life, that no longer existed. Luke was right, they couldn't go on pretending like this was temporary. Truth be told, she thought Ed's venture a waste of time. Even if he found his son, then what? It didn't change anything. They still didn't know how to stop the Adita.

"I spoke to Roxanne," Ed commented.

Madison's head jerked up. "She spoke to you?"

"Um, yes. She was very nice. And Caleb. Wow, that boy is smart." Ed stopped short of saying and weird.

"He spoke to you." Madison was bewildered.

"Yeah. We talked about the merits of beef. Why?"

Madison shook her head. "I...um... I haven't had much luck communicating with either one of them."

"She's very personable. In fact, I think she's really hit it off with Charlie."

"Did she tell you anything about the Adita?" Luke asked.

"I didn't want to be rude. After all her husband is in a coma."

Luke had his doubts about this woman claiming to be Roxanne but kept them private. Granted she looked like the woman in the pictures, but he still didn't trust her. And as far as the boy was concerned, he didn't know what to think. Two months ago Austin's son was an infant. Humans didn't age seven years in two months.

"I'll talk to her," Zack interjected. "We have to find out what the Adita are planning. If she knows anything, even if it's minor, it's still more than we know."

The subject drifted back to Christmas and babies. Ed suggested bringing the prospect up for a vote at dinner. Zack was against majority rules, stating no one should be forced to go along with the masses if they didn't want to. Madison teased Zack, saying he must have been a hippie in a previous life.

"I was a bird soaring free," he corrected her.

To which she agreed. Zack was a free spirit and her polar opposite. Maybe that's what attracted her to him. Madison quickly struck this thought from her mind and joined back in the debate.

In the end, they decided to bring it up and whoever wanted to celebrate was welcome to do so. No one expected dissent or mutiny over having Christmas. Ed thought it would be a good distraction for the younger people. To which Madison brought up a sensitive subject.

"Birth control!" Luke laughed and turned red. Sex was not something he wanted to discuss with Madison or anyone at that table.

"Yes, birth control," Madison reiterated.

Zack jumped in. "She's right. We aren't really equipped to handle babies. We'll do fine with the ones coming, but I agree it's best to avoid any more for the time being."

"Who's gonna talk to them about it?" Ed grimaced at the thought.

No one volunteered.

"I'll do it for heaven's sakes," Madison huffed. "But only the girls. One of you guys has to talk to the boys."

"Sex ed. My favorite subject," Zack joked. "I'll talk to them." He looked at Luke. "If things get hot and heavy, use a condom boy. Got it." This advice was almost verbatim of the speech ole Bobby Londergan gave him when he was nine. He didn't even like girls when he was nine.

Luke choked and nodded.

"There. What's the big deal?" He winked at Luke.

"Whatever. Guys never grow up," Madison replied.

"And you young lady." Zack wagged his finger at Madison. "You make sure you take those little white pills everyday cuz us guys can't be relied on," Zack teased.

Madison's expression changed as if she suddenly remembered needing to be somewhere. "Let me out Luke." She nudged him and he slid out of the booth. "I gotta go." Madison hurried from the diner.

"Shit. Did I hit a nerve?"

Ed nodded. "Don't worry about it. You didn't know."

"Didn't know what?" Zack demanded.

"Nothing. I mean I can't say." Ed shrugged and sighed. "You know, ghosts from the past."

"Bastards," Zack muttered and kicked himself for having upset Madison when all he wanted to do was make her laugh.

Ed guided them back to making plans for their first flight. Zack fetched the map from the command center and soon they were deep into planning and plotting. Wyoming would be the first stop on the search.

"A landing strip sits right here." Zack pointed on the map. "About fifty miles from that circle."

"Are you sure?" Ed frowned.

"Sure as we have three damn suns in the sky," Zack replied. "I used to fly pot out of there," he added.

Luke's brow shot up. He knew Zack had been in the pot business but didn't know much else about his former life.

"What?" Zack responded to their stares. "I never claimed to be a law-abiding citizen."

"I thought your business was legit?" Ed asked.

"It was. Sort of. You know, mostly in Colorado. What does it matter?"

"It doesn't," Ed replied.

They went back to analyzing and detailing out their plans.

10 EVE

Roxanne sat next to Austin's bed, her hands folded in her lap, a blank expression on her face. Caleb sat on the floor playing with toy dinosaurs. However, where normal seven-year-old boys used their hands Caleb used his mind, making the dinosaurs fight and run about. A pterodactyl flew from the opposite side of the room, swooped down and attacked T-Rex.

"Where did dinosaurs come from?" Caleb looked up at Roxanne.

"From a faraway place."

"How'd they get to Earth?"

"Your great-great-grandfather brought them here."

"For food?"

A soft smile graced her lips. "Yes."

"For the Svan."

Roxanne's forehead creased and smoothed over. "Yes. I told you about the Svan. Do you remember?"

"Yes, mother. The Svan are..."

The dinosaurs fell over and the pterodactyl crashed down from the ceiling, right as a knock on the door interrupted them.

"Open the door for Mr. Taylor," Roxanne instructed.

Caleb turned his head toward the door but did not move to get up. The knob began to turn.

"Caleb," Roxanne scolded.

Caleb threw her a smile and ran over to the door.

"Come in Mr. Luke." Caleb stepped back being the perfect gentleman.

Luke stepped into the room and was quickly pushed out of the way by German. "Hey, mind your manners dog."

German lay down at Roxanne's feet, ignoring Luke.

"It's ok. My dad likes having him here," Caleb informed Luke.

"He does? Did he wake up? Did he speak to you?"

"Not yet. I just know..."

Roxanne cleared her throat before Caleb could finish. He gave her an 'I'm sorry' look and went back to playing with the dinosaurs, this time using his hands.

Luke stood staring at Roxanne, not sure how to ask what he wanted to ask, so he decided to spit it out. If he was wrong, he would spend the rest of his life apologizing. "Who are you?"

Roxanne feigned surprise. "What do you mean?"

"I mean who are you? Are you really Austin's wife?"

"Yes. Who else would I be?"

"I...I don't know." Luke scratched his head. Ever since her arrival a colony of ants had built a hill on top of his head. "How'd you get away from the vampires? I mean the Adita?"

"Eve helped us."

"Why?"

"For Austin. She did it for him."

"What about Ed's wife? Did Eve know who she was?" Luke wasn't convinced Eve or any Adita would perform an act of kindness for a human.

"I don't know her reasons, but I think it was because Jenny is a mother," Roxanne offered.

"A mother? So were a lot of the women those bloodsuckers murdered. What makes her so special?"

"I don't know. She must have felt something for Jenny. Compassion or empathy or," Roxanne shook her head, "or I'm not sure. She didn't say."

"Do you know anything about the Adita? I mean were you in the warehouse with the others or did they keep you somewhere else?"

"All I remember is waking up and seeing Eve. It was all very confusing, and we had to hurry."

"Hurry? Why?"

"She didn't say."

Frustration built inside Luke, but he couldn't take it out on Roxanne. If her claim was true, that she was Austin's wife, the captain wouldn't take too kindly over Luke harassing her.

"I'm truly sorry I don't have any more to offer." Roxanne stood up.

"No. No, that's ok. I shouldn't have bothered you. It doesn't make sense is all." Luke walked to the door and opened it. "You'll let me know when he wakes up?" Luke nodded toward Austin.

"Absolutely."

"Thank you," Luke replied before closing the door close gently behind him.

Roxanne sat back down. She took Austin's hand and held his wrist to her lips, but resisted sinking her fangs into his skin. Her longing wasn't driven by the need to eat, despite her growing hunger. Food was not an issue, being that stored in a giant cooler under Cheyenne Mountain were hundreds of vats filled with human blood, all compliments of General Roth. Her longing came from a different part of her brain, a part she seldom used or understood.

Her son was not having any problems with his diet, having maintained a healthy carnivorous appetite that didn't include human flesh or blood. His only interest in the humans seemed to be as new friends. He was the future of the Adita and as she watched him play, she wondered what the future had in store for them, for him. Her green eyes darkened to black, her skin lost some luster, as she longed to shed her human form. Caution advised against doing so. The boy, Luke, was suspicious of her, of the Adita's motives, so pretending to be Roxanne would be necessary for a while longer. However, Luke was not her main concern. The woman, Madison, posed a bigger danger. Her mind was sharp, her eyes quick to observe. When people spoke, she listened as much to their words as to the feelings and actions behind the words. These things were not what made her a threat. No, love was something Eve knew nothing about but had witnessed humans doing tremendous things in the name of and Madison believed she loved Austin.

Eve faded back into Roxanne. She placed Austin's arm back under the blanket. He was regaining full color and before long would awaken. For a moment Eve's brow creased. She shouldn't have been surprised that his body fought the change but hadn't expected the strength he exhibited. Having had time to consider her situation, Eve felt Austin being human served her better for now. Still, no human she'd bitten had ever survived the change. In the past, rather than killing them right off, she had at times watched them fight to live, curious to see what they might become after the transformation was complete. No one ever came through. No one ever lasted as long as Austin or required being bitten more than once. Humans were resilient, she'd give them that much. They had a strong desire to live, but desire and ability were two different beasts.

Eve turned her attention toward her son, who was busy twisting his toys into contorted shapes. On the outside he was every bit human, his father's son, but the outside did not matter. His mind mattered, his strengths, his power, these things would determine his survival and that of the Adita. In nine moons, the Elder's time will have run out. If Agra had not found Austin so many years ago, there would have been no hope for the Elders or the Adita. Now they were guaranteed to live for a long time, if not forever. Few things meant absolute death to an Adita, and Agra had taken measures to ensure one of those would never take place. Caleb was one of those measures. An experiment Agra had called her son. One to be terminated if the results did not turn out precisely as the Elders expected.

Caleb jumped up as if poked. "Can we mother?" His hands flew up to his face and covered his mouth.

Eve shook her head. "Caleb. You have to be more careful."

Caleb ran over to her. "I will I promise. Now can we go for a walk? I'm tired of playing with these toys."

"Yes, but you better mind me and act like a human child."

"I will. Even you won't be to tell." He jumped up and ran for the door where he stopped to wait for her.

She joined him at the door and knelt in front of him. "Do you remember what to say?"

Caleb rolled his eyes. "Yes, I remember. Agra kept me locked in a room where I had no contact with anyone except you, I mean Eve. I don't know about the harvest or the people in the warehouses or much of anything because I'm only seven. How's that?"

"Very good." Eve stood up. A vision appeared before her causing her mouth to turn downward.

Caleb grasped Eve's arm. "You won't let them die, will you?"

Eve's brow furrowed. She tried to absorb her son's compassion for the humans, thinking it would help her better understand him and them. Empathy was something Agra considered a weakness, as he did all human emotions, and not something she discussed with her father. "I'll do what I can," she told him, uncertain how far she was willing to go to save them.

Eve listened before opening the door. Madison was in her room preoccupied with cleaning her weapon. A good thing as Eve did not want to run into her. She'd a difficult enough time pretending to be Roxanne without having her every movement scrutinized. Luke and the others she handled with ease, but Madison required more finesse, which did not cause concern. If, however, Madison ever became a problem, Eve would take appropriate measures.

11 FLYING UNDER THE RADAR

Zack sat behind the wheel of the Monster. Luke road shotgun while Ed took the back seat. They traveled the deserted road staring out at the nothingness their world had become. Each had his own thoughts, but one commonality was the desire to feel the warmth of the sun, and for the moment they didn't think about where they were headed or the risk they were taking. They all carried thoughts that were far away recollections of the past.

Luke was on Florida's Gulf Coast, staring out at emerald green waters and running his toes through warm white sand. His parents had a beach house in Destin and every summer the family reunion was held at their place. Every summer for the first fourteen years of his life Luke went with his parents down to Destin. He'd met Emma Ryder during one of those summers and fell in love in the first blink. Where the Taylor's were comfortable money, Emma's family was big money and big everything. The Ryder's beach house, or mansion as most referred to it, was located about a mile down the beach from the Taylor's. Etched in his mind was the image of her walking toward him on that stretch of beach between their homes. She'd worn a light orange sarong over a blue bikini. Her hair was pulled back in a loose ponytail. She'd stopped directly in front of him and introduced herself. He was fourteen, she was eleven, but she didn't look or act like an eleven-year-old. For the next two weeks, they spent every moment together. It was the best summer of his life.

Then football took over and instead of basking in the sun with Emma, he was doing drills in ninety-five-degree temps and one hundred percent humidity. More than once a teammate had been hospitalized for dehydration or heat exhaustion. Coach always made sure to be at the hospital when the principal arrived, making sure nothing was said that might cause trouble or interfere with the practice schedule. Luke hated those summers and truth be told, he hated football. The fans, the reporters, his dad, his coach, they all wanted a piece of him, and the better he performed, the more they took from him. The only good feeling he had about football was Emma. She always came to his games. She never wanted anything from him.

While Luke was holding hands with Emma on the beach, Ed was hiking a volcano in Hawaii with Jenny. They'd gone to the big island for their honeymoon. Cliché destination maybe, but Jenny had never been, and he wanted to make the moment a magical time for her. After all, she was marrying a tax attorney. The odds of their daily life being exciting weren't good. Turned out he was wrong; Jenny, who was so full of energy, had made every day an adventure. Anniversaries were filled with surprises, holidays with joy, even going to the grocery store had been fun. And just when he'd thought life couldn't get any better, Ryan had come along. He was the first grandchild and what an ordeal that had been for the entire family. Throughout all the baby showers and hoopla that took place, Jenny had made sure Ed still felt needed and loved. Although Ed would never know the physical pain of a knife piercing his heart, he thought now he had a pretty good idea and would go so far as to surmise that a real knife wouldn't cause near the pain as the metaphorical.

Zack, who had traveled the worldwide and spent time in some of the most exotic places, didn't imagine himself in Bali or Tahiti. He was in Disney World, on a once in a lifetime trip that had not included the old man. Compliments of mom's great aunt Carmella, who died at the ripe age of ninety-seven and in her will, she'd left her favorite niece a little money. Not enough, but a little. And if there was one thing his old man appreciated, it was free money. Mom gave the bastard all but a couple grand of the cash, a bribe, so he would let her take the boys on a vacation without him. How that conversation might have gone Zack would never know. He'd always wanted to ask her how she'd convinced him to let them go alone. Maybe he knew she didn't have enough to not come back. Maybe that's why he took such a big cut, greed and insurance. If Bobby loved money, he hated being embarrassed. No wife of his was going to leave him, not breathing she wasn't. That trip had been the highest point in Zack's childhood. A moment in time when he'd pretended their family was normal. A year before someone decided to blow half of Bobby Londergan's head all over the driver's side of his custom Cadillac.

A highway sign announced the exit for the airport was two miles away. Vacation time ended, the memories faded back into the recesses of their minds and they returned to the present, to focus on the task at hand. The shoulder of the off-ramp was cluttered with abandoned vehicles. They drove by a school bus. Both Luke and Ed stared and wondered.

"It's empty," Zack informed them, knowing what they were thinking.

They didn't ask how Zack knew this. How didn't matter. Thoughts of Lamar were never far off, could never be buried deep enough in their subconscious, safe from the slightest instance that might conjure up the macabre images once again.

They drove off the ramp onto the main road to the airport, also obstacle free. The results of work Zack and Colin had spent endless hours on completing during the aftermath of the invasion. Zack had kept Colin's time and mind busy clearing the main roadways of vehicles while he handled the removal of the bodies. The task had taken almost four months. When they'd finished, Zack decided to bury the deceased was better than burning them. At the time he'd still held a hope that the missing might return and when they did, they would want to know what happened to their loved ones. He'd dug a mass grave and covered the bodies with snow and dirt. On top of the mound, he'd planted a cross, not because he was a religious man, but as a marker. The image of those mutilated bodies piled up in that hole haunted him as much as Lamar haunted his friends.

The airport loomed up ahead. Zack bypassed the main entrance and continued down the road to the hangars where the private jets were housed. A buddy of his had a nice six-seater that would be perfect for the trip. A first-class, top of line jet. If they were flying to their death, Zack was going to do so in style.

Once inside the hangar Zack inspected the plane, which was in impeccable condition and the fuel tanks were full. Fortunately for them, the owner, unlike Zack, had been an organized responsible individual. While Zack checked out the interior, Ed and Luke opened the hangar doors. Ed backed the Monster into the hangar and Luke hooked up the towing cables. Ed pulled the plane into position on the tarmac. The Monster was unloaded and then secured inside the hangar. They stowed their gear, guns, food, and Zack's specialized tasers that could emit a small electromagnetic pulse, in the back of the plane. In theory, Zack hoped the pulse would disable the Sundog's electrical system. When packing for this trip, he'd thought this untested theory of his might be given an opportunity to prove him right or wrong. Something he wasn't sure he should be excited about, but he was.

They sat at the end of the runway preparing for takeoff. It was almost noon. The flight to Wyoming would take fifty minutes from start to finish. Once on the ground, time would be of the essence. The circle on the map was over forty miles from their landing zone. If a road to the spot existed, they would consider this a sign of luck. If not, the search would be like finding the proverbial needle in the proverbial haystack. Only one way to find out. Zack put the plane into motion and within seconds they were airborne. The radar screen was blank, but Zack could fly without it and didn't think air traffic would pose a problem. He maintained an altitude high enough to avoid skimming any mountain ranges, but low enough to stay under the white mass. The question of what would happen if he flew into the mass crossed his mind and that of his companions, but no one was ready to find that out. That point of desperation, where a person is willing to try anything regardless of the consequences, had not yet been reached.

People always speculated on what they would do and how much they would put up with in dire circumstances, but when faced with making those tough decisions, survival, at a minimum, came out on top of the list as the most important outcome to consider. With living to see another day in mind, Zack flew the plane with extreme caution.

As they flew over Wyoming, Ed and Luke kept their eyes glued on the ground for anything giving the appearance of a being a large building or simply looking out of place in the Wyoming landscape.

"Nothing," Ed announced as Zack circled the plane around. "Nothing, but white."

"I'm sick of the snow," Luke grumbled

"Me too man," Ed agreed.

"Strap in. We're gonna land and it might be bumpy."

"Might be?" Ed asked.

"Will be," Zack corrected, "and stopping might also be a problem."

Ed and Luke shared an expression of concern before strapping in extra tight. Ed had never flown in a private jet and knew nothing about the dynamics of a plane, so how Zack would stop the plane on the icy landing strip hadn't crossed his mind until now. Too late Ed my man. Don't panic or start acting like a cupcake. No room for cupcakes in this here *per-dic-a-ment*. Ed continued channeling his father's voice inside his head, much like Madison's imaginary conversations with her mother, Ed relied on his father's ghost to keep his nerves in check.

Despite the uncertainty, Zack wasn't concerned as he eased the plane down on to the narrow landing strip. The jolt from the wheels initial contact put their safety restraints to the test, but all belts and buckles remained secure. The reverse thrusters kicked in and the plane began to slow. Outside the scenery transitioned from a blur of white and brown to a more detailed view of the landscape.

"We might run out of runway," Zack announced.

"What?" Ed tried to see out the cockpit window, but couldn't from where he was sitting and wasn't about to unbuckle his seatbelt.

"Don't worry."

"Don't worry!" Luke repeated in dismay. Sitting in the cockpit he had a front-row seat. "We're gonna crash into the trees."

"We'll stop," Zack said sitting back relaxed.

Luke looked at him like he'd gone mad and glanced back at Ed who now had his head buried in his lap.

Zack smirked. "Dude, chill. I've done this before."

"You know we'll stop?" Ed yelled from his crash position.

"Yes," Zack answered exuding confidence despite not feeling one hundred percent certain, but nothing was one hundred percent guaranteed. A time or two he'd landed during a winter storm, but the field had only been covered with six or seven inches of snow and, as he recalled, no ice was in that mix.

The plane rolled along jerking whenever the wheels gripped something dry and the brakes caught. The interval between slides was not going to be enough. The trees at the end of the runway loomed closer. Although the plane's speed had slowed to the equivalent of thirty miles an hour, the impact wasn't going to be gentle.

The plane began to slide sideways. "Brace for a crash," Zack warned and applied the reverse thruster again. The force of this action shifted the plane back on course but didn't stop the slide. "Shit." Was all Zack could say before the nose connected with the trees. The plane plowed a path fifty-feet into the trees before coming to a stop. They sat quietly for several seconds. A tree limb fell on top of the plane, making them all jump. Ed unbuckled his restraints and fell forward before standing on shaky legs. Luke wobbled out of the cockpit. His face had an ashen tinge, his eyes a slightly glazed look.

"How are we gonna get back?" Luke asked.

"Get back," Ed snorted. "How are we gonna get outta here? We're in the middle of no fucking where."

Zack powered down the plane and spun his seat around. "Ye of little faith. Didn't you both hike halfway across the US before finding the bunker?" Zack nodded. "And now you're worried about a short romp through the woods? Come on dudes. We got this."

Skeptical, but having no choice, Ed and Luke followed Zack to the back of the plane where they'd stowed their gear. In twenty minutes they were dressed and loaded down with weapons. The emergency slide was activated, and they slid to the ground below. Zack, first to the bottom, jumped off and looked back down the path of destruction toward the runway. He didn't bother inspecting the plane. It was never his intention to use the same one to go home.

Luke dropped his backpack of supplies on the slide and followed down after. Ed came down last. He and Zack helped Luke into his backpack which was weighted down with extra survival supplies, in case they had to spend the night or two. Something Ed had hardly given much consideration but was now weighing heavy on his mind.

The trek out of the woods took under fifteen minutes and from there they walked across the runway and back into the woods. Ed and Luke followed Zack, both wondering and hoping he knew where the hell he was going. It wasn't long before they entered a clearing and there, half hidden under a snowdrift was a small log cabin. A crude path was forged through the snow to the door and smoke rose from the single chimney.

Zack stared at the path trying to determine how fresh the tracks were and if more than one set was present. Ed and Luke had similar thoughts as they approached the door.

"What are the odds?" Zack wondered out loud.

"Should we knock?" Ed asked.

Zack shrugged. "Might as well." He didn't want to get excited over the possibility his old friend might have survived the attack, but if anyone could. Zack knocked on the door and held his breath. From inside they heard a rustling noise, something crashed to the ground and a string of curse words let loose.

Zack banged on the door. "Ray open up. It's Zack. Zack Londergan." Inside, a shotgun opened and closed. Zack motioned for Luke and Ed to stand to the side.

"Ray put that damn shotgun down and open the door. It's your old buddy Zack."

After several seconds of silence, the cover over the peephole slid open and a black pupil peered out. "Zack?"

"Yeah Ray." Zack removed his face mask. "See. It's me."

"How do I know you ain't one of them alien things in disguise?"

"Would an alien know you have a tattoo of a purple fairy on your left bicep?"

"Maybe."

"Would an alien know you have that tattoo because you lost a bet when you were in the Army?"

"How the hell do I know what an alien knows?"

"Damn Ray. Open the door. I'm freezin' my balls off out here."

"How'd you get here?" Ray demanded, still not convinced.

"I borrowed a plane. You can see it for yourself. It's parked under the trees at the end of the landing strip."

"You crazy Irishman." The peephole slammed shut and a series of locks clicked and slid open. The door opened revealing the man behind the voice, a slim white-haired, dark-skinned ancient man.

"Well come on in before them alien demons feel the heat and come lookin' for a meal." Ray waved them inside, slamming the door and sliding all the locks back in place. "Go on, go stand by the fire."

The fire was a welcome sight. Ed and Luke removed their outer gear and stood close to the toasty blaze.

"Sit boy. Sit." Ray waved Zack to a chair near the fire.

"Can't stay long Ray. Gotta get back before night." Zack sat on the edge of the chair.

"What's your hurry?"

"It's a long story."

"Who're your friends?" Ray waved his hand at Ed and Luke.

"Yeah, sorry man, where are my manners? Edward McGrath and Luke Taylor," Zack said, "this is Ray Longhorne. My Wyoming connection and close friend."

Both Ed and Luke took turns shaking Ray's hand. Despite his frail appearance, he had a strong grip.

"What brings you to the wilds of Wyomin'?"

"We're looking for a warehouse or several warehouses that might have people inside. You wouldn't happen to know of any nearby would ya?" Zack asked.

Ray stared at Zack for a long time. His eyes closed, he began to rock back and forth. They thought he might have fallen asleep standing up, but his eyes popped open. "They aren't bein' kept in no warehouses. More like concentration camps. But you don't want to go near those places. That's where death resides."

"Whatta ya mean like concentration camps?" Zack asked.

"Like back during the war boy. Don't you read your history books?"

"You mean like the German camps."

"No boy. Like the Japanese camps right here on American soil. The Krauts weren't the only heartless bastards during the war."

"What are you talking about?" Luke asked.

"After the Japs bombed Pearl Harbor. The gov'ment decided all Japs in the great United States were a hazard to the nation. They rounded 'em up like cattle and locked 'em up behind barbed wire fences. They called 'em internment camps, but they's concentration camps yassir. In fact, and I only deliver the facts, there was one right here in Wyomin'."

This was blowing Luke's mind. US concentration camps weren't covered in his school books. In *fact*, if he were to have a long conversation with Ray about the country's history, he'd learn a whole lot more about things Mrs. Glover didn't cover during his sophomore history class.

"Is that really true?" Luke asked Ed.

Ed nodded.

"Course it's true son. What you callin me? A liar?"

"Take it easy Ray. Luke's from Louisiana. He doesn't know any better." Zack said.

"Very funny asshole," Luke replied, not amused.

"And what is it we're dealin' with Ray?"

"Like I said they's like camps, but these are more sophisticated. No barracks, but cinder block buildings, like a sanitarium. Inside, everything's white reminds you of pictures of heaven, but it ain't heaven, no sir. No angels, but lots of demons."

"So you've seen these camps?" Ed interrupted.

"Yeah, I'd seen 'em. Had a short stay in one," Ray replied, snickering. "Them beins' didn't know who they was messin' with."

"What happened?" Luke asked. "I mean how'd you get away from them?"

"I got strange blood son. They stuck all kinds of tubes and junk in me, but ain't none of it worked. I waited until they was gone and unhooked all them contraptions and then I walked out the front doors." Ray cackled and pretended to spit. "I was trapped for near a week, but got out."

"Were there other...other people?" Ed couldn't bring himself to ask if he'd seen any children.

"Oh yeah. The place was packed full. White tables were lined up in a row with people layin' on 'em all hooked up lookin' like octopuses. I ain't seen nothin like it. Not even durin' the war."

Now which war Ray referred to was uncertain, since he looked to be one hundred years old if not older, but his age didn't matter. That he'd been captured by the aliens and survived was all they were interested in hearing.

"Was it the Sundogs that took you?" Zack asked.

"Don't know nothin' about no Sundogs. Know them aliens are the damn creepiest folk I ever dealt with."

"The Adita," Ed said.

"Names don't mean nothin' to me boy. Never mind that. It was them soulless black eyed beins'. They visit the houses, but it's the winged demons that fetch folk and guard the place. The aliens come in and took blood from folks. I'm no doctor or scientist, but it appeared, to my simple mind, they were running tests on the blood. Every so often the winged demons would take bodies away and bring new ones in."

Zack glanced at his watch. It was almost two o'clock. "How far are the camps?"

"The closest one is thirty miles as the crow flies."

"How many if the crow walks?"

"Don't know why a crow would walk when he could fly, or in your case, drive just as easy." Ray chuckled at his wit but sobered when he saw the grim look on Zack's face. "You could get there usin' one of them all tear rain type vehicles. Take you maybe an hour or so. But don't know why you want to bother."

"Because those are human beings in there and the Adita are bleeding them dry. We can't leave them there to die," Luke replied in an elevated condemning tone.

"You think I didn't try to save em? Is that what you think son?"

"No sir." Luke looked embarrassed.

"I tried to save em." Ray declared, beating on his chest. "The first one, a young man about your age, died before I could get him back to the cabin. The second one, were a middle-aged woman. I carried her out over my shoulder, but she came to and started screamin'. Them winged demons come swooping in like lightnin' out of the sky. I only escaped because they were too preoccupied tearing her to pieces to notice an old man. I didn't try no more after that."

"You're saying we can't save anyone?"

"I'm not saying that at all. All I'm sayin were I had no success doin so." Ray threw another log on the fire causing a few embers to pop out onto the floor. He extinguished the embers with the toe of his boot. "I'll tell you the way, but yer on yer own gettin there."

"Thanks, Ray," Zack replied, patting the old man on the back.

"Don't thank me none for showin' you the way to yer death." He gave Zack a hard stare. "I'll fix us somethin' to eat."

Zack checked his watch. "Shouldn't we be goin?"

"Ain't goin today. Gonna have to wait 'til the suns rise. You get caught by the night there ain't gonna be no mornin' for you."

Zack, Ed, and Luke shared a worried glance. They'd told Madison they wouldn't be gone longer than a day or two if it could be helped. After the crash landing, getting back to the bunker at all was more of a concern than when it might actually happen, but still further delaying their pursuits only served to add to the apprehension felt.

Resolved to make the best of their situation and knowing Ray was right, Zack offered to help with dinner, while Luke and Ed volunteered their wood chopping services. The latter being a welcomed respite for Ray, who dreaded the task more than dying. At least in death, his old body would be eased of its aches and pains.

12 UNLIKELY ALLY

Zack awoke before daybreak, unable to sleep. His restlessness was as much due to the looming task ahead of him as the dying fire which allowed the cold to creep in all around. Zack set a couple of logs in the embers and stirred them around. Sleep clung to his mind, encouraged by the warmth creeping out from the revived fire. Zack shook it off. Life was a bitch, he thought for no particular reason other than it was truer now, in this fucked up world, than in the fucked-up world he'd once known. Running the streets of Boston with the old crew almost appealed to him, almost and only if certain conditions were met. One of those being ole Bobby Londergan would have to remain worm food.

A pocket of moisture fizzed and an ember popped out of the fireplace landing near Zack's foot. He pushed it back into the fire with the poker. Soon blue and orange tongues danced about the logs as embers turned to flames. Before long the room was toasty again and thoughts of Boston faded away. Zack entertained crawling back into his sleeping bag for another hour but knew he wouldn't wake up in an hour. They had to get an early start if they had any hope of getting home before nightfall. A hope he didn't hold tight. And even less so the hope that they would be saving anyone that day. Heartache was all they were inviting, heartache with the chance of death. Not a forecast for the meek.

"Cup a coffee?" Ray asked from the doorway of the kitchen, keeping his voice low.

Zack nodded and stepped over the snoozing bodies of his friends, relieved they were able to sleep despite the world falling down upon them.

In the kitchen, two steaming cups of coffee sat on the small table. Zack took a seat opposite Ray and sipped the warm brew. A wood stove kept the small kitchen comfortable. Ray sipped his coffee. His hands were covered with waves of wrinkles, revealing as much about his age as his full head of white hair. They were an unlikely pair born in worlds far apart, yet, despite their cultural differences, common life lessons bridged the gap and a lasting friendship had been formed.

"How's the diabetes?"

Ray wagged a finger and shook his head. "Funny thing about it bein' was after escapin' them alien bastards, my sugar fits stopped comin.' But I ain't grateful to em. No sir. They weren't considerin' my well bein' when they stuck me like a pin cushion."

"Did they inject you with something?"

"I reckon so. Somethin' right potent to the rest of those poor folks, but made me sleepy is all. Felt like when you stuff yer self too full on Thanksgivin'." Ray peered at Zack from over the rim of his cup. "You sure 'bout this thing yer gonna do? Kinda like temptin' fate ain't it?"

Zack gave a short laugh and shook his head. "They're my friends. I can't let em go alone."

"Don't go to that camp boy." Ray set his cup down. "There be things you don't want to see. Things you can't remove from your mind. Them horrors that want to come callin on you in the middle of the night." Ray's voice trailed off with his gaze.

"Ed needs to know if his kid is in one of those warehouses."

Ray shook his head. "Ain't no chillren' is them death buildings. Ain't no chillren'."

"None?" Ed stood in the doorway. "You said no children?"

Ray turned to look at Ed. "You heard clear."

"Are...are you sure?" Ed couldn't believe and didn't want to believe Ray's statement was true.

"Sorry son. Only adults hooked up lookin' like human octopuses. No chillren'. I couldn't a left no kiddies behind. They'd been better off goin' to see the Almighty, than bein' drained of life by them soulless beins."

The weight of this revelation was too much for Ed to shoulder, to bear, to comprehend. He shrank an inch or two and would have fallen had the door jamb not been there to support his weight. Ray's words were paralyzing. Memories of the initial days after the attack bombarded Ed with emotions that up until that very second he'd kept under tight wraps. The room wavered out of view. He grabbed the door jamb, his knuckles turned white. From far off Ed heard his name being called, but he didn't want to come back. He wanted to succumb to madness, to the mistress of the insane. Let her take him deep into her lair of murky existence where he'd be protected from pain. Pain, the insistent bully who'd held him captive since that first snowflake fell. Pain that waited around every corner to sucker punch him with a load of grief so heavy he'd never recover.

"Ed!" Zack grasped Ed's arm. "It's alright man."

Ed shook his head, trying to clear his mind. The room did one more wobble and wave, before regaining its edges. "I'm ok. I'm ok."

Zack helped Ed to the table and poured him a cup of coffee. Ed grasped the cup but didn't trust himself to bring it up to his lips. The mistress wailed for him to come to her, while the bully rejoiced with threatening fists waving in the air.

"Ed, man, there are more camps all over the country. You can't give up because the first one doesn't pan out."

Zack's words struck a chord with Ed, hitting him hard where he needed it most. He looked up at Zack, and lucidity returned. "You're right. You're absolutely right. It's just... I wanted it to be this one..." Ed couldn't finish.

"We'll find him. We'll search every damn camp. And we'll find Ryan," Zack promised, not knowing why he did so given he didn't believe it himself, but something in Ed's expression, something so desperate and sad, had scared him into lying.

Ray coughed but held his tongue. Some folks were better off believing lies than trying to face the harshness of the truth. They'd spend an entire lifetime avoiding the truth, some going to great lengths, others doing so without realizing the intent of their actions. For Ray the truth was always best, telling it and hearing it. He'd never been one to judge a person by how they approached living and wasn't going to start now. That death was the obvious outcome of their quest didn't play a hand in this. Death, as is in life, was not his to decide.

Refocused now, Ed picked up his coffee without shaking the liquid over the brim and took a sip. He took another sip and then another. This repeated action soothed his nerves and a sudden craving struck him for a bagel smothered in thick cream cheese that oozed to and over the edges. He refrained from asking their host if he had such a thing. He felt Zack's eyes watching him, waiting for the fissure in his sanity to crack wide open.

Zack was watching Ed, but not because he worried about Ed falling off the edge. Zack had seen desperation like this only one other time in his life. A time he didn't want to think about right then. Drudging up that memory brought with it the old man. Zack almost chuckled. It would almost be worth it for Bobby Londergan to be alive today, so that Zack could have the pleasure of killing him, as he'd planned to do only days before someone beat him to it. Zack shook away the past and turned his attention to the task at hand.

"Is Luke still sleeping?"

Ed gave him a blank stare. His mind searched and remembered who Luke was and why they were in the cabin in the middle of the woods. "Yeah. I think so. I'll go wake him." He swallowed the last of his coffee and shoved back his chair.

After he left, Ray turned to Zack. "His boy has most likely passed on. You know that don't ya?"

"I know."

"And you can't help them there folks neither. They's been hooked up to those tubes and machines for longer than I consider to be the humane thing. Course we ain't dealin' with beins that are humane in nature, now are we?" Ray continued on not expecting an answer. "Them folks was barely alive when I tried rescuin' 'em. No tellin' what shape they's in now."

"Ed's gonna have to figure this one out for himself. But I'm not letting him go it alone," Zack replied. "You really think there's no hope?"

Ray reached inside his shirt pocket and pulled out a cigarette. He wet the end and placed it in his mouth, but didn't light it. He'd given up the habit years ago, yet still enjoyed the taste and smell of the tobacco. "How long we been knowin' each other?"

"Five, six years. Why?"

"Have you ever known me to present things in a better light than what was shinin? To paint somethin' rose pink when it were really shit brown?"

Zack shook his head. "You're the most honest person I ever met." And this was the truth. Ray had a heart bigger than the state of Texas, but he'd never tell you a lie in order to avoid an uncomfortable truth. He'd given Zack more words of wisdom and sound advice than all the shrinks in the world had managed. Ray convinced him to get out of the pot business, to quit being prideful, to stop wasting the talents he had been blessed with and most important to do something that would make his mom proud.

"You never got the chance to tell her did you?" Ray asked.

"Nope." Zack turned away as if this action alone could prevent him from thinking about his mom and lost opportunities. While Zack silently battled his ghosts, a stray thought wandered in, one he'd never entertained before this very moment.

"Sometimes decidin' the better of two bad things is almost more than a person can handle," Ray commented. "If you decide for the betterment of the other person, rather than yer own self, you can't ever make the wrong choice."

"I hear ya old man," Zack replied. For once he was glad Colin was afraid to fly and hadn't wanted to join the party. If by the slimmest chances of fate Zack did find their mom plugged up to the alien's machines, he didn't want to fight with his brother over what they should do. The answer was clear. He wouldn't hem and haw over it. If the time came he would pull the plug.

Zack gave Ray a pat on the back. "You got any of them all-terrain vehicles stashed on the property?"

"Does a bear shit in the woods son?" Ray snorted. "Get your coat and I'll show you what I got."

Zack checked in on Luke and Ed before grabbing his coat and following Ray out the door. They walked down a hidden path to an old metal building. Ray pulled the door open revealing three brand new ATVs.

"Sweet," Zack whistled. "Where'd you get em?"

"Don't worry none about things that ain't none of yer biznax."

"Same ole Ray."

* * *

An hour later the guys were loaded and ready to go. Zack was on one ATV, while Ed and Luke road on a second. Ray had wanted them to take all three, but Zack refused to leave him without a means of transportation. Before departing the guys chopped enough wood to keep the house heated for months to come, probably years since Ray would use it like a miser spends money.

It was nine o'clock before they were on their way. If all went well they would arrive at the camp by ten, if all went better than well they would still be alive at ten-o-one. A lot was riding on all things going well, but they didn't think about this. In fact they didn't think about much other than the path in front of them.

As they neared the place where the camp was supposed to be located, Zack held up his hand for Luke to stop. A hundred yards ahead the trees thinned and gave way to a clearing. Nothing they saw gave an indication of what was in that clearing. The only way to find out was to keep going. Zack motioned for Luke to proceed slow and easy. If Austin had been along he could have filled in some of the missing pieces, eliminated some of the fear of the unknown, but not all. Knowing what evil waited didn't take away the trepidation of that evil and what it might be capable of doing.

While Austin had met the devil a few times over and Zack thought he'd been born the son of Satan, Ed and Luke were choir boys who believed good eventually triumphed over bad. Facing something of this magnitude was a hell of a way to graduate into the realms of evil. Zack only hoped if things went south that he wouldn't be left standing exposed, that Ed and Luke would have his back.

They drove at a turtle's pace into the clearing. Across the way they saw a double barbed wire fence stretching in front of the woods. Two gates capped with double rows of concertina wire formed an entrance. Through those gates, they could see several large gray block buildings. Zack motioned for Luke to follow him. They drove around the clearing and back to the opening where they'd entered. The ATVs were parked facing down the path, back the way they came. Zack wanted to be damn sure if they had to escape they would have a better than a slim chance.

Once the engines were cut off, the place turned silent as death. The crunching of snow underfoot was magnified by the heavy silence. Although full knowledge of the alien's powers was unknown, they had no misguided notion on sneaking in unseen, or unheard, yet here they were hoping to do so. Ray was right, Zack thought, they were on a death mission.

A faded red, white and blue metal sign hung on the gates warning trespassers this was US Government property and no unauthorized personnel allowed past this point. Zack ignored the sign and, using the wire cutters Ray gave him, cut an opening for them to climb through. They continued on toward the first building. No sirens went off. No guards rushed out waving automatic weapons, yelling for them to drop to the ground or be shot. Seeing someone in camouflage would have been a welcomed sight considering the alternative.

The buildings were windowless and, after walking all the way around one, they found only one set of doors. Zack walked up to the solid double metal doors. Another red, white and blue metal sign warned trespassers the installation belonged to the US government and deadly force was authorized. Ed and Luke stood next to Zack staring at the doors, looking for the handles or a way to open it. Zack reached out and pushed on the door. At first,, nothing happened. He pushed again, and this time like he meant it. The doors swung open and Zack tumbled inside. Luke and Ed hurried in after him. Behind them, the doors closed with a soft swish and a loud click.

The three men stopped and stared. They stood inside a large bay, white and sterile, exactly as Ray had described. A glass-enclosed walkway went down the center and, on each side, white tables lined the floor. On each table was a naked body with a small white cloth draped over the mid-section. A multitude of tubes extended down from the ceiling and into each body. Through some of the tubes they could see blood, but whether it was being drawn or added was impossible to distinguish.

"Their eyes are open." Ed had walked up to the glass to get a closer look. "And they're breathing."

Zack and Luke looked at the body of a young woman. She had auburn red hair and small perfect breasts that rose and fell indicating that yes, in fact, she was breathing. Green eyes stared up at the ceiling, but even from their viewpoint, it was clear she didn't see anything through those eyes. Her skin was translucent and reminded Zack of the Adita.

Luke tapped on the glass. They waited for any sign of movement, but none came. Zack pointed toward the end of the corridor where steps led to the next floor. At the top of the next landing, they were faced with another glass corridor and another stark white bay full of human pin cushions. They climbed eight more flights of steps and found more of the same on each floor.

At the top Zack removed his face mask and took in a deep breath. Even the air tasted sterile. Luke removed his mask and leaned against the wall, while Ed plopped down on the top step sinking his face into his hands. Numbers ran through his head, five thousand people in this building, at least twenty buildings in this camp, and thirteen circles on the map from Roth's office. That was over a million people. Four hundred million people lived in the US before the aliens arrived. Where were they all being kept?

As Ed number crunched, Zack wondered what in the hell the government had been up to when building these camps. What were they anticipating needing them for? These questions and many more plagued him, but most disturbing was what to do about these people? Could they save one? Could they save any?

"We should go," Zack said in a low voice.

"What about these people?" Luke asked.

"There's nothing we can do," Zack replied, bracing for a fight, but neither one of them argued back. Maybe they'd thought it through and reached the same conclusion he had, that any attempt at this point would be futile. They needed transportation, medical equipment, and knowledgeable staff. The list of things they did not have and could not get went on and on.

"Let's go. If we get to an airport by noon, we'll be home well before dark. In enough time to drive back to the bunker." Zack pulled his ski mask down over his face.

The men traveled down the steps feeling heavy hearted and ridden with guilt. Zack thought of the redhead. She looked to be eighteen or nineteen years of age, not far from Colin. What if that was Colin lying behind the glass, with his life being sucked out of him? No way in hell Zack would leave him behind. And despite his earlier decision concerning his mom, he knew he wouldn't leave her behind either.

They exited the building not looking back. Outside they stood for a long time saying nothing. The situation was dire, but they were powerless to make changes and no amount of wishing or good intentions mattered to the fact. They were leaving those people behind. Luke knew doing so would haunt him for days, probably weeks, probably forever. The redhead's green eyes would come to him in the dark, her lips would speak to him, plead with him to set her free.

Luke turned to Zack and Ed. "There's got to be something we can do. I mean we can't leave 'em like that."

"We could come back," Ed replied.

Zack shook his head. "And then what? Take 'em off their life support system? Watch 'em die before we get 'em out of the building. We're not trained for this shit. Not me. Not you. None of us are." Zack began walking toward the gate. He wanted to get back and, damn it to hell, he wanted to see Madison.

Ed and Luke shared a defeated look and followed Zack down the path. Nothing more was said about saving anyone. They'd be lucky to save themselves at this point and they knew it. Still, the doubts continued to linger while the guilt ate at them like a termite on a piece of wood.

Once through the hole in the fence, Zack put some effort into camouflaging where he'd cut the wire. He didn't imagine the Adita took kindly to trespassers any more than the US government might have at one time. He reviewed his handy work and figured even a blind bat could see someone had cut the fence. He stared at the hole, trying to decide whether or not he should do a better patch job, but he wasn't seeing the crisscrossed wires or thinking about how to fix them. He knew it didn't matter. The Adita would know. They'd know and then what might they do? Read the sign dumbass. Use of deadly force is authorized. Zack smiled under his face mask. Old Bobby Londergan might have been a rotten bastard, but he was no dummy. Luke tapped Zack on the shoulder, startling him from the trance he'd settled into.

Luke raised a finger to his face mask and pointed to the sky. Zack and Ed turned to listen. From far off and high above, a strange sound came to them, strange to all except Zack. Zack recognized the sound of death approaching and was frozen still by the chill it delivered.

The sight of the great-winged Svan, the Sundogs flying high above, made Ed feel like a character from The Wizard of Oz. Except these weren't winged monkeys obeying orders of the wicked witch. These were fierce predators with razor-sharp talons and pointed teeth capable of tearing through human flesh and bones as if made of paper. Their master was a demon who had come from the deepest pits of hell.

Zack pulled out the modified taser gun and aimed it upward. The Svan screeched, flying at lightning speed toward them. Zack didn't wait to see the whites of its eyes, or black in this case before he squeezed the trigger. A strong pulse emanated from the taser, but to their utter shock and dismay, the Svan didn't slow. The electromagnetic pulse had no impact. A second round resulted in the same. Zack shook the taser, banged it against his hand as if these simple actions might prove to be the catalyst in garnering the desired results from the weapon.

"Fuck you," Zack yelled at the Svan. He grabbed Luke and Ed and they ran for the forest. A worthless effort, he knew, but what else were they to do? Watch death approach without so much as moving a muscle to save themselves? He didn't know about his companions, but lying down wasn't Zack's style. He didn't live this long to go out like mindless prey, too stupid or scared to fight back. He was a Londergan damn it! Zack ran faster, cursing his weak lungs.

They ran across the frozen ground, lumbering along in their heavy gear. No one thought why they ran for the trees. The trees offered no protection but seemed to be the only option. Logical thinking was a luxury seldom available to those facing life or death situations. Fight or flight, those were the choices within this situation, the former fell under death rather than life and the latter a hopeless cause.

Ed looked over his shoulder. The Svan had landed in the exact spot they had only recently vacated and were now charging after them. In seconds they would catch up. In seconds it would be all over. Ed urged his legs to move faster. Despite having spent the last month training, Ed was no runner. He didn't possess natural speed, not even now with the adrenaline flowing through him faster than Niagara Falls.

The Svan were close enough Luke heard them breathing, heard them talking in their odd language, felt their breath on the back of his neck, on that one place between his collar and ski mask where his skin was exposed. He risked a glance over his shoulder, something he should have been accustomed to doing while running, a movement he had performed without thought thousands of times. A twisting of his head was something that had never been a problem, not even when mere inches stood between him and being flattened by a three-hundred-pound lineman. But exceptions were possible, and Luke's exception came when least desired and least able to recover. His eyes met those of the Svan, his feet twisted underneath him and down he went, tumbling hard for several feet. Motion ceased, Luke lay still on the ground, frozen by the certainty of death. No visions of his past life flashed before him. In fact, no thoughts came at all and when he felt himself being lifted in the air his mind went blank.

"Asta!" a woman's voice yelled out.

Luke was dropped to the ground where he lay silent and motionless, certain he was dead.

"Asta!"

Luke heard the voice say again. This time the Svan moved away and his mobility returned. He slowly rolled over. By now Zack and Ed had rejoined him. Ed helped Luke to his feet.

"You ok?"

Luke nodded his head in reflex only, as he didn't know if he was or wasn't ok. He was still alive and being alive or ok held little if any meaning these days.

"Where'd she come from?" Zack asked, but wasn't expecting an answer from either of his companions.

The men stood watching as the Svan bowed down to Eve, not knowing if they should stay or continue on their way to the forest, to the ATVs, to a perceived escape. Having removed the immediate threat of death, logic stood a chance at making a decision and without discussion, they turned to go.

"Wait," Eve said, reaching out to grab Zack's arm.

"Oh shit!" Zack jumped out of his skin. "How'd you get over here so dang fast?"

"I did not mean to frighten you," Eve offered as a means of apology, but not the answer Zack wanted. "I must return you to the bunker. The Adita will be here soon."

"Great. I've been wanting to meet with them again. You know, invite them over for supper. The last time we met was so brief and the circumstances were, how shall we say it? Less than desirable," Zack replied, but his sarcasm was lost on Eve.

"I don't have time to explain," Eve said. "You go now or you die now. It is your choice."

Luke, with his senses as near to normal as allowable, stepped up to Eve. "Who the fuck are you? And why the hell should we listen to you? You infect Austin with your sickness and now we're supposed to blindly follow you? Fuck no."

Eve ignored his outburst. "If you stay you will be killed."

Not to be pushed aside, Luke grabbed Eve's arm. "I asked you a question you bloodsucking freak of nature. Who are you? What did you do to Austin?"

Across the field, the Svan took notice but held their place watching and waiting for a sign from their mistress. Eve turned her black eyes upon Luke. "You know nothing of your origins, yet you assume humans are the rightful heirs of this planet, that humans are the species Nature showered her favors upon? You are a silly boy."

Luke released her arm. He didn't care about her opinion of him or the human race. "Tell me he won't die."

"He will live forever," she responded.

"No one should live forever," Zack argued. "It's not natural."

Eve ignored Zack and spread out her arms. A vortex of energy stirred the snow around them into a funnel. A tunnel leading to nowhere appeared and the men were sucked inside. The tunnel vanished as quickly as it appeared, and the snow settled back to the ground.

Eve returned to where the Svan waited. She looked across the field to a spot where the landscape wavered like a Vegas highway in the month of August. Out of the waves, a male Adita and three females materialized. Eve recognized the male, but could not remember his name or purpose, other than he was a member of the council. She waited for them to come to her. As they walked to her, Eve felt her father's invisible fingers reaching out to her, probing her mind. A sensation she'd experienced many times in her previous life and had welcomed. Welcomed like someone starving for food, dying of thirst, desperate for companionship. She was no longer desperate and blocked her father from delving deeper.

"Agra has instructed that you remain on Earth until he calls for you," the male announced.

"Remain here? Why what has happened? What is wrong? Tell me Za" Eve said, remembering his name.

"It is not for me to question his orders. They are thus, and you are to obey," he replied with an air of superiority above his station. "It is not a request."

Eve glanced at the females standing behind Za, giving them more attention, noticing who they were and what they represented. The force within her threatened, but she calmed the beast, now wasn't the time to unleash or reveal that which she herself did not understand. A human would have described the force as rage and, in its infantile state within an inferior mind, this would be accurate, but Eve did not feel on the level of a human.

"When the human recovers you are to deliver him to the Svan for harvesting," Za said.

"I will bring him to Paru."

Za pursed his lips. "This is not what your father has instructed. The Svan are to take possession of the man. If you disobey, your father will be very displeased," he added thinking this might intimidate Eve.

"You do not need to tell me what displeases my father," Eve said.

"No, I suppose I do not, but I will tell you this, the harvest is fast approaching. Need not I remind you what this means for the Adita," he responded, his tone that of a teacher instructing a pupil he considered dimwitted.

Eve only nodded her head, ignoring the snickers coming from the guards. She had many questions, but would not ask them of a mere messenger. As for the females, the guards sent by the council, Eve knew she was superior and took great satisfaction in the fact. If she'd decided to act upon her desires, they would be lying headless on the ground, their smug expressions frozen upon their faces. Today she would allow them to live for no other reason than killing them now did not serve her purpose. In the future, she hoped for the opportunity to take action against them, perhaps on the battlefield. A smile teased at Eve's lips and the guards tensed.

"When will the human be ready?" Za asked.

"Thirteen days."

Za, unsure if he should press for more, decided to let it go. Agra could deal with the insolent girl. And she would have to be dealt with soon, for the council grew weary and had deep-seated doubts about her son. The child had been created for a sole purpose, but his purpose could not be allowed to cultivate into something more powerful than the Elders themselves, thus eliminating their necessity altogether. This would not be allowed to happen.

"The child will not be harmed."

Za started but quickly reclaimed his stolid demeanor. "Careful where you tread daughter of man," he replied, his words dripping with contempt. With that obscure warning, he turned on his heel.

Eve watched them until they disappeared into the shimmering air. Perhaps she shouldn't have spoken out to Za's thoughts, but regret wasn't in her to have.

Actions led to reaction. Eve's thoughts had moved on to the next actions necessary. Her father was growing erratic as the time grew shorter. She sensed desperation in his actions but was not yet skilled enough to reach the cause without detection. Whatever his fears, he had suppressed them to the deepest recesses of his mind. She could not concern herself over her father when other things required her immediate attention.

13 BEST WESTERN

The F-350 Ford pick-up truck glided down the deserted Alaskan highway toward Anchorage, toward hope. Kyle and McKenna didn't talk about finding survivors, not directly. Talking about something resulted in unwanted doubts creeping in, the hope-stealing, soul-crushing, killing type of doubts. So they talked of nothing in particular, of things that mattered at the moment, and never of things from the past.

They stopped at a gas station. Inside Kyle snooped around for anything of use while McKenna used the restroom in the back, shouting to him the whole while. On the counter sat a jar of pickled eggs. The eggs floated around in pinkish red formaldehyde liquid. Kyle leaned in, taking a closer look at the eggs. Through the pinkness, Beethoven's face swam in and out of view. He pushed the jar aside revealing a rack filled with CDs. Along with the master, as McKenna called him, were a consortium of artists ranging from rap to country. Kyle grabbed them all, shoving them in his pack before McKenna returned.

"Ready Freddy," she announced.

"Let's hit it then Freddy Ready," Kyle kicked back at her and she laughed at him. "What? That's not right?"

She shook her head. "Don't worry about it. You're too old to understand."

Once back on the road Kyle surprised McKenna with the CDs. Her squeals of delight almost broke his eardrums while bringing an ache to his heart. His hand absently went to the picture in his breast pocket. He pulled it out.

"What's that?" she asked.

"A picture of my mom and sister."

"Can I see?"

Kyle handed her the photo. "That was three years ago."

McKenna examined the picture. The girl looked to be Kyle's age at the time the photo was taken. They stood in front of a sign that read Welcome to Cheyenne Mountain. Kyle's mother was very pretty but looked as if a brisk wind could whisk her away. McKenna wondered if she'd been sick, but didn't ask Kyle. He always looked so sad whenever he took out the picture.

She returned the photo. "What's their names?"

"My mom's name is Gisela, she's German, and my sister's name is Grace. She's my twin."

"What about your dad?"

"Died when I was five. He was a pilot. Small planes, crop dusters, what have you. Anyway, he was caught in an ice storm and crashed somewhere in the Rockies. They never recovered his body."

"I'm sorry."

"Don't be. Life happens the way it does in the order it does whether we agree with it or find reason in it. Shit happens."

"Right. Shit happens," she agreed.

"No cussing young lady."

"Shit is not really a cuss word," she informed him.

"So you know the origins of the word shit?" he asked.

"Who doesn't? Duh."

And over the next thirty miles, Kyle learned more about the word shit than he ever thought possible.

"You sound like a human Wikipedia."

"A Wiki what?"

Kyle glanced at her. "You've never heard of Wikipedia?"

She shook her head.

"Wow. No internet in the wilds of Alaska?"

"We didn't have it. Dad said he could provide nourishment for our bodies or mind-numbing crap from the internet. We chose nourishment."

"So no internet," Kyle mused.

"Jessica Hornet's Nest had internet."

"Hornet's nest?"

McKenna laughed. "That's what I called her. Her last name was Horne."

"You weren't friends?"

She shook her head but said no more and Kyle didn't pry. He remembered grade school and high school. Kids could be mean. They sank into a relaxed silence as the truck's speakers kicked out Symphony No. 9 by Dvorak. Kyle had no idea who the guy was, but his symphony wasn't too bad, and Kyle found himself developing a new appreciation for classical music. McKenna wiled away the miles writing out Beethoven's piano concertos or rewriting the tunes of famous rappers, turning them into hilarious country songs. Kyle discovered not only was McKenna a wiz on the piano, but her vocals had a range that would put a Mockingbird to shame.

The day and the miles flew by in a state of relative ease. They'd stayed the night in a small town the night before, but this stretch to Anchorage was too long and they would have to camp in the truck. Kyle had discussed this with McKenna before they hit the road. She'd accepted the news in a calm manner, reasoning through it until it settled in her mind as being the only option.

Ahead Kyle spotted an abandoned tow truck. He eased the Ford up alongside the truck and peered inside the cab. He breathed a sigh of relief that it was empty and pulled the Ford in behind the tow truck. He backed in at an angle to give the appearance of randomness. He didn't give much thought to the intelligence of the aliens and without having any solid facts to go on he applied common sense and hoped for the best. Besides if his logic was off base McKenna was quick to point out the flaws, advice to which he accepted without argument. Her average so far was one hundred percent accurate. He didn't bet against those odds.

"Here you go." Kyle handed her a peanut butter and jelly sandwich. "What do you want to drink?"

McKenna shook her head.

"Nothing?"

"I'll have a little water right before I go to sleep. There's no bathroom and I'm not using the bucket."

"Ok." Kyle bit into his sandwich and chugged down some water. "What about in the morning? You'll have to pee then."

"Gross. I'm trying to eat," she exclaimed.

"Sorry. Forgot how sensitive you little chicks are."

They finished their meal and climbed into the backseat. Kyle set the battery powered heater between the front seats and turned it on low. McKenna secured the foil curtains that covered the windows before propping up against her pillow and curling up her legs to allow Kyle as much bench space as possible. Kyle did the same on the opposite side, except his legs stretched all the way to McKenna's end where they rested on a Styrofoam cooler wedged between the seats. They would have been more comfortable in the back, stretched out under the camper shell, but Kyle didn't want to be where he couldn't jump into the driver's seat if need be. If he'd known the Ford was no match for the aliens he might have opted for comfort instead.

Kyle crossed his arms and McKenna propped one of hers over his boot. "What's Cheyenne Mountain?" McKenna asked.

"Huh? Why do you ask?"

"The sign in the picture, behind your mom and sister."

Kyle chuckled, not surprised she'd noticed the sign. "It's a military base built inside a mountain. We were going on a tour. It was right before I left for Germany."

"Is that where we're going?"

"For starters. The last time I spoke to my mom they were gathering up civilians to take to the mountain for safety. She was afraid they wouldn't take her because of her cancer." Kyle's voice trailed off. He'd never told anyone about his mom's illness, not even Will and Ada. He didn't have a reason for hiding this from them, other than he didn't want to be consoled or told things like she was in a better place and he shouldn't worry. Her being in a better place was not what kept him awake at night. The ghosts haunting him and the sorrow McKenna saw in his expression was for the suffering he felt certain she'd went through prior to breathing her last breath. His only solace bring in the fact Cheyenne had a highly advanced medical facility and her status as a soldier's mother might have at least garnered her a warm bed.

"I hope we find your mom and sister," McKenna replied in earnest.

Kyle turned to fix his pillow and to hide his shamed face. What a giant self-absorbed shit ass he was, never once asking about her family. All he knew was her mom wanted her to be a country music star and her dad worked his ass off. He thought back to the layout of the house, trying to remember how many bedrooms were in the house. Did she have any siblings? He had no idea. He turned back to apologize, but she was already fast asleep. Kyle sighed. An entire year she'd been alone and the first human she encounters is asshole Kyle Bosch. He'd have to do better by her and promised he would from then on out. He reached over and pulled the blanket up to her chin. Sleep didn't come for him until many hours later.

The next morning McKenna made Kyle sit in the front and promise to not move while she took care of her personal needs. He shook his head at her after she'd jumped out of the truck. Women, even at a young age, were queer complicated creatures.

"Ready Freddy," she announced and slammed the truck door.

"Time to roll Freddy Ready," Kyle answered back.

"We should arrive in Anchorage by noon. They have a Best Western Hotel. I want my own room. I'm going to stretch out on the bed and order room service. Hot chocolate, blueberry pancakes, maple syrup, scrambled eggs." She licked her lips. "No scratch that. I'm going to order one of everything from the menu and eat a little bit of each. Like the buffet we went to every Sunday after church at Terry's Wilderness Room. It was my dad's favorite place."

This reminded Kyle of his self-made promise, but despite his good intentions, he had no idea where or how to start being a sensitive guy. He glanced over at her. She was elaborating on about all the exciting things she would do at the Best Western and paying no mind to his discomfort. He let it go for the time being and listened with interest to her visions of grand hotel living. All pretend of course. Neither one had expectations for anything good let alone grand, fun or exciting.

The miles flew by, the truck cruising along at a safe speed of forty, only slowing if Kyle had to maneuver around an abandoned vehicle. They stopped once to get gas and stock up on water. The sign for Anchorage loomed ahead. It was a quarter to twelve. McKenna's odds were still spot on. The knot in Kyle's stomach twisted tighter. He almost hoped there wouldn't be anyone alive. A crummy thing to hope for, he knew, but finding survivors in the post-apocalyptic US was a crap shoot. People acted funny in good times. Bad times turned funny into crazy. These times were worse than bad and would most likely bring out the mean in folks, in particular, those who prior to the alien's arrival had lived according to society's rules only out of necessity. Removing the constraints of polite society was like removing a straitjacket from a nut case, crossing your fingers, and hoping for the best. A crap shoot for sure, Kyle thought again as he eased the pick-up off the highway onto the exit for Anchorage.

The first sights on the city outskirts promised all they had expected. Corpses enclosed in coffins of ice cluttered the roadways. Kyle wanted to tell McKenna to not look, but she was less fazed by the macabre than he and gazed out the window at the passing dead. Her face remained expressionless until Kyle turned onto Caribou Avenue and the Best Western sign came into view.

"There it is!" she hollered.

"I can see."

"Sorry," she replied without taking her eyes off the prize.

Kyle pulled into the semi-circle drive leading to the entrance and eased the pick-up around an abandoned station wagon that was blocking half of the drive. By the looks of things, he knew room availability wouldn't pose a problem. He backed into an open parking space and shifted into park but didn't cut the engine. Looking out the window at the empty street in front of the hotel, Kyle felt the city's desolation enveloping them. In the distance, he saw a lone figure standing in the middle of the street. He squinted and opened his eyes. It was a woman, maybe, dressed in black with eyes blacker than night. She seemed to float down the street toward them.

"Mr. Kyle?" McKenna tugged on his sleeve.

"Huh." He turned away for only a second, but the figure had vanished. "Did you see that, that person?" He wasn't even sure it was a person.

"What person?" McKenna jerked around in her seat, looking around in all directions. "I don't see anyone." She turned back to him. "You ok?"

Kyle shook his head. "Never mind. I'm just tired."

"Let's go inside then silly." She reached for the door handle.

"Wait." Kyle grabbed her arm.

"What's wrong?"

Kyle pulled a small handgun from his backpack. "Do you know how to use one of these?"

"Sure. My brother showed me."

"You had a brother?" Kyle blurted out and felt his cheeks flush.

"Yeah. He was older than me, but he taught me a bunch of stuff anyway. I know how to skin a deer and shoot a bow and arrow. I don't like killing animals, but dad says either you kill them or go hungry."

"I'm impressed," Kyle replied. He didn't know how to do either of those things, but he did know guns. He checked the gun's safety, flipped it around and handed it to McKenna. "If you have to use it, do you think you can?"

"You mean on a person?" She held the gun in both hands feeling its weight. "I don't know."

"If you get in a bad situation, aim low and pull the trigger. Ok?"

"Ok." She placed the gun in her backpack. "Can we go inside now? I'm hungry."

"Sure."

Kyle killed the engine. They grabbed their gear and he locked up the truck. Before going inside, they kicked snow onto and around the tires hoping to give the truck the same settled appearance as the other vehicles in the lot. As a last added measure Kyle tossed some snow on the windshield. They could always find another vehicle, but he liked this one. It was new, no remnants of a previous owner to worry about. At the door, Kyle stopped and looked up and down the street. Satisfied it was deserted, he went inside where McKenna waited for him by the reception desk.

"Should I ring the bell?"

"I don't think so." Kyle still had reservations on the merits of finding more people. Taking on a twelve-year-old was manageable, but an adult could not be predicted to act one way or the other. "Let's see what's available."

Behind the desk Kyle found the room keys, realizing they probably weren't going to work without access to the hotel's computer system. He thumbed over the white plastic cards thinking of what to do. He glanced behind him at the two office doors standing ajar. From where he stood he could see one was definitely empty. He suggested to McKenna they set up camp in the office. This was greeted with much protest and Kyle withdrew the suggestion. McKenna wanted to go to the top floor but changed her mind when Kyle pointed out the elevators weren't working. Elevators aside, Kyle was thinking of escape routes and safety. The second floor near the interior steps seemed the most logical location.

Using a crowbar he found inside an abandoned vehicle, Kyle jacked open the door to one room. Once let loose McKenna was like a kid on vacation, jumping on the bed, running between their rooms, praising the wonderful amenities of the Best Western. While she examined each nook, Kyle went about getting settled. He placed the portable heater and an extra cylinder of propane next to it, which should be enough to get them through the night. He looked over at the window and wondered if the hotel's kitchen might have aluminum foil. He would need to go scavenging before dark set in.

McKenna's scream startled him. He sprinted into the other room. She wasn't there.

"McKenna!"

"There's no hot water," she yelled from the bathroom.

Kyle expelled his breath. "Shit." He walked over to the bathroom. McKenna stood at the sink shining her light on the running water.

She flashed her light at him. "There's no hot water," she said in a quiet more matter of fact tone.

"I told you there probably wouldn't be," Kyle reminded her.

"I guess I won't take a shower," she sighed.

Her disappointment was heartfelt and Kyle, still feeling guilty for being a shmuck felt compelled to do something about the water. "Maybe the tank is on a backup generator. I might be able to get it working."

"Really?" Her face lit up.

"Don't get your hopes up." He returned to the room

"I have faith in you." McKenna sat on the bed watching him assemble the battery powered lantern. Soon a soft circle of yellow was cast about the room.

"Doesn't mean anything," Kyle replied. "I've had faith in a lot of things and they still failed me." He closed the curtains tight. No need to cast a beacon for anyone to see.

"They?"

"They. It. Whatever. People and things are not more reliable or liable to do things simply because you believe in them."

"I bet you a million dollars we'll have hot water tonight," she persisted.

"Funny girl. Ok, I'll take that bet and raise you another million that I won't."

"No sandbagging," she warned.

"Don't worry. Hot water is worth two million. Now if you'll stay put, I'm going to see about losing a bet."

Kyle walked toward the door, but McKenna jumped off the bed and ran after him, grabbing his arm. "I'm coming with you."

Kyle looked down into her frightened eyes and nodded. At times it was hard to remember she was a kid and, in their circumstances, what kid wouldn't be afraid. Truth be told, he didn't want to leave her behind anyway. With guns in hand, the pair eased the door open checking the hallway before exiting the room. Kyle guided the door until the broken lock touched the jam. They waited and listened to the silence of the hotel. A shiver ran the length of his spine.

Down in the lobby they passed by a golden lion encased in a glass cage. McKenna didn't look at the lion. She hated stuffed animals. Their eyes always seemed to follow you. Her dad had a shed full of stuffed animals out in their backyard. She'd only been in the shed one time. She shuddered and didn't think about it anymore. Reaching for Kyle's gloved hand, McKenna grabbed hold not looking at him when he turned questioning eyes down upon her. He thought her brave, but she really wasn't.

After thirty minutes of wandering around, Kyle located the boiler room at the back of the kitchen and took a look around inside while McKenna waited in the doorway. The room was like a concrete cavern. He located the high-pressure steam boiler at the far end of the room. Kyle flashed his light over the complex control panel and swore under his breath. Hot water was officially out of the question. Kyle headed back toward the door his thoughts churning. Maybe he could heat enough water for a bath using the portable heater.

McKenna's scream again startled him, and this time he knew it was serious. "McKenna." He ran for the door, but it slammed shut in his face. Kyle yanked on the handle. Locked! He heard McKenna screaming his name. She was still near. It wasn't too late. He yanked the shotgun around and fired at the lock. The force knocked him back a step. He fired again and then turned to hit the knob with the butt of the gun. After what seemed like an eternity the knob gave way and Kyle yanked the door open.

Kyle burst into the kitchen gun raised, but no one was waiting for him. He ran from the kitchen into the dining room. "McKenna!" From outside he heard her screaming. Kyle plowed through the dining room and out into the lobby like a raging bull. He ran out the front door, where a man was struggling to put McKenna in the back of his truck. She made this as difficult as her tiny frame could by kicking and flopping about. Kyle saw red when he grabbed the man and threw him down on the ground. He pointed the shotgun at the man's head his finger itching to pull the trigger. "You ok." He asked McKenna, not taking his eyes off the man.

She sniffled. "I'm...I'm ok."

"Come over here behind me." He jerked his head over his shoulder. "Who are you?" Kyle asked the man, thinking it didn't matter who he might be. Kyle ached to smash in his face in.

The man stared back at Kyle and sneered, but said nothing.

"I asked you a question." Kyle poked him with the double barrels.

"Let's leave." McKenna tugged on his arm. "There's time before it gets dark," she begged.

Kyle glanced at the fading suns, knowing he had little time for anything.

"Better think fast boy," the man spat.

"What'd you say?" Kyle stepped on the man's neck.

"You'll never make it out alive," he choked out, cackling afterward.

The man's laughter was dwarfed by the sound of a gun blast followed by the shattering glass of the front door of the Best Western. Kyle grabbed McKenna, threw her over his shoulder and ran inside the hotel as a second bullet whizzed close by them. Kyle took the steps in twos and threes to the second floor. Behind him, he heard more than one pursuer gaining on them and kept going right past their room, past their supplies. He'd the foresight to keep the truck keys in his pocket and knew if they wanted to stay alive reaching the truck was their only chance. At the steps on the other side of the hotel, Kyle set McKenna down telling her they had to make a run for the truck. He took the handgun from her and when the first pursuer's head popped out into the hall, Kyle fired off a shot. Not waiting to see how many were coming after them, Kyle again took the steps two at a time landing on the bottom with a thud.

Outside darkness had fallen, causing McKenna to hesitate in the doorway, but Kyle yanked her through. If he'd seen what she'd seen, he might have reconsidered who or what was the bigger threat. They fast walked blindly across the parking lot not stopping until they almost collided into an abandoned vehicle. Kyle heard the hotel door open and pulled McKenna down by the tire. A ray of light scanned the parking lot, but wasn't strong enough to reach them and was turned off not to come back on. Whoever was after them knew not to come out, to not make a sound, for Kyle didn't hear a word spoken, but did hear the door close. Now that one threat was removed he had time to consider others and wonder if he'd made the right decision.

It was too cold to think over choices. He had to get them to the truck and fast. Kyle grabbed McKenna's hand and felt his way around to the back of the car. They moved toward the front entrance going car by car. If their pursuers were afraid to come outside, then he and McKenna could make it to the truck. The question was, did he dare turn it on? The obvious answer being he had no choice. The heater was in the room. Most of their provisions were in the room. Kyle cursed himself for not being smarter. An eternity seemed to pass before they reached the back of the pickup. Kyle fished the keys out of his pocket, his hands shook so bad he almost dropped them.

"Shit." Kyle took a deep breath and forced his hands to ignore the cold long enough to find the right key and insert it into the lock.

They scurried into the back of the truck and closed the doors without making a sound. At least under the camper they were protected from the wind and prying eyes and whatever else might be lurking in the darkness. The camper had no side windows which allowed Kyle to turn on the flashlight.

"Are you ok," Kyle whispered.

"I can't feel my toes."

"I know. I can't feel mine either," Kyle replied. "I'm going to start the truck. I want you to stay back here ok?"

"No. No. I'm coming up front with you." She grabbed hold of his hand squeezing hard enough to make him wince.

"Ok. Ok. But let me go first." He pried her hand loose. "It's going to be ok McKenna. I promise. We're gonna get outta here."

"Ok," she replied, sounding unconvinced.

Kyle turned off the light and slid open the windows leading to the cab. He looked in the direction of the hotel lobby but saw only the black abyss. He squeezed himself through the opening and up into the driver's seat. He heard McKenna land on the back seat and slide the window closed. With the key in the ignition, Kyle held his breath and turned the key. The sound of the engine coming to life reverberated across the parking lot. Inside the hotel, a light came on and a beam flashed out panning the lot. Kyle ducked when it hit the windshield. The beam waved back and forth one more time before being turned off. It was now or never. Pulling forward meant driving right past the front entrance. Behind them was a small curb and what at one time might have been hedgerow, now a hedge of snow. Kyle thought for a few seconds, before shifting into reverse and hitting the gas pedal.

Several beams of light came on inside the lobby and then exited bobbing and weaving in pursuit. Kyle cranked the wheel and shifted into drive when the first bullet hit the side of the truck.

"Son of a bitch." Kyle floored the gas pedal making the tires spin. Another bullet hit the camper and McKenna screamed. He let up on the gas until the tires caught traction and the truck catapulted down the street. The rear fishtailed wildly before straightening out. Kyle checked the side mirror, letting out a sigh when all he saw was the dark night.

"Are you ok?"

"I'm ok."

"You can come up here. It's safe now."

McKenna stuck her head in between the seats and stared out the windshield, trying to see beyond the glow of the headlights.

"It's ok. Those men aren't coming after us."

"I'm not worried about them," she replied.

"Oh."

McKenna climbed up front, peering into the dark looking for things, or beings, that didn't belong. She'd heard the aliens at night on the roof, their long nails scraping and clicking along. On those nights she slept under the bed if she slept at all.

"Maybe we should find somewhere to stay," McKenna suggested.

Kyle glanced over at her. The glow from the dashboard lights was enough to see her frightened expression. He reached over and squeezed her knee. "We'll be ok."

The 'k' of ok coincided with a loud screech that shattered the night. McKenna dove into the back seat and pulled the blanket on up over her head. Kyle slowed the truck to a stop, cut the lights, and was debating on whether to turn off the engine when something bumped into the passenger door. Kyle caught his breath but didn't dare turn to see the cause, somehow knowing that bump came from something not of this Earth. McKenna didn't make a peep. Another bump to the hood, to the back, to the roof. The bumping stopped. A minute ticked off the clock and then another. Kyle's grip on the steering wheel eased up, allowing blood to return to his fingers. He leaned back against the headrest and stared into the pitch black. The air trapped inside his lungs was expelled, slow and deliberate. The engine fan kicked on startling him. He released the steering wheel and lowered his hands. Another minute ticked off the digital clock. Kyle grasped the light lever between his fingers. Two clicks forward were all it took. A slight flick of the wrist and he would know for sure if they were alone. But what if he was wrong? He dropped his hand and shifted his eyes to the glowing numbers on the dash.

Five fifty-three.

Five fifty-four.

He again took hold of the lever. At five fifty-five he would cut on the lights. His eyes were glued to the clock, glued to the number four until it changed to five. Kyle turned the lever two clicks.

"Oh shit."

Outside, surrounding the truck was maybe twenty Svan, maybe thirty, maybe too many to count. To Kyle, they were alien creatures, the things that went bump in the night, the monster under the bed. Without turning around, he instructed McKenna not to move, not to make a sound no matter what happened, no matter what she heard. And then Kyle began to silently pray, to beg God to hear him, to spare McKenna, if not him. He stopped praying and breathing when a Svan walked up to the passenger side of the truck. Kyle shook to his core, his teeth chattered uncontrollably. The alien grabbed the door and ripped it off, tossing it a hundred yards down the road.

"Holy Mother help us," Kyle whispered.

The alien spoke to one of the others standing close by using what sounded like a series of short grunts. The alien reached inside the cab. Kyle backed against the driver's door, but the being's long clawed fingers grabbed his leg and pulled him out of the truck. The alien dangled Kyle high up in the air like a prize for the others to see before lowering him and sniffing his hair. The fiend sniffed all over his head and then turned Kyle so they faced each other, so they were eye to eye. In the alien's large black eyes Kyle saw his terrified face looking back at him. The alien opened its mouth wide revealing sharp fangs and a black tongue. It brought Kyle closer and sucked in the air around his face.

Kyle closed his eyes and tried to lean back, to free himself. In a brief moment of clarity, he realized the futility of any effort to escape. Tension fell away and his muscles received the signal to surrender. Hanging there like a rag doll, he thought this was it, he was going to be eaten by this thing, this killer of man. He prayed a final prayer, not for himself, but for McKenna. He begged and cursed God at the same time; begging for McKenna to be spared and damning God if he didn't.

Amidst a string of curse words running through his head, Kyle felt his feet touch the ground, but before he could rationalize and find his legs, the alien released him. His knees buckled and he crumpled to the ground. He remained in his haphazard kneeling position, head bent down, not daring to look up. All around him the Svan chattered amongst themselves. Kyle listened and wondered if they were trying to decide how to kill him. Suddenly the chatter stopped. He held his breath, waiting for them to strike, bracing for the pain. Out of the silence, he heard a voice, a female voice and she spoke in the beast's language. An instant later the Svan took to the air, swift and thunderous, hundreds of giant wings flying upward, carrying them away into the darkness. Silence again filled the night.

14 UNKNOWNS

While Kyle was picking himself up from the road in Anchorage, Zack was flying through space at the speed of light. Upon reentering the present, he somersaulted across frozen ground, landing hard on his shoulder. Luke followed in much the same fashion, with Ed seconds behind him. Zack struggled to his knees only to fall back down. He wished whoever was sticking giant needles into his body would please stop. A sharp pain shot through the back of his head and straight into his eyes. He cursed out loud. Luke answered with his own curse words and Ed simply rolled about clutching his sides and groaning. After long minutes of what felt like torture, the pain subsided and then dissipated altogether. Ed stopped moaning. Zack stopped clutching his head and opened his eyes, realizing for the first time it was evening.

"Ed," Zack whispered into the darkness.

"Over here," came his weak response.

"Luke you there?" Zack said a bit louder.

"I'm here." His voice came from a different direction than Ed's.

Zack fished out a small flashlight from his pocket. "I'm gonna flash this light and you guys walk to me. Ok?"

Zack flashed the light until Ed and Luke were close enough he could hear them breathing.

"You guys alright?" Zack kept the light on. He didn't think the Sundogs would bother them again, at least not that night.

"Holy mother fucker!" Luke said.

"Did we just time travel? Or something?" Ed asked.

"Or something is right my friend." Zack patted him on the back. "And now we need to figure out where the fuck we landed." He looked around, but without the stars or the moon, they were no better off than a blind man. The wind picked up velocity and howled around them. "We are fucked," Zack announced. "All my shit's on the ATV. Compass, spotlight, thermal blankets. Every damn thing."

"Mine too," Luke added.

"All I have is a granola bar," Ed offered.

"What're we going to do? We can't stay out here." Luke's voice was a mix of panic and anger. "We could walk for miles. We have no fucking idea where we're at."

Eve appeared on the edge of the circle of light. "I will guide you."

"Oh shit!" Zack shined the tiny light toward Eve, avoiding hitting her directly in the face. "I wish you'd stop doing that."

"Follow me." Eve turned and walked out of the light.

Not one to look a gift horse in the mouth, Zack hurried after her, dragging Ed and Luke along before they had time to protest. She was the only chance they had. Zack didn't fancy freezing to death and she'd already saved them once, so the chances of her killing them off now were unlikely. After ten minutes of walking Eve halted without warning, causing Zack to dodge left or run into her. Had he been asked, he would have admitted that jumping off of a cliff might be preferable to having direct contact with her.

"You are safe for now," Eve said. "Stay away from the housing units. You cannot help those people."

"What'd ya mean can't help them?" Ed demanded.

"It's the barn," Zack announced, surprise in his voice.

"We were that damn close?" Luke asked, sounding pissed off.

"Did you want it to be farther?" Zack joked.

Luke didn't answer. What he wanted was to not have to rely on the vampire bitch. As soon as he thought this, he looked around. "She's gone."

"What?" Ed spun around looking in all directions. "Wait," he yelled out to the dark, "come back."

"Forget it Ed. She's gone." Zack turned back to the barn door. He took off his glove and reached his fingers behind a loose board. Within a few minutes the lights came on and a few more minutes the locks were being undone and the door was sliding open. On the other side, Colin and Madison waited for them.

"Shit man. What the hell happened?" Colin asked once they were inside and had closed the doors.

Zack pulled off his ski mask.

"Oh my God," Madison gasped. "Zack, you're bleeding

"What?" Zack touched his face.

Ed and Luke removed their masks as well.

"Your faces." She pointed at them.

They looked at each other. All three had dried blood around their noses and mouths.

"Must have been our mode of travel," Zack noted.

As they rode the platform down into the bunker, the travelers took turns explaining what had transpired over the past twenty-four hours and even to their ears it sounded wild and preposterous. Madison and Colin had no trouble believing it was true. In this new world they existed in, surprises were hard to come by, and seldom welcomed.

"Sick man," Colin exclaimed. "You were that close to a Sundog dude?" he asked Luke.

"Yeah. That close," Luke replied and couldn't help smiling at Colin's misguided admiration. He had no idea what they were up against. In a way, Luke envied him and wished life in the bunker satisfied him.

They stopped to clean up before heading for the command center. When Colin opened the door, they were swarmed by a welcoming committee of the bunker's residents. A hail of questions followed with everyone talking at once. Apparently, the nature of their trip hadn't remained a secret for long. Zack sought out Colin through the swarm. Colin shrugged his shoulders at his brother's raised eyebrows. It hadn't been Colin's doing. He'd only told Charlie, who only told one other person. Who told whom what after that was anyone's guess.

Once the hubbub died down to a quiet murmur, and Zack and Luke were the centers of attention, Ed quietly slipped out to see Jenny. He tried not to be concerned that she was not part of the welcoming crowd. He would have been more surprised to see her up and about. A gnawing fear ate at his mind, but he wasn't going to think about it just then. For right now, all he wanted was to see his wife.

Madison was the only one to notice Ed's departure and figured he was going to see Jenny. She'd gone to see her after Ed had left, not wanting her to be alone, worried about how she might be handling her return to the living. Jenny had insisted she was ok, but Madison stayed with her during Ed's absence. She had Colin bring them dinner, so Jenny wouldn't have to eat alone. Madison knew Jenny was having a hard time adjusting and tried to draw her out, but she wouldn't talk about what happened, claiming she couldn't remember. The one thing she had been animated about, was their son Ryan. Saying his name brought more than a spark to her eye. Madison's experience told her Jenny remembered more than she was letting on, but she didn't press the issue.

Thinking about Jenny brought Madison's thoughts around to Roxanne. Madison had gone to see her first, before Jenny, but no answer came when she knocked on the door. Later Madison ran into Caleb playing video games with Zoe. Although Zoe was thirteen and obviously knew the games well, Caleb beat her time and time again. When Madison asked if he ever played before he'd replied yes that he'd played many times, but his response sounded rehearsed. She was sure of this, but what was she going to do? Grill a seven-year-old? She let it go. All things would come to light, Madison was sure of it. She was also certain these things would not be revelations of the good sort, but only time would tell. Madison snapped out of her meanderings and looked up to find Zack staring at her from across the room.

Her fickle heart beat a little bit faster and she longed to go to him, to tell him she loved him. If he was the only man on her mind, she wouldn't have hesitated, but he wasn't, and Madison wouldn't inflict heartache upon him for her own selfish desires. That her aloofness was doing exactly what she intended it not to do never occurred to her. That he wanted her, even if it meant only having a part of her, also eluded her. If her momma had been there she would have pointed out the obvious and maybe saved Madison the unnecessary anguish she was feeling.

Across the room, Zack fought a different battle. He had told himself to give Madison time, she would figure out what she wanted, but now he thought to hell with waiting. Time was running out. He felt it deep inside and at times not deep at all, but right there on the surface ready to burst out into the open. The Adita were coming soon. That their return didn't bode well for what remained of the human race was also irrefutable. He didn't want to spend the last days of his life watching the woman he loved from across the room, hoping she would realize one day what a wonderful guy he was. One day would be too late. It was now or never.

After about fifty minutes of answering their questions with answers that were founded for the most part in speculation, Luke had had enough. He wanted to go see how Austin was doing and, more so, to check on Roxanne. The feeling that she wasn't who she claimed wouldn't let go of him. He thought about talking it over with Madison, but in thinking of what he might say, in each and every way he approached the topic it sounded absurd. Intuition fought against guilt and came up the loser. Austin was his friend, his family, and Luke couldn't betray him, but he would be damned if he'd let his guard down. With his conscience somewhat settled, Luke made his way over to Madison and let her know where he was headed. She gave him a quick hug and asked if he was ok. A charming smile, after a not so convincing yes, kept her from asking more questions. Luke left knowing he hadn't gotten one off, knowing that not much, if anything, got past her and she would find him later. Later, after she had time to dwell on it all, and then he wouldn't be able to dodge her questions.

* * *

Eve stood over Austin, her hand on his forehead, fingers spread wide curled over the top of his head. Za's visit and delivered pronouncement disturbed her more than she liked. Changes were coming that she could not foresee and waiting for Austin to recover on his own was no longer a viable option. She looked across Austin to where Caleb stood staring at his father's face. He glanced up at her, but not for long. Eve knew he was anxious to meet Austin.

Caleb was more than anxious, he was filled with great anticipation. Soon his father would leave the darkness and open his eyes. He wanted to see the very moment this happened, to see his father have eyes like his own. Caleb didn't know why this mattered, not yet, only that his father must be human for a little while longer. Eve withdrew her hand and rested it on Austin's forearm. Caleb watched Austin's eyes as they moved underneath his eyelids. Back and forth, fast and slow, slow, and then they opened. Blue eyes blinked, looked at Eve, blinked again, looked at Caleb, and then looked around at the ceiling, the walls, his expression one of uncertainty.

"Where am I?" he asked.

"Under the ground," Eve responded. She knew the humans called it a bunker, but it reminded her of Cheyenne.

"Mr. Londergan's bunker," Caleb added. "In Pueblo," he continued when Austin turned to look at him, pleased to have his father's attention. "We arrived last week."

Austin reached out and touched Caleb's face. "Caleb?"

"Yes, father."

Austin stared at the boy. Was this child his son? His son, he repeated this and decided he must be dreaming. This couldn't be his son, the baby Eve had presented to him a few months prior. Had so much time been lost that his son was already a boy? Austin tried to recall what happened. The last memory he had was falling to the floor. Needles and blood also played a part. Austin shook his head. This motion created the opposite effect of what was intended. The lines of the room blurred.

"Easy, your body is still adjusting," Eve said.

Austin turned to look at Eve. The sound of her voice, of Roxanne's voice, made its way through the fog. He pushed his body up into a sitting position. "What happened to me?"

"You were in a deep slumber," Eve replied.

"For how long?"

"Twenty-nine days."

An entire month he'd been lying in bed. He flexed his leg muscles. They felt stronger than he would have expected. He tossed the blanket off and swung his legs over the side. Placing his hands on the mattress, he pushed himself up. The room didn't spin, his knees didn't buckle. In fact, he felt a surge of energy sweep through him, which was frightening more than pleasing. He rubbed his face, his eyes. And then he remembered and rushed to the bathroom. An unshaven face greeted him, and eyes that were blue as the sky with no signs of black specs. He ran his hand over his beard and then over his head through his hair already an inch long. He returned to the bedroom.

"You're still human," Eve said, noting his expression of relief.

"Is that all I am? When you bit me, what did that do to me?" He rubbed his wrist where the marks were no longer visible to the naked eye.

"It was supposed to change you, to become an Adita, but your body rejected the transformation. You are stronger than I'd thought possible for a human."

"Why do I feel so strange?" Austin asked.

"Parts of your brain, those once dormant, are no longer. Your body is also functioning on a higher level. You are an improved human."

"That's why I feel so... so strong?"

Eve nodded.

Austin thought this over. He had so many more questions but didn't know where to begin. "How old is he?" Austin nodded at Caleb.

"I'm seven," Caleb announced, not content with being ignored after having waited so long to meet his father in person.

Austin turned to Eve. "How is that possible? We were on Bliss only two months ago."

"He will be fully grown by the ninth moon," Eve responded.

"And when is that?"

"By the ninth month of Earth's calendar," Caleb replied.

Austin marinated on this for a moment. "That doesn't answer my question."

"You want to know if he's human," Eve stated. "He's not. He's Adita, with a few human traits. Those that were the best of you."

"I'm a species that has never existed before," Caleb announced in a proud voice.

Austin knelt on one knee and looked Caleb in the eyes. They were the same clear blue as Austin's, not a speck of black anywhere. His hair was blonde and his complexion healthy, human. He saw nothing of Eve and despite his desire to find something of Roxanne, she wasn't visible in the boy's features either. In him, Austin only saw himself. Austin pulled Caleb to him, hugging him tightly. His heart ached for many reasons. This was his son, yet he felt him a stranger. As a father, he would never experience sleepless nights, diapers, or first steps to video and send out to friends and family. Austin leaned back from Caleb. He hadn't thought about his own mother in a long time. She'd abandoned him as a child, never to be heard from again. He'd never tried to find her, and she'd never contacted him. She was Caleb's grandmother and he'd no idea if she was alive. He hugged Caleb again, vowing his son would not grow up without his parents, like he and Eve, like...like Roxanne.

Roxanne. He repeated her name, pondering over his thoughts, over a specific thought, one he hadn't considered until now. Roxanne had been born in Russia and was orphaned when only a baby. An American couple adopted her, but again tragedy struck when she was five and they were killed in a plane crash. From there Roxanne bounced around the foster care system until she turned eighteen and vanished from the state's records. No one cared. It was one less in millions for the overworked, underpaid social workers to worry about.

Agra had said Austin never knew the human Roxanne. Had he been the maestro behind her parent's death, planning for Austin to fall in love with her and have a child? Had Agra targeted Roxanne because of her lack of family ties? Or was Agra responsible for the tragedies that orphaned Roxanne? The questions swarmed around inside his mind. He didn't have the answers, but she did. Eve did.

Austin kissed Caleb on the forehead and stood up. "Who are you? Who are you really?"

Eve heard his unspoken questions, understood his anxiety over the past. "If truths are what you desire I will tell them."

"Yes. I want to hear them, all of them," Austin replied without hesitation.

Eve didn't mock him with a doubtful smile. In her experience, humans were skilled in denying the truth, were quick to turn deaf ears to the truth and, even more so, were incapable of comprehending the meaning of such. For Austin, though, the truth might be all that was acceptable, no matter how difficult hearing the words might be for him. He would listen with an attentive mind and understand the meaning behind her words. She directed him out to the living room where they sat, he on the couch, and she on a chair facing him. In between, Caleb, who knew most of the story, occupied himself with his toys.

"Most all of what I am about to share I learned after arriving on Paru. Some parts were told to me by Agra and Arati, others I found through listening to those around me. I have few memories of my own from the time before my people left Earth," Eve began. "Agra told you the Adita are one of the oldest civilizations to exist and the first to occupy this planet. This he spoke in truth. As he did about the human disease that caused my people to flee. However, in the period prior to the spread of the disease, the Adita prospered and multiplied. Not all unions were pure. Many Adita males took to keeping human females as servants. Many of these ownerships produced offspring, as the males often mated with their servants. In the beginning, the Elders granted permission for these offspring to live. But from these unions, a stronger human evolved, one that questioned their place in the evolutionary chain. The Elders decided having them continue to breed was a threat to the Adita's way of life. From then on all Adita males were forbidden to reproduce with humans. The Elders took this decree a step further by ordering all humans carrying the Adita gene to be eradicated."

"Eradicated?"

"Beheaded and burned. Any Adita caught disobeying was beheaded. Humans were burned, usually alive."

"Like the witch hunts back in the fifteenth century."

Eve nodded but knew that witch hunts, in one form or another, occurred all throughout human history, including modern day. "Shortly after the eradication, the disease began to spread. Thousands of Svan and Adita perished. My people evacuated the planet, leaving me behind. At this point my own memories begin, at this point, I first heard the voice. My father of course, but I didn't know who or what he was, only that I should listen and obey his commands."

"And it was Agra that led you to me?"

"Yes. Although many were tested before you, I knew as soon as I saw you, and smelled your blood that you were the human he'd been searching for."

"And Roxanne?"

"Agra's doing. He instructed me to take on her persona, her features, her characteristics. He identified her as being a good match, one you would be attracted to."

Austin mulled this over. "What about Caleb? How was he possible?"

"Our union was the first of its kind. An Adita woman would never consider carrying a human's spawn. It was beneath them. My father didn't tell me this until after we met face to face."

Austin laughed, sarcastic and disbelieving. "Otherwise you never would have," he paused, "never would have mated with me."

"No, I would not have. Not in those days anyway." She looked over at Caleb. "Things do change."

"Was any of it real?" Austin asked and wished he hadn't.

"You want to know if Roxanne loved you. I was her, so the answer is no."

"Ouch, that hurts." Austin's hand went to his heart in jest, but the pain he felt was genuine.

"Adita do not love, we survive."

"Charming people." Austin couldn't keep the sarcasm out of his voice, the wounds of the past were too fresh.

"Charms get you nowhere. Knowing your place in the universe is all that has meaning. Humans do not know why they exist. You function on emotions and without real purpose. We function on instinct, our purpose is to survive above all others. You squander the strongest agile specimen on fields of sport, playing silly games. You hunt not to provide food, but for sport. Your soldiers are led by governments not generals, and are ill-equipped--"

"Hold up there," Austin interrupted. "Our military is not ill-equipped."

"On a level playing field I would agree with you, but you are no longer on that field and the rules have changed. You have no idea of what is out there, beyond your planet, beyond your comprehension. Do you think the Adita was the worst thing that could have happened to your people?"

After a minute of thought, Austin shook his head. Eve was right, things had changed. Up until a year ago, he'd never given the universe much thought, but he now understood how little he knew about anything out beyond the stars. "What happened before you came to Deadbear?"

"I walked the Earth from the deserts to the seas to the mountains searching, for what I did not know. I knew not who I was or where I came from, but I knew I wasn't like those around me. I listened to a voice that guided me and at times abandoned me. During the dark years, the voice was all I had for company."

"The dark years?"

"Many thousands of years after my people departed the planet, the human population had dwindled close to extinction. Only a few thousand remained. My life source was vanishing before my eyes and I was powerless to stop the ebb. With no other means of survival, I faced a death, but in the worst imaginable way."

"What about animals? Couldn't you survive on their blood?"

"The seas had diminished to almost nothing, turning the planet into a barren wasteland. Few animals remained, but the humans needed those to live. Survival is a powerful motivator." Eve paused, recalling Chase and admiring his strong desire to live. "The voice told me to leave, to travel in search of food. The only way I knew how to travel was on foot. Knowledge of my powers was kept hidden from me. I trusted in the voice like a blind child."

Austin took notice of her tone, the hint of tension in her voice. Her face was relaxed and her eyes, as always, unreadable, but he knew he hadn't imagined hearing the underlying anger, maybe even hatred. "Go on," he encouraged.

"I traveled from the only home I knew, the place you call Egypt, to a place named Cape Dezhnev located at the tip of Russia. I walked nonstop for one hundred and fifty days, seven thousand miles, leaving behind my only source of food. It was a death march through the land of the dead. At the point I thought the journey a failure and my death imminent, I came upon a small pack of humans. They were struggling to stay alive and losing. The smell of their blood was so overwhelming and my hunger so consuming, but —"

"But you didn't kill them," Austin finished.

Her lip turned up at one corner, not in a smile, but maybe something denoting twisted amusement. "No. I didn't kill them. I persuaded them to journey with me to the Cape. Three hundred miles remained before reaching my destination. If I had arrived at the Cape and found it no more hospitable than the land I'd left behind, my future would have been decided."

"They were your backup plan," Austin noted. "To ensure you wouldn't starve to death."

"Bravo captain," Eve commended him. That he understood the gravity of her situation was not surprising, that his voice carried a note of empathy she had not expected. Most would have called her actions inhumane or barbaric, to which she would have pointed out she was neither.

"What did you find at the Cape?"

"An abundance of life. Colonies of people, wildlife, crops, everything needed for sustained living. They were saved and so was I."

"I guess ten thousand years ago Russia wasn't the frozen tundra it is today?"

"It was lush and thriving. Like the planet where my people currently wait. Bliss as your generals called it. Paru as we know it."

"Why won't the Adita stay on Bliss or Paru? Why come back here?"

"This is home."

This answer seemed too simple, but Austin sensed she didn't have another to offer. "So what happened next?"

"I lived amongst the humans in Russia. They worshipped me as a god, offering up their own as sacrifices. I did not ask of them to do this, they did so on their own accord. They thought of me as their protector, which suited me better than hiding in the shadows, taking lives at random. I stayed for several thousand years, before returning to Egypt and then to America. The humans in your Russia grew in number, spreading out, repopulating the planet. Soon racial lines blurred, new lines were created while others faded away." Eve glanced over at Caleb. "I knew the old from the new, the strong from the weak."

"How?"

"Your genetic code, DNA sequence you might call it. Each unique to the owner, and what you can't see, I can. Those with the strongest genes are easy to distinguish and always prevail." Eve took Austin's arm and turned it over. Using her fingertip, she traced his vein. "Your genetic sequence is very old. It's the strongest human sequence in existence, to ever have existed. You are descendent of a great warrior from a tribe of great warriors. They survived the dark days on Earth, but as is always the case with your species, they didn't safeguard their lines. Eventually, the superior genes were lost amongst the inferior. Except for yours."

Austin stared at his vein unimpressed. "How does Caleb fit into Agra's plan?"

"His plan," she paused, choosing her words with caution before continuing. "His plan is to protect the Adita's way of life by improving their DNA sequence, making it stronger than before."

"You don't sound like you're on board with his plan."

"On board?"

"That you agree with his vision for the preservation of life," Austin clarified. "You say 'their DNA' not 'our DNA'. As if you don't think of yourself as one of them."

"I am one of them. And I believe in the preservation of life."

That wasn't his question or the answer he was looking for, but it occurred to him that she knew exactly what he'd asked and answered by saying exactly what she'd meant. Eve didn't mince words.

"Tell him about the Svan mother," Caleb suggested without looking up, continuing to play despite her displeasure and reluctance to discuss the subject. He didn't know why it had to be secret. He wanted to know more about them as well, but his mother wouldn't discuss these things with him until he was an adult.

"What about the Svan?" Austin asked.

"They're a very old and an important part of the Adita's culture. There isn't much more to tell."

"Are they part robot or computer? Zack dissected one that had died. Inside he found wires and something like a computer chip."

"Some of the Svan have been mechanized, but I don't know much about that process," she finished abruptly, having said more than she wanted to about the Svan. Caleb did not fool her pretending he wasn't hanging on her every word.

Austin sensed her unwillingness to discuss the Svan, and rather than press for information, he asked to hear more about Roxanne.

"When I arrived at the hospital where they'd brought Roxanne, I was too late. She'd been in an accident and her internal organs were badly damaged. Although they tried, your doctors couldn't save her."

"You could have saved her," Austin said.

Eve shook her head. "It doesn't work like that. If I had saved her you two never would have met, for she would not have been human any longer. An outcome that would not have served Agra's purpose and is against Adita laws."

"Of course. Always Agra's purpose," Austin replied, knowing his sarcasm was wasted on Eve. The memories of Roxanne were so real to him. Roxi was so real to him. "Why?"

"My natural form did not make me desirable for procreation. Agra instructed me to become human by absorbing Roxanne's thoughts and memories. I used her physical features to appeal to your human desires."

"When you came to Deadbear, I never knew if you were real or not," Austin said, feeling guilty, and not sure why. "You never spoke to me. And when you came back, you showed me death and destruction and nothing else. But you never explained any of it."

"I was preparing you for the future. For the end of mankind as you know it."

"As I know it? What does that mean?"

"Evolution. Nothing lasts in the continuum. Species evolve and change. The strongest of these will survive. The Adita are the fittest, but we have not always been such and if we do not take measures we will not remain as such. I know you are not so naive to think your species will survive the test of time without trials, without the possibility of extinction. If not us, another would have eradicated you or you would have destroyed yourselves."

"Mr. Luke is on his way to see you father," Caleb interrupted.

Austin heard footsteps approach and stop outside his door. He heard Luke talking to himself.

"Why don't you let him in?" Eve instructed, to which Caleb ran to the door.

Eve turned back to Austin. "I must resume my guise as your wife." She transformed into Roxanne.

"My wife? What..."

"You're awake!" Luke exclaimed.

"That I am." Austin spun around, hiding his shock behind happiness at seeing his friend. They hugged. Austin stared over Luke's shoulder at Eve or Roxanne, he wasn't sure anymore who he was seeing. When Luke stepped back, Austin continued to glance in her direction, expecting the image of his wife to vanish.

"Hello, Mrs. Reynolds." Luke nodded his head her way.

"Please call me Roxi," she said, giving him a sweet smile. "How was your trip to Wyoming?"

Austin looked away from her. "Wyoming. When did you go to Wyoming?"

"It's ok dear." Roxanne placed her hand on Austin's arm. "Luke can take care of himself."

Austin looked into her eyes, now green and lively. It was more than he could take and he looked away. Her hand tightened on his arm and a familiar rush of energy passed through his body, washing away his sadness, replacing it with tranquility. Luke watched them, guilt rising up over his awful thoughts and accusations. Seeing the two of them together, and Austin being awake and healthy, made him question his instincts. How could he have doubted she was Roxanne? He absently scratched his head wishing the ants would go away.

"When did you wake up?" Luke asked.

"Um, I guess about thirty minutes ago," Austin replied, sounding dazed as Luke would expect, but not for the reasons Luke assumed.

"I'm sorry I didn't come for you right away Luke," Roxanne apologized. "It happened so sudden and we had so much to catch up on." She smiled, charming and warm.

"Oh no ma'am that's perfectly ok with me. He's your husband, not mine. I mean he's not my husband, obviously right. He's my friend, you know. Anyway, I'll leave you two alone," Luke stammered.

"Don't go, man. I want to hear about Wyoming and everything else I've missed in the past month."

"You sure?" Luke glanced at Roxanne.

"Don't worry about me. Caleb and I are going to get something to eat. You two catch up. And be sure to tell him about Jenny's return."

Austin was stunned. She sounded so much like Roxanne in the way she talked and moved and her expressions. Knowing that it was Eve didn't change the impact it had on him. He watched her gather Caleb and head for the door. Before leaving she turned back.

"Can I bring you anything dear?"

Unable to form a coherent sentence, Austin shook his head.

"Luke?"

"No, ma'am. I'm good."

"We'll be back in a little while." They disappeared out the door, leaving behind a bewildered Austin.

Roxanne walked slowly down the corridor while Caleb ran ahead. She was fully aware of the cameras and the many eyes watching her on the video screens. One set of eyes watched her movements with great interest. Roxanne's brow creased and the hair rose on the back of her neck. Although not a worthy adversary, Madison was a prime specimen of her race, thus eradicating her would be wasteful, but if necessary she would not hesitate.

15 CHRISTMAS

Zack walked the corridors of the bunker enjoying the quiet. With Christmas only a couple of days away, the bunker was a constant buzz of excitement. Not the usual holiday glitz and glam, but as close to festive as the residents could manage. Colin and Ed had scavenged decorations from stores in Pueblo and most everyone pitched in to put them up. They could have found more in Colorado Springs, but Austin had been adamant they stay close to the bunker and Zack had seconded that motion.

Adding to the holiday spirit was the early arrival of Anne's twin girls. The delivery had proceeded without a hitch or a hiccup, but Zack for one was relieved the ordeal was over. The idea of birth control was even more prevalent now that the actuality of having to care for babies was smacking him in the face. He made a note to discuss contraceptives once more with Colin, who had laughed at him the first time he'd broached the subject. Maybe he would fill everyone's stockings with condoms.

Although the newborns were welcomed with open arms, Zack felt a certain amount of unease. Zoe was the youngest member of their group and if need be could defend herself. How long would they have to wait for the babies to do the same? Five years? Six maybe? Zack didn't have the answer. A child wielding a weapon might seem insane to most, but ole Bobby had taught him to handle a revolver when he was seven and a shotgun not long after. Unconventional as that might have been at the time, Zack didn't think the same standards existed in the world they lived in now. As far as he could tell or was concerned, convention had flown out the window after the Sundogs arrived.

"Couldn't sleep?"

Zack turned to see Madison catching up to him. She looked beautiful in the green dress she was wearing, one of those sweater types that hugged every curve. He stopped short of whistling his appreciation. She'd either punch him or walk off or both.

"No. You?"

Madison shook her head. "Mind if I walk with you?"

Zack stuck out his arm and Madison looped hers through his. "So what do you think of Austin's sudden recovery?" Zack asked.

"I don't know what to think. I mean he seemed so normal at dinner. Like he'd never been in a coma or whatever it was."

"I've been debating whether to ask him for another blood sample."

"Maybe he'll offer and you won't have to."

"Maybe so."

They walked through the bunker completing the entire loop talking about nothing in particular, wanting to say something specific but neither knowing where to begin. Upon reaching Madison's door, Zack released her arm and bowed. "Goodnight Madame. It was a pleasure."

Madison swallowed hard. "Did you want to come inside?"

Zack straightened up slowly. He looked her in the eyes. She stared back unwavering and he knew without having to ask that she was sure. Zack stepped closer to her, still no signs of hesitation. He reached around her and opened the door, being careful to not make any sudden movement. He held his breath expecting at any moment for Madison to bolt inside, and slam the door in his face, but she didn't. She stepped aside allowing him to enter and gently closed the door behind him.

* * *

Later that night, Zack lay awake listening to Madison sleep. He looked over at her again, confirming and reconfirming her presence, unable to believe this magnificent woman wanted to be with him. He wanted to ask why the change in heart, but once her lips touched his, talking had been put on hold. A sudden fear gripped his heart, a fear of this not being real, and a onetime deal, of her waking up hating herself for the things she whispered in the heat of the moment. Zack couldn't live with that, not after being this close to her.

"Do you ever sleep?"

Madison's voice startled him, and he was relieved to hear nothing in her tone resembling regret. He turned over to look at her.

"Not if I can help it."

"You must be superhuman, cuz you never seem tired," she mumbled through the blankets. It had been eons since she'd woken up with a man in her bed and she'd forgotten how to act. However, Zack, who had plenty of practice, was perfectly at ease. The fact many had been in her place didn't make her feel any less awkward.

"Not superhuman. Just don't like wasting too much time sleeping. I did plenty of that before things went haywire." And he'd missed out on too many opportunities, spending time with his mom being the main one. This round was most likely his last and he didn't want to screw it up as well.

"Do you want some coffee?" Madison asked.

"I do, but let me get it. You stretch out and enjoy the quiet while it lasts."

Madison grimaced. "Ahg, today is the big shopping day."

"Yep." Zack patted her on the leg before sliding out from under the covers as naked as the day he was born. He crossed the room and retrieved his jeans from the chair where he'd tossed them.

Madison watched him move about the room, looking very much at home. She admired his lean figure, which, despite his claims of being allergic to anything healthy and all forms of exercise, was surprisingly muscular. Not the same as Austin's, but... Shit! She swore in her head. Why'd you go and ruin a good thing by bringing him up? She placed her hands over her face blocking out the light coming from the other room.

Last night had been wonderful. She'd bit the bullet by telling Zack she loved him and wanted to be with him. She'd assured him that although she cared deeply for Austin, she wasn't in love with him. And that much was true. She hadn't gone so far to share that she was still very much attracted to Austin, because it was on a weird unexplainable level she couldn't talk about. The attraction was almost animalistic in nature and she'd finally concluded that what she felt wasn't love. She knew not what to call it, but discussing this with Zack served no purpose. His confidence in her love was all that mattered.

Madison removed her hands and smiled. Having someone to care about, to love that loved you back was an elated feeling, like being a teenager again. Her smile quickly faded when reminded of her duties for the day. She was taking the girls shopping for Christmas presents. The guys were going as well, but the plan was to split up once they reached the mall in Pueblo. As a side thought, Madison hoped Jenny would feel up to going out. She hadn't come out of their suite much and Madison knew it wore on Ed.

"Why the frown." Zack returned with steaming cups of coffee, handing one to her.

Madison sat up and took the cup. "I was thinking about today's duties."

Zack sat on the bed, legs stretched out in front of him. "Seems kinda weird. The whole Christmas thing."

"I know, but the kids are happy and occupied."

"What happens afterward?"

"As in the future? You want to get into that now?" Madison looked over at the clock. "At four am?"

"Not really, but Luke was right. We can't go on like this is permanent. It's not."

"No, it's not permanent," Madison agreed. "The Adita will return. And soon."

"So true. And how will they top the first show? Sequels never measure up to the first, especially in horror flicks. They're usually pretty fucking bad. Pardon my French. But in this case, knowing who's directing the picture and the main actors, I would say we can be certain the follow up will be a hell of a show for us captive moviegoers."

They sipped their coffee in silence, neither of them wanting to attempt to answer the questions hovering over them like a thunderstorm brewing on the horizon in the middle of August. A thunderstorm packing an EF5 tornado. All hope of surviving had not yet been abandoned but holding on was a delicate balance and easier to manage while the winds were calm. After seeing the camp in Wyoming and receiving Eve's warning, Zack knew this better than Madison.

"I always wondered what it would be like to shop like a rich person." She glanced at him. "I guess you already know what that's like huh?"

Zack laughed, happy to talk about money, a much safer topic. "I can't lie to you, having a shit load of money was nice. Living that lifestyle. I had no complaints. I mean how many guys my age are invited to the White House to play chess with the president?" Zack laughed at the absurdity. "I'm not even going to tell you it got old. It was the best time of my life." He sighed heavy and sad. "But none of it matters now, right? It's a level playing field. No rich. No poor."

"A silver lining?"

"Nah. Breaking it down to the nuts and bolts is all. Faced with the condition of death, it's the one thing that trumps everything else. Puts it all into perspective."

"You played chess with the president?"

"Yeah. I even let him win."

He took Madison's empty cup and set both on the side table. "If you aren't in a hurry, I thought we could do something more constructive with our remaining moments of peace."

"I like your way of thinking Mr. Londergan."

* * *

At breakfast later, Madison tried to act normal but felt her feelings must be written all over her face. She was an adult for goodness sakes, she thought, why was she acting like a teenager? The door to the dining room opened and worries over her behavior vanished when Roxanne walked in followed by Austin and Caleb. The moment of truth had arrived. Madison waited for her heart to betray her. Under the table, Zack squeezed her hand and she squeezed back, letting her breath out at the same time. Right then she knew her world would never turn upside down again because of Austin.

Roxanne took the chair opposite from Madison, while Caleb sat next to her and Austin on the other side of his son.

Austin looked over at them. "Morning."

"Mornin'. You're looking good," Zack replied.

"I feel good."

"What do you want for breakfast?" Zack shoved his chair back.

Austin held up his hand. "Sit man. You don't have to wait on us."

"Can I have some chocolate chip pancakes?" Caleb asked, jumping up from his chair. "With whipped cream?"

"You most certainly can, young man," Madison answered, surprising Caleb.

"Caleb, sit in your chair." Roxanne touched his arm.

"Yes, ma'am." Caleb slid back onto his chair and turned to Roxanne. "Can I have pancakes mother?"

"Yes, you may." Roxanne smiled at her son and turned to look across the table at Madison. "If you don't mind."

Madison met her gaze. "Not at all." She pushed away from the table.

"You don't have to Maddie. I can make pancakes," Austin said.

"Why don't you help her dear? That way Zack and I can get to know each other," Roxanne suggested.

Austin paused, looking to Zack for approval. The two men stared at each other and at that moment, Zack knew Austin knew his secret. Zack nodded, but he wasn't thinking about Madison or pancakes. His mind was moving fast in another direction. Austin looked normal, but Zack suspected if he drew a blood sample those cells would be far from normal.

"Maybe we can talk later if you're not busy," Austin offered.

"Ten work for you?" Zack asked.

Austin nodded and turned to Madison. "Now, how about we whip up some pancakes?"

"I want to help." Caleb sprung from his chair before Roxanne could get a hand on him.

"It's ok. He'll be fine," Madison said, laying her hand on Caleb's head when he came to join them. She snatched her hand back. "Ow."

"You ok?" Zack asked.

"Yeah." Madison rubbed her hand. "Static electricity I guess." But the sting felt more like she'd been zapped on an electric fence than static electricity. Sensing everyone watching her, Madison put on a smile. "I'm fine. It was nothing."

"Come on. I'm starving." Caleb reached to grab Madison's hand making her flinch, but this time no shock flowed from the boy.

Roxanne watched the exchange with a straight face that didn't belie the storm brewing behind her eyes. Killing had always been a matter of her life over another's, nothing more. She didn't want to kill Madison, but something about her brought out feelings Eve had little knowledge or experience in dealing with.

Zack glanced at Roxanne and paused. Her eyes appeared to have changed from light to dark green, almost black.

"Zack?" Madison repeated his name.

Zack looked over at her. "Huh?"

"Did you want pancakes?"

"Sure."

Madison gave him a puzzled look before allowing Caleb to lead her into the kitchen. Zack watched them go, all the while wanting to look back at Roxanne.

"Tell me about the bunker," Roxanne said.

This gave Zack permission to look at her. Light green eyes stared back at him and he felt stupid. "I'm sorry. What was that?"

"The bunker. Tell me about the design. Austin said you're the mastermind behind it all," she said, using flattery and charm to distract him.

Zack smiled back. He was probably imaging things. After all, the lighting in the dining room was set for mood, not for sight. Zack relaxed and began telling Roxanne about the bunker, a topic he could talk about for days. Roxanne turned out to be a good audience, asking intelligent questions and keeping up, even when Zack got too deep into the details. He found her fun to talk to and almost let himself think she was a beautiful woman. And she was, but the image of Austin exploding into the hulk and pounding him into the ground stopped cold that line of thinking.

A half an hour flew by and the cooks returned with stacks of chocolate chip pancakes, orange juice, hot coffee, and cinnamon buns. The mouthwatering smell permeated throughout the bunker and no sooner had Austin set the platter down when the door opened. Colin, Charlie, and Jeremy were the first in, followed by Zoe and German. German, as was his habit of late, lay near Roxanne's chair.

Charlie took a seat next to Roxanne, while Zoe sat down next to Madison and hugged her arm. "When are we leaving?"

"As soon as all of you girls are ready."

"Oh God, that's like gonna take forever," Zoe sighed.

"Ok then, how about we leave at ten, ready or not?"

"Awesome. I'll let everyone know." She stuffed a fork full of pancakes in her mouth, grabbed her plate and hustled from the room.

"Bring that plate back when you're through," Madison hollered.

"You're sticking to Pueblo, right?" Austin asked.

"Right. We should be able to find everything we need there," Madison answered

"Pueblo? Why can't we go to Colorado Springs?" Colin complained.

"Because you can't twerp," Zack responded.

"It's not safe," Roxanne added, which raised several eyebrows since she rarely spoke and most of the bunker's residents didn't know what to make of her.

"Why do you say that?" Madison asked.

"It's the truth," Roxanne replied, offering little else. From behind Roxanne's green eyes, Eve observed Madison with interest. Most human females Eve had encountered were silly creatures, but this one was different. "The Svan patrol often, and not only at night," she added, wanting to say they shouldn't leave the bunker at all, not now, not for a long time, but she kept silent. They would not listen and she felt no compulsion to act as their protector. As a species, they were still very young and had yet to learn the most valuable lessons of survival.

"Aren't you hungry?" Madison pointed to Roxanne's plate, where a stack of pancakes sat untouched.

"I don't usually eat this early in the morning." Roxanne smiled at her.

Roxanne's smile held not an ounce of warmth and Madison could have sworn the room's temperature dropped a few degrees. She turned her attention back to her food, which had turned from hot to cool. Stirring her pancakes around in the congealed syrup, she wished she hadn't been born with a sixth sense, the one telling her to pay attention, to watch her back. The justification for this wasn't within her grasp, not yet, but it was close. She knew this without a doubt, and knew, as in the past, that her intuition would prove to be right.

Madison ate a few more bites and excused herself from the group. Forgetting Roxanne and her odd behavior, Madison hurried to her suite to get ready for shopping. Even saying it in her head sounded wrong. The planet was buried under ice, and they were on the cusp of becoming an extinct species. What were they doing going Christmas shopping? It was insane.

She looked at herself in the mirror. "You have no one to blame but yourself." She nodded. "You're right. Why'd I open my big mouth?" She pointed at her reflection. "Because you were feeling all happy and shit and decided to be Ms. Susie Social, which you're not. And now you're stuck going shopping. So suck it up, sister."

Madison gave her reflection the middle finger before turning off the bathroom light. In her bedroom, she stopped to look at the bed, still disheveled from the night before. A smile replaced her scowl. All was good for the moment. If the Sundogs came for them, at least she wouldn't die a lonely bitter woman. No sir, not her. This woman was happy and so what if her sister had planned to marry her ex-fiancé. Her smile faded. She hadn't thought about Sydney in months. She'd thought of her mother often, but not Syd so much.

Guilt was vicious and if allowed free reign it could destroy a person, heart, and soul, so she kept a tight lock and key on those memories. The only person who knew her story was Ed, who was a vault for keeping secrets and why she'd trusted him. He hadn't passed judgment but insisted she was vindicated in being pissed off at her sister and even more so toward her ex. Who wouldn't be angry if they found out only a month after having a miscarriage, that fiancé was in love with another woman, who happened to be her sister?

Madison couldn't speak for how other women might react, but she'd been furious when Sydney broke the news to her. Later, after stewing over the news, murderous thoughts had plagued her on a regular basis. She hadn't confessed so much to Ed, that on more than one occasion she'd sat in her car outside her ex's house, waiting for him to come out. She'd held a loaded gun in her lap, safety off. She wouldn't have shot him, he wasn't worth prison. She'd only wanted to scare him, to make him feel some of the pain she'd felt. In the end, she'd done nothing. In the end, she'd buried her pain in her work and shielded herself behind a hard-nosed persona. In the end, her last conversation with her sister was an argument. Regret was a bitch to live with. This time absolution or redemption was not an option to ponder.

Madison heard a knock on the door and grabbed her shoes from under the bed. She checked her watch before answering the door, 9:30, they were early.

"I'm almost ready— Oh. Jenny. Hi," Madison said. "Is everything ok?"

"Yeah fine. I'm fine. Thought I might go shopping with you. If it's ok."

"Sure of course it is." Madison glanced at Jenny's sweatpants and t-shirt. "Maybe we should find you something warm to wear?"

Jenny let out an embarrassed laugh. The hint of a smile brightened her face. "Oh please do, that would be great. Ed didn't have much to offer in his wardrobe."

"I have some things that would fit you perfectly." Madison stepped aside allowing Jenny to walk in. She looked down the corridor and spotted Ed watching from his doorway. She gave him a smile and thumbs up. He smiled back; his relief obvious even from where she stood.

Fifteen minutes later Jenny stepped out, transformed from shabby to chic. Ed leaned against his doorway staring in disbelief at his wife, who was starting to look like her old self again. He made a mental note to buy Madison something special for Christmas.

Ed walked up and hugged Jenny. "You look great. How do ya feel?"

"Good. Not tired at all," Jenny replied and for the most part, this was true. She didn't feel tired, but she felt something better than good as if a dense fog had been lifted. She felt invigorated like she was twenty years old again. It was strange to feel this good after having been close to dead for over a year. It didn't make sense and at the moment she didn't care, she had more pressing things to worry about, things like finding her son. After Ed told her about the building in Wyoming, she'd made up her mind to find her son, with or without anyone's help. This with or without resolution included Ed, but she already knew he wanted the same.

Jenny's motives for going to Pueblo were not driven by Christmas shopping alone. She needed survival gear and although the bunker probably had more than a few things stored about, she didn't want to ask Zack for help. Voicing her plans out loud meant answering questions and listening to why she shouldn't look for her son. She wasn't going to listen to such talk.

They met up with the others and everyone talked at once. Grace wished them fun as they loaded into the vehicles. Jeremy joked with her about not having their baby while he was gone and then finding his joke not so funny after all offered to stay behind. Grace insisted she was fine and that he should go on. It was only after Zack assured the young father to be that he had nothing to worry about, Jeremy relented and closed the door.

Ed was behind the wheel of a brand new metallic gray Jeep Grand Cherokee, the latest addition to the bunkers vast array of vehicles, while Madison drove a new black Range Rover. Both were top of the line models, fully equipped with all the bells and whistles one could want, but would never use. Ed put the Jeep in gear and was about to put foot to gas pedal when he spotted Caleb running toward them. Ed lowered his window.

"What's up, Caleb?"

"May I come with you, Mr. Ed?" He smiled up at Ed. "My mother said it was ok."

"What about your father?" Ed's desire to not anger Austin outweighed keeping the mother happy.

"He agreed with my mother," Caleb replied without hesitation.

Although Ed thought it strange Austin wasn't present, he nodded his head and told Caleb to jump in the back. Once the boy was secure, Ed again shifted into drive and crept up the ramp. Zack hit the button raising the door at the end of the ramp. He watched until they were out of sight before hitting the button a second time. A sense of foreboding washed over him when he heard the soft thud of the door hitting the ground.

He shook the feeling away. This wasn't a suicide mission to the mountain or a manic trip through a wormhole to planets unknown. They were going shopping. His thoughts turned from doom and gloom to Madison's Christmas present, which turned his stomach into a sailor's knot. Was he insane for even thinking she'd want to marry him? Absolutely he was crazy and stupid on top of being crazy. Zack sighed. If he'd met her in another life things would be different. As soon as he finished this thought Zack laughed out loud. If they'd met in another life Madison would have arrested him, doing so without probable cause. Hell, who was he kidding anyway? It wasn't like he'd been the marrying type, far from it.

That was the past Zacky boy. You're not that spoiled kid anymore. No, he wasn't, he amiably agreed with that thought. He was a man responsible for the lives of thirteen people. For the first time, since he was five years old, Zack felt fear, but this was different. When he was five, Bobby the monster had given him plenty to be afraid of, but the old man was only human and outsmarting him hadn't been hard to figure out for a boy genius. Zack wondered if the aliens could be outsmarted. And he wondered if he was smart enough to do so.

16 LIFE FOR DEATH

Madison pulled the Range Rover up in front of the mall. On the way, they'd discussed the possibility of bodies being inside the mall and in the stores. A site everyone was accustomed to seeing, but no one wanted to see, not while Christmas shopping. Sitting in the parking lot, Madison laid out the plan and the ground rules. They would stick together no matter what. No shouting or screaming and if anyone became separated from the group they were to return to the vehicle and wait. Madison put the spare keys under the floor mat.

The girls piled out of the vehicle anxious to get started. They had exactly three hours to shop, not a minute longer. Everyone had a flashlight, a two-way radio and a shopping partner they were to stick with at all times. They waited at the doors for the guys to catch up. Madison pushed through the doors first, pulling out her gun as she walked inside. Ed, who also carried a weapon, followed in behind her. As they were expecting, a few corpses could be seen inside the doors. Other than that, it appeared safe and the others piled inside. The girls went to the right and guys to the left. Charlie and Colin spent an extra thirty seconds kissing goodbye as if they were going to be separated for weeks and not a couple of hours.

Madison watched them, not with envy or disgust, but with understanding as she also felt giddy in love like a teenager. She wished Zack had come with, but he had a more serious matter to attend to. She smiled to herself happy in knowing thinking of Austin no longer caused her anxiety. This pleased her, as much as it provided needed relief from the guilt.

"Ms. Madison?" Caleb tugged on her sleeve making her jump.

"Yes, sweetie."

"I would like to shop with you if you don't mind very much."

So polite, Madison thought and so not normal. "Why of course you can. And you can call me Maddie. Ok?"

"Ok." He took hold of her hand.

Madison looked down at the boy's curly-haired head. This was Austin's son. He looked like Austin, no doubts there, but he didn't act like a normal child. Her common sense and her lack of nerve had stopped her from asking Austin about the boy's age. As much as Madison didn't want to take the cop walk at that moment, she couldn't stop her mind from strolling down that path. She scratched her head, wishing to satisfy the itch, but no such luck. If only it were that easy, she thought and sighed out loud.

"Are you bothered by something in particular?" Caleb asked.

"Hm?"

"You sighed. I thought something might be troubling you."

"Not at all, dear. Now, what do you think you want to buy for your mother?"

Caleb thought about this for a minute, but more for effect than something to ponder. His mother didn't celebrate Christmas or expect gifts. The Adita only celebrated victory by drinking the blood of the conquered. The thought of drinking blood made him queasy. His grandfather had called him an unsophisticated barbarian when watching him eat animal meat. Caleb wasn't so sure drinking the blood of humans or others for that mattered was all that sophisticated. He would never say so out loud or allow the thought to surface from the depths of his mind, but the Adita seemed more the barbaric creatures than the humans.

"I'm not sure," he answered. "I'll have to see."

"What about Aust... I mean your father?"

Caleb knew the answer to this one but shrugged his shoulders. His father wanted Roxanne back, his human wife, but that was beyond anyone's powers, even his grandfather's. Not that Agra would grant such a thing to a human. If Caleb had the power he would make his father love his mother and forget about Roxanne. That would heal the hole in his father's heart and then his father would love him the same as Edward loved his son. And more important, his mother would no longer be sad. They would be a family, like humans. He liked the way the humans interacted, although he didn't always understand their feelings, being he was more Adita than human himself.

Behind Madison, the girl's flashlights bobbed up and down with their footsteps. Had this been a normal shopping trip they would have been giggling at boys and squealing each time they passed a storefront containing the latest heartthrob boy band's life-size cut outs. As the situation demanded, they spoke in hushed tones and huddled close together. At each store they hesitated, debated and then decided to not go inside.

Madison knew they were worried about stumbling over corpses. Hell, couldn't say she blamed them. With the cold and dark, it felt more like a morgue than a mall. They walked the entire mall not entering one store and, upon meeting up with the guys back at the front of the store, found they had not managed to find anything either.

"Well this was a bust," Ed noted, looking around the group.

"I don't feel like shopping," Charlie said and went to stand next to Colin.

"Maybe we should go back to the bunker," Ed suggested.

"Is that what you all want?" Madison asked.

They nodded.

She shrugged. "Ok. Let's load up then."

They walked in somber silence back to the vehicles. Madison opened the door and fished the keys out from under the mat. She leaned out and paused keys in hand. The ground was vibrating a slow unsteady sensation at first and then more rapid.

Madison turned to Jenny. "Do you feel that?" Jenny shook her head. Madison walked to the front of the vehicle. The ground shook violently, and Madison grabbed the braced vehicle's hood to keep from falling. "What the hell?"

Ed hurried to his wife's side and took hold of her arm. "You ok?"

"Yeah." She held onto Ed's hand for balance.

Ed looked around the parking lot. "An earthquake?" he asked.

"I don't know, but we better get back to the bunker," Madison replied.

Another rumble, stronger than the first, knocked Charlie to the ground and Colin had to twist his upper body, then dance in a circle on one leg in order not to fall on top of her. He knelt down, helping Charlie to a sitting position, brushing the snow off her back as he did so. "Some crazy shit happenin' folks."

The tremors eased and then stopped, but no one felt relieved. Relief was not a luxury in this world. Madison felt the hair rise on her neck and took a few steps away from the vehicle to get a better view of the parking lot. She shaded her eyes and squinted in the direction of the highway. No signs of movement, coming or going.

A third shock rocked them all sideways. Everyone knelt on the ground except Madison. In that very moment, she saw, out on the highway, something that was there and then it wasn't. Something wavering in the distance, like a mirage. Ed crawled over to her and stood up.

"Do you see it?" She pointed.

Ed shaded his eyes and looked out toward the highway. He saw it. "It's them. It's them. The Adita. Don't you see them?"

"The Adita? What are you talking about Ed?" Madison switched back and forth from looking at Ed to the shimmering highway, stopping suddenly when she saw the 'them' Ed was referring to. From across the highway, the Adita wavered in and out of view, getting closer without seeming to move at all. Za was in the lead followed by the three guards who had accompanied him to Wyoming, plus five more.

"Oh shit." Madison pulled out her gun, but Ed grabbed her arm.

"You can't shoot them."

She pulled her arm from his grasp. "Why the hell not?" she demanded, preparing to pull the trigger.

"You can't kill them with bullets," Caleb answered from behind.

Madison and Ed both turned, neither one having realized the boy was standing next to them.

"Caleb honey go back to the vehicle with the others," Madison instructed. Caleb didn't move. "Please Caleb," she begged.

"It's ok Miss Madison," he replied with a smile. "They can't hurt me."

Madison looked down at the boy, noticing for the first time he wasn't wearing his coat or hat or gloves. Before she could ask him about this, he was running toward the Adita.

"Caleb no!" She grabbed for him, but came up with air and went running after him.

Ed tried to stop her, but he was also too slow and couldn't grab hold of her. Jeremy's hand on his arm kept him from following after her.

"There's nothing you can do," Jeremy said. "You can't protect them now."

"Damn it." Ed stomped his foot in the Adita's direction. Ed knew Jeremy was right. He knew he was powerless. They were all powerless and all they could do was watch to see what happened next.

Across the parking lot at the edge of the highway, Madison came to a sliding stop behind Caleb, who was only feet away from Za. She reached for the boy's hand. "Come on Caleb."

Za raised his hand, picked Madison up in the air, and flung her through the air like a rag doll. She landed several hundred feet away, rolling and coming to a stop in a motionless heap.

"Where is your mother?" Za asked Caleb, unaware of the storm brewing behind the child's eyes. As a rule, Za avoided looking at the child and even more were his efforts to not look into those freakish blue eyes.

"She's not here," Caleb replied. "And you shouldn't be here either." He addressed Za as a man would have, not as the child he appeared.

Za snatched Caleb up by the hair. "Who do you think you are speaking to?" He held Caleb inches from his face, bearing his pointed fangs.

Caleb was calm and focused. "A corpse," he answered.

Za hissed and shoved Caleb away, sending him farther than he had Madison. The boy, however, landed on his feet and disappeared.

"You shouldn't have done that," Caleb said from behind them. They all jumped and turned at once to face him. Caleb had positioned his hands in front of him palms facing each other, with about a foot of air in between. "You will leave now and return to Paru."

Za, angry beyond reason, moved forward past the assassins, but stopped and fell to his knees moaning in pain. Caleb squeezed the air between his hands, crushing Za's thin frame as he pressed his hands closer. The guards moved to stop him and were met with the same force. They writhed about on the ground running out of air unable to escape the crushing pressure.

"Caleb!" Eve's voice carried across the parking lot and then she was standing next to them. "Caleb, let go." She laid her hand on his head.

Caleb lowered his hands, releasing them. Mere seconds were all they had left. Had Eve chose to not interfere, Za and his trash would have been turned to dust and blown away.

"I'm sorry mother." Caleb appeared shaken and dazed. "I don't know what happened."

Eve pulled him to her. She knew he was not playing games, he was telling the truth. Much like her, Caleb had no idea the strength or the power he possessed. Eve knelt next to Caleb and whispered in his ear. He nodded. Eve stood and watched Caleb return to the humans. She waited until they loaded Madison into the vehicle and drove away, before turning on Za.

"You overstep your position Za."

"Who do you think I represent? Myself? I am a member of your father's counsel, his eyes, and ears. I am here on his behalf. You question my authority? You are very stupid."

The guards snickered. Eve ignored them, for the day was not far when they would snicker at her no longer. "You are nothing more than an errand boy."

Za bristled. "Agra has asked that you stay here on Earth. He does not want the human brought back to Paru until he is ready for him."

Eve stood still for a long moment.

"Do you understand? Or are you dimwitted like the humans?" he demanded. "Have you lived so long amongst them you've lost the ability to think? To speak?"

Eve folded her hands behind her back and looked in Za's direction, but not at him. She heard more of what he was not saying over the drone of his lecture. A piece of information was missing, a piece not being shared with her father's lackey. Agra was hiding something important, something that made him on edge about the time, about the harvest. Za might have an idea what it was, but Agra was shielding him from her. In the same manner Eve shielded Caleb from Agra.

"If you do not answer I will be forced to tell your father you have disobeyed him and you—"

"Why didn't Agra ask me himself? Why send you?" Eve asked, her contempt obvious.

"I do not question his actions and neither should you. Now, do you understand this order—"

"I understand. I will wait to hear further instruction from my father," Eve replied, cutting him off.

Za's shoulders relaxed. "Agra will be pleased." With a wave of his arm Za and the guards vanished in the same way they had arrived. Eve waited several minutes to be certain they had returned home. Soon Agra would search and listen. Eve waited, but Agra did not come to her. That he trusted Za to carry out something as important as delivering this order confirmed Eve's suspicions. She was tempted to follow Za, but other matters required her attention.

* * *

Inside the bunker's infirmary, Zack stood over a bruised and unconscious Madison. Behind him, Luke and Ed wore expressions that said everything about what they were thinking and feeling. In the corner Jenny watched, quiet and unnoticed.

"Why don't you do something?" Luke demanded.

Zack didn't respond. He stared at Madison's still body, her face, once beautiful, now a swollen purple and red mess. Zack reached out pushing aside her hair.

"Zack," Luke called to him. "Zack man, don't just stand there."

Zack slammed his fist into his palm and turned. "What do you want me to do, damn it? What? I'm no fucking doctor. I had one year in medical school. One fucking year."

"You can't let her die," Luke insisted.

"Take it easy Luke," Ed said.

"Take it easy? Are you fucking kidding me? She's going to die because ya'll had to go Christmas shopping. Fucking Christmas shopping."

The door to the infirmary opened, hitting Luke's pressure release at the precise moment before an emotional explosion erupted. Austin rushed in followed by Roxanne. The sight of Madison stopped him in his tracks. "How bad is it Zack?"

Zack lowered his head and covered his face with his hands. He shook his head back and forth. "I think it's really bad. I don't know for sure, but I think there's internal bleeding. I have nothing. I can't fix this. I'm not a goddamn surgeon."

The weight of the world landed on Austin's shoulders. In fear and anger, he turned on Roxanne. "You heal her," he demanded.

"It's not that simple," she replied.

"It is that simple. Just do it."

"You don't know what you are asking?"

"I do, damn it," Austin insisted. "You did it for me, for Ed's wife, why not Madison?"

"You and Jenny were not damaged internally. It is as I explained to you before. To do this would mean changing her into something other than human."

"What did she do for Jenny?" Ed interrupted, but was ignored.

Austin walked up to Roxanne and grabbed her by the shoulders. "You have to do something. I know you don't care about them, but if you ever cared about me, then do this for me. Heal her. I'm begging you."

Roxanne stared up into Austin's eyes. If ever she wanted to understand a human's emotions it would have been right at that moment. His thoughts swirled in a rapid chaotic manner that was difficult to follow. She sensed guilt, anguish, and love. The latter annoyed her at some level, but she didn't understand why. Eve looked away toward Madison. She was going to die and soon. Only a few minutes remained before the blood would fill her lungs. Roxanne removed Austin's hands from her shoulders and walked over to Madison, stepping out of Roxanne and becoming Eve as she did so. She laid a hand on Madison's mid-section.

Turning to Zack, she said, "I can't save her as she is, as a human, but I can save the baby."

Zack's face rushed through a gamut of expressions; everything he'd witnessed over the past year threatened to rush forth and derail his sanity. "What baby? She's not pregnant. We only, it's only been..." He glanced at his watch. "Are you sure."

"I am sure," Eve replied. "The baby can be saved, but a host is needed."

"Host? What do you mean?" Zack pulled on his hair, turning back and forth between Madison and Eve.

"A womb to carry the baby."

"A womb? Where the fuck do I get one of those? Oh, wait I have a spare in the back room. Are you fucking kidding me?"

From the corner of the room, Jenny spoke, "I'll do it." She walked up to Zack. "I'll do it if you want me to."

Zack stared at Jenny, speechless, unable to make sense of what was happening, of what they were asking him to decide. Madison wasn't pregnant. What an absurd notion.

"Jenny you can't," Ed protested.

Eve turned to Ed. "Yes, she can. She is in optimal shape for reproduction. Her body is healthy and free of disease. She would serve well as the baby's carrier," Eve replied, turning back to Zack. "Her time is running out."

Eve knew the decision Zack would arrive at, but she could not wait for him to get there. If Madison died before she removed the baby, the baby would also die. She gestured for Jenny to come and stand next to her. Eve laid one hand on

Madison's stomach and the other on Jenny's. From all around she pulled forth energy, using her newly discovered powers to control the force. The life energy flowed from her fingertips into Madison first and from her into Jenny's body, glowing brighter as each second ticked by. A sphere of brilliant light surrounded the trio. The room came alive, the walls expanded outward allowing space for the immense amount of energy being generated.

Jenny screamed from inside the sphere. Ed tried to reach her, but the force drove him backward. She screamed again, a tortrous scream that shattered a glass sitting on a nearby table and brought Ed to his knees covering his ears.

Inside the sphere, Eve's entire body glowed. From her hands flowed a life-giving source older than time itself. She transferred the baby from Madison's womb to Jenny's and in the process improved the baby's genetic code sequence. There would be consequences for breaking the laws of the Adita, but for that instant, she didn't care. Eve withdrew her hands in a slow and precise manner. As she moved away from them, the light dimmed until it went out. Ed rushed to Jenny, catching her before she collapsed to the ground.

Eve staggered and almost lost her balance. Saving the baby required more strength than she'd anticipated, and proved much more taxing than Jenny's transformation had been. Exhausted, Eve fell to the floor.

Austin rushed to Eve's side. "Are you ok?"

Eve knelt, head bent, motionless. From behind them, Zack moaned, Austin left Eve to go to him, to Madison. Eve felt Austin's pain and something akin to rejection pierced her heart. She sank further to the floor, too exhausted to protect against the rise of human-like emotions threatening to overcome her.

Jenny stared up at the ceiling before rolling dazed eyes over in Ed's direction. Something was wrong with her tongue. It felt too big, too heavy. "Am I ok?" This came out slurred.

"Yes. You're fine."

"Don't...lie," she replied using great effort to form these words. She tried to frown, but her facial muscles refused to move. She tried to move her hands, her legs, but nothing responded. A panicked look filled her eyes. "Wrong...what's...can't move." Her eyes darted around the room.

From the corner Eve spoke, her voice weak. "Tell her to be calm. She will regain control in a few hours."

Ed repeated this, ensuring Jenny she was going to be ok and to trust him. He held and stroked her hand. Jenny tried to reply, but her lips felt sloppy on her face. Using what little control she did have Jenny squeezed Ed's hand. Behind him, Austin and Zack stood on opposite sides of each other looking down at Madison's lifeless body. She was no longer bruised, as Eve was at the least able to heal her exterior wounds.

"I can't believe this is happening," Zack said, quiet and more to himself than anyone else in the room.

Luke came to stand next Zack.

"Hey man, is she ok?" Ed tapped Austin's shoulder, pointing to Eve who was crumpled over.

Austin went to her and knelt down. "Are you ok?"

Eve pushed herself into a sitting position. "I need blood," she whispered before falling over into Austin's arms.

Austin picked her up and carried her into the adjacent room, closing the door behind him. He lay her on the examination table. From his side pocket, he pulled out a small knife and sliced open the palm of his hand. He didn't feel the pain as he held his hand over Eve's mouth, allowing his blood to drip onto her lips. It only took a few drops before Eve's eyes snapped open. She grabbed hold of his hand, bringing it to her lips, but she didn't sink her teeth into the open cut. As quickly as she grabbed him, she shoved him away from her. The desire to take more was almost too much, the consequences too great.

"I could have killed you," she said.

"I knew you wouldn't."

Eve swung her legs over the side of the table and slid to the floor. Her instincts were on edge, awareness aroused to its peak. Something had changed in her, an energy existed that she'd only before experienced through the feelings of another, but was now feeling first hand. Eve resisted the urge to circle Austin as the female Svan would do to her chosen mate. Now was not the time for such pursuits.

Austin also felt the charge between them but was too wrapped in grief to take much notice or make sense of what it meant.

"You loved the woman?"

"Madison? Yes, I loved her."

"But not the same as Zack. How you loved her was different?"

"She was... she was like family to me. We went through a lot together."

"And different than your feelings for Roxanne."

Austin paused at the mention of Roxanne. Hearing Eve say her name, in a voice that had been Roxanne's once upon a time, created a painful longing in his heart and soul.

"I loved Roxanne, she was my life, but she wasn't Roxanne, she was you. And you have been in my life always, you're a part of who I am." He looked up at her. A sudden desire to be near her, to hold her close, surprised him. That he had these thoughts brought guilt and shame. How could he be thinking such things when Madison was lying dead in the other room? While his friends grieved and needed him, he was thinking about Eve and how much he wanted her.

"What you feel for me is not love, but something purer."

Austin didn't care what she called it. He grabbed her arm and pulled her to him, knowing she wouldn't resist. He kissed her hard on the lips, holding her thin frame against his unconcerned if he hurt her, knowing it wasn't possible. He kissed her on the mouth and neck, his touch far from tender.

Eve welcomed his touch, experiencing it for the first time and feeling somewhat surprised by the intensity. During the time she'd been Roxanne, Austin was never rough. He'd treated his wife like a delicate flower, always using great tenderness, always holding back for fear he might hurt her. No such restraints held him now. Eve felt her body responding to his demands.

Eve pushed away from him. "Caleb is coming."

No sooner had the words left her mouth when their son burst into the room. "Mother!" He stopped short, noticing his father's expression, sensing his mother's energy.

"What is it Caleb?" Eve asked, distracting the child from thinking too deeply about them.

"Nothing."

"What do you mean nothing? I don't have time for your games."

"I can't hear grandfather anymore."

"What do you mean?" Eve demanded.

"I can always hear him, even when I'm not listening, but I can't anymore. Do you think he's alright?"

"If you can't hear him it's because he doesn't want you to. I've told you about eavesdropping Caleb. Not only is it against the Adita law, but if your grandfather ever caught you he would be beyond angry."

"Yes, mother I know. He would terminate me."

"He would what?" Austin asked.

"Nothing," Eve snapped.

"Nothing?" Austin looked from one to the other.

"Agra threatens many things, but terminating Caleb is not one he will ever carry out." She knelt in front of Caleb. "Grandfather is fine. I would know if something was wrong, so stop worrying."

"But mother."

"This conversation is over." She stood and turned to Austin. "I must go to Russia."

"I'll go with you," Austin said, stepping toward her. "I want to go with you."

"It's easier if I go alone. Besides you need to keep your son out of trouble."

"And what about you?"

"I can take care of myself and will do much better not having to worry about you or Caleb. Your people need you here and I'll only be gone a few days." Eve would have preferred having him with her, but she had no idea what to expect. Agra's intentions were constantly shifting, she couldn't get a clear handle on them. Caleb's announcement bothered her more than she let on. She knew Caleb was aware of her concerns and was relieved he didn't press the issue in front of Austin

"What's in Russia?" Austin asked.

"I don't know, but before coming back to Earth, I saw an image in Agra's mind. His thoughts were on returning to Russia. There was more, but not within my reach." Eve moved toward the door. "It is urgent that I leave immediately."

"What did you see?" Austin walked over to her.

"Many things. Agra traveling to Russia alone. Which I can't imagine why he'd risk such a thing with his fear of disease. I saw Agra traveling with the Elders, which makes less sense. He wouldn't leave the safety of Paru before the harvest."

"Why not? What happens at the harvest?"

Eve opened her mouth to speak, closing it without saying a word.

"Tell me," Austin pleaded.

"It will only serve to cloud your judgment, to give you false hopes of winning a battle already lost. The Adita will come and they will thrive. You are powerless to stop them."

"I don't believe that," Austin argued. "When I was in my coma, I had visions of armies of Svan fighting against the Adita. Humans fought alongside the Svan and I was leading them in the battle."

"It was not you leading them." Eve nodded at Caleb. "Your dreams were a glimpse of one possible future, but one that will result in bloodshed and death for your race. Please hear me when I say this, the Adita do not lose."

Austin ran his hand over his head. "The harvest. What is it?"

"She won't say in front of me," Caleb informed him.

"It doesn't concern you, Caleb."

"It will one day though. Father's dreams are truer than you allow yourself to believe or admit." He smiled up at his mother.

Speaking the truth came naturally to her son and was not meant to provoke Eve, this she knew as much as she knew her son was right. She turned back to Austin. "I will be back in a few days, maybe a week."

"And you're leaving Caleb with me?" Austin asked.

"Yes. He's to stay here with you," Eve replied. "Agra sees Caleb as a threat. I can no longer predict how he will react and will not risk his life."

"What if he decides to come here? To get Caleb?"

"He wouldn't risk being exposed to so many humans. He'd send Za or his guard and Caleb can handle them," Eve replied.

"If they come down here I will eradicate them," Caleb added his voice heavy with confidence and maybe a touch of something less noble.

A chill ran down Austin's spine hearing his son speak this way about taking a life. He thought of the kid in the movie The Omen, but quickly shrugged those thoughts away.

"I will come see you as soon as I return." Eve touched Austin's arm.

Austin tore his eyes from his son. He wanted to tell Eve to be careful but refrained. His sudden desire to protect her was befuddling and unnecessary.

"You don't have to worry."

Austin nodded, wanting to take her in his arms, to kiss her, to finish what they'd started, but before he could act or speak she vanished from the room. With her departure, the spell broke, and guilt washed over him. He returned to the other room, to his friends, who were in a state of shock. They needed him now.

17 CHANCE MEETING

Kyle and McKenna crossed the Colorado state line a week after Madison's coffin was lowered into the ground at the Pueblo cemetery. For the pair, the three-thousand-mile trip had been tense, but uneventful. As the road sign welcoming them to Colorado came into view, Kyle breathed a huge sigh of relief, whooping out loud when they entered the state. His exclamation of joy, however, held little vim or vigor. The sights they'd seen along the way gave him little hope of finding anyone alive, let alone finding his family.

McKenna, though relieved, was even more skeptical than her companion on what they might find. Her near kidnapping at the Best Western kept her on edge for hundreds of miles and haunted her more than Kyle's standoff with the aliens. In her mind the aliens didn't want them, she worried little about a return visit. Kyle had other thoughts about the aliens, most of which centered on hoping to never see them again. He'd gone over and over in his mind what had happened, what he'd seen and marveled at the fact he was still breathing.

The place had a clean look about it. Too clean, Kyle thought to himself and was certain his sharp as a tack travel companion had already picked up on this incongruity. They passed a sign which read Colorado Springs 52 Miles, Exit 142A. The roads along the way were clear of vehicles and they hadn't seen a frozen corpsicle for several miles. Kyle had coined the term corpsicle back in Alaska, which had evoked a reproachful raised eyebrow from McKenna.

"It's really clean here," McKenna noted as if speaking to Kyle's silent thoughts. Her breath fogged the window as she pressed her nose to the cold glass.

"I was thinking the same thing."

She gave Kyle a nervous look and turned back to watching the tedious landscape.

"Doesn't mean they're bad people."

"I know," she replied, "but don't leave me alone."

"I won't. Promise." Kyle reached over and squeezed her leg. A sorry excuse for reassurance, but the best he could offer. What did he know about talking to kids, especially the female kind? He hoped they found more people, and more so he hoped one would be a parent.

"Are we going to Cheyenne Mountain?"

"I guess that would be the best place to start."

"Do you remember how to get there?"

"What? Are you kidding me? Agent Kyle Bosch knows how to get there." He nodded his head in an exaggerated fashion, pretending to be insulted.

McKenna almost cracked the tiniest of smiles, but then pursed her lips and frowned at Kyle. "Do you really?"

"Yes really, but I'm about out of gas," he noted, "so first things first."

Apprehension returned to McKenna's expression. Gas stations were held in low regard in her mind, almost superstitiously so. Bad things happened at gas stations. Her brother Tommy had been robbed at a gas station. Someone had beat him over the head, knocking him out cold next to an overflowing dumpster in the back of Kwiki Pete's. If not for a hungry dog nosing around for a scrap to eat, Tommy might have died in that squalor. No, McKenna did not like gas stations and with the very real prospect of running into people, she liked them even less.

Kyle pulled up to the tanks and shifted into park. The truck was a diesel, so he left the motor running. "You can stay in the truck. It's warm and you can lock the doors."

McKenna thought this over and finally nodded ok. She agreed, she would be safer inside the truck.

"You remember what I told you if anything happens to me?" Kyle asked and lifted the top of the console dividing the seats.

"Yes," she replied.

"Say it." He pulled out a small handgun.

"I should drive away." She took the gun from Kyle, checked the safety and laid it in her lap.

"And?" He pulled out a second larger handgun and stuffed it inside his jacket.

"And not come back." She stroked the barrel of the gun with the tip of her finger.

"Because?"

"Because you'll probably be dead." Her finger stopped and she clenched her hand into a fist.

"Good girl." Kyle jumped out of the truck and waited until she climbed into the driver's seat and clicked the locks before heading for the rear of the vehicle. He had two gas cans to fill, plus the dual tanks. He caught sight of the price sign. Five dollars and fifty-nine cents would forever be the price per gallon or at least until the sign gave way and fell over. Good thing he didn't have to pay for it.

Kyle walked toward the entrance of the station. The gun was now in his pocket. He gripped it with his bare hand; the cold weighty steel gave him comfort and courage. At the door, he leaned into the glass bracing his weight with his gloved hand. The place appeared empty. After one more scan of the parking lot, and up and down the highway to be certain they were alone, he pushed open the door.

Once inside the station, Kyle didn't waste time but went straight to the pump switches. The setup was a bit different than the last station, but the concept was the same and it wasn't difficult to figure out how the pumps worked. With that out of the way, he went in search of any type of fuel additives. The gas, after sitting for so long, sometimes needed a boost.

* * *

While Kyle was perusing the shelves of the Kwiki-Mart for additives and maybe a candy bar or two, forty miles up the road, outside Pueblo, a black Hummer sat idle on the side of the highway with a flat tire. At the back of the vehicle Luke pulled out the spare tire and necessary tools. He handed the tools over to Ed. Colin and German stood near the utility pole and watched from the side of the road.

"Have you ever done this before?" Ed asked.

"Many times," Luke assured him. Ed's expression blatantly said he doubted this assertion. To which Luke gave a 'watch and learn' look. Luke's dad had made sure his son knew how to take care of things that mattered. Like fixing a leaky faucet, trimming tree limbs and most importantly changing a flat tire. He'd always say, "*You never wanted to get stranded parking somewhere with your girl and not know how to fix a flat tire.*"

Luke never had the heart to tell his dad parking was a thing of the past. Besides, Emma would never go for a thing like that. Luke paused in his task. He hadn't thought about Emma in a long time. He couldn't remember when he'd stopped or what his last thought had been, but he guessed it was that she was dead. Once he'd gone down that road, he'd stopped thinking about her at all. Burying Madison brought back a lot of things from the past he'd rather not think about.

A familiar emotion stepped out of the wings where it waited with anxious anticipation for another opportunity to take front and center. Luke swallowed back the bitter anger. Being pissed off was pointless. Being pissed off at Austin was a waste of energy. The captain hadn't invited Eve into his life; she'd always been there. She'd used him and tricked him into believing she cared about him, but Luke didn't buy into her game. She was only looking out for herself. At times he wondered if she cared about anyone, even her own people. His suspicions kept him from giving

Eve any credit at all. None for bringing Jenny back or for saving Madison's baby. If she'd wanted to save Madison, Luke thought she could have done so.

Luke knelt next to the tire and focused on cranking off the lug nuts, but his mind wouldn't let go. He didn't trust Eve or her intentions in regards to Austin or them. Something about her, that he couldn't put his finger on, bothered him and he knew couldn't be ignored. Madison would have called these instincts or his sixth sense. Eve, who existed on instincts, would have been inclined to agree with that conclusion.

The last lug nut popped off and rolled across the road. Luke lurched after it on hands and knees. He grabbed the nut and looked up. A pick-up truck was heading in his direction. He jumped up and returned to the Hummer. German heard the truck before the others saw it and tugged on his leash, letting out an anxious bark.

"Who's that?" Ed peered down the road at the truck which had slowed to a stop.

"Don't know. Don't recognize it," Colin replied.

Luke pulled three shotguns from the back of the Hummer and handed them out. Standing at the back of the vehicle, they peered through the windows, watching and waiting for the truck to make a move. It eased forward a foot or two.

"Where are the binoculars?" Luke asked Ed.

Ed pulled a small set from his pocket and handed them over. Luke peered through the lenses adjusting the focus. "It's a girl. A young girl and guy, maybe my age."

"What should we do?" Ed took a turn looking through the set.

"The kid could be a decoy," Colin warned.

"I don't think so. She looks scared. I think she wants the driver to turn around."

"Do we have anything white?" Luke asked.

"I have a hanky." Ed pulled a white hanky out from inside his coat. "It's clean," he replied to Luke's grimace.

Luke grabbed the hanky and walked out into the middle of the road waving it over his head. He removed his ski mask and continued waving. The truck sat idle, not moving in one direction or the other. "Colin, bring German out here."

"No way man. What if they shoot him?"

"Go on Colin," Ed urged. "They won't shoot him. I'm telling you, they're good people. I have a feeling."

Colin pulled German's collar tighter and walked out into the road. He commanded the dog to sit. "If they shoot my dog some serious shit is gonna go down. Kid or not."

"Chill man." Luke continued to wave the hanky, getting more excited by the second. Other survivors! This was huge.

Down the road, Kyle and McKenna debated on what their next move should be. Kyle wanted to drive forward, to see who these people were. McKenna wanted nothing to do with them and argued they should turn around.

"What are we going to do? Run the other direction every time we come across people?" Kyle tried reasoning with her.

"Yes," she replied, sticking her chin out and crossing her arms.

"McKenna come on. They look safe. And they have a dog."

"So what. Could be a vicious man-eating attack dog."

Kyle nodded, but knew better; he'd noticed her sit up when the boy walked out with the dog.

"I had a Husky," she said. "Ok." She was more curious than she let on, having assumed the aliens had killed all animals.

"Ok?"

"Yes."

Kyle threw the truck into drive and eased down the road toward the strangers, the survivors. Thinking of people as survivors was a foreign concept he hadn't grown accustomed to using or hearing. As he pulled the truck up to where the men waited, he doubted they had much difficulty with the idea of being called survivors. With his nine-mil tucked away on the side, Kyle lowered the window a couple of inches. That all three men carried shotguns made him more than a little apprehensive.

"Hi ya'll," Luke greeted them in what he hoped was a friendly I'm not going to hurt you voice, Southern accent included for its extra down-home comfort effect. "Luke Taylor," he said to Kyle and nodded his head at McKenna.

"Kyle Bosch and McKenna..." Kyle looked to McKenna

"Markovo. My last name is Markovo. Is that your dog mister?" McKenna asked.

"German. No miss. That's Colin's dog." Luke pointed to Colin. "But we all kinda share him."

"Is he a man-eater?" she demanded.

"McKenna!" Kyle chastised.

Luke smiled. "It's ok. And no, he's not a man-eater. But he's a darn good guard dog."

McKenna nodded her head, agreeing with him, as if yes, she could see that the dog was indeed a good guard dog. The thought occurred to her to ask what he guarded. It also occurred to her that no dog was going to protect them from the aliens, but maybe monster men who hung out in empty Best Western Hotels.

"Where'd you all come from?" Luke asked Kyle.

"Me? I came from Germany. Cologne, Germany."

Luke opened his mouth and then shut it, unsure if he'd heard right, unsure what to say or ask

"On the Rhine River near Frankfort? Dusseldorf?"

"Sorry. You did say Germany, right?" Luke didn't care that he sounded like a dimwit.

"Yes. Germany."

It wasn't that Luke had never heard of those places. He'd been to Germany a couple of times. Never to Cologne, but Frankfurt and Berlin sure, the former one with his dad, the latter with a friend before he went off to college to become a superstar quarterback. He'd almost not come home. But that was another time and meanwhile, Kyle was staring at him.

"Are there people in Germany? I mean still alive?"

"Yeah. All over Europe. China, Russia, all still intact."

"All this time. Unbelievable," Luke muttered. "Ed, Colin, come over here."

They joined Luke at the driver's side, shotguns slung over their shoulders.

"How do you do. Edward McGrath, but you can call me Ed." He tilted his head at Kyle.

"Kyle Bosch and McKenna...," Luke faltered on her last name.

"Markovo."

"Sorry and McKenna Markovo."

Colin stepped forward. "Colin Londergan and this here's German, the last surviving canine." German barked.

"Nice to meet you," Kyle replied.

"He came from Germany," Luke said. "Said there're people. All over Europe and more. Alive."

Ed and Colin would have been less shocked had Kyle sprouted horns from his head and spit fire at them.

"That true?" Colin demanded.

"Yes. At least it was a few weeks ago. I haven't had contact since I left."

"How'd you get here?" Luke asked.

Kyle gave a small chuckle. "I walked and then swam across the Bering Strait, to Deadbear, Alaska. That's where I found this one." He jerked his thumb in McKenna's direction.

"Are you an Eskimo girl?" Colin asked.

"Chukchi," McKenna corrected him.

"Chew what?"

"Chukchi. Northeast Siberia," she replied. "You know, Russia."

"I know Russia." Colin had no idea what a Chukchi was or if he'd ever heard of such a person in his geography class, but he wasn't going to insult her by saying so, or worse, have this little girl make him look stupid.

"Deadbear. That's where Austin's from or lived when he was a kid," Luke remarked.

"You didn't find anyone else?" Ed asked.

"No. It's been pretty damn dead all the way here, pun intended. Except for a few unsavory gents we met in Anchorage."

"I'm hungry," McKenna interrupted on purpose, stopping Kyle from telling the story of her kidnapping.

Kyle glanced over at her and lowered his window, hiding his gun as he did so. "Look, we've been on the road for a long time and—"

"And where the heck is our manners. You can come back to the bunker with us. We've got plenty of room and food," Ed offered. "And we won't take no for an answer," he added on Kyle expression of doubt.

"How far is it from Cheyenne Mountain?" Kyle asked.

"About fifty miles that way," Ed replied, pointing, "but you don't want to go there."

"Why not?"

Ed glanced at McKenna who sat at attention waiting to hear Ed's answer. "You don't want to, leave it at that."

"It's ok. McKenna can handle it," Kyle assured him but wondered if he could handle the bad news that was about to be laid on him.

Ed pursed his lips and grunted. "There's nobody there. They killed them all." He stopped at that. *'They'* covered a lot of ground and wasn't a conversation he would have in front of a child, no matter how accustomed to the bullshit of their new world she'd become.

Kyle's chin sank to his chest. He'd traveled all this way for nothing, risked everything for nothing. His mom, his sister. Gone. McKenna laid her hand on his and squeezed. Heartbreaking disappointment threatened to overcome him, forcing Kyle to gather his strength, to focus on reason. Coming here wasn't a total waste. He'd found McKenna. That in itself was worth the trip, worth risking his life for wasn't it?

"I'm sorry. Were you hoping to find someone? Family?" Ed asked.

Kyle nodded. "Where is this bunker?" Talking about what he'd been hoping for didn't matter, not if all hope was gone.

Ed gave brief directions and as soon as Luke finished changing the tire, they were off. Conversations in the two vehicles landed on opposite ends of the spectrum. Colin and Ed talked fast and over one another, speculating, postulating, and debating the possibilities of civilization still existing in other parts of the planet. Luke wondered, but not out loud, if this would change Austin's mind.

While their conversation continued on and on, silence reigned in the truck following behind. Kyle stewed over the facts, chewing the inside of his mouth to keep obscenities from spewing forth. For her part, McKenna worried about meeting new people and what she would say to them. In school she'd been too smart for her grade, surpassing the standard curriculum and that of some college-level studies. Her classmates, because children were often mean without knowing why resented or ignored her. Her teacher, because he lacked grit and nobility, left her to her own devices.

For McKenna, this meant long solitary days spent filling time and the state's attendance requirement. She hadn't minded being alone. It allowed her to think about things that were important, topics that never came up amongst her babbling peers, who, in her opinion, yapped on and on, like little toy dogs, and did so in the continuum. On a good day, her mom would allow her to stay at home and study, but those days were rare. This time though, she wanted things to be different. She wanted to be outgoing, not shy. And she could be whoever she wanted. Having made this decision, she turned her restless mind onto worrying about Kyle for the remainder of the trip.

When Luke came to a stop in the middle of the once upon a time cow pasture, McKenna leaned forward anxious and eager for things to come. Curiosity turned to wonder when the ground rose up revealing a ramp leading underground. Kyle followed Luke down the ramp watching in his rear view as the ramp closed down blocking the outside and any chance of escape.

"You stay near me ok?" Kyle said.

"Ok," she replied. "But I think they're good people."

"Maybe so," Kyle agreed.

At the bottom of the ramp, Luke pulled the Hummer into a parking space and indicated for Kyle to pull up in the next empty space. Colin was the first to come over, bringing German with him. McKenna, having overcome her earlier misgivings about the dog, didn't wait on an all clear from Kyle before opening the door and sliding out.

"McKenna, right?" Colin verified.

McKenna nodded, having suddenly lost all of her planned bravado and newly found outgoing personality.

"This is German." Colin brought German forward. The dog stood at McKenna's shoulder. He wagged his tail and licked McKenna's face making her laugh. "He likes you."

McKenna reached out touching the dog's head, stroking his ear. He was a beautiful dog. She missed her dogs, sometimes more than she missed her family. And now, with German standing there in front of her, she felt at peace, something she hadn't experienced since the aliens took everyone away. Colin would have understood and although he shared German with everyone, he very much thought of the dog as belonging to him.

Kyle came around the truck and stood next to McKenna. He wasn't surprised by her change in attitude. A dog could melt a person's heart like nothing else and he liked to believe the animal's warm behavior was an indication of the kind of people Luke and his friends might be.

"Come on. They're all waiting to meet you," Colin said. "We haven't found anyone in a long time."

"How many live down here?" Kyle asked.

"We were up to eighteen with the babies, but," Ed paused, "but not anymore."

"What happened?" Kyle asked.

Colin and Luke exchanged weary expressions, Ed kept walking, not looking at anyone. "We lost a family member last week," Ed answered. "There was an accident. There are no doctors, just Zack, so…" His voice trailed off.

"I'm sorry." Kyle offered.

"Yeah, so are we," Ed replied and walked on.

After a few moments, Kyle asked, "You sure you have room for two more?"

"Did you say babies?" McKenna asked.

"Space is one thing we do not have to worry about," Ed assured him. "And yes babies. Anne had her twins and—"

"We're here," Colin announced and opened the door to the diner.

The newcomers were overtaken by smiling faces and friendly greetings of the bunker's residents. Everyone welcomed the distraction after the past week. Two new lives to fill the void of one special life lost. New life brought new hope for survival when they discovered Kyle had traveled from Germany.

18 THE GREATEST ODDS

That afternoon Kyle and McKenna settled into their rooms. Charlie, who kept to herself unless with Colin, took an instant liking to McKenna and invited her to be her roommate. Charlie didn't have a roommate and, although she enjoyed spending time with Colin, she thought having a friend would be nice. Leery about being away from Kyle, McKenna needed only a little prodding before she'd accepted Charlie's offer. She couldn't help feeling elated at the prospect of having friends. Kyle gave her his blessing, which eased her guilt over feeling as if she was abandoning him.

If Kyle had known McKenna fretted over him, he would have assured her that guilt was not necessary. He was beyond relieved to have found this group of people with kids young enough for McKenna to feel comfortable with, for him to feel comfortable enough to allow her out of his sight for longer than a few minutes. More than that, if he had to leave her behind he could do so with a clear conscience. It was the first time since leaving Germany he felt able to relax.

Kyle's suite was across from Austin's, who along with Zack, hadn't been part of the welcoming committee. Later when Kyle opened his door to step out for dinner, he did so at the same time Austin and Caleb opened theirs. The two men stared at each other.

"You must be Austin," Kyle stepped across the hall extending his hand.

"And you must be Kyle." Austin shook Kyle's hand, thinking he was a kid, not much older than Luke, if he had to guess. "Nice to meet you."

"Same here. The others talked you up quite a bit. I half expected to see a giant S on your chest," Kyle joked.

"You're disappointed?" Austin teased, knowing it wasn't fair since he could hear the man's thoughts, but he hadn't asked for the ability. Eve herself had been unaware of the small side effect until he'd brought it up.

Kyle choked a bit. "Not at all."

Austin smiled, easing Kyle's discomfort. "This is my son Caleb."

"Now that I could have guessed. Nice to meet you Caleb."

"Very pleased to meet you Mr. Bosch." Caleb shook Kyle's hand, careful to not squeeze too tight.

"You ready to eat like a king?" Austin asked, hoping to distract Kyle from thinking too much about how Caleb knew his last name.

"Sure, but I need to find McKenna." Kyle turned but wasn't sure which way to go.

"She's already in the dining room," Caleb announced.

"Oh, well let's eat." Kyle glanced down at Caleb. Cute kid he thought, cute and a bit off, but wasn't sure why he would think the latter.

The two men walked down the corridor while Caleb ran ahead. They were shoulder to shoulder in height, Austin being the broader of the two. They walked in silence, although both had a thousand questions to ask the other. They entered the dining room and were almost the last to sit down. Caleb was quickly grabbed up by Jane and the other girls who thought he was too precious for words. Caleb didn't mind the attention. The humans were fun, like playing with a new toy.

Colin sat at the head of the table taking Zack's place as host. He'd tried to convince his brother to come out of his room, but he'd declined. Ed had taken a shot at coaxing him out as well but also failed. Not even the prospect of new people could persuade him to join them. Over the past year, during the entire ordeal, Colin had never seen Zack miserable or depressed and now he was both. This scared Colin more and more each passing day. The only thing easing his fears was Austin's promise to talk with Zack. If anyone could get through to his brother, the Captain was that person.

Ed and Jenny were handling dinner, which meant it was Irish night. Beer, cottage pie, and corned beef were on the evening's menu. The only other residents not present were Anne and Grace. Anne was nursing, and Grace, after her last checkup, had been put on strict bed rest. Austin made excuses for Roxanne, but other than Charlie, no one cared much that she decided to not join them. The others thought Roxanne an odd sort, cold at times, but would never voice their opinions out loud.

No one had thought this more than Madison, something Austin had been fully aware of, as well as being cognizant of the uneasiness felt by the rest of the group. If the truth were told about Eve, about what occurred the day Madison died, if told about many things, he'd no doubts of their reaction. Keeping secrets had never been his way or how he liked dealing with people, but their circumstances were different, their situation unique and delicate. Keeping balance amongst them remained key to a peaceful coexistence.

Austin turned his attention to the end of the table where Luke sat alone wearing a permanent scowl. Since Madison's death, he'd become more reclusive and incommunicative. Jenny seemed to be the only person able to draw him out from under the dark cloud he walked under. Talk of the baby brought light into his eyes, animation into his voice, but these were always fleeting.

They hadn't announced Jenny's pregnancy yet but would need to do so soon. As with anything where the Adita were involved, time never came and went in the same manner they expected. Pregnancies were nine months, not six as Eve had warned Jenny to expect. Austin had discussed the timing of the announcement with Ed and Jenny. If planned right they could push the news out so that when the delivery day arrived appearances would seem Jenny had carried the baby about eight months. A few weeks premature wouldn't raise suspicions with anyone, except the one person who was no longer with them. Austin smiled to himself. Madison had had an eagle eye for details and a nose for sniffing out the truth. She was missed. He missed her and he knew Luke missed her more than the rest.

The kitchen doors swung open drawing everyone's attention. Ed and Jenny pushed out two carts loaded with comfort food. "Dinner is served," Ed announced, using a watered-down version of his usual enthusiastic attitude. Even he, who could find the silver lining in the darkest of clouds, couldn't make sense of Madison's death.

The meal took center stage and for the next hour conversation centered on eating and the Irish. Safe subjects. McKenna couldn't get over the abundance of food and, as she popped another bite of pie into her mouth, she hoped to never eat another peanut butter and jelly sandwich ever again. She caught Kyle watching her and gave him a big smile. He winked back at her.

Jane and Sue sat on either side of Caleb taking care of his every need. They couldn't help being drawn to him, because, though they hadn't discussed or even thought about it, he reminded them of their younger brother Mike, who would have been his age. Caleb understood this, as did his father, who kept a watchful eye on his son.

Zoe, who usually talked nonstop, sat stirring her food around her plate. Of all the girls, she was the only one not completely scarred by what took place in Section Seven. Being too young had saved her from the horrors the others experienced, which in turn allowed her to move on and eventually forget. Having a carefree attitude also made her more vulnerable and ill-equipped to deal with Madison's death.

Austin added little to the conversation. No one expected him to talk much and he was fine with playing that role. Tonight, more so than any other, he was impatient for the evening to end. He absently stirred his food around on his plate. The conversation around him and inside his head turned into a dull hum. Thoughts of Eve commanded his attention. He laid his fork down, propped his elbow on the table, and placed his hand on his head.

Charlie watched Austin and wondered what bothered him. Those who knew him best would have suspected something other than Madison's death weighed on him this evening. By Ed's expression, she could tell he also worried. *What does it matter what's bothering him?* She asked herself. It wasn't like he gave a damn about her anymore. Charlie almost dropped her fork when Austin looked up and his piercing eyes bore into hers. *You can hear me*, she thought and despite it sounding silly, even absurd, Charlie couldn't help thinking this was true. She stared into his eyes unable to look away and for the briefest of moments felt like she was seeing two people. Austin on the surface, but someone darker, more ominous behind him.

"Girls turn to clean up," Ed announced, drawing Charlie's attention back to the table and away from Austin.

Charlie jumped up, happy to be on cleanup detail. Before the aliens arrived, she wouldn't have been caught dead doing the dishes. *That's why they had servants*, she would have told anyone who dared to suggest she wash a dish. Those days were long gone and Charlie, more than the others, looked forward to the menial tasks. Colin teased her about how clean she kept her room, but he didn't know any better. If he'd paid attention, maybe looked past the stars in his love-struck eyes, he might have realized her compulsion to clean was more than a weird quirk. But he couldn't have known she sometimes stayed up until the early morning hours cleaning, any more than he could have known the reason why. For Charlie the reason was simple, keeping busy was the one thing standing between her and breaking her promise to Austin.

Once the table was cleared, the dishes washed, and everything returned to its rightful place, Austin asked Kyle if he wouldn't mind telling them about his journey to Colorado. At this suggestion, the room grew quiet and they turned their attention on the new guy. His story was what they'd all been waiting to hear, but didn't want to be rude in asking before he finished eating.

Kyle began his story from the time the massive cloud first dropped down over the US and Canada and fifty minutes later paused after telling them about his excursion across the Bering Strait and what he now believed was the Svan visiting him on the island.

After dessert was served, Kyle continued. "I crawled into Deadbear, Alaska on a wing and a prayer. And that's where I found McKenna."

"Deadbear?" Austin asked.

"Yeah. Looked to be a shithole of place even before the aliens wiped out the population."

"I was born there," Austin replied.

"Aw hell," Kyle said, embarrassed. "Man, I'm sorry. I mean I'm sure it wasn't all that bad."

"It was worse."

Kyle felt like a heel. What were the odds of coming across someone from Deadbear? They had to be worse than winning the lottery. Yet here sat a man born in that godforsaken place. The image of the yellow newspaper clipping taped to the window of the gas station came back to him. What was that name? Reynolds? D. Reynolds. Austin Reynolds. "Shit," Kyle said under his breath.

"My father was Donny Reynolds," Austin said. "He died when I was nine."

Luke and Ed, who were hearing for the first time about Austin's father, were somewhat taken by surprise. They knew so little about Austin's past, or his family. Ed had joked with Luke that he thought Austin had been born a grown man.

"You said all of Europe is still there and operating as normal?" Austin asked.

"Yeah. I mean things were rough at first, but you know they returned to normal. Sort of normal anyway."

"We can go back the way you came then," Luke said. "We might have a chance against the Adita."

"Who are the Adita?"

For the next hour, Kyle heard about the incredible journey they'd taken, from Drop Day to Cheyenne to Bliss, and how they'd wound up living in the bunker. At the end of their tale, he sighed and shook his head, finding the entire thing almost too hard to believe, except he'd seen the Svan up close and knew it wasn't bullshit.

On the other side of the table Ed was shaking his head over a thought he was stuck on. "I'm not going anywhere," he blurted out. "I'm going to find my son."

"I'm with Ed," Luke said.

"Why'd you leave Germany?" Austin asked before the discussion turned to expeditions across the US.

Kyle's hand moved to his pocket. "I was hoping to find my mother and sister, Grace. The last time we talked they were going to Cheyenne Mountain."

"Did you say Grace?" Ed asked.

"We have a Grace," Zoe announced.

"What do you mean you have a Grace?"

"I mean, like, we have a Grace, she lives here. She's didn't come to dinner cuz she's really pregnant," Zoe explained but wished she'd kept her mouth shut when Kyle's face turned pale.

From his pocket, Kyle pulled out the picture he'd kept close to his heart for over a year now. He handed it across the table to Zoe. She didn't have to look twice before nodding her head. She handed the picture to Ed. This was too big for her to handle, let an adult say it out loud.

"That's our Grace," Ed confirmed.

"Where is she?" Kyle could barely speak. "Is she ok?"

"She's fine. Her blood pressure has been elevated is all," Austin assured him.

"When's the baby due?"

"Three weeks," Jeremy spoke up.

Kyle looked at the young man and knew without asking that he must be the father. "You're her husband?"

Jeremy shook his head. "I'm...no it wasn't—"

"There wasn't time and it didn't seem all that important," Ed interjected before Jeremy could spill his guts. Some things were better left unsaid until the timing was right or maybe not said at all.

"But you want to marry her, right?" Kyle demanded.

Jeremy turned red and fumbled for an answer. Marriage didn't hold much, if any, importance in their new world, and never crossed Jeremy's mind, but he couldn't confess this to Kyle. Kyle hadn't suffered their fate. He wasn't part of their common thread, a survivor of shared horrific events. Without first-hand experience, he wouldn't understand.

Austin came to the rescue before Jeremy decided to spill his guts. "He does, but Grace refused to get married while she was pregnant. Something about being fat and the wedding dress not fitting." A complete fabrication, but Austin didn't care. If Kyle knew the whole truth he wouldn't care so much either.

"Can I see her?" Kyle asked, afraid to believe he'd found her without visual proof.

"Sure. I'll take you to her," Ed offered, pushing back and getting up from the table. "Do you want to come with?" he asked Jenny. "In case the shock is a bit much for her?"

Jenny nodded and stood up.

"You better go too Jeremy," Austin suggested, Jeremy agreed, casting a nervous glance in Kyle's direction.

Soon after their departure, the others cleared out of the dining room leaving Austin to think in peace, but all he found was his tormented thoughts. Visions of Roxanne and Eve meshed together, separated and swirled around his mind. He forced those images away and thought about Kyle's journey. If he was able to cross the Bering Strait to come here, couldn't they cross it to leave? What would that take? Would the risk justify the result? The Adita wouldn't stop until they had world domination. If they escaped to Russia or Germany, would they then die once the Svan were sent out to harvest more humans?

Too many questions without answers remained, and Austin couldn't help thinking about the one person who knew the answers. He glanced at his watch. She'd been gone for a week. An unsettling thought that she might not come back crossed his mind and put a knot in his stomach. He rubbed his head. She would come back. She had to come back.

Austin dropped his hands. What was he doing to himself? She wasn't human. She didn't have feelings like a human. He looked at the palm of his hand, no mark, no scar was visible. Was he human anymore? Yes, of course he was. He felt emotions, he hurt, and he loved. Eve wasn't capable of love. Love? Austin stood up, almost knocking over his chair in the process. Was he so desperate to have Roxanne back he would think himself in love with Eve? How could he love Eve? That would be foolish. Ah, but you are a fool, for maybe you already love her and have since you were nine years old.

Austin leaned on the table gripping the edge so hard he felt it begin to crack within his grasp. The picture Kyle had given to Charlie caught his eye. He reached across the table and picked it up. He looked at the picture, not seeing the images for being blinded by his thoughts. He didn't see the tall petite woman standing with her arm draped around Grace's shoulder. He didn't see the woman until he focused and then he saw her. First, her long blonde hair, braided and hanging over one shoulder, caught his eye. Styled similar to how he remembered his mom wearing her hair. She wore hers like...she looked like.... just like his mother.

He set the picture down and pulled out his wallet. From behind his driver's license, he slipped out a photo. It was old and frayed around the edges. Although his hands were steady, his heart thumped hard and fast against his rib cage. He picked up Kyle's picture and compared the two. The similarities were undeniable, removing any doubt that the woman in Kyle's photo was the same one in his. The same woman who had abandoned him when he was five, leaving him behind with an alcoholic father, leaving him to fend for himself, leaving and never coming back.

Bitter pills were the hardest to swallow and Austin had taken his fair share, but he never thought he'd be faced with this biting rancid truth. As a child he'd pictured her living a miserable lonely life, or dead, and not coming back for him because she was unable. But she'd gone on to start another family, never returning for the one she'd left behind. He'd been replaced and forgotten. Austin's hand itched to crush the picture, but he laid the photo gently down on the table. He would ask Kyle who she was before jumping to conclusions. He needed that validation first, because maybe, yes maybe, he was wrong. The odds were not good; in fact, the odds were the greatest odds in favor of him being dead on right.

*　*　*

The lighting in Grace's room was dim, but they could see she was asleep. Kyle looked at the girl lying on the bed. Tears welled up in his eyes. He walked over to the bed and gazed upon his sister's sweet face. For so long he'd given up hope, thinking she had to be dead. He touched her hair, her face. She was real. *She's real*, he thought, trying to assure himself he wasn't hallucinating or dreaming.

"Grace," he said.

Grace stirred and murmured in her sleep.

"Grace wake up. It's Kyle."

Grace's head turned back and forth fitfully, perhaps hearing Kyle's voice in her dream. Her eyes opened. For a few seconds, she lay there not moving, waiting for sleep to subside, waiting for her dreams to subside. She frowned remembering her dream and turned her head.

"Hey, kiddo."

Grace rubbed her eyes. "Kyle?"

"In the flesh." He smiled.

"Kyle?"

"Yeah, it's me sis."

"Oh my... How'd you get here? When?" Grace frowned. "Am I dead?"

Kyle laughed and leaned down giving her a big hug. "Not at all. I arrived by pick-up truck, well by foot, then a truck. It's a long story. Anyway, what about you? Gonna be a mommy I hear and see." He pointed to her stomach.

Grace looked away from Kyle, embarrassed. Not for being pregnant, but for how it had happened. "Did they tell you?" Her voice wavered.

"Tell me what?" Kyle didn't like the sound in her voice. If that kid hurt Grace he wouldn't live to see the end of the day. "Did that boy hurt you?" Kyle demanded.

Grace turned back to look at her brother. "What boy? You mean Jeremy?"

"Yes Jeremy," he spat out the name, already planning the various ways he would torture him.

"He didn't hurt me. It wasn't his fault I got pregnant. I wanted to. I needed to."

"What? Why? I mean why would you need to get pregnant? Help me out here sis."

Grace sighed. Where was she supposed to start? When General Roth's men rescued her and their mother? When they wouldn't let her bury their mother? When Roth lost it and turned their safe haven into a den of nightmares? The entire past year existed of bad things, bad news, and bad all around. Except for Captain Reynolds killing Roth and bringing them all to the bunker, but a silver lining around a pile of shit didn't change the pile from being shit. This brought her back to Kyle's question and still not knowing where or how to start.

"It's probably not a good idea for Grace to relive all that right now," Zack said from the doorway. No one noticed Zack coming in, but his disheveled appearance was a sight to behold. "Zack Londergan, bunker physician of sorts, nice to meet ya." He held out his hand to Kyle.

Kyle shook his hand. "Maybe you can tell me what the hell's going on."

"Be glad to, but not right now," Zack replied, holding his ground. Kyle was under a lot of stress and needed to process having found his sister before he heard the circumstances of that which brought her to the bunker.

Kyle turned back to Grace. "Where's mom?"

Grace looked broken. "She died. The cancer was too much. She was too weak and without treatment..."

"When?"

"About a month after the Sundogs arrived. She didn't suffer. She died in her sleep," Grace said, hoping to ease his pain. "I was with her. She didn't die alone." Grace would never tell him about the deplorable treatment she'd received, his wounds were deep enough without that knowledge.

19 THE HARVEST

While Kyle was wondering why life must always turn out bittersweet, Austin sat in the dark of his suite wondering what to do about the picture. When he'd first seen Kyle something familiar had struck him, recognition maybe, but he'd brushed the feeling away. The chance that they were related, brothers even, was irrefutable. Although Austin reasoned, Kyle could be a stepchild and no relation at all. This was plausible, but a theory Austin disregarded immediately. He knew they were brothers and the blood ties ran deep.

Austin felt the air around him stir and the hair on his arms popped. Eve had returned. "You came back," he said, trying to sound casual, trying to ignore the way he felt when she was near.

"Why do you hide your feelings from me?" she asked.

"I don't know. Human nature I guess," he replied and wondered if that might sound stupid to her.

Eve touched his arm. "I would like to take you somewhere. A place I used to go before everything changed."

Austin nodded and thought to ask if they were going far, but distance wasn't a relevant measure where Eve was concerned.

She reached out and took Austin's hand, pulling him from the bed. "We'll only be away for the night."

The air around them expanded and contracted like a giant breathing entity. Eve held Austin close to her as she whisked them through space. Moments later Austin found himself standing in the middle of an imposing bedroom. The walls were made of hefty stones, the windows stood floor to ceiling, and the furniture was built for a man of immense stature. An immense canopy bed sat in the center of the room and two fireplaces took up entire walls on opposite sides of the room. Several tall candle pillars provided globes of dancing light.

"Where are we?" Austin asked, watching his breath mist in front of him.

"Eastern Siberia."

Austin walked to the window, pulling aside the heavy drapery, he peered out over a vast wilderness of mountain peaks and valleys covered in snow and ice. "How high up?"

"Eight thousand feet."

"Is that all?" he joked.

"I don't understand."

"Nothing. I was being... nothing." He turned back to her. "I thought you didn't want me to go to Russia with you?"

"I am going to another place not far from here and I will go alone."

"Why did you bring me here?"

Eve considered his question but had no answer that would satisfy him, other than the truth. "Because I wanted to be alone with you." With that, she raised her hands, palms outward, and gave a gentle push. Soon both fireplaces were crackling with fire, spreading heat into the frigid room.

"How do you do that?"

"Transfer of energy."

"Where does the energy come from?"

"Everywhere." Eve walked over to Austin. "We don't have much time. Are these the questions you wish to ask?"

Austin shook his head. He didn't want to ask questions or talk, he only wanted to kiss her. Eve stepped into his arms. Their lips met, tender at first and then more demanding. Austin picked her up and carried her to the bed. Inside, hidden behind the black velvet curtains, their bodies entwined, becoming one with each other.

For the first time in her long existence Eve experienced the ecstasy of physical contact. She'd never desired to mate with a human, not even as Roxanne. During her years as Roxanne, she'd become her and had relied upon her memories and desires in order to behave in a manner appealing to Austin. She'd performed an act, one she'd been mentally removed from, one she treated as a necessary means to an end. However, tonight she was being Eve, mentally, physically and without a hidden agenda. And she found the experience to be unlike anything she'd ever felt or imagined. The satisfaction was not unlike her first kill.

These were not the words Austin would have used to describe what took place between them. The only word going through his mind was more. He wanted more of her. And later, as he lay on his back, bathed in sweat, he wasn't thinking of anything other than his desire to have her. He didn't notice his heart rate being normal; the beats per minute being no indication of the efforts expelled over the past hour. That his heart rate was normal and that the cause was related to his mutated genes, were not in his thoughts. Eve's hand touched his, sending a spark through his body. He pulled her on top of him, losing himself again.

They spent the better part of the night with few words passing between them. In the early morning hours, before dawn's first light, Eve lay in Austin's arms listening to him breathe. She'd observed the human mating ritual many times and always thought the process complex and strange. The efforts taken by the male to entice the female were often covert and she didn't wonder why they seldom came away with the fittest female if any at all. The Svan mated in the year of the ninth moon. The strongest female chose the strongest male to produce the fittest of the species. Humans applied no such consideration into selecting a mate. Their process was driven by visual attraction first and foremost. For the males, especially the young, the need to satisfy the desire outweighed the need for procreation. Although after tonight Eve felt she better understood this drive, she still couldn't grasp their unwillingness to strengthen their species, as the Adita did, as other civilizations did.

Austin pulled the heavy blanket up to his waist. He knew Eve didn't feel the cold air, but he was still human enough that his body temperature fluctuated.

"What is this place?" he asked.

"A fortress, or castle if you like, built by my great-great-grandfather Sattya. It has been here in these mountains for centuries, but no human has ever been here," she paused, "until now."

"Should I be honored?"

"Be whatever you like," Eve replied.

Austin smiled over the fact his sarcasm fell on deaf ears. He never thought pure honesty would unnerve him, but delivered by Eve had an unsettling effect on him. Many things about Eve were unsettling, but not all were negative.

"Would you like to hear more about the Adita and the harvest?"

After several seconds Austin replied, "Yes."

"You will not like what you hear about the harvest."

"I know."

Eve spread the drapery aside to allow in the warmth of the fireplace and rolled over on her back, keeping a hand on Austin's arm. Touching him gave her a sense of being something different, something she imagined being human might feel like. Feeling at peace was not a sensation Eve recognized, all she knew was the hunger inside was satisfied for the moment.

"The history of the Adita is known only by the Adita. The secrets I share go far beyond those of the Adita alone. By giving you this knowledge, I give Agra more reasons to kill you. Are you sure you wish to know?"

Austin nodded. "I think Agra was going to kill me anyway, but I don't want to put you in danger."

"It doesn't matter now. I have already broken many rules and fear I've outworn my welcome with my father," she replied. "But let me begin before the day appears and we have to return."

I don't want to leave, was his first thought, which he pushed aside, feeling disgusted with himself for thinking such a gutless thing. Obviously, they would go back. Hiding from the Adita wasn't an option and he wouldn't abandon his friends.

"We will return to your people," Eve assured him and then began her story. As she spoke Austin forgot about the bunker and his guilt.

"The Adita's arrival on this planet took place in the middle of their extensive history. For you to understand the middle, I must start at a point earlier. We don't have time to go back to the beginning as the history in-between is vast and made up of events too numerous to relay in the few hours we have. Thus, I will tell you those that are most important. The first thing you need to understand is the structure of the universes. There are seven." She drew seven perfect circles in the air that radiated light from the energy force within her. "These seven are separated and connected by dark matter." She indicated the black space surrounding the seven circles. "Earth is here, in the third." She pointed to a circle in the middle. "The universes are commanded by a Council. They control everything within this realm. The suns, the moons, the winds, life. For countless years they were in agreement and wars were non-existent. The Adita lived and commanded the second and third universes. They lived in the second on a planet much like Earth, but smaller in size."

"Why did they leave?"

"A vicious battle took place with the Mahat, a species from the fifth universe who make the Svan look less dangerous than your domestic cats. The Mahat had lost their Elders in an unsanctioned war with the Adita. The remaining Elders held a meeting to discuss the appointment of a new governing group for the Mahat. During this time the Mahat attacked the planets of the second universe in retaliation. A grievous departure from the laws, but the damage was done. The Council desperately wanted to prevent an all-out war and asked the Elders to give the second universe to the Mahat as reparations. Our Elders acquiesced and in turn, kept the third universe. Sort of an appeasement for their losses."

"Earth was the only inhabitable planet?"

Eve nodded. "The Adita have not always been in the advanced form you see them today. The first of our kind evolved from a more primitive species. A *savage beast* as you humans would say. They were the first inhabitants of Earth. When they arrived only the twelve Elders and maybe fifty guards remained; all others had been lost in the battle. As I told you before, Earth was inhabited only by the wildlife, and an abundance of it. Within a few months, the Elders had settled into their new home. Unfortunately, it wasn't long before the Zari, also an unprincipled group discovered the fertile planet. They arrived and with them brought the first humans."

"Brought them here? From where?"

"They were purchased from the trade colony. The Zari used them as servants and some were kept as pets. They were not as advanced as you are today."

"Meaning?"

"They were like your pet dog, but slightly smarter and more obedient."

Austin nodded.

"The Elders avoided the Zari and the humans, keeping to the caves and only coming out at night. Food was plentiful, they had no need to fight. But then one of the Elders was caught stealing a goat. He was discovered by a male human tending his master's property. Naturally, the man tried to fight, to defend his master's possessions, but he was no match. The Elder, as was custom for the victor, drank the blood of his kill. This fateful encounter was the turning point in the Adita's future. An event whose consequence changed our way of life forever. For you see, the blood he drank was the rarest of types. One they'd never tasted before. The Elder shared this blood with the other Elders. Their physical form took on a rapid transformation, turning them from a beast into the Adita as you see them today. The change took thirteen hours. Within ten years they'd multiplied from twelve to twelve thousand and did so without the Zari's knowledge."

"That's a thousand babies a year."

"Our reproductive process is only forty-five days. The latter part of those years saw the biggest surge in reproduction. Without the Zari realizing it, they were sharing the planet with the Adita. And by the time the Adita outnumbered the Zari, it was too late. On the night of the ninth moon, they waged war, killing all Zari that had not manage to escape, but sparing the humans."

"And claimed Earth as their own."

"Yes, and then some."

Austin nodded for her to go on.

"For millions of years the Adita thrived on Earth. They learned the difference in your blood types and sought out the rare blood they needed and only took selections from the fittest humans. The Adita grew stronger, more intelligent as the years went by, and at their peak they were the strongest species in the universes, defending the third universe from all others. They reclaimed the second from the Mahat, forcing them to become nomads. They elected themselves supreme leaders of the Council of Elders. They thought they were invincible."

"They found out otherwise?"

"They discovered just how vulnerable they'd become," Eve replied. "When the plague hit, they were unprepared and never fully recovered. Now they are weak and without the blood they so desperately need in order to regain their former power. If they were challenged in battle they would most likely suffer great losses, if not total defeat. The only thing saving them is their ability to shield their weaknesses from the prying eyes of their enemies."

"Who would challenge them? The Mahat? Humans?"

Eve smirked at the very idea. "Humans would lose. No, the Adita have many enemies, Mahat being only one, but none so near as the very species they evolved from," Eve responded. "You see after the plague forced the Adita to leave the planet, their blood supply was cut off. The Elders had tried to prepare for this by taking a handful of uninfected humans with them when they left, but it wasn't enough. When the blood supplies diminished, and for the Elders to live, some were left to starve. But they didn't starve. They reverted to original form and turned on the Adita. The Adita were still superior in every way and an uneasy truce was established."

Eve paused to listen, waiting for Agra to reach out for her but he didn't. Relief was not to be hers, for it was better to know when your enemy was coming then to sit and wait for his attack. This was not the first time she'd thought of her father as her opponent.

"The Adita attempted to reconvert those who had changed back, but it was too late. The transformation seems to only take place once. Those that did not agree to the Adita's terms were controlled through other methods."

"The Svan," Austin said. "The Adita evolved or transformed from the Svan?"

"That is correct."

"It was human blood that turned those savages into advanced beings?" Austin asked, stunned at this newest revelation.

"Certain human blood, not all. A particular strand of DNA was the missing link. Once that was added, the Adita came to be. And what you consider savages are still far more advanced than your species. The language the Svan speak is older than this Earth. Their DNA the most complex and highly developed in multiple universes, second only to the Adita."

"Ok." Austin's mind was reeling. The discovery of wormholes and Paru and alien beings had been mind-boggling in itself. He'd barely given that much thought other than accepting they existed, but now he was confronted with tales even more astounding.

"It is much to take in, even for you."

"What does that mean? Even for me? What makes me special?"

"Your blood is pure. The first pure sample found since the plague. The rarest in existence. From you, Agra felt we could evolve to an even higher level."

"And that's why we had Caleb?"

"Yes. I thought he was to be the first of a superior race of beings," Eve said, hesitating to say what she really thought.

"But?"

"I don't know. Agra is hiding something from me. He seems displeased with the results."

"Is Caleb's life in danger?"

"Maybe, but I won't allow him to be harmed." She paused. "Agra is waiting for something, but I don't know what."

"You haven't explained the harvest."

Eve hesitated. Thus far she'd kept to the simple facts, avoiding any detailed accounts of how the Adita used humans to survive. However, knowing Austin wouldn't like hearing the truth didn't weigh in on her decision to divulge the family secrets. He wanted to know so she would tell him.

"The harvest takes place every ninth moon or ninety-nine years in Earth time. The coming year is the ninety-ninth. Prior to the moon rising the Svan will give birth. Of the offspring, the fittest will be chosen for transformation. In times past, humans were harvested in advance of the birthing in order for their blood to be purified and ready for the transformation. Although the blood type was rare, having shortages wasn't a concern. One human could provide enough blood to transform seven hundred Svan. Each ninth moon the number transformed declined due to the blood shortage. The Svan's numbers continued to grow, while the Adita, who were forbidden to reproduce, their numbers dwindled. The Elders fear the Svan will rise up against them. I believe Agra used this fear to convince the Elders to permit our union and ultimately Caleb."

"But if Agra wanted a superior race why not just use me to produce more. Why not just come and get me? Why the big charade? Why Roxanne?"

"As I told you before, an Adita female has never mated with a human before. Agra wasn't sure of the success and couldn't come here for risk of contamination."

"Then he used you as a guinea pig?" Austin asked. "A test subject," he clarified.

"Yes. He knew you wouldn't willingly become my mate."

"But why all of the killing? People, animals, everything?"

"The planet had to be purged of the disease before the Adita would return. The Elders would take no chances."

"The planet? There's nothing left?" Austin's shoulder's sagged, knowing before she answered this was the case.

"The Svan have been instructed to complete the process."

"What about the people in the warehouses and the camps?" he asked trying to not think about the deaths being suffered at the hands of the Svan as they spread out across Earth.

"Those on Paru will be used for the harvest. They have the blood needed to transform the Svan. Those here on Earth are being used as test subjects, guinea pigs as you called them."

"I don't understand. I thought I was the only one with pure, or clean blood."

"You are the only one, but before I found you, the Adita had perfected a method for extracting the mutant gene from those with your blood type, but who were not pure. The process requires many months to complete and isn't full proof. It was meant to be an alternate survival strategy."

"You don't sound convinced."

"There's much I don't know, which is why I must find Agra. I must find out why he would want to come here." She turned to face him. "You will stay in the bunker. Protect your brother and sister and the others, but more than anything watch over Caleb."

"My brother and sister? I don't have any..."

"You know it's true and who they are. Why do you lie to yourself? You are not such a person to lie. You have always been honest with others as well as yourself."

Austin mentally shrugged. "I know. It's a lot to take in. A lot I don't understand. Most of it goes against everything I know or makes sense."

"You learn, grow and evolve all of your life. This is no different."

"Yeah, but... never mind." He stopped, knowing he would lose in a debate with her. "So how did Agra miss that I had siblings? I thought he saw or knew everything?"

"Their blood, although quite exceptional for a human, is not the same as yours and, quite simply, because I never crossed paths with them until recently. Agra would not have been able to see them unless through me. He can't see them now and won't see them unless I allow him."

"The Svan let Kyle live. Won't they tell Agra?"

"The Svan owe no allegiance to Agra or the Adita. They allowed him to live because I ordered them to do so."

"You were there?"

"I've been keeping an eye on your brother, yes."

Austin was silent for a long moment. "He was wrong," Austin remarked. "Agra was wrong about what I would have done. Who I would have chosen."

"Are you saying you would choose me as a mate?"

"That sounds really primitive."

"You humans are peculiar about your words. If it is the truth then say so. Changing how you say it, doesn't make it any less so. Does it?"

"No, it doesn't. So yes, I would, I do choose you as my mate," he replied and pulled her to him for a kiss.

Eve tensed and pushed away.

"Did I do something wrong?"

"We're not alone." Eve dressed and pounced from the bed like a nimble cat, returning to Austin after a few seconds. "Get dressed. Hurry."

Austin did as she instructed.

"They will be here soon. You must wait here, behind the drapery. It is the only way I can protect you."

"I can protect myself," Austin argued.

Eve kissed him hard on the lips. "No, you cannot. Not against what's coming." She pulled the drapes closed around the bed, leaving Austin to massage his wounded ego.

Eve waited in the middle of the room listening to the silent thunder grow louder as it rolled toward the room. The force burst through the massive doors sending hundreds of knife-like shards of wood and jagged-edged rocks flying across the room. Eve stood amid the storm unscathed. When the three female Adita guards entered in the wake, Eve was ready for them.

The predators surrounded their prey. They carried heavy swords with edges that gleamed wicked sharp. The weapons were forged from the strongest metals found on the remotest planets in the seventh universe. Only Adita guards used such weapons and only when sent to assassinate one of their own. They held the swords high, grasping the handle with both hands. Eve stood perfectly still, unafraid of death, for she knew death would not be hers this day. She licked her lips in anticipation, having looked forward to this moment since their first encounter.

"Look at her," the first guard spoke.

This was Talina, she was the leader and would die last.

"What's so special about her?" the second asked.

She was the weakest of the group and would die first.

"Nothing. She's the child of a whore. A child of man. Weak and pathetic," the third replied, sniffing the air around Eve. "She even stinks like one."

Talina sneered. "Stupid little girl. Wandering around listening to voices. Do you hear them now little Eve?" she taunted. "Do you hear your master's voice now?"

Eve had never been made fun of or bullied, and that they mocked her now she cared little. In her mind, she envisioned each move required to end their lives, lives lived too long. As they continued to taunt and mock and tease, Eve planned. First, she would take the sword of guard number two, the weak one, and cut off her head. Second, she would remove the head of guard number three and third... and third, Talina, the one who wouldn't shut up, Eve had special plans for her.

Eve breathed, the walls of the room breathed with her. The guards paused in their onslaught to pay attention, thinking maybe Eve was more than what they'd first assumed, and maybe she was dangerous. Before they could decide, two were dead on the floor, exactly as Eve planned, but Talina had vanished from sight, although not from the room. Eve listened for her and hissed through her teeth upon locating her.

"I found your pet," Talina said and threw Austin across the room toward the roaring fire. Eve extinguished the fire leaving cold embers, rather than burning flames, to provide for his landing.

"I would have thought you better trained Talina," Eve remarked. "My father must have been desperate. Oh, but wait. You aren't here under Agra's orders," Eve noted. "Za sent you. He knows I'm returning home soon, and he sent you to stop me. Agra's puppet, as you are Za's."

"Funny you talk of marionettes when Agra has held your strings since the day you were born."

"Silly Talina. Do you not know?" Eve paused. "The bylaws state, and very concisely, only the leader of the Adita can instruct a death by beheading? An assassination? Do you believe Za, a mere member of the council, has the authority to send you to do such a thing?"

Upon hearing this and knowing Eve spoke the truth, Talina lowered her sword. Za had assured her Agra wished for his daughter to be killed. Now she knew she'd made a dreadful error in judgment, but the deed was done. She would rather die here than face Agra's wrath. Talina raised her sword and charged toward Eve. From the corner of her eye, she saw the blade swinging toward her, but it was too late. Her head and body were separated from one another.

Austin stood over the headless corpse holding one of the swords with both hands, his muscles strained from the weight. Talina's blood dripped from the end.

"You are quite capable, but stupid for doing so," Eve said.

"You're welcome."

"I don't need your help. If she'd been paying attention it would have been your head on the floor and not hers." Eve picked up Talina's head and tossed it into the fire.

"Are you scolding me?" Austin asked, laughing at the notion.

Eve turned to him. "You forget what you are."

"I don't know what I am," Austin replied, no longer amused.

"You don't know what you want to be is more accurate, but for now you are human," she said. "The question you must answer is, do you want to be human or do you wish to be something more?"

"But I'm not human? Humans can't hear people's thoughts," he argued.

"You consider yourself less human because you can hear other's thoughts? Or is it because you feel stronger and an improved version of your former self? You are a better human, but still very much a human. And you haven't answered my question. What do you want to be?"

The answer should have been easy and quick, but Austin hesitated to reply, to consider what he wanted. Not long ago he was cursing her for infecting him, and now he fumbled over making a decision. He couldn't claim he knew for certain about remaining human, she would know it a lie. He knew this to be a lie.

"I can change you."

"What would that mean?" he asked.

"I don't know. It could mean your death, but I don't foresee that happening."

"Have you ever turned anyone before?"

"Not with success."

Austin laughed out loud. "What makes you think you can change me then?"

"You were close before, but you fought against it. Your desire to be human was very strong. You'd have to want to change or this time you will certainly die."

"Do you want me to change? To become like you?"

"No."

Her abrupt answer surprised him. "Why not?"

"We live only to live, to survive, we stop at nothing to safeguard our way of life. I don't want you to become like me."

"But you're more than that Eve," he replied, taking her arm and pulling her close. "You're much more than that."

He was wrong, but Eve did not argue and let him kiss her. "We have to go," she said, but not letting go of him.

"What happens now?"

Eve shrugged. "The future keeps changing, more than ever before. I'm not sure what to make of this and mustn't delay my departure any longer."

Eve took them back to the bunker. She was anxious to be on her way. Things were moving and changing at a rapid pace, time was shortening.

20 BLOOD TYPING

Zack pounded on Austin's door again, stopping to listen only for a second before resuming his assault. At the next pause, he was surprised to hear the lock being turned. The door opened, Eve stepped aside for him to enter. Although one of the few who knew her as Eve, seeing her this way always caught him off guard. Zack eased by, avoiding any contact with her.

"Glad you're here man. We need to talk and don't have much time," Austin said, coming to meet Zack at the door.

"Not much time before what?"

"I have to leave," Eve interrupted.

Austin walked over to her. "You'll be careful?"

"I will."

They kissed goodbye, embracing briefly before Eve vanished from the room.

"What was that?" Zack asked.

"Nothing," Austin avoided looking at him and sat on the couch.

"Can you explain nothing that looked like something?" Zack sat down across from him. "Last time we talked you were desperate to find a cure, now you're playing house with the devil's spawn."

Austin's cheek twitched, subtle enough it went unnoticed by Zack. "You think her inherently evil?

"I think for Eve, for the Adita, the line between good and evil is razor thin and even sharper. Inherent or not," Zack replied. "I think if you came between her and something she wanted, you wouldn't stand a chance. She'd kill you without remorse. Right or wrong doesn't exist for them. In most situations a human might consider the difference, weigh the consequences, whereas an Adita considers neither, nor do they care." Zack took a breath and then shrugged. "Obviously this is only an opinion based on what, I haven't a fucking clue."

"I understand you'd think that way about them, about Eve, but she's the mother of my son. I have to believe there's something more to her than basic survival instincts."

"Maybe so," Zack replied. "I guess you could argue nature versus nurture. And considering Eve's been on Earth, separated from the Adita for thousands of years, I guess it's possible she's picked up some of our traits. Not sure if that changes who she is, but it's possible."

"Do your feelings have anything to do with Madison?" Austin asked straight out. "That maybe you doubt Eve and think she could have saved Madison had she wanted to?"

Zack dropped his head finding the floor easier to look at than those piercing blue eyes. "Yeah, I guess in some ways, yes. I'm sorry. I wasn't trying to be an asshole. And you know I'm grateful she saved Madison's baby, our baby."

"Then why all the hostility?" Austin knew his answer but wanted to give Zack the opportunity to let it out.

"It's been so fricking hard. I miss her so much. The emptiness. I didn't want her to go that day." Zack squeezed his hands together until his knuckles turned white. "I shouldn't have let her go."

"You can't do that to yourself, Zack. It won't change anything," Austin replied. "You're going to have a child; a daughter Eve tells me. You need to live for her. Don't chase ghosts. You can never catch them."

Zack looked up. "A daughter? Holy shit. I'm gonna be a dad. Now that's fucked up." A hint of a smile teased at his lips.

Austin smiled back. "Cut Eve some slack will ya?"

"Yeah..."

"But?"

"But I don't trust her. There I said it and I'm sorry if that hurts your feelings or pisses you off. Hopefully, you won't pummel me into the ground for being honest, but that's it and, well that's all," Zack finished, holding his breath.

Austin couldn't say much to this. Trust was something he himself hadn't given to Eve. He couldn't expect those who knew nothing about her to do more than he was willing or able.

"And from your silence, I'm guessing you don't either," Zack added. "Which means you won't pound me into the ground."

"I don't know what to think," Austin admitted. "And no one's going to pound anyone into the ground for being honest."

Zack looked up, a spark in his eye. "Do you love her? Is that what this is about?" It was Austin's turn to stare at the floor. "You do. Damn." But he couldn't berate the man for falling in love, even if she wasn't human.

"It's not love. Eve is not someone you fall in love with." Austin stopped short, unsure of what to say or how to explain his feelings for Eve.

Zack snorted. "Not love, then what is it?"

"I don't know. Look, Zack, things are changing. Eve's not certain anymore what Agra plans to do," Austin said. "She's gone to Russia, where she thinks Agra is headed."

"What do you mean plans to do? Were there alternatives to taking over the planet?"

"That's still going to happen or is happening. That's what I wanted to talk to you about. The Svan have moved overseas. There's nothing left of Europe except for a handful of survivors. They've ramped up their search for humans. By the end of the week I expect they'll have covered the entire planet," Austin replied, knowing how awful it sounded, but dousing a pile of shit with perfume wouldn't change it from smelling like a pile of shit. At least not according to Donny Reynolds' philosophy on life.

"But how do you know this?"

"Eve told me."

"And you believe her? Just like that? Eve said it, so it must be true?" Zack argued for the sake of arguing because he didn't want to think about what this meant.

"She has no reason to lie. Do I think she's told me everything? Probably not, but what she's shared about the Earth is the truth."

"So what now? What do we do now?" Zack asked.

"I don't know," Austin answered. They were always looking to him for answers, but this time he didn't know what to do, not now, not with the playbook always changing. Warlords, militants, even the gorillas followed certain behavior patterns he could pick up on. Blood drinking, organ stealing aliens weren't in any of the government's training sims.

"Do we wait? Like sitting ducks?" Zack pressed.

"We wait for Eve to return. I know it's asking a lot to trust her, but even if she doesn't have your best interest in mind, she won't allow harm to come to any of you because of me. I know it's not the best solution, but if the Adita are taking over the entire planet, what does it matter where we go? If they want to find us, they will find us. If we fly to Germany or to Japan, it wouldn't make a difference. If for some reason Eve lied and life still exists as Kyle described, what do we do then? Warn people? Would they listen? Would mass hysteria follow?"

Zack marinated on this for a few seconds. "Maybe I can figure out a way to stop them. Maybe Eve would help me do that. She must know how they die."

"The Adita don't die," Austin said, knowing this was not completely accurate.

"Oh, bullshit. Everything dies. Everything," Zack emphasized the last word.

Austin considered telling him decapitation was effective, but only if using a weapon made of a rare metal from a universe they had no means of reaching. "The Adita are not like other species and they aren't the only ones out there."

"They aren't? Shit and fuck me over twice."

"I would have expected you of all people to already have considered we aren't alone in the universe."

"Sure I have. I've thought about it, but it was you know, the dope. Smoke a joint, sit on the hood of your car, gaze at the stars and ponder shit. Never meant anything."

Austin understood Zack's reluctance to believe. "Whether we like the facts or believe in them doesn't matter. The Adita are real."

"Ed will want to keep looking for his son. He won't stand for being trapped down here." Zack replied, giving up on debating other life forms. They were a done deal, and if the Adita existed, logic dictated others probably did as well.

Austin decided against telling Zack about the harvest. What did it matter now? Ed's son, Madison's sister, Luke's mom, they were nothing more than corpses kept alive by machines, if they were alive at all. He would never say this to Ed, even if it was the truth. With Jenny's return, Ed had renewed hope for finding his son. "You realize that his son is probably dead or close to it."

Zack sat back. "And you know this how?"

"I don't, but I've seen the people in the warehouses on Paru. You saw for yourself the people in that camp. It would be suicide to go after him. And for what?"

"For closure man. Ed needs to know Ryan isn't hooked up to a machine somewhere, alive enough that he might still have dreams. That he might still remember and think about his parents. Think about it, man. You risked everything for your son. How can you expect him not to do the same?" Zack demanded, getting slightly perturbed.

"That was different. I didn't know what I was up against?"

"Bullshit man. That's pure bullshit. You would have fought King Kong with your bare hands to save your son. Don't give me that crap. I deserve more respect than that. Ed deserves more."

"You're right. You're right. I'm sorry." Austin took a deep breath, letting it out slowly.

"Eve could save him. She saved Jenny. Why not Ryan?"

"And what about your mom or Luke's mom? Aren't they all worth saving?"

"My mother's dead."

"How can you be so sure?"

"I can't. It's a theory. An almost educated guess, but not really."

Austin waited, again blocking Zack's thought from his mind. A skill he was getting better at, allowing him to control what came in. He had more than enough going on in his own mind to be sorting out other people's thoughts.

"It's nothing."

"Tell me."

"She had AB negative blood."

"And?"

"The bodies dropped back to Earth, they all had AB blood. No variations. I tested hundreds of samples. Each time it was the same type."

"What does that prove?"

"The Adita can't use the AB blood type."

"What type are you?

"O positive. In fact, everyone in the bunker, except you and Grace, is an O plus. Grace is O negative and I don't know what type you have or had. I thought it was O negative, but I don't know anymore. Not sure about Kyle and McKenna. I haven't tested them yet, but my money's on O. The thing is ABs can receive from anyone, but can only give to other ABs, where an O can give to anyone, but an O negative is super rare and can only receive from another O negatives. Thus my theory is this..."

"Zack," Austin interrupted. "What does it matter if you figure it out?

Zack looked at Austin like a spiked horn had sprouted from the center of his forehead. "What does it matter? What does it matter? It matters that if those bloodsuckers can only survive on O negative, which is rare, then, unless they have a production line somewhere capable of replicating human blood, they will..." Zack stopped. "That's it isn't it? They've figured out how to make more blood."

Austin didn't answer. Based on what Eve had told him, Zack was close to being right. He would have liked to share what he knew, but he couldn't put Zack's life in more danger by fostering hope in defeating the Adita.

"Anyway, Madison's sister was AB negative and so was Luke's mom. Oh and Ryan's an O negative, but I don't know what that means. Maybe the Adita are O negative, or something like O negative, or maybe they can mix O negative with other types. We can't, but they might know how..."

Austin held up his hand to stop Zack. "You need to prepare for a long stay underground. In fact, we might want to consider returning to the mountain."

Zack balked at this idea. "Cheyenne? Oh hell no. The girls will refuse. We're better prepared here than anywhere else."

"I guess that puts us back at square one," Austin replied.

"I guess it does," Zack agreed, his thoughts going out to Ray and if he was still alive. Maybe he could go get him, but then again not. The thing was Ray most likely wouldn't leave. *'Them damn aliens don't want nothin' to do with an old cuss like me,'* he would argue and refuse to go.

"We'll be safe. Eve will protect us." Austin said, knowing this didn't comfort Zack. "I don't have any answers right now, but you have to trust me," Austin said. "Eve will protect us. The Svan won't come down here. She won't allow them to. They obey her, I've seen it. Besides, right now they are occupied overseas. Only a small group was left behind to guard the camps here."

"What about Ed?"

"I'll talk to him. I feel for him, but he can't go traipsing around the country. Eventually, a Svan will kill him. I don't want him or Luke acting like run and gun cowboys. They'll both end up dead." Austin's hand went to rubbing his head. "I'll look for Ryan."

"How will you know where to find him?"

"I don't know. I'll ask Eve. She may know where to find him."

The two men sat lost in their own thoughts. Nothing about their discussion sat well or promised a good outcome. Zack caught himself wondering when a good time might be to give up, to throw in that towel and surrender. Maybe they could re-enact Guyana. He could take on the role of Jim Jones. They would name the bunker Zack-town and they would all drink the Kool-Aid or Gatorade or maybe whiskey. Yes, whiskey. If he was going out, he was going to do it right. Jack Daniels or Southern Comfort, and to hell with the kid's stuff.

Zack stood up. "I'll catch you later."

After he left, Austin went into the kitchenette. He opened cabinet doors, not sure what he was looking for until he came across a bottle of Southern Comfort. He grabbed the bottle and a small glass before returning to the couch. With the lights down low, he poured the caramel brown liquid into the glass and set the bottle on the table. Old Donny Reynolds had started drinking at the ripe old age of ten and never stopped. At his wise young age of twenty-seven, Austin Reynolds was about to have his first drink.

Austin took a sip and grimaced. He took a second bigger swallow and waited as the liquid burned down his throat into his chest. He finished off what remained in the glass, took a second and a third before setting the glass next to the bottle. Soon his face felt warm and his eyelids heavy. He stretched out on the couch allowing the alcohol to do its thing. This wasn't so bad he thought and wondered why his father had always been so pissed off when he drank. Austin didn't feel angry, he felt sleepy. As he lay there, close to feeling relaxed, Austin went over his conversation with Zack. If he could tell Zack everything they might be able to figure out a way to stop the Adita, but if he told Zack what he knew he would be betraying Eve's trust, not to mention putting Zack's life in peril. Whether Eve was trustworthy didn't matter to him. He'd always prided himself on holding true to his values and didn't think now was the time to forgo them. Austin knew he'd have to figure this out alone. Going it alone meant making hard decisions.

'Do you want to be human?'

He heard Eve's question again and asked himself the same thing. Did he want to be human? What would it mean if he wasn't? Could he then fight the Adita as one of them or would he end up like them? What about Caleb? By this time next year, he would be a young man. He'd already grown two inches since arriving and Austin could see his face changing, losing its baby softness, starting to show the man he would be someday.

The warmth of the alcohol left him, Austin felt very much awake but continued to lie still with his eyes closed. Thinking was easier in the dark. His teammates had always relied on him to devise the perfect plan of attack. When they'd rescued that village in Africa so long ago, Austin had led the charge. He found the warlord hiding deep in the brush. He rescued the girls from the underground prison, saving them from a life of rape and torture. He'd done all these things and many more seemingly with ease. At least that's how things appeared to his teammates. But he knew their picture of him wasn't complete. None of those things were accomplished without Eve's help. Eve had guided his hand, making sure he knew when to attack, where danger awaited and when to get out. Her motives were pure in her desire to protect him but went no further. He was not so blinded as to believe she felt anything for the people he saved. And to Zack's point, he wasn't foolish enough to think she would help him against her own people and he wouldn't ask. No, this time he truly was on his own.

"Do you sneak up on your mother like that?" Austin opened his eyes to see Caleb sitting on the coffee table staring at him.

"Yes."

"Does she get angry?"

"Sometimes. Sometimes she laughs."

Austin sat up. "She laughs?"

"She only smiles, but I know she's laughing."

"I didn't think Adita laughed at all."

"Grandfather doesn't."

"Tell me about him."

"He's afraid of dying and he's angry, but I don't know why. He's also afraid of mother."

"Do you know why?"

"She's more powerful than he is, but she doesn't know how to use all of her powers yet and Agra, I mean grandfather, fears she'll turn against him when she learns his secret."

"What is his secret?"

Caleb shrugged. "I don't know. I can just feel it is all." He spotted the bottle. "Can I try some?"

"No."

"Why not?"

Because I said so, almost slipped past Austin's lips. "I don't think your mother would approve, besides it's not all that great."

"You don't have to tell her."

Austin laughed. What kind of secrets could he keep from Eve? "Come on Caleb, you know better than that."

Caleb smiled, happy to see his father wasn't easily swayed. He thought to thank him for making the baby but knew his mother would not laugh if he told. He wasn't even supposed to know, but her thoughts sometimes entwined themselves with his so that he couldn't help hearing her. As was the case with Agra's thoughts, but lately Caleb had put great effort into blocking Agra from his mind. He wasn't always successful and when a random thought did slip through, it was never pleasant in nature.

"Would you like to talk about it?" Austin asked.

Caleb looked at him, first surprised, then with understanding. "If you were to change, aren't you afraid you might become like grandfather or worse, like Za?"

Eve had warned him about Caleb's powers and his tendency to listen when he shouldn't. "I haven't decided yet what I'm going to do, but I think I would still be me. I don't think it would change who I am as a person."

"The Adita's DNA doesn't work that way. If mother transforms you, her DNA will dominate and eventually take over completely. Only the very best of your genes will survive."

"So you're saying I wouldn't have a choice in how I want to act? Kind of like eavesdropping on folks?"

Caleb shook his head. "But it's not a choice father, it's quite the opposite. My mind is much stronger than yours, which is why hearing, or not hearing, is difficult to control."

"Explain."

"It's like energy. I have more than you and the same or maybe a little more than mother. I'll have a lot more than mother and grandfather by the time I become an adult. Now though, the energy flows fast."

"Like an ocean's current?"

"Yes. And it brings many thoughts all at once. They arrive before I know it and then you hear a voice you recognize, and your mind tells you to pay attention, so you do," Caleb explained. "But you haven't answered my question."

"No, I didn't," Austin said, "because I don't know the answer."

Caleb shook his head. "We always know the answer, it's choosing to not hear what the mind tells us that keeps us from making decisions."

Austin laughed. "And what do you know that you're not telling me? Something about your mother?"

Caleb was again caught off guard. "Yes, but she doesn't know I know and I would be in a lot of trouble if I told."

Austin's brow creased. He'd never tried to listen to other's thoughts, they came without warning, as Caleb described. That his son could block him from hearing what he himself was thinking was obvious. "You can tell me," Austin said. "I'll deal with your mother."

Caleb crossed his legs underneath him and folded his hands, resting his chin in the center over his thumbs. He didn't speak the words but thought them rather than saying them out loud. If he didn't say them out loud, he couldn't get in trouble.

Austin's eyes grew wide. "Are you sure?"

Caleb nodded.

"Does Agra know?"

"Not yet, but you don't have to worry. Mother is very good at hiding things from him."

"What will he do if he finds out?"

"I don't know. He might try to harm her. She's stronger than grandfather, but she won't fight him."

"Why not?"

"I don't know. I guess she hasn't made up her mind yet."

"About what?"

Caleb shrugged. "I can take you to Mr. Edward's son." Caleb changed the subject, a skill, or trick, he was well practiced at and one his mother wouldn't have let pass, but his father didn't know him as well. His father still thought of him as a child and assumed all children had short attention spans.

Austin knelt in front of Caleb. "Do you know where he is? Where Ed's boy is?"

"I know the way to him."

"Is he here on Earth? Is he still alive?"

"He's not here, but the way to him is here. I'm not sure what stage he's in. Would you like to go see him?"

Austin nodded, but his mind was moving at breakneck speed over the possibilities, the risks involved, and the logic of listening to a seven-year-old, even if that seven-year-old was an exceptional being. He didn't like making decisions on the fly, could be a quick way to the grave. Special operations took weeks of planning and this was no special op. If they were going to the camps or warehouses or anywhere the Adita were holding bodies, then the mission was most likely a death sentence.

Caleb tugged on his arm. "We should go right away, father."

Austin made up his mind in that instant. "Let me call Zack first. I want at least one person to know we're leaving. Then we'll go. Five minutes."

Austin went into the bedroom and dialed Zack's number, having no idea what he would say. He had to do this, and he had to go alone. He thought about lying to Zack, but when he answered Austin told him the truth. He was going to find Ryan and would be back as soon as he could. And they weren't to say anything to Ed. Zack argued about the sanity or lack of Austin going alone or going at all. Zack's protests were duly noted and duly ignored.

Austin returned to where Caleb waited. "Let's go." Caleb took his father's hand and they vanished into the air.

Out in the hall, Zack was running toward Austin's suite, but when he opened the door he was too late. Zack spotted the open bottle of Southern Comfort and an uneasy feeling settled in the pit of his stomach. "Damn it, man." Zack pounded on the door frame.

"What's wrong?" Luke asked, having walked upon the scene.

"Austin went somewhere," Zack answered.

"Whatta ya mean went somewhere? Did the bloodsucker take him back to Bliss or Paru or whatever the damn place is called?"

"No. No. No. He went somewhere with Caleb," Zack replied. "Somewhere in the US. He didn't say where."

Luke relaxed some. Caleb was better than the bloodsucker, although he had his doubts about the boy as well. He wasn't buying the reason for the kid's growth spurt. He wasn't buying any of the explanations they'd been pushing.

"Why do you hate her so much?" Zack asked, seeing the disgusted expression on Luke's face.

Luke's lip turned up in a sneer. "Why do you like her so much?"

Zack blew air through his lips, frustrated. "What are we, in high school?"

Luke shook his head annoyed with Zack's inability to see Eve for what she really was, and that was evil. "The bloodsucker's going to get Austin killed or worse. Why don't you see that?"

"She saved Jenny's life," Zack reminded him. "And the life of my unborn child."

"She didn't do it for you. Austin begged her to. She doesn't give a damn about you or me or anyone in this bunker. When are you gonna wake the fuck up."

"You don't know that," Zack argued. "She must care some or why bother with us at all?"

Luke raised his hand for Zack to stop. He was tired of their ignorance. He knew Eve would stop at nothing to preserve her way of life. They would all see, but they would see too late. "Let me know when he comes back." Luke walked off before Zack could say more.

Zack let him go. He knew Luke was more upset over Madison's death then he let on, but what ate at him went deeper than Madison. Out of everyone in the bunker, Zack worried about Luke the most. He'd never grown close to anyone except Austin and this thing with Eve was eating at him. If he knew the recent development in Austin's relationship with Eve, he would come unglued.

Zack returned to Austin's empty living room. He picked up the bottle and was relieved to see only a small amount missing. He took a swig, grimaced as it burned down his throat and then took another. "Hope you know what you're doing big man." Zack took one more swig before twisting the cap in place and setting the bottle on the table. Knowing he couldn't do anything more, Zack closed the door and headed for the command center. He decided Austin and Caleb had used unconventional travel methods and didn't hold much hope of seeing anything on the monitors. The bad feeling from earlier returned, reminding Zack of an old blues tune by R. L. Burnside.

"*It's bad you know,*" he sang. "That's right R. L. I know it's bad. All the way bad. Flip it, turn it, spin it around. It's bad you know."

21 SAVING RYAN

Austin and Caleb stood outside the open gates of the Port of Los Angeles, once upon a time billed as the busiest in the US, but its glory days were a thing of the past. Austin gazed out over the vast sea of containers. Thousands of cargo containers held goods that would never leave the port would never reach the intended destination. All those items were slowly deteriorating. All those things people couldn't live without.

Caleb took Austin's hand and led him through the gates. They walked by an abandoned truck. The driver's door hung at a forty-five-degree angle, clinging to the truck by one hinge. Inside, the driver lay slumped over the steering wheel facing the door. The expression on the man's face, still apparent after all this time, caused Austin to pause. The man might have been in his forties. A silver wedding band hung on his finger.

They came across a few more corpses, all in a similar pose, caught in their last breathing moments. Upon reaching the containers Austin followed Caleb through the maze of metal boxes. The port was the size of a small town and they walked near one hundred yards before reaching the end of a row. Parked here, where the port met the ocean, was an industrial size crane. Dangling from the end of a cable attached to the crane was a blue cargo container. Each time the breeze stirred, the metal moaned, echoing its lonesome sound throughout the port. The doors of the container had come open, spilling its contents on the ground below.

Austin picked up one of the boxes that had tumbled away from the pile. Inside were several smaller plastic boxes that held self-tapping metal screws, one hundred per box, good for use in brittle material. Austin tossed the box back toward the pile. At one time the world needed such things. He looked around for Caleb and found him a good twenty yards ahead waiting for him in front of a yellow container.

"This is the container." Caleb said.

"This container? Ryan's inside this container?"

"No."

Caleb didn't explain with words but opened the container doors using his mind. Austin braced, expecting the worst, but the container was empty. Caleb walked inside to the back where he waited for Austin to join him. Austin wasn't surprised his son could see in the dark. There probably wasn't much his son couldn't do, an odd sense of pride washed over Austin, which struck him as almost humorous. He imagined comparing his boy to other children, bragging about him to other dads.

"Ok. What are we doing in here?" Austin asked.

"When I open the door, you will see a portal--."

"A portal?"

"Yes, father. The portal will take us to a where some of the children are being kept. Once we arrive we must hurry. You can't talk. And try to think about something else, other than what you're looking at. If we are very careful they won't hear us."

"Who is *they*?"

"The Svan."

Caleb placed his hands on the container wall and pressed. The wall slid open revealing a portal, different than the one in Cheyenne in shape, but having the same murky center. Caleb pulled Austin through the center. On the other side they arrived in a stark white room, so brilliantly bright Austin had to blink several times before his eyes adjusted. Upon focusing he was able to take in the magnificent and horrid scene before him. A scene of make-believe so remarkable it strained acceptance. A marvel of technology, of human preservation, of something so macabre it fascinated and repelled the mind. Thousands of coffin-sized rectangle boxes stood upright lining the walls of a cavernous room that went on forever. The pods appeared to be made of a thick white colored metal. On the front of each, a pane of glass giving a view to the inside. And what Austin saw behind each pane made his stomach turn. He stared at the children's faces, captivated by a sick fascination.

Austin reached out to touch one, but Caleb grabbed his arm and shook his head, reminding him they needed to be quick about their task. He followed his son past the silent faces of hundreds of children. Their eyes were closed and for this Austin was thankful. About halfway down Caleb stopped in front of a pod and motioned to Austin that this was the one. Caleb tapped a number sequence into the keypad positioned below the glass and then stepped back. The case filled with a white vapor. After a couple of minutes, the locking mechanisms engaged, and the door swung open with a pop and a hiss. Austin stepped forward to catch the occupant from falling out onto the ground. Austin held the boy his arms and recognized Ed's son Ryan from the pictures he'd seen.

"You'll have to carry him," Caleb whispered in his father's ear. He shut the case and tapped in a different sequence of numbers. Following this, the interior went dark and a solid metal blind covered the window. If they were lucky, the Svan would not notice one more child had died. But Austin noticed, and as they rushed back to the portal, he noticed several cases with closed windows. He didn't need Caleb to tell him what that meant.

They entered the portal, exiting on the other side through the container and into the dim light of a fading day. Austin glanced down at Ryan, but his eyes remained closed. He hoped the boy stayed in his current state of unconsciousness until they returned safely to the bunker. Caleb closed the container doors and they continued on down the row back to where they initially dropped in. If they wanted to stand a chance of moving undetected it was necessary to start and stop from the same place. This created the least amount of disturbance in the space continuum and would attract little or no attention. Having no knowledge of how space or time travel worked, Austin didn't over think this but did as instructed.

"Will he survive the trip?" Austin asked.

Caleb touched Ryan's head with his fingertip, holding it there for a few seconds. "He will live, but we must hurry."

Austin wrapped his arms around Ryan while Caleb took hold of his father's hand. "Ready?"

"Ready."

Caleb squeezed tight and they vanished into the air, returning to Austin's suite in the bunker. Austin laid Ryan down on the couch, checked that he was still breathing and went to call Zack. He returned seconds later unable to contact Zack.

"I can't reach Zack."

"He's in the recreation room."

"How'd...never mind. I'll be back. Stay here with Ryan. Ok?"

"Yes, father." Caleb didn't try to stop his father from rushing out of the suite. Humans seldom spent the appropriate time thinking things through, they were always in a hurry. If his father had paused in his thoughts, he could have found Zack on his own. If he had paused to assess the situation, he would have considered his own abilities or that of his son's, but he hadn't.

Caleb knelt by Ryan's side and placed a hand on Ryan's head and chest. He'd experimented on the animals on Paru and knew he had the power to regenerate smaller life forms, but Ryan was not a small animal. It wasn't that being human mattered, but Caleb's strength, his power, mattered. It mattered a whole lot, but he couldn't worry about that right now. Time wasn't the boy's friend and he wasn't sure when his mother would return. With his mind made up, Caleb closed his eyes and focused. As when Eve applied her energy to regenerate Jenny's cells, Caleb performed the same process on Ryan.

A few moments later Austin and Zack were hurrying down the hallway, stopping when they saw the bright glow of light shooting out from every crack and crevice around the door.

"Is Eve back?" Zack asked, stopping short from standing in front of the door.

Austin didn't sense that Eve was back. "Caleb," he said almost too soft for Zack to hear him.

"Your son?"

Austin gave Zack a cautious look. "Yes."

The emanating light retreated from the door. The men listened and were shocked to hear voices, children's voices. Austin grabbed the knob, which turned under his hand and Caleb opened the door.

"Come in father, Mr. Zack." Caleb swung the door open. "Ryan's doing very well."

Ryan sat on the couch looking a bit disoriented, but very much alive. His eyes were human and his cheeks rosy.

Zack walked over to him and knelt down eye level with the boy. "Hey Ryan. How ya doin' buddy?"

Ryan rubbed his eyes, maybe thinking Zack wasn't real, that none of this was real. "It feels like ants are crawlin' on me." He rubbed his arms, looking at his skin to confirm he didn't have ants. "You don't suppose cancer termites are eating my bones do you?"

Zack and Austin exchanged a confused glance. "No cancer termites buddy," Zack said

"The healing will continue for a couple of hours," Caleb informed them. "He will feel various sensations as his body fully acclimates to the change."

Zack glanced back at Caleb and then up at Austin. Who was this kid? What was this kid?

"Eve's son. Our son," Austin replied.

Comprehension dawned on Zack's face. His mind began to wander down the path of the boy's mother and vampires. "Do you know your name?" Zack asked Ryan, cutting off his thoughts before they got him into trouble.

Ryan stared at Zack and then replied, "My name's Ryan McGrath. I live in Plainfield, Illinois."

"How old are you Ryan?"

"I'm eight."

Ed had told them he was seven when he'd been taken. That Ryan knew a year had gone by brought more unanswered questions and raised the moral dilemma bar a bit higher.

"Where's my mom and dad?" He peeked over Zack's shoulder at Austin and Caleb. "Are they ok?"

"They're fine Ryan and they're here. Would you like to see them?" Austin asked.

"Yes. I'm sure they've been very worried about me."

"I'll go get them," Zack said.

Austin walked with him to the door.

"What should I tell them?" Zack asked.

"Tell them the truth. Best they know before walking in here."

"Right, that should be easy. Be back in a few."

Austin closed the door behind Zack but held onto the knob for a long time afterward, thinking too many things at once to focus on any one thing. *Ryan had memories*, kept circling around in his mind. The implications of this fact ran deep and wide.

"May I have something to drink please?" Ryan asked.

Austin snapped out of his trance. "Sure thing." He grabbed up the whiskey bottle, noticing for the first time it was still on the table, and went to the kitchenette. "Water? Juice?"

"Do you have Coke?"

Austin scrounged around in the fridge. "No Coke. How about Berry-Ade?" He held up a bottle of purplish-blue liquid.

Ryan smiled and nodded his head.

Austin sat next to Ryan and poured the purple-blue drink into a glass. He set the bottle down. "Is it ok if he drinks this?" He looked to his son, noticing his skin had become pale and clammy.

"Yes. His body has recovered enough to process the liquid chemicals," Caleb answered.

Austin handed the glass to Ryan. The contents did look a bit like something you'd find at the local auto supply store. "Are you ok Caleb?"

Caleb nodded. "A little tired is all."

"Can I get you anything?" Austin was thinking about what Eve had needed after saving Madison's baby. Did his son also require human blood?

"No. I'm fine father," Caleb replied.

Ryan drank the contents and asked for more. Austin poured him another glass which the boy swallowed in two gulps. He set down the glass and covered his mouth before letting out a loud belch, followed by another.

"Sorry," Ryan said, embarrassed.

Austin laughed. "That's ok Ryan. Gotta let that air out." He patted him on the back, inducing another round of belching.

They were still laughing when Zack opened the door.

Ed and Jenny stood inside the doorway wide eyed, mouths open, for a moment doubting the image before them.

"Mom! Dad!" Ryan jumped off the couch.

They met in the middle of the room. Ed fell to his knees before Ryan. He touched his face, his arms, and his hair. He was there in the flesh, warm and alive. Jenny knelt with them, tears streaming down her face.

"Ryan honey." She hugged him tight, kissing his face, the top of his head. "Oh, sweetie I've missed you."

Ed turned to Austin. "How? How'd you find him?"

"It's a long story Ed. We'll talk later. Why don't you two take Ryan to the Diner? I think he might be hungry."

"I'm starving," Ryan confirmed, and his parents laughed through their tears.

"May I go with them?" Caleb asked.

"Sure," Austin replied, paying closer attention to Caleb. "You ok?"

"Just hungry." He flashed his father a smile.

Austin raised an eyebrow. He knew that charm worked on the girls, but he wasn't fooled by it. "You'll come back as soon as you're finished?"

"I'll make sure he gets back," Ed replied.

Ed picked Ryan up in his arms and carried him out the door followed closely by Jenny. "I can't believe you're here." They heard Ed say before the door closed behind him.

22 NOWHERE TO HIDE

Austin had Zack call Luke and Kyle. He wanted to meet with them here in his suite. It was time they discussed the future, their future. The news about Europe and the rest of the world wasn't going to be easy to hear. While waiting, he told Zack about his journey to find Ryan. He described where the children were kept, an incredible scene he still found hard to believe himself. Zack asked the obvious question about saving more.

Austin shook his head. "Caleb can't save them all. It was a risk just in taking Ryan. If we took more the Svan would be alerted."

"How did he do that? How did Eve, you know save my daughter? How do they do that?"

"Transfer of energy or harnessing energy. I'm not sure exactly, but that's the best way I know how to explain it. I know it takes a lot out of them. Eve near fainted afterwards, and Caleb wasn't looking too great."

"So... this is a conversation I never thought I'd be having," Zack said and cleared his throat, "Your son...he's...what is he?"

"He's human and Adita. I guess you can say he's a new species," Austin answered, knowing he shouldn't say anything, but wanted Zack to understand, to not think Caleb was a freak. "The Adita thought they could start a new superior race of beings."

"But?"

"But I don't know. Agra doesn't seem happy with the results. He wanted a superior being, and Caleb is that--"

"But aren't they already superior beings?"

"Only to humans and only if you consider a diet of blood superior."

"Only to humans," Zack repeated in deliberate fashion, letting the words simmer a bit.

"Think about it, Zack. We can live on a variety of things. Meat, vegetables, fish. They have one choice. If oranges were the only thing you could survive on wouldn't you do everything in your power to preserve those trees?"

"Yes, but we aren't fruit."

"We are to the Adita." *A crop to be cultivated and then harvested*, he finished silently.

"You sound like an advocate for their plight to conquer and destroy."

"They don't want to destroy us."

Zack nodded. "My friend I do believe you're correct. However, they don't want to preserve our way of life either. I'm afraid what they want is heck of lot worse than anything we want to envision."

Austin held his tongue. He couldn't argue for or against without giving away he knew everything. Despite not knowing the facts, Zack's assumptions were right on target. Their options were not inviting. Dead, the preferable option, or vacuum sealed for eternity while having your blood cleansed for the harvest of the next generation Adita. It was on the tip of his tongue to share with Zack all that Eve had told him, but he'd promised.

"Does Caleb... is he like Eve? I mean what does he eat? Ah, I mean..."

"He doesn't desire human blood if that's what you're driving at. He doesn't need it to survive like Eve does," Austin replied.

"And what about you man? What are you? I mean I've seen your blood cells and they are pretty fucking out there. Like the incredible Hulk or something. Crazy super cells on a crazy super train. Superman cells--"

Austin cleared his throat, stopping Zack from rambling on. "I'm, well I'm a new improved version of myself, but still fully human."

Zack pursed his lips and shook his head at the irony of that statement, new and improved, as if Austin needed improvement. "And telepathy comes along with being new and improved?"

Austin wasn't so self-assured to not be embarrassed. "Hey man if it helps any, I don't hear everything clearly, sometimes it's more seeing than hearing and I can block stuff," he said, going to the door. "They're here." He waited until Luke knocked before opening.

Luke walked in, suspicion in his eyes and thoughts, but he held back any biting comments. Kyle came in a few minutes later and Austin couldn't help staring at him. This was his brother. They looked nothing alike, Kyle favored their mother, yet Austin saw the resemblance clear as day. Given time he felt certain the others would pick up on the similarities. Madison would have noticed for certain.

"So why are we here?" Luke asked.

Austin turned his attention on the group, settling his eyes on Kyle. "The Adita have resumed their course of reclaiming the planet. The Svan moved into Europe a few days ago. Only a handful of people were left behind. Same as here."

"Are you sure?" Kyle asked, his voice unsteady, his expression of someone about to throw up.

"I'm sure." Austin went over to Kyle and placed his arm around his shoulder. "I'm really sorry."

"What does that mean for us?" Luke asked.

"I don't know." Austin sighed.

The group sat quiet and solemn, facing the fact of having no way out. Before, when they'd believed the entire world had perished at the same time, the situation had been tolerable. Discovering life had gone on in other places gave them new hope, a new breath of life, but then as hope went, it was snatched away from them. Your best friend and your worst enemy. Ed could have attested to that had he been present to attest. He'd been on and off the hope wagon, more times than a Hollywood star checked in and out of rehab.

Looking around the room, Austin knew the fall of Europe had slapped them in the face and hard. The sort of slap that left marks and turned an ugly yellow before fading away. It meant admitting the Svan were unstoppable. It meant admitting defeat. This was something Austin could not accept. Everything had a weakness, even the Svan and the Adita had a weakness. For the Adita their strength was also their weakness. The very liquid that made them invincible could also bring them to their knees.

The Svan were another beast all together. They were carnivores and intelligent. Austin almost preferred them as an enemy over the Adita. That they could not see through aluminum hardly counted as a game changer or an advantage. This had been something Austin had wanted to ask Eve about, but other things had been on his mind. He had a fleeting thought for her safety but brushed the concern away. Agra needed her as much as they needed him and Caleb. He wouldn't hurt his own daughter.

"Why Earth?" Luke asked, breaking the silence.

"It's their home," Austin answered, leaving out that they had a right to reclaim their home. No one would understand, or care, and Austin didn't have answers for the questions that would follow such a statement.

"We should fight them," Luke said suddenly.

"How? We have no way of defeating them," Zack argued.

"I don't care. I would rather die fighting then live in this fantasy world ya'll have created down here. Christmas shopping. Are you fucking serious? Madison's dead because everyone wanted to pretend that we aren't fucked."

"Shut up Luke," Zack said, standing up, an expression crossing his face Austin had never seen. A look the kids in Boston had known well and feared.

"I won't shut up and I won't lie." Luke ignored Zack's glare.

"Luke that's enough." Austin stepped over to him taking his arm. "Please."

"You should tell him," Luke insisted.

"Tell me what?" Zack asked, growing more concerned by what they weren't saying.

"Damn it, man," Austin said.

"Damn it nothing. What don't I know?" Zack demanded.

His words hung heavy in the room

"I'm sorry Zack. I should have told you, but you were... I didn't want to upset you more than you already were."

"Well tell me now then. Tell for fuck sake."

"The baby's DNA was altered," Austin replied.

"Altered? What the fuck does that mean? Is she my kid or not?"

"Yes. Calm down." Austin threw Luke a look. This could have been handled in a better way at another time. "

"Calm down? What does that mean? Will she be human? Will she be an Adita? One of them?" Panic arose in his voice.

"It's not like that," Austin replied. "She'll be human. She'll be a better human. That's all. Eve altered her DNA during the transfer in order to ensure her survival. In order to ensure she was born as fit as possible, but she is still very much your child."

"Better how? In what ways better?" Zack asked, taking his anxiety down a notch, trying to see the benefit in this.

"Stronger, smarter, faster. I don't know for sure, but she'll be better in a good way." Austin wished he had more to tell him.

Zack examined Austin's face, unsure what to say or think. DNA and how it worked wasn't an unfamiliar topic. They'd studied DNA sequencing in one of his advanced courses, so he knew the lingo, understood the concept, but that was as far as it went. The nuts and bolts of DNA testing wasn't something Zack had pursued or took an interest in but was thinking he'd do some research and learn more about it.

"Couldn't Eve do that for all of us? Make us all stronger? Give us somewhat of an advantage?" Luke asked.

Austin shook his head. It was legitimate to ask, but not as simple as he imagined. "I don't know if she can."

"Why not?" Luke demanded. "The bloodsucker could if she wanted to."

"Luke, man, take it easy," Zack warned, seeing Austin's jaw stiffen.

"She would if it was possible," Austin replied, keeping his cool and giving Zack a warning look to not say anything more. His relationship with Eve was not something Luke was ready to hear about.

"That's not the answer anyway," Zack said. "Unless we become an Adita, we'll never be strong enough to fight them and even then, who knows. And I don't know about anyone else, but I like being human. So, we have to figure out another way."

Luke protested with a grunt but said no more.

"I'm going back to Germany," Kyle announced, rejoining the conversation. "If people survived, if there are even a few, maybe Will and Ada..." His voice trailed off.

"I'll go with you," Austin said, surprising everyone.

"So am I," Luke said, his tone daring anyone to say otherwise.

"I can't ask you to do that," Kyle said.

"You're not asking. We're volunteering," Austin replied. "We know the Svan better than you. And it's never a bad idea to have someone watching your back."

"How will you get there? The same way Kyle came?" Zack asked.

"We could fly," Luke offered.

"Let me handle that part." Austin replied.

Kyle felt somewhat comforted by the knowledge he was at least going to make an effort to find out if Will and Ada were alive. Trying was the least he could do after all they'd done for him. They deserved that effort and he wasn't going without any hope. Various underground places were scattered about the country and he knew of one stockpiled full of provisions. He knew this because shortly after the US did its disappearing act, he'd gotten busy stashing necessities.

"I know a place they may be hiding. Under Wetterstein Mountains," Kyle said. "There're a series of tunnels. One of those leads to a secret facility built by the German government. Kind of like the Section Seven you mentioned in Cheyenne. It's self-sufficient, has a medical facility, a small grow center, everything you need to survive. The German's used it during WWII for testing biological pathogens."

"Sounds charming. Like a basket full of rattle snakes," Zack commented.

"The Germans weren't the only ones." Kyle replied to which Zack nodded in agreement. "Anyway, the place was converted to a science lab for petrology about fifteen years ago," Kyle continued, "but they closed it down a few years back. I guess no one was all that interested in rocks. Prior to closing they spent a mint upgrading the place with state-of-the-art equipment until the funds ran dry. Will told me about it. I guess at one time they thought there might be evidence in those rocks of early civilizations, maybe even aliens on Earth." Kyle half smiled at the irony of it all. "I don't guess they ever found any."

"Had you been there recently?" Austin asked

"When the cloud of confusion rolled over the US, I started stockpiling supplies. No one traveled anywhere. Everyone stuck close to their homes. No one wanted to get caught outside when the clouds came storming in, so I knew my things would be safe."

"Do many people know about it?" Zack asked.

"Nah. Those who used to work there are most likely dead. And like I said, rocks weren't high on anyone's list of things to learn."

"Maybe your friends went there," Zack said.

"Maybe. But it's a two-hour drive from Cologne." Kyle sighed. "They could have made it if they were watching the radar, but Will wouldn't have left people behind to save himself."

"Maybe he sent Ada and some others to the mountain." Zack offered trying to sound positive if only to ease the pain and uncertainty he knew Kyle was dealing with.

Everyone wanted to be positive but hidden behind their good intentions was the truth of the situation. Keep hope alive meant little, if it meant anything anymore. They'd already survived the purge and the drop and General Roth. The Svan were brutal in their attacks, non- discriminate in choosing who lived, who died. Rhyme, reason or natural selection hadn't been deciding factors. Death, and lots of it, ruled the day. Kyle was the fortunate one. He wasn't alone in his grief and misery, wandering aimlessly about hoping he wasn't the last human alive.

Each one in that room had faced the ultimate challenge and came out the victor in the game of survival. No easy feat for even the strongest of souls. This game came with all sorts of options and no rules. It required skill, luck and something most did not possess on a good day. It required true grit. It was putting the gun barrel in your mouth and not pulling the trigger. It was sitting in the bathtub with a sharpened razor in one hand and a bottle of Jack in the other and not slicing open your veins. It was pouring your fifth cocktail and not using it to wash down a handful of sleeping pills. It was not listening to the devil's call for surrender. Each one had battled the ultimate demon and decided life was still worth living, but no one shared those tales of woe. Rather they offered Kyle false hope, knowing he would figure it out eventually, but at least he wasn't doing it alone.

"I need some fresh air," Kyle stood up. "Is it safe to go outside?"

Austin checked his watch. "Two hours left till dark. Mind if I join you?"

"Suit yourself," Kyle replied, although he would have preferred being alone in his misery and grief.

"I don't talk much," Austin offered.

Kyle smiled. "Neither do I." He held the door open for Austin.

As Zack watched them go a random thought occurred to him, one he quickly, but not completely, dismissed. Anything was possible. If it had teeth, it would nibble at him later. The important stuff always nibbled and sometimes bit hard, usually at three in the morning. A popular time to bite into those ideas that hadn't warranted the proper amount of attention during the day.

Zack got up with Luke trailing behind, quiet and uncommunicative. Zack noticed and worried but left him alone. He'd tried finding him after Austin left with

Caleb, but couldn't and, upon deciding this was intentional, he'd stopped searching. They parted ways at Luke's suite. Zack went on, but not to his suite, instead he went to Madison's, where he'd spent the past week drowning his sorrows. It was time to figure things out. To come to terms with life's latest blow. Time was short, and Austin was right, his daughter was going to need him. A thought occurred to him and he laughed out loud. He wished his mother was there with him, to know he was going to have to deal with raising a child genius. And he knew what a pain in the ass he'd been. Ah the poetic justice of it all.

* * *

Austin and Kyle stood inside the open barn door looking out over the frozen landscape. Kyle took a swig from the bottle he'd grabbed from his suite on their way up. Austin declined his brother's invitation to join him; having tasted whiskey once was all he needed. Watching Kyle chug the liquor like it was water reminded him of dear old dad.

Ole Donny would toss back his first bottle in under a half an hour. 'Just getting' warmed up,' he'd say before cracking the cap on a second. Austin could judge the evening's outcome by how many bottles the old man had before teetering off to the local, and only, watering hole in the wall. Where they served non-alcoholic beverages. Wink. Wink. And the town's one and only trooper was a regular.

On a good week, when the old man held onto a paycheck, he'd stock up. Not on anything quality like Southern Comfort or Jack Daniels or Crown, not for Donny, he was strictly bottom shelf. If Austin was lucky, stocking up might include a pack of bologna or some of those red hotdogs from the gas station, but never bread or buns. Those were extras and a boy shouldn't expect to eat like a fucking prince when the king of the castle needed to stock up. No, if Austin wanted bread, he had to find it himself. This usually meant a trip to the dumpster behind Kwiki Pete's gas station.

All that changed when Eve came into his life. She'd made sure he never went hungry. Austin often wondered how she'd managed her hunger while living in Deadbear. The community was too small and tight knit for people to go missing for long and often. The occasional drifter wandered through, lost or running from the law. Those sorts wouldn't have missed. Maybe that was how she'd survived.

"How's Grace doing?" Austin asked to take his mind off things he'd rather not think about and Kyle's mind off returning to Germany. They were going to find death and probably nothing more.

"Really good. I mean, considering the circumstances." Kyle's hand gripped the bottle tighter.

"She'll be ok," Austin assured him.

"I hope so."

"Has she picked out a name yet?"

"Gisela or Emil."

It was Austin's turn to feel like he'd been punched in the stomach. Gisela was his mother's name. Austin closed his mind to Kyle's thoughts. It would have been too easy to listen in on the memories Kyle had of his family and growing up. It would have been easy, but it would have been painful. Austin didn't need to spy to know his brother had lived a better life than he had, and most certainly never dug through a dumpster looking for food.

"You were the one who killed Roth?"

"Huh?"

"Grace said you killed General Roth."

"Yeah. Shot him in the head," Austin replied, unapologetic.

"Thank you. You know for saving her. She's all the family I got left." Kyle choked on his words.

"You're welcome," Austin replied, having trouble himself getting the words out over the lump in his throat. The pain Kyle's statement caused squeezed his heart to the breaking point. Kyle was suffering himself and it would have been so easy to tell him, to say, 'Hey, guess what man? We're brothers', but Austin refused to give in to self-pity or selfish desires. Kyle and Grace's safety had to come first.

"So, you were a Marine?" Kyle asked.

"Still am."

"Ed let me borrow that book, Africa Rising. Pretty impressive."

Austin groaned. He was going to have a talk with Ed about all this sharing. It was embarrassing to say the least and the most. Austin never would have agreed to do the story if his teammates hadn't insisted. And the photo was never supposed to make it into the book. It had compromised his safety and that of his team. He remembered sitting at the kitchen table holding the book, groaning over that picture. Roxanne had sat on his lap, kissed his cheek and told him not to worry.

"No one can touch you. I won't let them."

That's what she'd said. *I won't let them.* He didn't think anything of it back then. She was his wife and being protective, was saying things a wife is supposed to say. How many other instances had he missed for not paying attention to his wife? He had a hunch there had been many.

"That was a long time ago," Austin remarked to himself as much as to Kyle.

"Still impressive."

"What about you? What were you doing before you went to Germany?" Austin asked, eager to change the subject.

Kyle smiled. It was a bitter sweet smile. They'd been living right here in Colorado for about a year when he'd decided to join the Army. He wasn't cut out for college and couldn't go on living off his mother.

"What about your father?" Austin asked.

"He died in a plane crash when I was five," Kyle replied. "One of those small two prop jobs. They never found his body."

"And your mom?" Austin asked, unable to resist hearing about her.

"My mom," Kyle paused. "My mom was great. She had this way about her that always let you know where you stood. She never sugar-coated things, but you knew she loved you. Anyway, right before I left for Germany she was diagnosed with cancer. I wasn't going to go, but she insisted. Grace said she died in Cheyenne."

Austin felt guilt upon hearing this, upon finding out Kyle's life hadn't been picture perfect and because he felt a small sense of joy or relief that his mother had suffered some. It was a jackass thing to feel and think, but it was there, and Austin wasn't one to apologize for having honest feelings.

"What about you?" Kyle was asking.

"Me?"

"Yeah. What about your mom?"

"She split right before my fifth birthday. Never heard from her again." The words sounded as bitter as they tasted.

"Ah man, sorry to hear that."

"Doesn't matter anymore." Austin replied and, until meeting Kyle, this had been true.

"No, I guess it doesn't."

The two men stood inside the barn door, the younger leaning against the jamb, the older standing arms crossed, both staring out at the blank white landscape. Kyle hit the bottle, taking a long draw this time. He'd hit the halfway mark but felt no number than when he'd first opened the bottle and asked himself why he kept trying. No amount of alcohol would make this thing any easier.

He glanced at Austin, curious at what made him tick. He knew guys like him back in Cologne. Rock solid no matter what kind of shit salad they got tossed into. Loyal and honest to a fault. Although, Kyle couldn't help thinking something about Austin was different, almost supernatural. A mental image of Austin with a large S on his chest and a red cape billowing out behind him came to mind. Yet that didn't quite fit. Superman was clean cut, wholesome. Austin was dark, maybe even a bit menacing, more like Batman or The Hulk.

Austin found his brother's ponderings amusing, having never considered himself a superhero of any kind. "We best get inside. The Svan will be patrolling soon." Austin grabbed the handle on the barn door. The smaller suns had faded into the gray. Soon blackness would fall heavy on the land. The night still belonged to the

Svan. Austin often heard them. They usually patrolled in pairs, out looking for stragglers, out protecting the land. Humans had nowhere left to hide, their home no longer belonged to them.

23 BROTHERS

A musical mobile spun small brown bears dressed in pink satin tutu's and pink satin ballet slippers above a sleeping baby Gisela, who was now a week old. The happy little tune plinked away as she slept unaware of the world she'd been born into. Next to her in separate cribs Anne's twin girls, Valerie and Kathryn, also slept.

Kyle stood looking down at his niece feeling elated, yet incredibly sad and scared. Grace had gone into labor two weeks early thus postponing their trip to Germany. Looking at Gisela, Kyle couldn't fathom leaving her behind, unprotected. Having gone through the agony of losing his family once already he didn't want to do it again. But, and this was a big but, Will and Ada might be alive. How could he turn his back on them? In either case, whatever he decided to do, he would feel like he'd abandoned those he cared about most.

The door to the nursery opened. "Can I come in?" Austin asked in a hushed voice.

Kyle waved him in. Austin walked over to the bassinette and took a long gaze at his niece. It was already evident she would have dark hair and a darker complexion than Grace and Kyle. He wasn't sure if that came from the Reynolds' side or from the baby's father who had similar features. Not that it mattered. He loved her all the same and again questioned his decision on not telling Kyle they were brothers. Austin tapped Kyle's arm and motioned for him to come out into the hall. Kyle nodded and followed Austin to the door, looking back one last time before leaving.

"What's up big man?"

Big man, big brother. It would be so easy. Austin rubbed his face and sighed. "I wanted to talk to you about Germany."

Kyle's face fell a little. "Yeah I know. Time is running out. We need to get going, I know. It's so hard to leave her behind." He tilted his head toward the door.

"Which is why I'm going without you," Austin said. "Luke and I are leaving in the morning, but I need a little more information about the facility where the science lab is located."

"Aw man. I can't let you do that. It's not your responsibility," Kyle argued although his heart wasn't in it.

"It's ok Kyle. I understand how you feel," Austin assured him. "You'll be distracted the entire time and that's a quick and easy way to get killed. Luke and I got this. It'll be good for Luke anyway."

"Is he ok. I mean can you trust him to have your back?" Kyle worried about Luke's mental state more than he did his own.

"He's fine. A little stir crazed from being cooped up down here, but that's all. Madison's death was really hard on him." Austin let it go at that, knowing Luke's issues ran much deeper. Taking him along to Germany was more to get him away from the bunker than Austin needing someone to watch his back. He had Eve to look out for him. Or at least he hoped so. She'd been gone two weeks now and he was beginning to worry. Caleb assured him she was fine and would be back soon. Austin had no reason to doubt his son, but all the same couldn't shake the nagging feeling something was wrong.

Kyle accepted Austin's offer, thankful to have that burden off his shoulders. "I owe you big time."

"No, you don't," Austin assured him. "You'd do the same for me."

Kyle nodded in agreement. He was glad it was Austin going and hoped he had success. He hadn't known him long, but he liked and trusted him, as if they'd been close friends, even like brothers.

Austin turned his head to hide a smile in hearing Kyle's thoughts. Maybe one day when all of this was over, he would tell him and Grace the truth. Maybe one day they could live as a family. His smile faltered as he pictured this. No point in daydreaming about a life he would most likely never have. The future was impossible to guess but didn't seem to promise good things.

They went to the command center, where Luke joined them to discuss details of the trip. It was the first time Austin saw a light in Luke's eyes and an uptick in his mood. Maybe he was doing the right thing by taking him along.

* * *

The next morning around four o'clock Luke and Austin, along with Caleb and Zack, met again in the command center. Zack was the only person who knew they were leaving. Austin didn't want a big send off. The less witnesses the better.

The plan was to leave at 5:30 am, putting them in Cologne around 2:30 pm. They had no idea if a time differential still existed around the planet, or if everyone was now on the same day and night pattern controlled by the Adita. Arriving in the middle of the afternoon seemed like the best way to go at it.

The plan was to search for Will and Ada in Cologne first. The question of other survivors had come up, and after a long tense discussion they agreed to only bring Will and Ada back to the bunker. Ed had argued they were picking and choosing lives. Austin stood his ground. The bunker was a safe place where they all got along, but every person they brought into their group threatened that balance. In the end Ed went along with the plan, although it left a sick feeling in his stomach.

Austin assured him they would help anyone they found. They would teach them how to survive, to avoid the Svan. Chances were if they survived the purge, the Svan didn't want them, but they wouldn't hesitate to kill them either.

"So how are we getting there?" Luke asked.

"Through space."

Luke groaned. "God that hurts. And how? Eve?"

"No."

"Then who?"

"Me," Caleb answered.

Luke turned at the sound of Caleb's voice, having forgotten the boy was present. He looked back to Austin. "You sure about this man?"

"I'm perfectly capable of transporting you both," Caleb answered.

"It's fine Luke. He can handle more than you and I put together," Austin added. "And we'll need him to help us find Kyle's friends."

Luke's expression said loud and clear he had his doubts, but he said no more. The boy was better than the mother.

Austin checked his watch. It was time to go. They donned backpacks and weapons.

"I feel like I'm always sayin' goodbye to you or be careful or some shit. Like I'm your wife or something," Zack joked.

"We'll be back man. Walk in the park," Austin replied and believed it. "You take care of everyone. Don't take any chances. Don't let anyone else down here."

"Yeah, I won't."

Zack held out his hand to Austin, who surprised him by grabbing Zack into a bear hug.

"See you soon," Austin laughed.

Austin and Luke joined hands with Caleb. The air around them swirled, shimmered and they vanished from the room. Zack shook his head. He still couldn't get used to the whole space travel thing and often felt he was living out some drug induced fantasy. Or maybe he'd ended up in a mental institution where he was catatonic around the clock and this was his mind's way of dealing with shit. Zack pondered various scenarios as he took his usual walk around the bunker checking that everything was in working order.

Along the way a random thought stopped him. What if he had killed the ole man like he planned, and his mind had slipped down the rabbit hole? Zack shook his head. No way. He wouldn't lose it over that douche bag. Over his mom yeah. Colin definitely, but not the old bastard. Certain he wasn't insane, Zack opened the door to his suite, and closed it. Since Madison's death, being alone wasn't something he looked forward to anymore. Maybe Jenny would be up soon.

Thoughts of his daughter helped temper the grief and many hours went by thinking about her. He'd already decided to name her Madison and hoped for her sake she looked like her mother rather than him. If he'd known Eve was going to do her voodoo on the baby's genetics, he would have requested this in advance. Considering the possibilities of what changing her DNA might offer, was as nerve racking as it was exciting. What their scientists could have come up with if they had that capability. A super human race?

Zack paused. But wasn't Agra after that very thing? A superior race of Adita? Although their methods to achieve this were not favorable to man, he couldn't in all honesty fault them. If humans could have altered DNA, they would have used questionable and even unscrupulous methods to accomplish the task. The government would have stepped in and fucked it all up anyway. With this thought and many others tossing about, Zack opened the door to the diner and was surprised to find Charlie sitting at the counter sipping on a cup of coffee.

Charlie spun around looking like a deer caught in headlights. "Zack!"

"Sorry, didn't mean to startle you."

She laughed, sounding nervous and insecure. "I was zoned out, you know, thinking about stuff." Charlie turned back to the counter and set her cup down. She didn't know why, but she always felt like an idiot around Zack and wished Colin hadn't told her about him being a genius.

Zack walked around the counter and poured a cup of coffee. He topped Charlie's off. "You're up early."

"I couldn't sleep." She sipped on her coffee, avoiding looking directly at Zack. "Do you have anything I can take? You know to help me sleep?"

Zack frowned. "What's wrong Charlie?"

About to raise her mug again, she paused mid-way and lowered it back to the counter. She clasped her hands together to keep them from shaking.

"You can talk to me Charlie. I'm good at keeping secrets." He reached out to her but stopped short of touching her hand.

A tear fell on the counter. She wiped her face, angry at herself for crying. Angry at herself for not being strong, like the other girls. They'd all suffered at the hands of her father. They'd all suffered, but for her the ordeal had been different.

Zack waited and watched while Charlie fought her silent battle for control, handing her a napkin to blow her nose.

"Is it Colin? Cuz I'll thump the little twerp if he's treating you badly," Zack offered in a joking manner, all the while hoping it wasn't Colin causing her problems.

Charlie shook her head and couldn't hold back a tiny smile. The Londergan brothers, when they were together, always made her laugh. Aaron would have liked them. Thinking of her brother took away her joy and the tears threatened again.

Zack reached out, this time taking her hand. "Life ain't easy Charlie, trust me I know."

Charlie raised her head. "I'm sorry about Madison. I know you miss her. I still miss my brother."

"Yeah, it hurts like hell. Makes me want to beat the crap out of something. Won't bring her back, but sure would make me feel a hell of lot better."

A full smile graced Charlie's face. "Don't you have a punching bag somewhere?"

"You know what? I don't. I'll have to put that on my shopping list." He pretended to look for paper and pen. "A punching bag. Perfect."

"You're funny."

"A real clown, right?"

"No. You make me laugh. Let's me forget about...about the past. About my father." She sobered on this comment. Just saying it out loud caused a panicky feeling deep in the pit of her stomach. Her father was why she couldn't sleep, why she was afraid to close her eyes. Chase, the beatings, the other men, these she could forget, but not her father. Those memories were embedded too deep.

Zack watched the emotions play out on her face and knew the damage was caused by something more than they had imagined. His stomach turned at the thought. "You want to know something I've never told anyone?" Zack asked. Charlie turned to him, nodding. "I was going to kill my old man. Yep. When I was seventeen, I planned to blast him with his own shotgun, but someone beat me to it. And you know what? I was pissed off that I didn't get the chance. I wanted to kill him so bad, it was all I thought about. And then he was dead. When I saw him there, in his coffin, I wanted to punch him in the face. Instead I stole his ring." Zack pulled a chain out from under his shirt. A ruby pinky ring hung from the chain. "The mob gave him this after he became a *made* guy. He prized this ring over everything." Zack took the chain off. "Here, you wear this. I don't need it anymore." He placed the chain over Charlie's head. "He can't ever hurt you again Charlie. You remember that ok?"

Charlie held the ring in her hand rolling it around watching the ruby sparkle in the light. "Thank you, Zack."

Zack came around the counter. "One day you'll be able to take it off. I promise." He hugged Charlie, shocked to feel she was not much more than skin and bones. "Is my cooking that bad?"

Charlie laughed and hugged Zack tighter. He held her close, hoping he helped her, hoping he wouldn't find her in a pool of her own blood, like his mother.

24 GERMANY

The streets of Cologne were empty save the bodies displayed in the same macabre fashion they'd come so accustomed to seeing. They made their way toward the center of town where Will's building was located. As expected, the place was deserted. They roamed the halls looking for anyone or anything. For Austin it was like having déjà vu. Memories of base headquarters flashed through his mind. After leaving the building they found a vehicle with a full tank of gas and an engine that cranked. They headed out of town toward the mountains. After two hours of driving the base of the mountain loomed ahead. The entrance of the facility was hidden behind a snow drift. A sign above the entrance hung haphazard, ready to fall at any moment. Caleb used his abilities to clear a path through the snow.

Austin tried the door. It was locked. The door was made of heavy steel, so he pounded with his fist. They waited. Caleb offered to open the door, but Austin wanted to try things the old-fashioned way first, so as not to scare anyone who might be holed up inside. After several minutes and several attempts at pounding, Austin stepped aside.

"You sure people are inside?" Austin asked Caleb.

"Positive. Can't you hear their hearts beating?"

Austin dropped his head and listened. He heard them. One, two, three distinct beating hearts. The third was beating faster than the others and the breathing seemed short and fast. He listened closer, heard them debating on answering the door. He heard a woman's voice and then a man's voice. The third person remained silent other than the rapid breathing.

"Are they Kyle's friends?"

Caleb listened. "The woman, Ada is one. There's also a man, he is much younger than she, and a canine."

"A canine? A dog?" Luke asked.

Caleb nodded. "A female, different in breed to Colin's dog."

Austin pounded on the door again. "Ada, if you can hear me, please open the door. Kyle sent us to find you," No answer was returned. Austin repeated in

German. This time the dog barked. The barking got closer, as did Ada's heart beat and that of the man. They heard the locks being worked on the other side of the door. The door opened slowly, and the barrel of a shotgun came out first.

"Who are you?" the gun holder asked, speaking in German, his accent thick.

"Austin Reynolds, Luke Taylor and my son Caleb. We're looking for Ada and Will Gaynor," Austin explained in German.

"Why?" the man demanded.

"Kyle Bosch sent us to find them. To take them to the US."

The door opened wider, but the shotgun remained held high by a boy-man, perhaps in his early twenties. An elderly woman looked out at them from behind the man. She held on to a yellow Labrador retriever with fur as white as the snow.

"Kyle sent you? Why didn't he come himself," Ada asked, imagining the worst had happened.

"He stayed behind with his sister Grace. She had a baby and he didn't want to leave her alone," Austin explained.

Ada's face melted. "A baby? Oh, my goodness." She covered her mouth, tears filled her eyes. "You can put the gun down Bruno. They're not here to hurt us." She smiled at Austin. "Please forgive us. I'm Ada Gaynor and this is my nephew Bruno." The dog barked. "And this is Josie."

Bruno lowered the gun but kept his finger on the trigger and a tight grip on the stock, ready to bring the barrel up at a moment's notice. Austin assessed the boy. He was a street kid, tough as nails, and fiercely loyal to Ada. Austin already knew they couldn't leave him behind, but that's where he would have to draw the line.

"Where's your husband ma'am?" Austin asked.

Her face clouded over. "I don't know. When the mass began moving this way, Will sent us on ahead. He promised me he wouldn't be far behind, but he never came," Ada replied, using great effort to maintain her composure. "No one came."

"You're from the United States? How'd you get here?" Bruno asked, his suspicions heightened.

"It's complicated and I don't have time to explain," Austin replied. "You're going to have to trust me for now." To Ada. "Kyle wants you to join him in Colorado. I'll take you two and the dog, but no one else."

"What do you mean? Are there others to take?" Ada asked.

"I don't know. We didn't see anyone on our way here," Austin answered.

"Shouldn't we look for others? I mean if you think there might be others, we can't leave them behind." Ada's brow creased.

"There's no time," Austin replied, refraining from adding that it didn't matter anyway, here, the US, one place was not safer than the other.

"Why not. What's going to happen?" Bruno demanded, using English this time.

"Some badass aliens are going to happen man," Luke answered. "The longer we stand here jarring with you the higher the chances of being found. We're offering safety, food, shelter. Pretty much anything you need. I suggest you trust the captain and accept our offer."

Bruno scowled at Luke and Austin. Ada took his arm. "They're right Bruno. We should go."

Austin was surprised she didn't argue to stay, to find her husband, and realized she'd already accepted he was dead. Austin glanced at Caleb, asking him the question without speaking. Caleb searched for Will but couldn't find him. They both knew what that meant, but better to let Ada believe he was dead.

"Can we go to my home first? I would like to retrieve a few things," Ada requested.

"Of course." Austin replied.

On the trip back to Cologne, Austin explained what had happened, leaving out some of the unbelievable details and most of the gruesome ones. When they arrived at Ada's house, he was still trying to decide how to approach their mode of travel back to the US. Bruno had not asked again, but he was thinking it over, that and many other things concerned him about the strangers from overseas.

"Please come inside out of the cold." Ada insisted.

They sat at the kitchen table while Ada went to gather a few personal possessions. Bruno stood arms crossed, brow furrowed. Trust wasn't something he gave out easy, if at all. "How do these aliens control the climate?" Bruno asked.

"It's simple science," Caleb replied. "You've heard of the ice ages. It's the same concept. Alter the Earth's winds and currents, decrease the ocean's temperatures, increase the water to land ratio."

Bruno stared at Caleb dumbfounded. Not only had he answered in a manner befitting an adult, but he used perfect German. Although Caleb had aged five years since arriving on Earth, to those first meeting him he still appeared a child of twelve.

Caleb added for clarification, "Shifts in the tectonic plates, changes in the atmosphere's composition, in the planet's orbit around the sun. The Elders manipulated all of these in order to create a new ice age." Which of course didn't clarify anything as far as Bruno was concerned, and this was simplest version Caleb could have given.

For Austin and Luke, the information wasn't new and having witnessed the powers of the Adita it wasn't difficult to believe. For Bruno though this simple science was not simple at all and having it delivered by Caleb made it all the more difficult for him to grasp.

At Bruno's feet, Josie suddenly sat up, ears at attention. She growled low. Bruno knelt next to him, stroking her head.

"What is it girl?"

"There are three men outside," Caleb said.

Austin peered through the curtains. Three unsavory individuals stood around their vehicle inspecting its contents. "Take her to the back of the house. Try to keep her quiet," Austin whispered to Bruno.

Bruno coaxed Josie from the room, by now the hairs on her back were raised. Austin kept watch on the men. He didn't like what he heard from them. If they tried to come in the house things were going to get dicey. Austin motioned to Luke to hand him the assault rifle. They waited, holding their breath. The front door rattled. Austin motioned for Luke to get down. They sat out of sight under the kitchen window listening to the men walk around the front of the house. They were scavengers, common thieves. Austin shook his head in disgust. Someone yelled out that he'd found something. The other two wandered across the street to join their fellow thief. From the back of the house Austin heard Josie bark. He looked out through the curtains. The men were across the street and hadn't heard. Austin went to the back to find Ada and Bruno. It was time to leave. He found Ada in her bedroom sorting through pictures.

"Ada, ma'am, we need to leave."

"I had planned on putting all of these on the computer, so that I'd always have them. But I never got around to it." She stuffed a few of the pictures into a small suitcase. "I'm ready."

Austin stepped aside for her. Out in the hall Bruno waited with Josie. They went back to the kitchen where Luke was keeping an eye out for the band of thieves who'd taken up residence in the house across the street.

"How are we going to get out of here without them seeing us?" Bruno asked.

Having no viable option, Austin decided to go with honesty. "We're going to travel through space."

Bruno laughed. "Travel through space? What the hell does that mean?"

"It means exactly that, and I know it's asking a lot for you to trust me, but you're gonna have to." Austin turned to Ada. "How's your health Miss Ada?"

"My health? Why it's...it's--

"She's fit enough father." Caleb replied. "But it will take her longer to recover due to her age."

"My age?" Ada sounded offended. "I'm only fifty-eight."

"Don't take offense," Austin said. "It's important that you're both in good health and that you understand this will hurt a little."

"Hurt?" Bruno asked.

"Traveling through space puts extreme stress on the body, especially the first time. You'll feel like you went rounds with a heavy weight boxer. But the very worst of the pain is brief," Austin explained.

From outside they heard the thieves. They'd returned. Josie ran to the front door, barking and they had no hope the men didn't hear her. Bruno went after her, pulling the dog back into the kitchen by her leash.

"Caleb, take Ada and Bruno to the bunker, then come back for us."

"Yes father." Caleb took Ada's hand and held out his other to Bruno. After a few seconds of uncertainty, he took Caleb's hand. "Pull your dog close and hold on to her." Bruno did so. The air around them wavered, space opened, and they were sucked away as the thieves busted in front door.

"Stay where you are." Austin aimed the weapon at the surprised men.

"We don't want no trouble," the first man replied, holding his hands in the air. "We're out looking for survivors."

"I know what you're looking for and it's not people."

The man sneered. "So what? Nobody around to care if we take a few things."

"Don't you get it man?" Luke asked. "What're you going to do with money? Or jewels? Or whatever it is you're stealing?"

The man shrugged. Stealing was all he knew, so turning his back on these perfect opportunities was pure stupid as far as he was concerned and had never occurred to him. Stocking up on things that held value in this new world, like water and food, also never occurred to him. The store had been left unattended and he felt it was his duty, as a thief, to take advantage of the situation before someone else beat him to it. That no one else was around to get the jump on the goods never occurred to him either.

"I thought I heard a dog barking?"

"No dog here," Austin replied, looking the man straight on.

"I guess we'll be on our way then." He waved for his companions to leave. He turned back, "You sure about the dog?"

"I'm sure," Austin answered.

"Hm." The man left closing the door behind him, not believing Austin about the dog and thinking there must be something pretty valuable in the house.

"They'll be back once it's dark," Austin said.

"We'll be gone by, then won't we?"

"Let's barricade the doors in case we aren't."

Austin and Luke maneuvered a heavy book case in front of the door and did the same to the back door. They walked through the house closing bedroom and bathroom doors, barricading windows with whatever was available. Austin was tired of killing and death. He'd rather hole up than fight, but he'd seen that look in men's eyes before and knew the thief wouldn't change his mind about returning. They sat in the kitchen to wait on Caleb's return. An hour turned into two and then three. The light outside was dimming. Austin stirred up a fire in the wood stove. Luke scrounged up some food. They ate in silence. In another thirty minutes it would be dark.

"Do you remember when you found me?" Luke asked.

Austin chuckled. "Sure do. Passed out in that gas station."

"Panic attack. I couldn't deal with everyone being gone, with my parents being dead. I thought I was the only one left."

"Yeah I know kid. It was rough."

"I wanted to say thank you. I don't think I ever thanked you, you know for saving my life."

"You don't have to do that."

"Yeah I do."

"You're welcome then."

They finished eating. Luke suddenly felt better. In fact, for the first time in months life again had purpose and he didn't feel as if he was swimming in muck. He finished his meal and gathered their plates. "Do you think there's running water?" He walked over to the sink.

The hair on Austin's neck rose. Time stalled, almost stopping, as he turned his head toward Luke. A shot rang out. Austin launched from his chair, right as a bullet slammed through Luke's temple, exiting out the other side, taking half his skull out. Austin reached Luke in time to catch him from falling to the floor.

"Luke. Luke. No! No!" Austin rocked him back and forth. "Luke."

More shots rang out, the bullets shattered the kitchen window. Austin laid Luke down, grabbed his assault rifle. At the front door he pushed the bookcase over with one shove and opened the door. Rage surged through him like he'd never experienced, igniting all his senses.

Outside was pitch black, but Austin saw every detail in clear definition. The millions of particles floating in the air sizzled, electrified by the energy surging through his blood, illuminated by the powers unleashed by his rage. The thieves fired at him, but the force inside acted as a shield protecting Austin from harm.

Austin raised his rifle and emptied the clip into the night. Each bullet met its mark, each man went down, three bullets through the heart and one through the center of each forehead. He stared at the bodies, watching reds turn to blues as the bodies went cold in their fresh state of death. Austin's anger subsided and with this the particles began to dim now that their source of energy had lessened in intensity. The night returned, swallowing up what light remained. The rifle slipped from his fingers, clanging down onto the concrete sidewalk, echoing loudly through the night. He left it lying on the ground and returned to Luke.

A pool of blood had formed under Luke's head. The sight was near Austin's undoing. He knelt next to his friend, his brother, hanging his head. He wanted to cry, to scream, but did neither. Not even now in this darkest of moments was grief his to own, to experience, to use as a means of easing the pain. Easy was not for him, only questions and guilt. How could this have happened? How had he not heard them? He cursed himself for failing Luke.

The wind blew the curtain from the window. Austin knew Caleb was back.

"Father are you ok?" Caleb stepped gingerly into the kitchen, uncertain how to deal with the emotions his father was feeling, wishing his mother was here to take care of things.

"Can you save Luke?" Austin asked.

Caleb reached out to Luke, probed around his mind, found no brain activity. "It is very difficult once the heart stops. And there's extensive damage to his brain."

"Can you save him?"

Caleb walked over to Austin, laid his hand on his shoulder. "I can't, but mother might be able to."

Austin turned to face him. "Has she returned?"

"Not yet, but I'll find her. I'll bring her back home." Caleb knelt next to Luke, laid his hand on his head, then over his heart, he shook his head. "She might be able to change him, but she won't be able to bring him back as human. There's too much damage." Like Madison, Caleb thought.

Austin hung his head, succumbing to defeat. Luke wouldn't want to live like that, but he couldn't make that decision. All he wanted was to have his friend back, at whatever cost. If he did this, brought Luke back as an Adita, he might never forgive Austin for choosing a life for him that was less than human. Austin needed help, he needed Madison. She would have been strong. She would have made that decision. The right decision.

Austin looked up. "How much time do we have?"

"Based on his body temperature, about thirty minutes, but I'm not sure. And the longer we wait the riskier it is."

"What do you mean?"

"The brain changes in death. He may not come back as the same person."

The news kept getting worse. "Can you take us back to the bunker?"

Caleb nodded

They wrapped Luke's body in a sheet and Caleb whisked them back to the bunker's infirmary. Austin called for Zack and Ed. They both arrived out of breath, having run the entire way. They wore grim expressions, as if they knew it was going to be bad.

"What happened?" Ed's eyes darted around Austin landing on the shrouded body of Luke. He and Zack walked over to Luke's body. They felt like they were reliving a bad dream. Ed pulled the sheet down, looked into Luke's face, and laid his hand on Luke's arm. It was cold.

"No. No. It can't...he can't be dead, he can't," Ed mumbled.

"Ed," Austin said, walking over to him. "Eve can save him."

Ed turned, confused. "Then do it. What are you waiting for?"

"She's not here. Caleb's gone to find her," Austin paused, "but that's not all. If she does this, saves him, he'll be like her, like an Adita."

"Like Eve? You mean he'll be a... like them?" Ed stopped himself from saying the word vampire out loud.

"Yes, in every sense of what that means," Austin replied.

Ed stared at Austin, allowing this to sink in before turning back to Luke.

"I can't let him go man, but I know Luke wouldn't want to be like them." Austin choked on his words, on his emotions. "I can't make that decision."

Ed knew what he was asking of him. Zack came to stand next to him, placing a hand on his shoulder for support. Ed thought it a bad idea for Luke to go with Austin, but he'd insisted, and Austin had encouraged him. Now here they were, trying to decide if he should die or come back as a blood thirsty freak.

"I'm sorry Ed, Zack. I shouldn't have let it happen. I should have been paying closer attention. It's my fault. It's all my fault." Austin replied, his voice cracking as he choked back the tears.

Zack put his other hand on Austin's shoulder. "Don't do that man. Don't blame yourself. Luke made his own decisions." These words came out sounding as hollow as they felt. Madison's death, now this, it was too much to ask of anyone to be strong.

Austin looked at him through bleary eyes. For a flash of an instant he hated him for being right, for doing the right thing, for being the stronger one. It wasn't fair to put this decision on them, but this was one time he couldn't put his emotions aside. The hate vanished, replaced by another feeling more sickening in its meaning and intensity. He was a coward.

* * *

The next day the entire group joined together again at the cemetery in Pueblo. Austin covered Luke's coffin with an L.S.U. blanket before Zack lowered him into the ground. His grave was next to Madison's. Everyone took a turn throwing a handful of frozen dirt onto the coffin and saying goodbye. When it was Ed's turn, Jenny walked by his side, holding him steady. Ryan held his dad's hand and cried, not from his own grief, but because he felt his father's pain and it was overwhelming. Ed knelt next to the grave, silently crying, staring down at the coffin wondering if they made the right choice. Jenny's hand rested on his shoulder, providing him the strength to not fall apart.

After they'd left, Austin stood alone at the gravesite lost in grief, shrouded in blackness. He sank to the ground, his eyes dry, but his heart aching a thousand times over. The wind wailed for him. The cold embraced his wretchedness. None of it mattered anymore, nothing mattered anymore. He'd fought all along the way to keep Luke safe, to keep Madison safe, but in the end, he'd failed. In the end he wouldn't be able to protect any of them. The hard truth of their situation numbed him. He had nothing left to give.

Nothing. Nothing. Nothing.

A thought spun around in his mind like a leaf spinning along in a brisk wind. The thought found a place to land in the murkiness shrouding his conscience. Slowly an idea took hold, and then hooked his full attention. He knew what must be done.

25 POINT OF NO RETURN

A custom designed Piper Seneca warmed up at the end of the only runway in Pueblo's small airport. The plane was somewhat of a celebrity in pre-Sundog days thanks to a philandering senator who desired to impress his latest girlfriend and had more money than sense. The wife discovered her husband's toy and, unfortunately for the plane, managed to spray paint the word **WHORE** in bold red letters on both wings. It was the biggest scandal in Pueblo history and remained a front-page story for several weeks. Ignoring the tasteless graffiti, the plane was an impressive machine. Two 220 horsepower engines provided maximum power at a ceiling of 25,000 feet. This particular model was made for flying over mountainous areas and wide expanses of water, of which Austin would travelling.

Austin sat in the cockpit half listening as Zack read over the basics from the owner's manual. His thoughts were on his mission, which appeared less and less a search and find. Search and find because the idea that Eve and Caleb needed rescuing was solidifying into more of a fact than a hunch. He couldn't ignore the warnings gnawing at him since Luke's funeral.

"What happens if you don't come back?" Zack asked. Austin looked over at Zack, his expression hinted of defeat. Seeing vulnerability in Austin's face scared the crap out of Zack. He started to get up, but a sinking feeling gripped his stomach. The real possibility that he might never see his friend again tightened around him like a giant vise. He sat back down and turned to Austin. "Their deaths weren't your fault man."

Austin gripped the control wheel tighter. "It was my responsibility to keep them safe, to keep you all safe. I can't do that anymore. I don't know that I ever could."

"You're not responsible for us. We're all adults."

"It was my duty to protect you, to protect all civilians. I took an oath to put that duty above all else. And I failed," Austin replied. "I put my feelings first."

Zack sighed in frustration. Blame for everything that had happened, and how fucked up their world had become, couldn't be placed at one man's feet, least of all Austin's. "You can't help who you love."

Austin shook his head. "It's not Eve's fault."

Zack frowned. Not Eve's fault? But that wasn't what he'd meant, so he wasn't sure what to make of Austin's statement. He didn't press the issue.

Austin changed the subject. "You know she was in love with you, Madison was. You made her very happy."

Zack stared at Austin and knew he was telling the truth but couldn't help the direction his thoughts went.

"What she felt for me wasn't love. It was something simple in its purity and dark in its nature. A darkness that wanted to possess her, but she refused to allow it. She fought the possession without even knowing she was in a battle for her soul. Madison was too good for this world we live in. She needed light to live by. You were her light. She chose you, she chose to love and to live in the light."

"What are you choosing?"

"The only choice left to me."

The realization of what this meant flirted with Zack, but he didn't want to believe, to acknowledge the meaning full on. "You don't have to walk that road man."

"I do. I can't exist in two worlds and be whole. I can't succeed if I have only one foot in the fight. I must have both in. I must commit fully to one way or the other. Victory is lost without commitment, without sacrifice. The Adita know this. They live by this creed without fail. They never choose. For them there is but one choice."

"Well that blows, and the Adita blow," Zack replied, wanting to say more, wanting to argue, but he knew Austin's mind was set. Unable to stall his friend's departure any longer Zack made his way to the exit, turning back one last time. "Come home ok?"

"I'll do my best." Austin saluted him.

Zack jumped out. As soon as he cleared the plane, Austin maneuvered around, taxied down the runway, picked up speed and took off into the gray sky. Zack shielded his eyes, watching the plane until it became a tiny speck on the horizon. He'd lost count of the number of times Austin had left to go on one mission or another, always returning in one piece with no more than minor scratches. But how long could one man's luck run? Madison had said Austin didn't believe in luck and maybe he didn't, but whether it was luck or skill or a combination of the two, Zack hoped it continued to work in his friend's favor.

* * *

    Ahead of Austin the sky was an endless expanse of gray, below the ground was not the usual patchwork blanket of farm lands and clusters of twinkling neighborhoods. Below was a mass of white, crisscrossed by the highways filled with abandoned vehicles holding the remains of the dead. Austin guided the plane along through the cloudless sky. He operated on instinct, on the foreign substance coursing through his blood. A power that supersized his abilities, his senses, allowing him to perform at a peak beyond that of even the most elite human beings.

    Life no longer made sense and despite the added energy, Austin felt exhausted. The strengths he'd come to rely on had failed him and he had failed his friends. Images of their faces at Madison's funeral and then Luke's, haunted him day and night. The overwhelming grief he'd caused everyone could have been avoided had he done the right thing, had he made the right decision when the opportunity was offered. And more than deciding wrong, the reason for his decision ate at him and was the cause of his exhaustion. Fear never drove him in the past, but he'd given in, allowed himself to be controlled by a lesser emotion. Lesser in its usefulness, but not in its power to drive a man in the wrong direction. Austin rubbed his head trying to clear his mind of the turmoil. Focus was key and something he never faltered in maintaining.

    "Tighten up man," he ordered himself. The sound of his voice in the silence broke him free of his mind and he continued to talk out loud. "You got this buddy. Find Eve and Caleb. Make the right choice. Save your friends, save the world." He nodded in agreement. "Pity is for the weak minded. You are not weak. You are a soldier. You are a Marine. You are proud, be proud."

    Most men would have faltered under such pressure, giving in and up. Austin was not prone to wallowing for long or at all. He'd stared unblinking down the barrel of the many guns life had pointed at him. The Adita had simply pointed a bigger gun, one that had thrown him off balance and he'd blinked. For a lesser man blinking was an automatic response to adversity, failure was always the expected outcome. For an elite man, like Austin, blinking created a fissure weakening the barrier. For the toughest man, like Austin, that fissure was never allowed to grow, to turn into a crack that broke the dam, and this time wasn't going to be the exception.

    Where fear was debilitating, resolve was liberating, and Austin had his resolve. He turned his thoughts on to the details of his plan. He'd reach Deadbear, Alaska before dark. Kyle had thought Alaska time was the same as anywhere else, that the amount of daylight was the same everywhere and it appeared this was true. At first light he would refuel and be on his way. The plane would serve as his hotel, as he had no desire to walk down memory lane, to see if his house was still standing. The sole reason for landing in Deadbear was his familiarity with the airstrip. Everything else there was dead to him.

The airstrip brought a back memories Austin had buried, long ago. A source of income when he was nine, Austin had spent many hours at the airport pandering to whoever would glance in his direction. Most days he worked for the owner, a drunken bastard with a bum leg named Barney. Barney paid Austin less than shit wages to do all the shit jobs. Wash planes, clean grease spills, clean toilets, whatever Barney asked. Two quarters, maybe a dollar, were often the result of his efforts. Fifty cents bought him a bag of chips or a candy bar from the vending machine. Not enough to fill his empty stomach, let alone refuel after a day of hard work.

Every so often a group of businessmen would arrive. On those days Austin made a fortune in tips carrying bags to and from. A fortune being twenty dollars. Twenty dollars turned into ten after Barney took his share. The remaining ten he hid from the old man. Ten he could stretch out for a month or more through strict frugality.

On one occasion a group of men from Texas arrived. They planned to ride the Dalton Highway on motorcycle. Randy Westlake was one of these men. He wore a Texas sized cowboy hat and a belt buckle the diameter of a hub cap. He'd tipped Austin a ten spot and clapped him on the back like they were best buddies. Later, while cleaning the plane Austin had found that man's wallet. He knew it was the Texan's by the driver's license picture. Austin tracked Randy down at the only hotel in town and returned the wallet. Randy, who only carried cash, was very, very appreciative. He tipped Austin two crisp fifty-dollar bills, said to call him R.W. and invited him to stay for dinner. Austin enjoyed the best steak Deadbear had to offer. Prior to Eve arriving, Randy Westlake had been the one and only redeeming memory he had of his childhood.

As Austin approached the runway of his home, old feelings surfaced bringing a rancid taste to his mouth. The wheels touched the icy ground and for a second he thought the plane would slide sideways off the runway. He willed the wheels to catch, to slow down, and for the plane to come to a stop in front of the lone hangar. He glanced over at the hangar wondering if Barney's frozen corpse might still be inside. His eyes moved over to the fuel truck sitting cockeyed about twenty yards away. The cab looked to be empty.

Leaving the plane running, Austin jumped out and checked the fuel truck. The tank was close to full, which was enough to get him to Russia and back. Packed in with his things was an additive Zack developed to cleanse fuel of debris. The chemicals were especially effective on fuel having sat for long periods of time. Austin dug this out and poured the gel like liquid into the fuel truck's tank, then emptied the contents of the fuel truck into the plane. He glanced at the sky. The crescent suns had faded into the gray, which meant he had less than thirty minutes to wrap things up before the black curtain of night fell.

Once the truck was moved safely out of the way, Austin went into the hangar through the personnel door, which opened up into a cramped office. A crappy faux wood desk took up one corner of the room. Stacks of paper covered every inch of the surface. Splayed over those stacks was Barney, or what was left of him, and what was left was more than should have been after more than a year of being dead, but the sub-zero temps were a rather effective inhibitor to decomposition.

Austin recognized the pinky ring dangling on the bone of Barney's right hand. The emerald sparkled in the beam of Austin's flashlight. Barney prized that ring over most everything, his whiskey sours, his bowling ball and most of all over his snappy wife Vera. Austin never knew the story behind the ring, but he imagined it must have been a gift from a girlfriend. He knew it wasn't from Vera.

Once upon a time Barney was thrown in jail for breaking Vera's arm, thinking she'd stolen the ring. Austin heard his old man talking about it, saying *the whore woman got what she deserved*. Later Austin found the ring sitting in the hangar bathroom, but he didn't touch it. He let Barney find it two days later, after Vera dropped the charges and he was released. Two days later Vera borrowed Barney's 38 revolver and decorated their mauve and baby blue bedroom with her blood. The coroner's report stated the cause of death as 'bleeding to death from a gunshot wound'. As fate would have it, Vera's right arm was the one Barney chose to test out the resilience of his Louisville Slugger baseball bat. Being right handed, Vera had to switch to using her left hand on account of the cast. Apparently, Vera's aim had been a little off and rather than dying instantly, she'd slowly bled to death while Barney was out celebrating his release.

Barney collected the twenty-thousand-dollar life insurance check wearing a Cheshire Cat smile on his face. He'd given Austin an extra five dollars that week. He'd treated Donny and some of the others to a week-long drinking binge in Anchorage. Austin was left behind to fend for himself. He welcomed the reprieve, all the while dreading when the old man would return, knowing he'd be surlier than ever. Surliness meant extra beatings. As fate went, at the end of that week Austin fell into the frigid water and died for thirty-four seconds. In a way, looking back, his near death was the precise moment he started living.

Austin picked his way around the junk cluttering the floor. Various owner's manuals lay in a haphazard heap on top of a rusted metal shelf. Barney knew each one inside and out, for despite his social shortcomings, the man had been a genius when it came to fixing an airplane. Austin found an old blanket and covered Barney's body.

Out in the hanger he assessed the size and decided his plane would fit. He shoved open the large doors to a pitch-black night and the lights inside the plane glowing like beacons. Time had gotten away from him, but he wasn't worried. He guided the plane into the hangar and shut the doors. Less than a foot clearance remained, which was a foot more than needed.

The cabin of the plane was maximized for comfort on long flights. Four large leather chairs faced each other. Austin sat in one facing the door and was pleasantly surprised to find it reclined. The temperature in the cabin was a balmy sixty-five degrees. Zack had assured him leaving the heater on was not a problem, since it ran on its own batteries. While munching on cold spam and crackers, Austin looked over a map of Russia. Oymyakon was his destination. An air strip built back during WWII was where he'd land. From there he would travel by whatever means he could find. By foot if nothing else was available. He knew at some point by foot was going to be his only choice. He folded the map and tucked it in his backpack. The recliner fit him perfectly and within minutes he was sound asleep.

Late into the night the wind picked up, crashing into the hangar with gale force gusts. The metal groaned, threatening to give. Inside the insulated cabin of the plane Austin heard a different wind, not from outside the hangar, but from inside his dream, walking on the Kolyma Highway in Russia.

M56 Kolyma Highway, the Road of Bones, ran through the Far East of Russia. Constructed during the Stalin era by labor camp inmates, the road stretched twelve hundred miles. Inmates were sent to the road to die, and thousands did perish during the construction period. The road signified the end of the Earth. Many years later, people settled there in hopes of striking it rich, only to become stuck, never to leave.

Austin walked down the Road of Bones, ignoring the wind's angry howls. The inmates who'd worked the road, faded in and out of view, ghosts of long ago, wearing expressions of hopelessness and desperation. Up ahead he could see the Lena River, where a ferry bobbed about at the shore. A hunched backed man, who had paper thin skin covered in dark liver spots, operated the ferry. Austin climbed on board, dropping a gold coin into the operator's outstretched hand.

Parking himself at the far end of the ferry, Austin stared out across the Lena to the opposite shores where more spirits moved about, dancing dances of lives lived long gone. He'd traveled between worlds before, between that of the living and the dead, but Eve had always been his guide. He did not feel her presence with him now. They floated across the Lena amidst thrashing waves and blustery winds threatening to toss them overboard. Austin stood solid on the deck watching the water rise and fall. This semi-state of consciousness caused him no fear, only anticipation. Not seeing Eve bothered him more than he cared to think about. If she wasn't guiding him, then something had gone terribly wrong and death might be all that he found at the end of this journey.

On the banks Austin caught a glimpse of a man dressed in white, who had solid white eyes and dark brown skin. Despite his unusual appearance and that he stood bent over leaning on a cane, Austin sensed he was an Adita. The man raised an arm beckoning to Austin, urging him to come along, to follow. The man jerked his head up to the sky. Out of the mist a Svan swooped down sinking its great talons onto the man's head, ripping it from his body. His arm continued to beckon before his body toppled over into the water.

Austin sat up with a start. The image of the man's headless body bobbing down the river stayed with him briefly before fading away. The man was familiar, but Austin was sure they'd never met. The man didn't look like an Adita, but Austin had no doubt he was, despite his unusual appearance. Austin sighed and laid back. Of one more thing he was certain, the man was there to help him find Eve. Of another thing he was certain, she needed his help and this time it wasn't on any premise. The only thing he still had no sense of was the whereabouts of his son. The boy seemed to have vanished. Austin shook away the fear this brought. If he found Eve, he would find Caleb.

Three hours were between him and daylight. Sleep would not be his anymore that night. He turned on the overhead reading lamp and pulled a journal and pen from his pack. He flipped through the pages stopping on a page dated November sixteenth. It was the day he'd found Luke. The words swam around on the page. He turned until the pages were blank, past all the moments and memories of Luke and Madison.

Putting pen to paper Austin began to write. He wrote about saving Ed, meeting Zack and Colin, about Charlie, and the Adita. He skipped writing about Madison's death. There would be a better time for that than at the present. After three hours his journal was caught up to the point of meeting General Roth and his watch read 4:57. The suns would make their appearance in a few minutes. It was time to fly. He'd put Eve and Caleb out of his mind while writing, intentionally leaving pages blank to return to later. He needed to approach this search like any other mission, unemotional, unattached, and focused on the details.

* * *

Austin opened the hangar doors pulled the plane out onto the runway using the refueling truck. He returned to Barney's office. He felt like he should say something, but in the end, he slipped Barney's ring from his finger and dropped it in his own pocket. He didn't do this out of spite or because he liked the ring, but because of the future. A future where nothing of what used to be remained, even if what used to be wasn't an altogether pleasant memory, Austin still wanted to remember.

Out on the runway Austin warmed up the plane's engines. After fifteen minutes the plane was ready for takeoff and he taxied down the runway. As the plane ascended into the gray, Austin didn't look back or feel regret over not visiting his home. The town of Deadbear was a piece of his history he didn't mind leaving behind.

Flying low over the Bering Strait, Austin imagined Kyle swimming through the waters, walking across the jagged ice, spending the night on the island of the dead. He took a moment to admire his brother's tenacity and bravery, to feel pride that they were family. As he approached Russia, Kyle's Mercedes came into view, sitting at the edge of the sea. A lonesome, desperate image.

Austin continued toward the ends of the Earth, toward the Lena River and a ferry boat run by the undead. On the other side of that river he'd find Eve and Caleb. Relying on hope, wishing on stars, praying to unseen gods, all of these were unnecessary conveyances and never his way. He would find them. His certainty in this was a feeling, an instinct, something that couldn't be explained with words.

The Oymyakon runway appeared in the distance. A narrow strip of land provided for a tight landing to work with, but at least the path was clear. The plane descended, touching down and coming to a stop without incident. A rush of relief didn't flood his senses, he'd no anxiety to wash away. He was calm and ready.

Inside a small hangar, a brief search turned up a BMW motorcycle with keys in the ignition and gas in the tank. Austin poured the last bottle of fuel additive into the bike's tank and jumped on. He carried a backpack, a sleeping bag and nothing else. If the bike started, he'd have a ride. If not, he'd walk. The bike turned on the third try to which Austin was appreciative but didn't take his gratitude so far as to thank anyone or consider himself lucky.

In no time at all he was riding down The Road of Bones, which proved every bit as treacherous as he'd read about and experienced in his dream. The inmates didn't visit from the afterworld and when he arrived at the ferry, a half-bent man wasn't waiting to take him across. No matter anyway, the river was frozen around the ferry and of no use in crossing over. The bike was another thing to consider. The river, although frozen, appeared a treacherous travel by foot, let alone on a bike. In the end the bike was left behind, hidden on the ferry just in case.

Crossing the river took longer than expected and when he finally reached the shores on the other side, Austin jogged in order to make up time. An hour later he approached a mining village where a handful of shacks remained standing. He chose the one at the farthest end closest to the foothills. The shack wasn't pretty or even weather proof, but he didn't care. The cold didn't bother him so much anymore.

Inside he found a single room sparingly furnished that served as the bedroom, living room and kitchen. To his surprise he also found a small bathroom, but no running water. He set his things in the corner facing the door. After another dinner of spam and crackers, Austin climbed into his sleeping bag and fell asleep, anxious to see the white haired being again. He wasn't disappointed as his sleep was filled with vivid dreams, of visits to the worlds in-between, of strange sights and stranger beings. Some worlds were misty and cold, others dry and hot.

In the latter he came upon the white-haired man. Wearing nothing more than a pair of shorts and a t-shirt wrapped around his head, Austin trudged across desert dunes. He stood upon one of the tallest peaks and gazed out over an endless sea of sand, a static brown ocean. Down below the man waited. He looked up to Austin and opened his arms wide. Before Austin could react, the desert swallowed itself, taking the man and Austin into its gaping black hole. They were deposited on top of the Siberian Mountains. He looked for the man, but he was nowhere to be found. This was not important. Austin knew this was where he would find Eve.

As soon as this thought entered his mind Austin awoke. He lay still waiting for his mind to clear. His watch read 2:05. He knew this without having to check. Outside the wind blew in gusts, each one rocking the shack's thin walls. Amazed the structure held up this long, Austin buried himself deeper in his sleeping bag and allowed his mind to drift back into a deep slumber. The man with the white hair did not return, he'd accomplished his task, all that remained was for Austin to follow through and do his part.

* * *

The Siberian Mountains weren't any less intimidating from the ground than from eight thousand feet up looking down. A narrow path led Austin into the hills. He walked for two hours listening to the sound of his boots crunching the snow. The place was desolate, where a man's thoughts might overwhelm him, but Austin didn't mind the quiet or his thoughts. He was focused on the task, the mission, on Eve and Caleb.

The path narrowed, winding its way up into the hazardous terrain of the mountains. A gentle mist swirled about his feet giving the illusion of walking on air. As when he'd entered the great temple hidden in the jungles of Paru, Austin felt the presence of the supernatural, which indicated to him Eve must be close. Although he sensed her, he couldn't hear her. The farther up and in he traveled, the stronger the connection became. Soon the mist was up to his knees, tugging at his legs with invisible hands, whispering to him in a sweet seductive voice. Gruesome images floated in and out of view. Austin kept moving. One step after another, turning a blind eye and deaf ear to the spirit world.

At the turn in the path, where the precipices rose to magnificent heights, diminishing everything below, a wave of pain so excruciating knocked the air from Austin's lungs. He fell to his knees gasping for air. Desperate seconds expired. *Focus man. Focus. It's not your pain. It's not real.* After repeating this over and over the pain subsided, and he could breathe again. From his pack he grabbed an energy packet and squeezed the contents into his mouth. His hands shook. He squeezed his fingers into a fist, opening and closing them until the shakes subsided. He swallowed the goo sitting on his tongue and waited.

From his kneeling position on the ground Austin sat with his head bowed. Remnants of pain lingered in his muscles causing him to hesitate, to not want to move too soon. A deep breath of crisp air burned inside his lungs. He released the air, went to draw another when a sudden awareness caused him to pause. He stared at the path beneath him, at the crystals making up each and every snow flake, every particle of ice unique in shape and design. The ice crystals did not interest him, they were a focusing mechanism. An excuse to not lift his head, to not see what caught his eye's view right before the pain struck him down. Minutes ticked by, but a second was all that mattered. The second required to raise his head, to look up and see. Austin got up on his feet, but he didn't look, not yet. Images of what he'd seen, although brief, were very clear. Images of Eve. He wanted to shake them away, to not believe what his mind was telling him, but the truth couldn't be dismissed.

Facing the truth was man's most difficult task and greatest weakness. Great amounts of energy were put into avoiding truths, into creating false realities in order to cope with the harshness life throws our way, at times seemingly at random. Austin didn't fall into this category of men, but sometimes even he wavered when faced with the unthinkable. Breathing in, he forced himself to look ahead.

Before veering off in another direction, the path he was on met a sheer wall of thick ice that extended up the side of the mountain. Spiked poles lined the path up to the wall and upon each pole a head was impaled. The eyes of the dead cried tears of blood. Blood oozed from the shredded flesh of what remained of the neck. Ignoring the heads, Austin moved closer to the wall. A gap, perhaps five feet in width, separated the mountain from the path. Austin stopped at the edge and gazed at Eve's face frozen behind the ice. He reached out to her, but his foot slipped on the edge, sending debris tumbling into the abyss below. A moment of uncertainty before reclaiming his balance went unnoticed. His mind repeated over and over. *This can't be. She can't be dead.* Yet he knew, with no level of uncertainty, if they beheaded her, and from all appearances this was the case, no other conclusion could be arrived at other than death. If Eve was dead, then what of his son? The answer to this he couldn't bear to consider.

Unsure how long he stood there, Austin became aware of the time. Dark would fall in less than two hours. If he hurried, he'd reach the bottom by night fall. Taking a last look upon Eve's face, Austin begged for her to respond, but his pleas went unanswered. He turned back, heading down the path. Each step drove a stake into his heart. He began to run, not caring about his safety, not caring if he fell to his death. Thoughts of Eve and Caleb drove him to recklessness. He'd accepted Roxanne wasn't real, which had made the pain of losing her manageable. Nothing made Eve's death acceptable. She was dead, gone forever this time.

***

Four days and nights passed before Austin crawled from his sleeping bag to face the day. Outside the shack nothing had changed. The landscape was still frozen, the sky still gray, the three suns still sitting above the horizon. But this wasn't accurate. Everything had changed. Caleb was missing. Eve was dead. Everything was dead. He returned to the protection of his sleeping bag, to the comatose state where he remained for another three days.

On the night of the seventh day Austin dreamt. He stood upon the deck of a majestic ship gliding through still waters of a vast ocean. The moon shown full casting a white blush upon the water. Out in the sea icebergs rose up from the water like colossal creatures of the deep. The moon's light turned the giant black shadow creatures into glowing blue ice sculptures. The ship passed near one of the towering pieces, close enough for Austin to see the boat reflected in the surface.

The ship approached another iceberg. This one different from the others with its glass like surface and smooth face. As they came up close Austin saw Eve suspended inside the ice. He climbed the railing and leaned out as far out as he could without falling over. The ship slowed, coming to a stop in front of the iceberg. Austin reached out, touching the ice over Eve's face, and felt a warm sensation under his fingertips. Loud voices carried over to him. Out beyond the icebergs, where the ocean appeared to drop off a sharp edge, another ship approached. Many figures moved about on the deck, and though Austin couldn't distinguish who they were, he sensed they were foe not friend. He turned back to Eve, this was his only chance to save her, and he must free her before they arrived.

The ship suddenly lurched forward, snapping Austin sideways, and he lost his grip. He fell hard to the deck and scrambled back onto the railing. The other ship had pulled up alongside the iceberg holding Eve. The Adita commanded the vessel, while the Svan worked the deck. A group of Svan hoisted a large metal claw out over the top of Eve's iceberg. They lowered the claw, sunk the teeth into the iceberg and plucked it from the ocean. Austin yelled out to Eve. The sound of his voice jolted him awake. Alertness arrived swift like a light turned on in the dark. She was alive. Eve was alive. He was certain of this, but whoever or whatever had placed her in the mountain would return soon. They were coming for her. If he allowed this to happen, she would be gone forever.

Three hours until daylight. If he headed out now, he could reach her before the suns appeared, but then what? *Think,* he ordered his brain. His brows furrowed, his hands rubbed his head, and he thought. If her captors were coming for her wouldn't they have to free her from the mountain? This might be his only opportunity to save her. Austin kept thinking this over, considering all that he knew, which wasn't much. Traveling through the foothills and up into the mountains in the pitch black was not a task for the meek. This mission lacked planning, supplies, logistics, thus based on statistics would fail and should fail, but Austin wouldn't allow failure. He wasn't alone in this, someone was helping him, guiding him, wanting him to save Eve as much as he desired to do so. For the first time in his life, Austin put his faith in chance, in hope, in the unknown.

As Austin approached the bend, the suns pressed through the ebony curtain. Black turned to gray, night to day, with minimal transition between. Austin removed the night vision goggles, allowing his eyes to adjust before moving on. He turned the bend holding his breath, exhaling when he saw Eve was still encapsulated in the mountain side guarded by the mutilated heads. He stepped up to the edge of the path, getting as close as possible. He examined Eve's neck, looking for signs that her body was still attached, but beyond her head the ice was solid white. Austin became aware of a presence and turned. On the path, not more than five feet away, stood the man with the stark white hair and solid white eyes. Although his slender frame bent at a slight angle, he was taller than Austin.

"It's you. You were in my dreams," Austin said.

The man tilted his head. "I must apologize for being rude, but she doesn't have time for explanations Captain Reynolds. If we are to save her, we must act now."

Austin was all for acting now. "What can I do? How do I get her out of there?"

"You must allow me to enter your body and mind. Do you allow this?"

Austin nodded. "And after? What happens then?"

The man stepped up to within inches of Austin. "You must give up your life for hers. Are you prepared to do so?"

Austin knew what the man was asking of him. "I'm ready."

"Good. You must act quickly, if you have any doubts, remove them. Once we extract her, she will have mere seconds before she's beyond saving. You must not hesitate. Do you understand?"

"I understand," Austin assured him. "I have no doubts."

The man took possession of Austin's body and mind. He raised both hands, palms facing Eve, and began chanting in a low voice. The ice cracked. Bits and chunks fell into the crevice below. Soon Eve's entire body was visible. The man inside Austin continued to chant, his words pulling Eve from the ice. Her body floated over the gap and came to lie at Austin's feet. The man returned control over to Austin.

Austin knelt next to her and pulled out his knife. Without hesitation he cut into his wrist. Blood spewed forth, coloring the snow bright red. He lowered his wrist to her lips and the point of turning back slipped away forever. As her teeth sank into the cut, a burning sensation ran the length of his arm and he blacked out.

26 AFTER

Austin opened his eyes. He stared at the white ceiling, listening to the noise around him, listening to them talk, waiting for them to notice he was awake, to speak to him, but they didn't. He turned his head, recognizing that he was back in the bunker in his bedroom, and that he was alone. He blinked several times. The room was empty, yet he could still hear their voices. He turned back to the ceiling and closed his eyes. The next time he awoke, no voices filled the room, or his head. The only sound he heard was the steady breathing of one person, who felt very close. Eve, he thought.

"I'm right here," she said, coming to stand next to his bed.

Austin looked at her, touched her arm, and squeezed her hand. "You're real? I'm not dreaming?"

"You're not dreaming," she assured him. "How do you feel?"

Although a simple question, Austin wasn't sure how to answer. "I'm not sure. Strange I guess."

"Do you remember what happened?"

Bits and pieces floated at the edge of his memory. Flying to Russia, walking the Road of Bones, searching in the mountains. "I found you in the mountain. You were frozen. I thought you were dead." He grasped her hand, remembering the desperation he'd felt upon finding her encapsulated in the mountain.

"You saved my life and that of our unborn daughter, Zevia."

"I did? Our daughter. You're pregnant. Yes. Yes. I remember. You named her Zevia. I think I knew that."

"You're going to feel disoriented, but it will soon pass."

More memories were returning. Images of ferry boats and icebergs flickered in and out, but he disregarded these as unimportant. The piece missing, the one out of his mind's reach, seemed to matter most. Austin retraced his steps over and over, filling in more details each time. He heard himself saying *"I have no doubts"* and saw himself pull out his knife. The blade sharp, the metal bright. The metal sliced into his skin. The pieces of the puzzle collided together.

He turned to Eve. "I survived."

Eve nodded.

"Are you angry that I did it? That I decided to change?"

"No. I knew you would eventually make that decision. It's who you are."

"Then what's bothering you?"

Eve folded her hands together as if in prayer. "When I was in Russia looking for Agra, I came upon a tomb built deep inside the mountain. I don't know the importance of the tomb or why I was led there. But before I could explore further, Za and several guards arrived. Za had Caleb. I had no choice. I had to surrender. Za's plan was to return later to kill me."

Austin sat up. The remaining memories flooded back. "Caleb. They took him?" Austin got up from the bed. "After he brought us back from Germany, I sent him to find you. It was Luke. Luke had been shot. It was too late to save him, but I sent him off to find you anyway. I was out of mind. He said he knew where you were, but he never came back. I couldn't reach him."

She went to Austin and took his hand. "He's no longer on Earth. I think Agra has taken him somewhere far into the seventh universe."

Austin didn't ask if she was certain. "How long before I'm fully recovered?"

"I don't know. I've never changed anyone before." She laid her hand on his chest over his heart. "You're very strong. Maybe two days, maybe less."

"Tomorrow we'll go to Paru."

"He's not on Paru and neither is Za."

"I know, but the answers are," Austin replied. "Someone there knows where Caleb is. I can feel this, or, or…I don't know how to explain it. It's like I see it in my mind." He recalled the white-haired man. "A man, or a male, he was Adita, he helped me find you. And rescue you. I don't know who he was, but he has the answers. And I'm certain he's on Paru."

The description of the man rang familiar to Eve. She saw him in her mind, as if looking at an old out of focus photo. His presence was significant, indicating his powers must be many and his position high.

"Does anyone know we're back?" Austin asked.

"No."

Austin got up from the bed and went into the bathroom to look in the mirror. The image of an Adita male stared back at him; solid black eyes, hair short and black, skin pale.

"You can change how they see you." Eve came up behind him placing her hand on his back. His appearance altered between old and new, from human to Adita. "It's a projection of what they remember, or what they expect to see."

"I think it's best no one knows about this." Austin turned to her. "I'm not ashamed and I don't regret my decision. But they won't understand. Especially the younger ones." He turned back to the mirror, not thinking about the bunker residents or becoming an Adita. It was Agra who occupied his thoughts. Agra who was responsible for Caleb's absence. Agra who would pay if Caleb was harmed in anyway.

Feeling Austin's unease added to her own sense of foreboding. "Things are changing rapidly on Paru," she said. "Agra's presence fades and shifts so often I can no longer hold on to him," she said. "We should leave as soon as you are ready. And you won't be ready until you nourish your body. You will need the strength."

Austin didn't shudder at the thought or find her words difficult to hear. This was part of the deal, something he would have to accept or die a slow death of starvation.

27 EVE OF MAN

The temple was quiet. Not a whisper, not a breath was heard as Eve and Austin traveled the dim halls. They passed through the judging chambers on to Agra's quarters, but Eve knew before pushing open the door that her father was gone. They were all gone. She'd come full circle, abandoned again by her people, her family. However, this time was different. This time she knew who was responsible and that knowledge cut deep, searing in her mind thoughts of revenge. A fissure began to take form.

  A fissure was seldom noticed until too late. Eve's thoughts engulfed her, she fell to her knees holding her head, digging her nails into her skin. Why, she screamed inside her head and slammed her fist on the ground, cracking the stone underfoot. The rage was almost uncontrollable, and she didn't know how to release these feelings, to subside the ebb. She ran from the temple out onto the steps, releasing a primal yell of rage into the night. The sound shook the temple to its foundation. Turning to face the temple, she raised her hands into the air. The rage boiled up inside her body, exploding in a wave of energy directed at the temple, at Agra, at all Adita. Austin didn't try to stop her, he understood, he felt her pain.

  The temple, a structure perhaps older than Eve, began to cave in upon itself. From the top a large section crashed down a few feet from where Austin stood. He stepped aside in time, an afterthought. The first felled stone released the raging demon inside of her. She continued tearing the temple down, down to its knees, just as Agra's actions had brought her to her knees. Each broken piece suffocated her, each piece broke her spirit. Why? This was the single question running through her mind. Why had he done this to her again? And worse, how had she so grossly underestimated Agra? When nothing to destroy remained, Eve sank onto an upturned stone, feeling ruined. Weariness overcame her, she wished for sleep, like a human. Respite from living belonged to humans, but never before had the consequences of the day impacted her so that she desired to be human.

  Austin knelt in front of her, taking her hand into his. "We'll find Caleb," he said and believed it.

Eve didn't have the strength to even shake her head, or to argue. Agra had left no traces of where he'd gone, where he'd taken their son. When Eve listened, the silence was deafening. Her future was never more uncertain than now, and Austin would also suffer her fate. He knew nothing of hunger, but soon he would understand and hate her for the curse she bestowed upon him. The curse of being an Adita.

Austin heard this and grasped her by the shoulders. "Don't think that. It was my decision to become part of your world. I'm going to be fine."

"You don't know that."

"I do know," he replied. "And I know we'll find Caleb."

"We have to," Eve said, "before it's too late."

Austin held her close to him, passing his strength to her as she'd done so many times for him. They sat amidst the rubble until night turned to day and the sun began to find its way through the jungle's canopy. A single ray fell upon Eve's arm, warming her skin. She lifted her face to that ray of light and opened her eyes. She looked through the sun out into the cold dark universe beyond, out to where the planet Kaja existed alone in the dark matter on the edge of the universes. That was where she belonged. A lone being, on a lone planet, with no people to call her own.

"You're not alone," Austin said, tilting her head to look at him. "You've walked alongside man for a very long time. You have more memories of my world than you do of the Adita's. You even have a child that is part human. I think that qualifies you as a member of my family, more so than of the Adita."

"Eve of man," she whispered, although doubting the humans would accept her as one of their own. Not as long as she was Adita and needed them for her very existence. A feather of a warning danced down her spine taking her mind off her woes. She motioned to Austin, who was already scanning the tree line for movement. They walked down the steps, over the rubble, and across the clearing, stopping a few feet from the jungle's edge. Shadows shifted in and out of view, words were whispered, too soft to understand.

"Who's there?" Austin demanded.

A large shadow moved forward, stepping out from the dense undercover into the clearing. A Svan, darker skinned than most, stood before them. He wore a type of battle dress upon his breast. Soon another and then another stepped out, until Eve and Austin were surrounded. The dark-skinned Svan bowed down on one knee in front of Eve and the others followed suit.

"Rise. I'm not your master," Eve ordered them.

They stood tall. The dark-skinned Svan spoke a greeting and to Austin's surprise he understood their language.

"My name is Pala. I am the commanding officer of the Elder's guard," the dark-skinned Svan said.

"I am Eve, daughter of Agra," she replied using the Svan's native tongue. "And this is Captain Austin Reynolds."

Pala turned to Austin and bowed to him. "I am honored to meet you Captain Reynolds. Your name is spoken in high regard amongst the Svan."

Austin looked up at Pala, who stood at least three feet taller than he. "I would like to say the same about you, about the Svan, but I would be telling lies."

"And I would hear nothing less than the truth Captain Reynolds. I do not pretend that we are friends now, but I think in time we might not be adversaries."

"I'll keep an open mind," Austin replied.

Pala turned to Eve. "The Elders request an audience."

Having been unaware of their presence, Eve paused before responding, "Of course we will see them."

Pala stepped aside. From out of the shadows the white-haired man from Austin's dreams stepped into the sunlight. He was followed by eleven more; male and female, dark skin, white hair, some bent over, most frail in appearance.

"Do you know who I am?" the man from Austin's dream asked Eve, using the Adita's ancient tongue.

Eve came forward for a closer look. He was familiar, from a time long ago, but she could not put a name to the memory. "I know you. I know you from my father's memories of long ago, when the Adita lived on Earth."

"I am Sattya. Your great-great-grandfather. And this is Matri, your great-great-grandmother." A female Elder stepped forward.

"Hello granddaughter. It is a pleasure to see you again. I know you don't remember me, but in time your mind will find the missing pieces."

Some experiences were amazing, others were truly humbling, and Eve was humbled to be in their presence, in the presence of her great-great-grandparents and the other Elders. She had Agra's memories of them, had heard the tales and legends about them, but none were hers to claim. Now here they were, here they all stood. Her ancestors. The beginning of civilization. Eve bowed her head to them. Austin, who had Adita blood coursing through his veins, blood that held Eve's memories, bowed his head in reverence as well.

"Raise your heads, we are not your masters." Sattya responded, his voice warm and tender. "We are an aged and feeble bunch, having outlived our usefulness."

Eve raised her head to look at her grandfather. "Why are you all still here grandfather? On Paru?"

"I'm afraid Agra gave us little choice when he left. We could join him in his quest or stay here to die. We chose to stay. We chose honor."

"Does he have Caleb? Do you know where he took our son?" Eve asked.

Sattya nodded. "He took him to the trade colonies."

Austin stiffened. "The trade colonies on Vazya?"

"Yes, on Vazya," Sattya replied. "A planet built on the backs of slaves and fueled by the suffering of many. It sits at the edge of life's very existence, beyond it there is nothing."

Austin recalled what Eve had told him of the first humans brought to Earth, and felt a knot forming in his stomach. "Do they still trade humans?"

"There are those who buy or trade them from time to time for," he paused, "for various uses, but the demand has decreased greatly over the past century. Other species have become more desirable."

"I thought the Adita weren't welcome in the colonies. Why would he go there?" Eve interrupted.

"There is much you do not know about Agra. I feel I must tell you, so you will understand. The words I have to say will not be easy to hear, but if you wish to know the truth and if you wish to find your son, you will listen."

"We have to find our son," Eve answered, her voice carrying more forcefulness than intended. "I'm sorry grandfather. I meant no disrespect."

"I know you didn't," he replied. "Shall we go inside?" He gestured behind them.

They turned to find a new temple standing in place of the one Eve had destroyed. The new structure was built of blue glass, and where the former promised evil, the present offered warmth and hospitality. They rode a glass platform to the top of the temple where they entered a room made entirely of glass. They sat at a round glass table. Below the jungle's canopy formed a thick green carpet, far off to the left and right the oceans sparkled like a million jewels, above them the sky was a brilliant blue. The views, although magnificent, only added to the surreal moment and a feeling of déjà vu for Eve. She turned her attention on Sattya, who was ready to tell them about the Adita, about her father. The truth this time.

Sattya began to speak. "Much of what Agra told you about the beginning is true. We were the first on Earth, where we lived in our true form for many years. We'd regained our strength and grown in number. Plans for taking complete control of the seven universes were being laid out. Those were very exciting times." Sattya sighed. "Then everything changed in a moment, in a single chance encounter on that fateful night." He paused.

"It was you?" Eve asked. "You were the first to turn?"

"That is correct. And it's a moment I will forever regret," Sattya replied and the other Elders nodded in agreement.

"Did you wish to live as Svan? Do you wish to be Svan again?" Austin asked, gripping the edge of the table. "They murdered almost the entire human race. Is that what you wanted? Our annihilation?" Eve laid her hand on Austin's arm, but he shook her off.

"Let him have his say dear. He has every right to be angry," Sattya said, turning to Austin. "Do not look down upon the Svan. They can be brutal, yes, but they are honest in who they are and aren't reliant on humans for survival. They have no pretenses. They killed many humans, but this was done under Agra's orders, based on the lies he wove."

Hearing that Agra was responsible didn't make the genocide any more palatable. "Why? Why did he do it? If it wasn't to cleanse the Earth, what was his reason?" Austin asked.

"His reason was for his own purpose."

Eve shook her head. "I don't understand."

"It is the story you do not know. The story I feel you must hear now." Sattya lowered his head and sighed. "Our wish was to become more human like, to evolve. The day you found Austin was a day of great celebration. Hope was ours once again. As he grew, we discussed the possibility of a union between an Adita female and a human male. We were blinded by our own desires, blinded by Agra's well-told lies. You were not the only one manipulated granddaughter." He looked over at Austin. "I feel I in turn did the same to you, but Eve had to be saved and time was not on our side. Can you forgive me?"

"My decision was made long before you came along," Austin replied and felt Sattya knew this without him having to say so.

"I thought my father wanted to advance the Adita, to provide a new way of life, one less dependent on humans?" Eve frowned, nothing was making sense. If he didn't want Caleb for that, then what?

"He lied to you. He lied to us. His intention was never to continue our evolution."

"What then? What is he planning to do? What is going to happen to our son?" Austin asked.

"Perhaps you should start from the beginning dear," Matri suggested.

Sattya smiled in Matri's direction and nodded. "Yes, that would be best," he replied, turning back to Eve. "Do you recall anything about the great purge?"

"Very little and what I know was told to me by Agra."

"And I assume the same of your mother?"

"Even less. Agra refused to talk about her."

Sattya and Matri exchanged a look. "Soon you will understand why." Matri said, nodding to Sattya to continue.

"As you know, a period in our history existed when Adita and humans formed unions and mixed offspring were born. Of those, the males went on to procreate with female human and Adita. By law only male Adita, as well as male Adita children, were allowed to mate with female humans. After many years of this cross breeding, we realized the Adita line was being weakened and the human's strengthened. A directive was sent out banning all further unions."

Matri picked up the story at this point. "This new law was met with great resistance, but the penalty for disobeying was death. About the same time the law came to be, your mother had fallen in love with a human."

"Fell in love? I thought Adita didn't feel love," Eve interjected, glancing at Austin.

"We feel love dear and your mother felt very strongly for the human. The human who was your real father."

Eve leaned forward, grasping the table. "What do you mean my real father? Agra is my father."

"No dear, Agra is your half-brother. His father was an Adita warrior who died in battle many years earlier. He is much older than you and, in many ways, more a father than a sibling. We never agreed with him not telling you who he was, but he insisted this was best for you and for the Adita. This is why no one outside our circle knows you have human ancestors." Matri smiled, but nothing in her expression gave comfort to her words.

Sattya took over again. "Adita law forbade your parent's union. When Agra learned his mother was pregnant with you, he became enraged and thus his profound hatred for the human race was born. And being that he'd recently taken over as head of the Saciva and as ruler of the Adita he was now in command of our people. He ordered all half-breeds to be brought to him. The parents, both Adita and human, were made to watch their loved ones slaughtered and burned. Your mother fled, taking you with her. Agra spent the next several years hunting her. He was relentless in his search and he eventually found her in Russia. You were seven years old at the time. When he returned, he'd only brought you back and refused to talk of your mother. We presumed her dead."

"Why didn't he kill me as well? Why bring me back?"

"You were the first of your kind and despite his hatred toward you, he sensed something unique in your blood. He wanted to wait, to see how you developed before deciding your fate," Matri answered.

"However, only a few weeks after his return, the Adita began dying. We realized, almost too late, the human's DNA had altered over time and that change, although slight, acted like a lethal virus. Evacuations began immediately. Agra spared your life on the condition that you remain behind on Earth. We tried to persuade him otherwise, but he was adamant."

"I thought I was left behind because I was immune to the disease. Is that not true?"

Sattya shook his head. "Agra didn't know for sure. He gambled with your life on a hunch that you would survive. He was of the opinion that if you didn't, the loss was negligible."

"I'm not a true blood? I have human DNA?"

"You're every bit a true blood now. Over time your transformation to Adita proved Agra's theory to be correct in that the Adita DNA will always dominate. Although some human traits remain, they are insignificant," Sattya explained. "I know this is a lot for you to take in and I'm sorry to be the one telling you, but we felt you should know the truth."

Eve sat back from the table and stared out the window. She'd misjudged Agra on every level. All this mattered little to her. She couldn't change the past and in time she would meet Agra again. They would have their day, but until then her main concern was finding Caleb.

"Agra believes strongly in preserving the Adita blood line. He has secured lands on Vazya and will breed humans for his own use. In doing so he secures the continuance of the Adita, but to stay as they are, and not to evolve."

Eve wasn't pleased with this. "What does he need Caleb for?"

"As another test subject, much like you were. When Austin was discovered, Agra agreed you could conceive and led us to think his goals were the same as ours. That he had the same desires for the evolution of the Adita, but this was all a ruse."

"Is Caleb's life in danger?" Eve asked.

"I do not know. Agra's mind became impenetrable. He's grown very strong and we are very weak. I do think he'll keep Caleb for as long as it takes to determine the outcome of his blood type. The best for the boy will be if the Adita DNA is the stronger of the two. As it was for you."

This did not diminish Eve's concerns. Caleb was headstrong, impetuous and still very much human. His humanity might be a frailty and his undoing or his greatest strength.

"But you aren't certain of his intentions?" Austin asked.

Sattya shrugged his shoulders, uncertain of many things since Agra's departure. Of one thing he did know, he and the other Elders were dying. He reached out, took Eve's hand in his. "We do not have much time left dear. We thought the blood of your son was our last hope, but you have news for us? A new hope."

Eve nodded, not surprised he knew of their daughter. "In three weeks we will give birth to a daughter. But you already knew this."

"Yes, we knew," Matri replied.

"I will not put her in harm's way," Austin said.

Sattya shook his head. "That will not be necessary. The amount of blood needed is very little. You must stay here on Paru. Have your child, allow us to gain strength from her blood."

Unease settled over Eve, causing her to wonder if she could trust Sattya and the other Elders. What if they were working with Agra? What if Agra knew about her daughter and the Elders stayed behind to trick her with their tales of despair? Agra knew she held more compassion in her heart than was normal for an Adita. He knew she would be desperate to find her son. He knew how to pull her strings, to manipulate her feelings, her human feelings.

Sattya watched Eve as she silently battled with her fears, her demons and doubts. These thoughts were expected and would be dealt with as necessary. "We would travel to Earth, but I'm afraid in our weakened state we could not survive the trip."

Eve's brows furrowed. She wanted to believe him. She wanted to think someone in her family was not going to turn on her when she needed them the most. In the end, having no choice, she decided to trust them, but on her terms. "I will bring her blood to you, but I will give birth to my daughter on Earth."

"I understand your need for caution. We respect your decision and will await your return, but please do hurry dear," Sattya replied.

Eve nodded and stood. The Elders also stood, sitting once she and Austin had exited the room. The Elders sat in silence until satisfied Eve and Austin had left Paru. Sattya was the first to speak. "I know what you're thinking. A sample is not enough, but it's a start and if the blood is pure, we won't require much more than a few drops."

One of the Elders, not at all pleased, spoke out, "You should have ordered her to stay here."

"I agree. What if the blood isn't pure or we need more?" another asked.

"The blood of the child will be pure," Sattya replied, although he too had doubts, but delicate matters required a delicate approach. Sattya sensed their displeasure and tried to appease them. "It will be enough to provide the strength we need to regenerate our own blood and give us time to plan for our future. We must keep in mind, Eve does not feel an allegiance to the Adita, but today we have given her reason to choose our side to align with. We must tread lightly going forward, lest we lose what little trust we have gained from her."

28 PROPOSAL

Eve stood alone on top of Mount Everest, looking out over the lands in a desperate effort to find proof that the Elders were wrong, that Agra hadn't betrayed her. She'd traveled across the universes searching for her people, for the Svan, but they had vanished without a trace. The compounds on Earth were empty, boarded up as if they hadn't been used in years. The Adita's exit from the planet had been thorough and complete. All that remained were a handful of humans, perhaps a thousand in total, scattered about the planet. How long could she live on their blood? How long could Austin survive this life thrust upon him? These thoughts darkened her mood and deepened the rage she felt toward Agra.

She returned to the bunker, to Austin, who anxiously awaited her return. "The Elders told the truth. They're gone."

"Everyone?"

"Yes, except for a few humans here on Earth and the Elders and Svan on Paru. I searched the seven universes and found nothing." Eve sank down onto the couch.

Austin came to sit next to her. "Can you hear Agra?"

She shook her head. "He's using his powers to shield Vazya so that I can't even come close. His efforts to keep me away are extreme, which leads me to believe that Caleb must be on Vazya with him."

"The Elders said he planned to cultivate the humans, to breed them like our cattle. What does that mean for them?" Austin asked.

"The males who are the best of breed will mate with the best of the females. From their offspring, only the top of the line will be chosen to continue breeding."

"What happens to those who don't make the cut?"

Eve turned to Austin. "They will be sold at auction."

Austin was silent for several minutes. He'd known the answer before he asked the question. They were no more to the Adita than a cow or pig to a human. He couldn't fault the Adita for being who they were, at least not in the beginning. Now though, when Caleb could have provided a solution, a way to eliminate their need for human blood, he thought different.

"Do you think it that easy?" Eve asked.

"If there's an alternate way, then yes it should be that easy."

"You would have passed up a meal of cow or pig for an alternative?" she asked. "No, you would not have. Although many of your kind declined being carnivores, most chose it as their primary means of sustenance."

"I get what you're saying, but this is different."

"No, it isn't."

Austin couldn't argue against her point, she was right. Humans didn't exist to the Adita in any other capacity than for their survival. They'd taken from Earth what they'd wanted and left. The meaning of this for those who remained, who had survived the nightmare, was a dim light at the end of a long tunnel. The survivors could start over, repopulate, and regain control of their lives. These were things Austin should have found solace in, but his concern wasn't just for those left behind. The more urgent concerns were for Eve and to some extent for himself. How would they survive? People wouldn't willingly line up to donate blood. This all paled against his worry over his son and again guilt washed over him for allowing Agra to take Caleb.

"It wasn't your fault."

"It was."

"I see you have not lost your ability to feel human emotions," Eve noted and not without feeling a measure of relief over this fact. "Had you been there you wouldn't have been able to stop them. Even now as you are, they are stronger than you. There is much you need to learn."

"Do you trust them? The Elders?"

"I sensed truth in their words, but they are skilled beyond my powers and could easily disguise lies as truth. But much is at stake for them, as well for Agra. I just don't know at this moment. However, if what they say is true and Agra's done everything they've accused, what choice do we have? At the very least we need them on our side."

"Keep your enemies closer," Austin commented, more to himself than Eve. "What do we do now?"

"After our daughter is born, you will take her blood to the Elders. I will stay here with her in case treachery is in their plans. In the meantime, I will teach you how to control the world around you and in you."

"And then we...?"

"We build an army," she replied, feeling renewed by the idea. "Many hundreds of Svan live on Paru, plus the Elders--."

"No disrespect, but the Elders could barely walk upright."

Eve smiled. "Don't be fooled by appearances. With the pure blood of our daughter, they will be unstoppable. Once others learn it is Agra we seek to destroy, they too will join in our quest."

"These others, can they be trusted?"

"No, but we'll need them. The Zari would like nothing more than to claim Earth for their own. The Jada, nomads from the fifth universe, could easily be persuaded if Earth was the reward for success."

"Earth? Wait a minute. We're not giving away the planet. This is our home."

"Your home will remain in this frozen state for the next seven centuries. Captain Chase spoke the truth about its impending demise. One of the few things he told that was not deceitful." Eve smiled, thinking of Chase's demise. "For you and I the cold doesn't matter, but for your friends it will. Do you wish for them to live as they have been? For your niece to grow up under the ground, never feeling the warmth of the sun."

The mention of his niece hit home, he experienced a strong emotional reaction, one he wouldn't have expected after the change. "No, I don't wish that," he said, turning to her "I feel more human than I thought I would."

"In time those feelings will diminish. The Adita side will become more dominant than the human side, but for you it will never be completely one side or the other. You will have to learn to reconcile the two. If not, this weakness will be used against you."

"I've a lot to learn, don't I?"

Eve nodded. Trust was something he would learn not to give out, not even to her. A lesson bestowed upon her, compliments of Agra and the Adita. One she would never forget and never repeat.

"Paru could be a new home for your people," Eve suggested.

Austin frowned at first, but admitted the idea had merit. "Can we convince them to go?"

"If it's in the interest of survival, I think yes, even a human can be convinced to do that which is best, despite their qualms."

"Will they be safe?"

"Safer than they are here. The Svan will not touch them at my request."

"What about Zevia?"

"She will stay here with us until I can be sure the Elders are not working against me, that they are indeed genuine in their intentions."

"Do you know if her blood will work? Do you know if Caleb's did?"

"I suspect Agra tested Caleb's blood, but on whom and the results of which I don't know. I cannot give an answer to your question, but the sooner we take Zevia's blood to the Elders, the sooner we can prepare for battle."

Eve stood up, extending her hand to Austin. When he touched her fingers, his appearance reverted to being human as did Eve, who changed back into Roxanne.

"It is best we continue in human form. Not even your friend Zack should know about you," she said. "And we shouldn't share with them the news of our daughter."

Austin agreed. Despite their talk in the plane and Zack's reluctant acknowledgment and understanding of Austin's intentions, seeing the results might be too much for even someone like Zack.

* * *

The bunker's residents sat around the table in the Viking room. They wore stunned expressions as they tried to digest the news about the Adita's sudden departure and the end to the threat of attack by the Svan, and more so they wondered about freedoms regained. After eighteen months of living in fear and uncertainty they weren't sure what to think. Was this cause for celebration or concern? They had no way of knowing the Adita's plans, whether they would return, or if the next time it began snowing the Svan would again attack.

"What about the climate?" Ed asked.

"The climate might stay this way for the next seven hundred years or longer." Austin answered. "Or it could begin thawing tomorrow. If it thaws too soon the planet will flood, the core will eventually overheat and destroy the planet."

"What's the plan?" Zack asked. "I mean, you sound like you have a plan."

"You could go to Paru," Austin replied. "The Adita have left and will not come back. Only the Elders and few Svan remain."

For Zack, who had been to Paru, this wasn't as much to digest as it was for the others. They all looked around unsure what to think or say. Moving to another state was more stress than the average person was usually capable of handling and handling well. They were being asked to move to another planet, to leave Earth.

"You as in us, not including you?" Ed asked.

Austin had to smile a little. Of anyone, Ed would have caught that. "Roxanne and I are staying here for a little while longer."

"But why?" Ed asked.

Austin looked around the group before answering, letting his gaze land on Zack. "Agra has our son and for reasons I can't explain right now, we need to stay here. At least for a month, maybe two."

Zack's eyes narrowed, his forehead creased in thought. "Two months could be several years on Paru. Or maybe it's the other way around," he argued, "but in either case the differential between here and there could be huge."

"I know, but you have to trust me. This is the only way for us," Austin replied, listening to Zack's mind as he recalled their past conversation. "Some things are best left alone."

This last comment pulled Zack's thoughts back to the present. "Will you visit?" he asked. This was not the foremost question running through his mind, but it was a safe question to ask in the current setting.

"If we're able to, we'll come to Paru," Austin replied.

"I don't get this at all," Ed said. "If the Svan are on Paru, what's to say they won't attack us as they did here?"

Eve addressed Ed's question. "Eve won't allow it."

Ed looked at the woman sitting at Austin's side. The woman, who was not who she presented herself to be, but for the others they'd kept up the charade. "And we should trust her?"

"They will obey her command and of this I have no doubt," she replied. "You are a very intuitive man Ed. I would have thought you to be more perceptive."

"How so?" Ed asked, surprised to be bestowed a compliment in any shape or form from a being of supreme intelligence.

"If you stay here and the planet thaws, you are certain to die. The waters will reach the highest peaks, not to recede for many years. You will not live through such harsh conditions. If you don't drown, you will starve, if not that, you will die of disease. If you go to Paru, you have a chance to live again, as you once did."

"You talk of the floods as if from experience," Ed noted, thinking Eve had most likely seen every natural disaster known to man and more.

"Experience comes from many places Edward, some have to be lived, and others you only read about." Eve smiled at him and as Roxanne that smile was warm and inviting.

Ed nodded and sat back in his chair, digesting her words and chewing on his tongue. He had so many questions swirling about in his head, but the others, who only saw Roxanne, would think he'd lost his mind if he asked any one of them.

Around the table, all were thinking about what was said and not too concerned with Roxanne and Ed. Although the picture painted was bleak, it was not without hope. They could travel to Paru through the portals. The planet had the natural resources they needed, plus they could take their technology, medicine, weapons, whatever they could haul through the portal. As they sat silent, contemplating leaving Earth, the idea began to take hold, to become a real possibility. Not only was this a real possibility, it was a chance to live, to breathe, to be free again.

"Can Gisela travel through the portal?" Kyle asked. "And what about Ada? She almost died coming over from Germany."

Ada reached out to Kyle, shaking her head. "Don't you worry about me dear. I'll be fine." Her English was covered by a thick German accent.

"She's right, she'll be fine. The portal is different. You'll travel in the pod, which shields your body." Austin answered.

"What about my dog? I'm not leaving Josie behind." Bruno said, mixing his German with English. At the sound of her name, Josie's ears perked up.

Austin paused to listen to Eve's thoughts before he answered. "The dogs can go but will have to be kept in closed quarters until we're sure they can acclimate to the environment."

Somewhat satisfied with this answer, Bruno leaned back in his chair, but he wasn't through questioning Austin. "There are other animals on this place, big animals no?" he asked.

"Yes. And yes, some are quite large."

"What stops them from eating my dog? From eating us?"

"Be smarter than the beast and you won't have to worry," Roxanne replied, speaking in perfect German.

Colin interrupted before Bruno could formulate a response, "It's going to take a long time for... how many people did you say were still on Earth?"

"About a thousand," Austin responded.

Colin tried to calculate this in his mind, giving up before too long. "I'm no math wiz, but that's a lot of trips in two pods that only hold two people isn't it."

Zack laughed. "You're not an anything wiz." This comment earned him a punch in the arm from Charlie.

Colin scowled at his brother. "Should have hit him in the mouth."

"A thousand divided by four is two hundred fifty." Ed answered. "Two hundred fifty times two is five hundred. That's five hundred trips. And that's for the people. What about our things? Clothing, electronics, machinery. How do we transport those things?"

"I'm terribly sorry sir, but one bag per person. Anything more and the portal will have to charge you extra," Zack quipped. "In addition, the portal is not responsible for lost luggage, so do not place any items of value in your checked baggage. As always, thank you for traveling with the portal and enjoy your trip through space."

They all laughed, and even Austin appreciated Zack's humor. It took the attention off Roxanne, which was a relief, since their feelings toward her were ones of suspicion, doubt and sometimes confusion. Charlie, who seemed to have a sixth sense about Roxanne, was the exception. She thought Roxanne wonderful and, other than himself, was the only bunker resident to spend time alone with her. He'd never felt at ease about their relationship, not as far as Charlie was concerned. Something about the girl appealed to Eve and he couldn't determine in what capacity she valued Charlie's company.

"When are we leaving?" Charlie asked, looking Austin in the eyes, interrupting his train of thought.

Austin met her gaze. For a mere moment, he thought he saw recognition in her expression and perhaps she saw past his human disguise. He answered without wavering, "The sooner the better. I think a week is all you'll need."

"What about other survivors?" Kyle asked.

"Eve will lead them to the portals," he replied. "There's one other portal in the US, but only the Cheyenne portal is usable. There're three more outside the US, in Australia, Russia and Brazil. Eve will divide up the other survivors."

"Five?" Zack asked. "Why five?"

"Not sure man. But if the Adita are responsible for putting them on Earth, be certain there's a significance to the locations," Austin replied.

Zack's mind spun into turbo mode thinking over the possibilities. Were the portals located at specific coordinates that maybe held some strategic importance to the Adita? Or was there an electromagnetic field created by the five points. But wait, a sixth portal existed in California, the portal Austin used to find Ryan. Zack leaned back in his chair imagining, theorizing, and breaking it down until he realized Austin was watching him.

"What?"

"I didn't say anything," Austin replied, giving his famous half smile, to which Zack mouthed the words fuck off. The two men shared a look, one of mutual respect, one that said it all without having to say anything. One that said goodbye, for they both sensed these might be their final days together.

The group planned into the night for their departure. The younger crew turned in after midnight, while the adults stayed up hashing out the logistics. At half past three Austin stood up, leading the way for the others to do the same. Zack was the only one staying behind, using the excuse of wanting a snack before going to bed.

29 GUARANTEES

Inside his living quarters Austin paced the room, thinking about his son being with Agra. The next time they saw Caleb, he would most likely be a young man, but right now he was a child and vulnerable. Although Eve felt sure of Caleb's strengths and that Agra could not turn their son against them, Austin feared this would happen. Losing his son a second time, was harder and easier in some respect, to the first time. Easier because he knew Eve was right about Caleb and that he would continue to grow stronger each day, that he would resist any attempts made by Agra to corrupt him. The hard part was losing what little time was left of his childhood. A silly notion considering Caleb was never really a child, but a notion none the less.

Before turning his back on being human, Austin had dreamed again of leading the Svan into battle. The first time he'd seen this possible future, he'd been in a comatose state. The second time was after discovering Eve frozen in the mountain. She'd thought in his first vision it was Caleb at the front leading the charge, not him. After sharing his second dream with her, the 'who' in charge appeared to have changed, the sides chosen were no longer certain. That father and son might be on opposite sides had become a possibility; a future Austin hoped wouldn't come to fruition.

However, dreams and speculations of their meanings would have to wait. They would begin moving people to Paru within a week, but he was no closer to liking the idea or trusting the Elders. He stopped pacing and turned around. "I'm going back to Paru, to speak to the Elders. I can't take a chance with everyone's life unless I have some guarantees. If they want our daughter's blood, they're going to have to give me something in return."

"You don't have to go there to speak to them."

"I don't? How then?" he asked, then the answer was there.

Eve walked over to him. "Close your eyes. I'm going to teach you how to see beyond your mind, into the universes."

He did as she instructed.

"Now clear your mind. See nothing, feel nothing, hear only my voice." She spoke inside his head, and everywhere around him. "Leave your body behind. See yourself below, see us below."

Austin had the sense of floating. He opened his eyes and looked down upon himself and Eve standing in the middle of the room.

"We're going to leave the bunker and travel out into the universe. It's going to be darker than you can imagine. You will feel the dark inside of you, cold and heavy, permeating every cell. Don't be alarmed." Eve touched Austin's arm with her thoughts. "We will find the Elder's energy. Light means energy, energy means life."

They traveled through a vast dark emptiness as Eve described. A place absent of sights or sounds to act as guides. A place of nonexistence. Eve kept her mind's touch on Austin, leading him along, providing him a point of focus. She knew it possible to lose your way, having almost done so when she'd first ventured out on her own. Agra had been her teacher of this lesson and many others. During her lessons she'd felt a bond with Agra, as if he'd let his guard down, allowed himself to relax, and allowed her to come in closer. Afterwards though, he always reverted back to being cold and distant, leaving her on her own, feeling more alone. At least now she knew why.

They were approaching the Elders. Eve let go of Agra's memory to guide Austin. "You will feel the energy before you see it," she said.

"That's good to know, since I can't see shit out here."

"You don't need to see with your eyes. You need to see with your mind," she replied. "Focus Austin."

He focused and before long he felt the air change temperature, transitioning from cold to warm.

"Focus on the warm air. Let it take you along its current."

With the next patch of warm air, they were pulled into the current and whisked along at a fast pace. The air grew warmer, almost hot like an open oven door. They sped along until a brilliant light appeared out of the blackness, blinding Austin.

"Don't resist," Eve said. "It will not hurt you."

Austin relaxed, allowing the sphere of light to draw them in. Once inside, all motion ceased and again it felt as if he was floating.

"Where are we?"

"Do not think in defined terms. We are everywhere," she replied. "Sattya and the other Elders are near."

Austin tried to get a sense of this, to see them. Obscure shapes formed on the edge of the light, becoming more solid as they approached. Out from the blackness beyond, the Elders stepped into the light.

"Hello again granddaughter," Sattya greeted Eve with a bow of his head. "It is good to see the captain's learning to use the gifts that have been bestowed upon him."

Austin nodded his head to Sattya, to the others. His bearings were settling in place, his attention becoming fine-tuned, his instincts telling him to listen and watch closely.

"Perhaps this would be easier in a more controlled environment," Matri suggested. Upon her suggestion, the nothingness solidified into walls and a floor. Austin found himself and the others sitting in chairs. They were positioned in a circle with Sattya sitting opposite him and Eve.

"Thank you for seeing us grandfather," Eve said. "I'm sure by now you are aware of the reason why we sought you out."

"Yes, we are," he answered. "We have discussed your request and concerns. Our desire is to allow the humans to relocate to Paru. However, there must be rules."

"On both sides," Austin added.

Sattya paused and looked to Austin. "Yes, on both sides. As I said, we've discussed your concerns thoroughly. We will honor an agreement between our people. The Adita and Svan will live as neighbors with the humans. They will live together in peace."

"And your rules grandfather?"

"If the humans wish to live here, the planet must not be harmed, the air and water must not be polluted, nor the wildlife exploited. They will take only what is needed to survive. Population growth will be controlled. These are only the basic rules. They are not our rules per say, but those by which the humans have not used in their stewardship of Earth. Therefore, I felt it necessary to note such out loud and let it be known at the very least we expect these to be applied. For these and one specific request, we will provide for all of their needs. They will have most all of the comforts they've grown accustomed to having, but in such a manner that Paru is not harmed."

Austin tensed, sensing and hearing what was about to be requested. Eve laid a hand on his arm, calming him, pulling him back into his chair.

"As I said, we have one specific request." Sattya glanced around the circle before continuing. "In return for all that we will provide, we ask for the humans to give of their blood, in order that we might continue our research into finding a solution."

"But that's not all you want it for," Austin said, leaning forward in his chair again. "You intend to use it for your own survival, in case the blood of our daughter is not enough?"

Sattya again paused before responding. "You perceive much for being so young. However, I hope you can understand our plight. I know you also understand our needs, having experienced them first hand as one of us. Although, I do admit, you have tremendous will power in ignoring the demands of your body. Very admirable captain."

"I'm not seeking your admiration, only your assurance that no humans will be harmed or killed." The sense that he was missing something important poked at him. "I want your word that the Svan will not be ordered to kill any humans."

"And of our request?"

It was Austin's turn to pause. "I will discuss it with them. If they are willing, then you can have what you ask for, as long as it does not endanger their lives."

"We await your answer then. If it is yes, a new home on Paru will await them," Sattya replied and the others concurred.

"We anxiously await the arrival of our granddaughter," Matri said to Eve. "We shall see you soon."

Eve's hands instinctively moved to her stomach. The Elders stood, the room vanished and the two were left alone floating in a bright nothing. Eve reached out and covered Austin's eyes for the briefest moment. When she removed her hand, they were back in the bunker, standing in their living room. The time on the clock indicated five minutes had lapsed during their absence.

"You need nourishment," Eve noted.

As if by the power of suggestion, Austin felt the cravings and they were strong. He rubbed his throat and licked his lips. The sensation was not unlike having hunger for food, except the desire affected more than his physical requirements. Where human hunger centered on the stomach, this clawed at his throat, feeling more like a thirst, than hunger.

Eve took his hand. "It's best to replenish before using your powers. You in particular need to pay close attention to your needs. It would not do anyone well if those needs were to overcome your ability to reason."

Austin shrugged off the sensation, the desire to drink, pulling his focus back onto the conversation they had with Sattya. "Can they be trusted?"

As Sattya had noted, Eve too was impressed with Austin's strength. "For now, yes, but only because we have something they need. After that I can't see. Adita aren't bound by their word. They feel no sense of loyalty or obligation to honor agreements. If the situation serves their purpose they will play by the rules."

"And when the time comes that they no longer need us, then what?"

"The rules will change," she replied, matter of fact. "And therefore, evolution is so very important. This is why complacency is so very dangerous. You understand this now."

A reply was not necessary. His reasons for changing weren't a secret or unfamiliar to Eve. "What are you suggesting we do?"

"Prepare, change, evolve."

He heard everything she said and that which she didn't say out loud. "You make it sound as if it's a simple decision to make, but it won't be for them. They'll resist."

"At first yes, but in the end, they will see reason," she said having complete confidence this would be the outcome. "What is not simple about change or die? One choice increases the odds and the other decreases them. I think it to be a very easy decision."

Austin almost laughed. "For as long as you have been around the human race, you know they don't function or think in simple terms."

He was right, but a time had existed when humans weren't so lazy about survival. And there would come a time in the near future when once again circumstances would require a different outlook. If they hoped to live, not thrive, but live, the humans needed to prepare now. If they waited until the threat fell upon them, they would perish.

"What do we say about Caleb?" Austin asked.

"The truth. That Agra took him."

Austin frowned at this, thinking news of Caleb's kidnapping would be too upsetting for the girls, but he would have to tell them something. "I'll speak to Zack first. See what he thinks."

"I'll come with you. Zack will need more than your words to accept and agree to what you are about to propose. He needs to see the outcome, to know what life will become if they say no."

"Freedom is a powerful motivator to overcome," Austin noted.

"Yes, it is, but some freedoms come with substantial sacrifice and one must weigh their choices and choose that which guarantees preservation of life."

Eve took Austin to Cheyenne before going to see Zack. Despite his assurance that he could wait, Eve insisted, knowing better than to risk an altercation. The smell of Zack's blood would have been tempting and maybe quite more than he could have resisted. She didn't want Zack's death on her hands as well.

* * *

The walls of the room were closing in on Zack. He paced from one end of the diner to the other, certain each time it took less and less steps. That Austin and Eve sat quietly watching him, didn't stop him from pacing, and didn't make it any easier to think this thing through. They were asking the impossible. They were asking for them to agree to become a food source for the Adita. He stopped pacing and stared at the back wall, not seeing the life-sized paintings of James Dean or

Marilyn Monroe. His last thought percolated through the natural progression of rationalization and logic. Humans were already their food source, which had occurred without invitation. This time they were asking first, giving them the opportunity to say no. If that was what they were offering, with no strings attached, Zack could maybe get there, but he had doubts, and none more so than in regard to the Adita's underlying intentions.

Putting all of this aside for the moment, Zack shifted to the second pressing decision his friend had presented to him. This one being more palatable than the first, but no less difficult and still filled with unknown consequences. If in turning into something better than human, were they only making themselves a bigger target? A tastier morsel? Were they taking a plain bowl of vanilla ice cream, adding whipped cream, chocolate syrup and placing a cherry on top, only to set it down in front of a sugar addict, expecting not to have consequences? A small part of him thought yes, this was exactly what they were doing if they agreed. He returned to the booth where Austin and Eve waited.

"I don't like it, any of it. Changing our DNA, volunteering to be a food source. None of it makes sense. In fact, it's way off key. If those are our options, I'd rather take my chances here on Earth," Zack said, putting it all out there in one breath. "I like my freedom."

"Can I show you something?" Eve asked, sliding out from the booth to stand next to Zack. He hesitated when she held out her hand to him. Austin encouraged him with a nod. Eve took his hand. "I will show you what freedom looks like if you stay here on Earth."

Before Zack could mutter a single syllable of protest, Eve whisked him into another time and dimension. Behind him, the diner remained visible, but as he watched, rising waters swallowed it whole. The water was murky black, having an oil like consistency. Eve touched Zack's arm and pointed to a mountain range that hadn't been visible a moment ago. The foothills appeared miles away, and the mountain peak disappeared into the clouds above.

In a blink they were high up in the mountain walking along an uneven path carved into its side. The path was three feet wide in most places, narrowing to two in others. Every ten feet they passed a cave opening. At one of these openings Eve stopped and again pointed. Zack followed her direction and saw water, vast and wide. It was everywhere, and everywhere he looked was the water. From behind him he heard a baby crying. His daughter's cries. Crying because she was hungry and cold and alone. The sound pierced his heart. At that very moment he felt the desperation of the entire planet. He looked back out over the water, left to right, as far as he could see. And not a single mountain range was visible from where he stood. They were alone. Zack fell to his knees and covered his face.

Once upon a time he'd experienced flooding. It was after torrential rains dumped six inches of water in less than twenty-four hours down on parts of Colorado. Mass flooding affected several places in central Colorado and Governor Parks had declared a state of emergency. Zack had done his part to help out those in need by sending boats, supplies, food and as much marijuana as anyone might want in such desperate times. Not surprising to Zack, he sold out all stock in the flood's first week. In desperate times he knew alcohol and drug sales went through the roof. That he'd been high through most of it hadn't inhibited his ability to grasp basic economics.

After three weeks went by, many places had remained under water. He and some buddies decided it a good idea to stock up and tour the flooded areas by boat. In the beginning it had been for fun. Avoiding the law was easy, selling the pot was easy, making money was easy. In the end Zack gave away his supplies, playing it off as being a Good Samaritan, as buying his way into heaven. The truth of it, which he wouldn't have shared with any of his so-called friends back then, was he had a conscience. The desperation on the faces of the people who had lost everything bothered him deeply. He'd gone back the next day and the next, trying to help in any way he could. He'd even rented out an entire hotel, paying for families to stay for as long as it took.

During those days he remembered coming home, taking off his clothes and falling into the bed exhausted. The next morning, he would pick up his clothes from the floor and the smell of the flood water would bowl him over. He'd thrown the clothes in the garbage. Not even Tide Extra Duty could do the job on that smell. A week or so later, he could still smell the stench of the flood waters, as if it was somehow ingrained in every pore. As awful as that had been, it paled in comparison to what Eve presented to him. In his clothes, in his nose, the stench of the water remained. A damp stinking odor that clung to him, much the same as the feelings of desolation clung to his mind.

Zack opened his eyes, bracing for the horrid sight, relieved to see they were back in the diner. "I can't do that to my daughter," he said, although he couldn't help thinking they were simply trading one impending death for another. A lesser evil? Maybe so. A quicker death? Maybe not.

"It's the right decision Zack," Austin said. "You'll be safe on Paru. You have my word."

Zack chuckled, a half amused, half sarcastic little laugh. "I'm not worried about you keeping your word. You I get. You're human. We think alike. The Adita not so much. The Elders? Haven't a clue. So, while I appreciate your word and know you'll honor it come death do us part, forgive me if it doesn't provide much in the way of assurance."

With that being said and nothing more to decide, Austin called Ed, Jenny, Colin and Charlie to the diner at which time Eve changed back into Roxanne. Three of the four reacted in much the same way as Zack; at first fear and concern and then arriving at the same conclusion. Charlie, who sat next to Roxanne hugging her arm, couldn't have been more excited about leaving the planet, starting new, meeting the Elders. Austin felt that familiar twinge of concern for Charlie's delicate mental state, for where her mind had settled. Upon hearing his thoughts, Roxanne reached out and touched his hand. A small unnoticed gesture, a touch that conveyed much and justified his concerns. Austin's hand went to rubbing his head. Charlie's problems would have to be addressed soon.

The next group was called to the diner, and they went through the same process, having the same reactions. When the news about Caleb was shared the girls were beside themselves with worry and tears were shed. Austin assured them Caleb was being well taken care of and that Agra's intentions were not to harm his son.

Two hours later all the residents were present and marinating on the Elder's offer. As was expected, convincing them to trust the Elders, to accept their deal, was the more difficult sale. In the end, the promise of life much as what they had been accustomed to pre-aliens clinched the deal. Unlike asking them to offer up their veins on demand, the decision to become improved versions of themselves seemed to be a no brainer for everyone. After all questions and concerns were exhausted, votes were cast on each. In each vote, the group arrived at the unanimous decision of yes.

30 CHANGE

Change never comes in neatly wrapped packages with specific instructions on the best way to handle. For the bunker's residents, preparing to move was filled with anxiety, doubts and one question after another. The full-blown realization of where they were going was sinking in hard and fast. They knew Paru wasn't an industrialized planet. They wouldn't have factories or corporations to work in, supermarkets to buy food, malls to shop at, and no electronics, so where would their necessities come from? For Austin to say the Elders would provide for them meant little to anyone, including on occasion, Austin. The Elders hadn't volunteered specifics and he hadn't asked for them. He'd witnessed their power to move and create, to build and destroy and was basing his trust on this knowledge.

Not all worries were of the same enormity in regard to consequences. For the girls, simple things like clothing and make up, as well as more complicated things, like tampons and razors were topics of concern. How much could they take? How long would things last? What happened when they ran out? Could they come back? The questions never ended, with one leading into another.

Jenny, who had stepped into Madison's shoes as den mother, took the brunt of the girl's questions. She did her best to keep everyone calm, but each unanswered question caused their anxiety levels to increase. At one point, while discussing the possibility of no indoor plumbing on Paru, she thought the girls would stage a mutiny. The fault wasn't theirs, and over the past week, for reasons of her own, she didn't feel as confident they were doing the right thing. She'd held it together while in front of the girls, but at night she would fall exhausted into Ed's arms.

On the day of the move Jenny chose quiet over pandemonium. She, with Ryan's help, sat in their living room neatly folding clothes and placing them into suitcases. On the outside she smiled and laughed with her son. On the inside she was in knots. Each time she thought about going back to Paru, panic reared its ugly head, threatening to overwhelm her. Ed had asked about her time in the warehouse, but she'd lied, telling him she couldn't remember anything before opening her eyes and seeing Roxanne standing over her.

But she remembered everything, from the very start, from the day the Svan came for her and Ryan. She could recall each minute detail of that morning when she walked into the kitchen and saw the Svan for the first time. She'd been holding a tray of mugs filled with hot chocolate, which she'd hurled at the hulking beast as it moved toward Ryan. Her only thought was for protecting her son, but the Svan moved too swiftly. One moment Ryan was there, the next he was gone, and then they'd come for her. She'd screamed for Ed. She'd heard him banging on the door and then the window, trying to get inside.

For a while everything was dark and quiet, almost peaceful, almost as if the entire experience had been a nightmare. When she awoke, she'd quickly understood the nightmare was beginning in earnest. The tubes stuck in her body, the Adita watching over them at first, then leaving them alone, to slowly die. Lying naked on that table, not feeling anything, not able to speak, only able to watch the life draining from her body. Somehow, even though surrounded by death, she'd held onto her will to live. Her strength came from Ryan, from knowing he lived. And from Ed, her pillar. She knew they were alive, that her son was alive, and he dreamed of her.

All of this remained vivid in her memories, not to be shared with Ed, not now. Maybe later she could tell him, when she felt certain he could handle it, but for now she must think of Madison and Zack's baby. Jenny's hand went to her stomach, where a small bump could already be felt. Soon they would have to make the announcement to the others, but that worry would have to wait until after the move.

* * *

On the other end of the bunker, Zack dealt with concerns of his own regarding the move, a primary worry being medicine. He'd made a trip to the Colorado Springs drug store, stocking up on everything and anything he thought might be needed in the future. To his surprise, Austin had gone with him. Not for any other reason than to spend some time with Zack before they left for Paru. That Austin wanted to spend time with him made Zack laugh, thinking back to when the captain had first arrived at the bunker. A dumb kid who sold pot for a living had been Austin's opinion of him. Zack had tried hard to impress him, without making it too obvious it mattered to him what Austin thought. Funny they should end up as close as they were, but life was funny that way. For a fleeting moment Zack thought about Madison but chased it away. Counting boxes of aspirin and wondering how long their supplies would last was a safer place to be.

Planning a move for eighteen people was logistically more challenging than keeping pot inventory up to date in a few stores. CVS or Walgreens didn't exist on

Paru and, despite Austin telling him not to worry, he worried. Worrying had never been his thing, a fact his mom would have attested to and explained being due to his inability to take responsibility, for anything. How times had changed. No shortage of things he'd taken responsibility for these days, and worried over plenty. The bottle of Jack had taken a back seat to a bottle of Rolaids, which he chewed on like candy. The chalky little tablets would be ineffective against what he knew was an ulcer in the making.

"Things have changed mom. Boy have they changed," Zack said, talking out loud to keep from hearing his own thoughts.

* * *

In the teen quarters, the noise and activity caused a buzz like a disturbed beehive. Out in the common area suitcases were propped open on the floor, clothes spilling over, leaving little room to walk. Every available space was covered with someone's things; the couches, tables, desks, nothing was spared. A madhouse of sorts fed by their nervousness over what was to come.

Sue and Jane helped McKenna pack her things, while Anne and Grace fussed over which baby toys to take. In a corner, away from the noise, Charlie sat folding her clothes and placing them in her suitcase. The move didn't bother her. She couldn't wait to leave Earth and start over. She wasn't worried about the Elders either. They wouldn't harm anyone, especially not her. She was Eve's special friend and soon she was going to be like her. The others could become improved versions of themselves, but not her, she was going to be better than everyone. Eve had said she'd think it over and let her know today. Nothing mattered more to her, more than becoming someone else, more than shedding her body for a new one, for one her father hadn't touched. Yes, she thought, new and fresh and clean. She glanced at her watch. Only a few more minutes and she would know her fate. Please, please, please say yes, she silently begged, thinking that if Eve heard her, she'd know how much it meant and couldn't say no.

"Charlie!" Anne said for the third time.

Charlie looked up. "Uh, sorry." She pulled her ear buds out. "What's wrong?"

"Do you have room in your suitcase for this?" Anne held a stuffed bunny rabbit out to her.

Charlie reached for it. "Sure."

"You ok?" Anne asked, observing Charlie closely. The captain had asked her to keep an eye on Charlie, to let him know if she was acting strange. A hard thing to determine since Charlie was kind of odd and withdrawn anyway.

Charlie smiled, an empty sort of smile that held no joy. "I'm ok. You ok?"

"Yeah," Anne replied and, after a moment of hesitation, turned away. She didn't have time to babysit a teenager; she had two real babies who needed her attention. Still, Austin seemed more than concerned and she couldn't, in good conscience, blow him off after all he'd done for them. She turned back, but Charlie was no longer there. Anne looked all around the room. No Charlie. Her shoulders dropped. Should she alert the captain? Was Charlie acting strange or just being Charlie? She wrung her hands together trying to decide.

"Anne, the girls are up." Grace called from the door. "Do you want help feeding?" And with the call of motherhood, Anne forgot all about Charlie.

* * *

The barn was empty when Charlie arrived, so she walked around looking in the stalls, waiting, and hoping. She paused at the door, running her finger along the metal bars. Replacements for the locks her father's men had destroyed trying to find her. A smile played on her lips. She'd outsmarted them. Each and every last one. She'd escaped and made them look stupid. Her only regret was not being able to see her father's face when they told him his prize possession was gone. When she'd heard that the captain had shot her father in the head, she'd wished it had been her pulling the trigger.

"Hey Charlie."

She spun around almost falling over. "Austin. What are you doing here?"

"I could ask you the same, but I already know why you're here."

"You do?" She regarded him with suspicion. Had Anne said something to him? Had Colin?

"Eve told me about your request."

Charlie balked. "She told you." Eve had betrayed her? How could she have told the captain? It was their secret, no one had to know. From behind Austin, Charlie saw Eve step out of the shadows. Tears filled her eyes, spilling over and down her cheeks.

"Please don't be upset," Austin said, stepping closer to her, wanting to take her in his arms, to make her pain go away. "She only wanted to protect you."

Charlie shook her head. "You don't understand. No one understands."

Austin took her hand in his. "I do understand Charlie. I understand what he did to you. I understand that you can't forget no matter how hard you try, no matter how much time you spend cleaning. You can never clean the memories away."

"How'd you know about the cleaning?"

"Colin made a remark, nothing much. And when Eve told me what you asked of her, I put two and two together. But it's ok. It's going to be ok."

She shook her head. "Does that mean you won't do it?" she asked Eve.

"I thought it would be nice to have you be like me, to have a friend Charlie, but we can be friends as we are now. You don't want to be like me."

"But I do want to be like you." Charlie walked up to Eve. "I want to be stronger than everyone. I want to not care about anything or anyone."

"Is that what you think being Adita means? Is that what you think of me?" Eve asked, knowing it was exactly what the girl thought and perhaps on some level it bothered Eve because it was true.

Charlie searched Eve's eyes, but only saw her panicked expression reflected back. "You promised you would change me. You promised!" She pulled up her sleeve and tore off a bandage wrapped around her wrist, revealing a fresh wound. "Here, I'm offering myself to you. Take my blood, take it all," she begged. "I'd rather die than live another day as his daughter."

Eve took Charlie by the shoulders and pulled her close. "You are no longer his daughter, you are mine," she whispered in Charlie's ear. "But not as an Adita, not that way." Eve stepped back and placed her hand on top of Charlie's head. "This will hurt." And with that she passed a bolt of energy through Charlie's body. Her entire body glowed, she screamed and fainted. Austin caught her as she fell. He laid her on the ground, cradling her head. Eve came to stand next to him.

"Will she remember this happened?" he asked.

"No. The pain of her father will no longer be her curse to carry. She is whole again. She is better."

Austin smoothed Charlie's hair from her face. "Is everything set?"

"Yes. We should leave directly after sending them to Paru. You have much to learn and we have many places to visit."

"Do you foresee any major problems? Any real resistance?"

Eve glanced over at him and said, "With your species, there's always resistance to logic when it does not meet expectations or fit neatly into preconceived notions. However, the proper motivation can subdue even the most stubborn of humans."

* * *

Charlie opened her eyes feeling disoriented. She stared at the ceiling trying to get her bearings. She was lying on a bed in someone's room, but couldn't remember how she came to be there or whose room she was in. The door stood ajar and she could hear the other girls talking. She'd been packing. That's right, she thought, and she'd been tired, so tired, but she wasn't any longer. In fact, she felt great, but that wasn't all, something more had changed.

Anne knocked and stuck her head inside. "Are you feeling better?"

Charlie swung her legs over the side of the bed. "I feel great. I guess I was really tired." She smiled at Anne. A genuine smile.

Anne smiled back. She couldn't help noticing Charlie seemed different, brighter maybe. As if her dark cloud had blown away. Whatever the reason, Anne was glad. "Everyone's meeting in the diner in five. Last minute instructions I guess."

"Ok. I'm coming."

* * *

The noise in the diner was a subdued murmur, as everyone waited for Austin to arrive. They sat in the booths, or at the counter, talking in voices above a whisper. Zack stood behind the counter, leaning over across from Ryan, who was working a bowl of cereal to the bottom. Every now and then Zack's eye wandered over to the booth where Jenny sat with Barbara and some of the other girls. He didn't gaze for long, not wanting Ed to catch him watching her, worrying over her and his baby growing inside of her. The whole surrogate pregnancy thing bothered Ed more than he let on.

The door opened, conversations halted, but quickly resumed, when seeing it was Anne and Charlie, not Austin. Charlie took a seat across from Roxanne, who sat alone in a booth at the back of the diner. For her part, Roxanne sat and listened while Charlie prattled off about this and that. From behind Roxanne's green eyes, Eve observed how her gift was affecting Charlie. So far all appeared to be going as expected, but only time would tell. This gift was unlike what she'd bestowed upon Jenny or that which Caleb had done for Ryan. At the thought of her son, a frown touched her lips and a crease formed in her brow. Had Charlie been paying attention, she would have noticed the sad expression on Roxanne's face. However, as it went with sixteen-year old's, attention that strayed far from themselves was rare.

A few minutes later Austin arrived. Eighteen expectant faces turned toward him. Eighteen heart rates went up in anticipation of what he would say. For Austin, who had worked with the roughest hardest men on Earth, this should have been a cakewalk, but looking out at the sea of faces drew his stomach into a knot. These weren't seasoned soldiers, or trained mercenaries, and aside from Zack and Kyle, they had little to bring to the table in means of survival. Within his team of Marines, they obeyed a golden rule; never enter a situation where the unknown outnumbers the known. Yet here he stood, about to send them off on a journey full of unknowns. The pitfalls they might encounter; unknown. Their safe being; unknown. The Elders abiding by their word; unknown. That last unknown was the biggest gamble and his prevalent concern. With a deep breath and squaring of his shoulders, Austin hid his uncertainty and addressed the group in the firm commanding tone they'd come to expect from him.

"I know you're busy packing, so I won't keep you long. I wanted to go over what Eve and I discussed as far as logistics of the move are concerned," he said, walking over to the counter and motioning to Zack for some water. "We decided it best for this group to arrive on Paru first. While you're busy laying the groundwork, Eve will visit the remaining survivors across the globe. This will take about two months start to finish."

"As we discussed, Ed will serve as the community leader." He nodded to Ed. "You'll need to choose a welcoming committee for the new arrivals. They'll begin trickling in a week or so after you, maybe sooner, maybe later. They will look to you and those you choose as the people in charge. No one will question your authority."

"Will they speak English?" Anne asked.

"No, but you'll be able to understand their languages. Which leads to my next point. We discussed the process that will take place to change your DNA. Eve will begin as soon as we finish here. Anne and Grace, you'll go first, the babies will go last. That gives you time to adjust."

Anne and Grace shared a nervous glance. Now that the time was upon them, having the alien girl touch what was most precious to them didn't seem like that good of an idea any longer.

"The process will hurt them less than it hurts you," Austin assured them. "Within twenty-four hours you will be functioning at full capacity. In twenty-four hours, we will load the vehicles and head for Cheyenne." He paused to let this sink in. "Are there any questions?"

Bruno raised his hand and stood up. "Are you absolutely sure about these old people, these Elders, keeping their word?"

Using English, Austin repeated Bruno's question to the others and then addressed him in German. "No, I'm not, but you can't stay here. You'll die. That much I do know."

Bruno scowled and replied, "Maybe dying ain't so bad Mr. Reynolds. I knew a man to hide from death, only to die a death ten times worse once it caught up to him again. Some things are worse than death, much worse. Sometimes you have to know when to say when." Having felt he said his peace, Bruno nodded to Austin and sat down, scowl in place.

Austin tilted his head in return, thankful to be the only one other than Ada and Kyle, who understood Bruno. It wouldn't do well to stir up the others with talk of death.

31 FINAL DEPARTURE

Their caravan cruised down the highway heading for Cheyenne. It was made up of an odd assortment of vehicles, ranging from a moving van to a stretch Hummer with tinted windows, spinner rims that sparkled and a license plate that read BDAWG. The contents of the moving van exceeded the allowable weight limits causing the wheel well to rub against the tire whenever they hit a dip in the road.

BDAWG's Hummer took the lead, with Ed driving and Jenny riding shotgun. Ryan, Anne, Grace and the three babies sat in back. Behind them, Kyle drove his black diesel pick-up truck, with McKenna in the passenger seat and Ada, Bruno and Josie in the back. McKenna had talked nonstop since leaving. The thoughts running through her head were too many and too interesting not to share. No one minded, since they could listen or tune her out. They had their own thoughts to process. Another stretch Hummer, this one driven by Jeremy, was second to last in line. This one had tinted windows, but no bling or personalized plates. Sue, Jane, Barbara, Zoe and German rode in the back. Bringing up the rear was a thirty-foot-long moving truck with Zack at the helm, Colin shotgun and Charlie sandwiched in the middle. Colin had fussed over being separated from his dog, but Charlie cajoled him into letting German ride in the Hummer.

Looking around, taking in the landscape, listening to the sound of the van's engine, Zack felt a little bit like Neo in *The Matrix*. Neo at the precise moment he realized he was 'the one'. Zack couldn't see ones and zeros, but he could see a hell of lot more than he had twenty-four hours ago. All things fuzzy suddenly become clear. He was blind and now he could see. He found himself singing *Amazing Grace* and even remembered all of the versus, not just the first. Colin and Charlie joined in and for the next few miles they sang old church hymns.

Being new and improved certainly had its advantages. Before leaving, Zack had dug through his things for an old notebook. Inside was a math equation one of his college professors had given him. It had been his nemesis for years, yet when he looked at the numbers this time, the solution popped off the pages. If only Madison had lived to experience it with him. He gave a little laugh. Who was he kidding? Madison never would have allowed Eve to touch her, let alone change her DNA. Sedation would have been the only way. Zack sighed, his smile fading away. He wondered if he'd ever stop missing her. Charlie commented about being able to feel the road's camber and Zack moved Madison to the back of his mind.

All too soon the sign for Cheyenne came into view. In each vehicle, as awareness set in, so did the silence. They approached the entrance tunnel with trepidation, as well as nervous excitement. This was it. They were going to travel through a space portal. They were going to a new planet. They were starting over with new people from all over the globe. They didn't wonder over anything more than the basics. They didn't think about exactly how or when the Elders would want to collect their blood. Austin had explained it wouldn't be any more painful than giving to a blood bank and to think of it in the same manner. Donated blood was used to save lives, the same as their blood might one day save the Elders from dying.

Zack followed the caravan into the parking lot. The others found parking spaces, while he looped around the lot, coming back to face the tunnel.

"Where are we supposed to meet them?" Colin asked.

"Right here. In the parking lot," Zack replied, looking around for signs of Eve or Austin. "They should already be here."

"Maybe they're inside."

"Yeah maybe," Zack replied. "I'm gonna go see, you two stay put."

"You're not the boss of me," Colin smarted back.

Zack swung his head around to look at his brother. "You know? There's no fixin' stupid. Not even Eve could improve that dimwitted brain of yours."

"Ha. Ha. Guess she couldn't make you less of an asshole either."

Charlie grabbed Colin's arm about to implore him to quit goofing around when she spotted Eve and Austin walking toward them. "Look. There they are. Let me out." She nudged Colin toward the door. He jumped out and Charlie pushed passed him. She ran over to Eve, who hugged her hello.

"What's that about?" Zack asked.

"No idea," Colin replied, shaking his head. Charlie's relationship with Eve baffled everyone, but no one more so than Colin. Seeing them act that way made him nervous, but he wasn't about to share his concerns with Zack. He shrugged and climbed back into the cab. "Where's Roxanne?"

"At the bunker."

"You ever notice she's never around when Eve's is?"

Zack looked out the window, pretending to semi-ignore his brother. "Never noticed that."

Austin walked around to the driver's door and waited for Zack to roll down the window. "You guys ready?"

"I guess. I mean who can answer that considering the circumstances."

"You'll do fine Zack. I have total confidence in you. And I'll be around more than you think. Don't worry man. You got this."

"If you say so big guy. But given the choice between this and growing pot, I'd take Mary J. Hey is there any on..."

"Don't even think about it man."

Zack looked offended, then disappointed before he smiled and assured Austin he was only kidding. Although, in the back of his mind he did wonder what type of plants might be available, but from a medicinal aspect rather than recreational.

Everyone gathered at the entrance to the tunnel. Zack handed out flashlights, while Austin gave last minute instructions.

"Eve will take care of everyone's personal belongings, so leave your things here." A few concerned looks were exchanged and murmurs about this. "Your things will be there before you are," he assured them. "So, follow me."

They proceeded through the tunnel and on into the tomb like facility. The girls didn't think about their days in captivity or General Roth. Charlie had a fleeting thought of Chase and nothing more. The mood was light, as if they were all under a protective shield, one that kept the bad memories at bay. Only Austin noticed the dog's behavior. German turned around several times, stopping to look back down the passage, ears alert, nostrils twitching. Each time German stopped, Josie waited on him. The hair on her back would rise, only falling back in place once German returned to her side. Under normal circumstances, Austin would have chalked the dog's behavior up to not liking the unfamiliar place. This wasn't a normal situation. Austin opened an ear to anything moving behind or lurking ahead but sensed nothing and pressed on. Eventually they arrived in the exterior room to the portal. Austin opened the door and stepped back allowing everyone in, taking one last look down the passage before following behind them.

After the expected oohing and ahhing subsided, and Austin answered several questions, they were ready to begin their journey. Zack and Jeremy would go in the first pod. Before climbing in, Jeremy gave his daughter a kiss good-bye and hugged Grace. Zack and Austin stood facing each other, neither knowing how to say good-bye.

"I hate long good-byes," Zack finally said, feeling like they were breaking up.

"Me too man," Austin said, and then pulled Zack into a bear hug. Stepping back, Austin took a deep breath. "I'll see you soon my friend."

Zack looked doubtful, but replied, "I hope so big guy. I hope so." With nothing more to say, at least not out loud, Zack climbed into the pod. Austin closed the lid and sent them on their way.

They were followed by Anne, Zoe and the twins. Grace, Gisela and Charlie were third in line, with the others following in twos. Last to go was Kyle and German. It took both Kyle and Austin to strap the unwilling dog into the pod seat. Once he was secured, it was Kyle's turn to climb in.

Turning to Austin, Kyle said, "So these have been, by far, the strangest weeks of my life, but in a good way. I mean, having Grace and the baby and, well, it felt like being home again. I don't know if that makes sense." He paused, uncertain of what he wanted to say, but knowing he wanted to say something. "I'll never be able to repay you for what you've done. The sacrifices you've made for us. Thank you." He held out his hand to Austin.

Austin stared at his brother's hand for a long time before taking it in his own. He looked Kyle in the eyes. "I'm glad you found your way to us. That we met, and I got to know you. Another time, another place, things would have been different." Austin gave Kyle a hug. "Stay safe…my brother," he said, too low for Kyle to hear the last part. Austin stepped back allowing Kyle to climb in the pod.

"Until we meet again," Austin said, lowering the lid, his heart heavy.

Once Kyle was strapped in, he gave the thumbs up. Austin waved and stepped back. The lights blazed, the pod raced down the track and into the portal. He waited several minutes to see if anyone returned, but soon the portal turned dark, the lights faded to off and the system shut down. It was done, they were gone. Austin closed his eyes and traveled to Paru with them. His lips spread into a smile. A smile of relief, knowing they'd arrived safely, and the Elders were being true to their word.

* * *

As the group had made their way through the dark narrow passage and into the portal room, Eve had taken care of their personal belongings. All of their things, as they remembered them, were already waiting on Paru. Their clothes, toothbrushes, books, everything would look and feel the same. Journals would have the same words and dates, toothpaste tubes the same squeeze marks, clothes missing the same buttons. Nothing would indicate they were not the originals. In Eve's mind, it was a small deception to replace their things with exact duplicates. Besides, in time those material things would become less and less important.

Eve closed her eyes and breathed in deep, smelling the various scents of blood, feeling the gnawing hunger growing more persistent. The past thirty-six hours had pushed her limits. Although improving the human's DNA turned out as she'd foreseen, the future of mankind remained unclear, which was disturbing, and even more so now that she felt responsible for their survival. The scars from Agra's deception pervaded deep into her very being, dictated her thoughts and decisions. Austin didn't trust the Elders. She didn't trust them either and felt justified in this mistrust. For now, though, going to Paru was the best option. Other planets existed where the humans could survive, maybe even flourish, but they would do so without help or protection. The small boost Eve had given them through their DNA change was not enough against that which existed in the universes beyond this one.

Eve opened her eyes as Austin emerged from the tunnel. Each time she looked upon him her body tensed, as if she'd suddenly been thrown in a tug-of-war with a powerful adversary. They were connected now. He with her blood, she with his. Before long the pulling sensation would vanish, their blood would be the same. The only way to break the connection would be through death. It was in this knowledge she found comfort, for though she no longer heard Caleb's thoughts, she knew he was alive. If he'd died, the piece of him that existed inside of her would have also died.

"I brought you something." Austin held up two small gray water bladders.

She took one, screwed off the cap and sniffed. "Your General Roth used to bring the very same to me." She tilted the bag to her lips and took a long drink. "He would wait days to bring one. Sometimes he spiked the blood with drugs. He spent hours mixing up concoctions, thinking of how he might put me to sleep." She finished the last drop and took the second, again sniffing before drinking. "His brain was exceptional, but, as with all humans, it was governed by emotion, not logic. Had he taken the time to think it through, he would have realized much sooner the impossibility of his quest." With that she finished the second bladder in one gulp.

"There's enough stored in the coolers to last at least three years, maybe longer if we're conservative," Austin said, trying to not sound concerned. Stored blood served its purpose, but not as a substitute for fresh. "We should be going," Austin said, anxious to get started, and not wanting to think about what the distant future might have in store for them. Other matters, more pressing matters, needed their attention. Although he was certain they could convince the remaining survivors to leave, traveling around the globe would take time. And time was a fickle thing on Paru, sometimes slow, sometimes fast, and always unpredictable. Vazya might be the same.

First things first, which meant Eve teaching him to move through space. A task requiring more skill and practice than mind jumping. The concept seemed simple enough, as she'd explained it. The displacement and replacement of energy, of all the particles around and in him. She'd no doubt he'd master this task with ease as he did each challenge presented to him since he was a boy. After a few attempts, and less failures, he did as she expected. He was able to harness energy, move within that energy without losing himself along the way. It was much like traveling on highways of moving particles, millions upon millions of them. After his fifth successful trip, Austin asked Eve about going to Vazya.

"We will go as soon as the humans are secure on Paru," she replied. "Don't you want to make sure your people are safe?" Our people, she added in thought.

"Yes of course. I only wanted to see it. To maybe…" He didn't finish, but she knew he too thought of their son.

Eve smiled, he had much to learn of his abilities. "You can see it anytime you wish, but with that comes risk of alerting Agra. I think it best if we don't go until we have finished here."

Austin nodded. She was right. He'd only wanted to get an idea of what they were up against. How many Svan were there? What other species would they have to deal with? What was the lay out of the terrain? He'd never went into a mission without doing basic recon first and didn't expect to handle this one any different. However, more than any of those things, he wanted to be closer to his son, on the off chance he might be able to hear him, to speak to him.

"Where would you like to start?" Eve asked, sensing his restlessness, his need to have every detail mapped out and under control.

"You said pockets of people were scattered to all corners?" She nodded. "We should start in China and work our way around the globe. It's the fastest route." Eve nodded again.

"Let's go." He took her hand, pulling her close. The snow stirred about at their feet, funneling upwards and bursting outward. Before the flakes settled back to the ground, the pair had touched down on Chinese soil.

32 PARU

Six Months Later

Zack sat on the front porch of the place he, Colin and his newborn daughter Madison now called home. A simple one-story white adobe structure, with a slanted roof and a covered porch. Nothing fancy to look at, that was for sure. The houses that lined both sides of the street and the next were all the same, as were the seven hundred and eighty houses that made up the town. Etched into his door was a symbol representing the number one. Ed and family, who lived to Zack's right, had a symbol representing the number two. Kyle, Ada and McKenna were number three, and so on. All of the bunker group lived in this neighborhood on the same side of the street.

Across from the Londergan's, resided Mr. and Mrs. Takaki, a thirtyish aged couple from Japan. Two Korean brothers lived with them, ages twelve and fourteen. No relation to the couple, but Mrs. Takaki never had children and the boys were orphaned. The Takaki's weren't the only mixed family living on Paru. Many adults who'd lost children or wanted children, were eager to adopt those who'd lost parents. No one cared about race. Zack had been surprised at the number of children who survived. He'd expected the count to be much lower, but it wasn't low and continued to rise. Apparently after arriving on Paru, everyone wanted to make up for lost time. He knew of fifteen women who were pregnant and suspected more would be before the end of the year when the population control rule went into effect.

The neighborhoods were divided by streets made of sand colored stones of all shapes and sizes. Not rough cobble stones, but an even surface, like unpolished granite. Trees resembling palms lined the street on both sides. In the center of town was a community center that also served as the town hall. A few blocks further, was the medical facility surrounded by a beautiful park. All things needed and none customary. On the outskirts were the farms where their food was cultivated. The farms were overseen by the Svan. A sight to behold in itself and one that always made Zack think of Dorothy in *The Wizard of Oz*. No sir, they were most definitely not in Kansas any longer.

Zack stood up and stretched. He glanced toward the end of the street, as he did every day, making sure the portal was still floating in mid-air. The last group of survivors had arrived two weeks prior. One of them had handed Zack a note from Austin. On it he'd scribbled *May sixteenth*. That was it, May sixteenth. This date held no special meaning that he knew, other than it had already past, but that's what the note had said. Maybe Paru was ahead of Earth by a month, being that June sixteenth was less than two weeks away. In any case, Zack planned to be planted on his porch on June sixteenth. Just in case something happened, or his friend decided to drop in for an overdue visit, a long overdue visit.

In the meantime, he had three deliveries to make today. Anita Chavez, Gertrude Heinrich, and Jaclyn Froste. All three were having girls. Zack went inside to grab his uniform and to check on Madison. Jenny would be over soon to watch her while he went off to do doctor things. Right on queue he heard the knock on the door and went to let Jenny in.

"How's my baby girl today?" Jenny asked when Zack opened the door.

"Sweet as a Georgia peach."

"You working a twelve?"

"Probably. There are several deliveries due and they all requested me." He was one of only four doctors on Paru, along with twenty-seven qualified staff who performed various medical type duties and another thirty or so floaters who came and went as needed or as they pleased.

"Imagine that," Jenny said with a knowing smile. "And the nurses?"

Zack shook his head and raised his hands. "I'm a dad now. Gotta be responsible. No time to play."

"Well don't become too grown-up." She kissed him on the cheek and sent him on his way.

The facility was about a mile away or fifteen minutes on foot. On foot happened to be the only mode of travel allowed, by Adita rule. Zack didn't mind the walk, it gave him time to think, to enjoy the peace and quiet. As he walked, he couldn't help marveling over his surroundings. Not because they were grandiose, quite the opposite. The house designs were simple and pleasing to the eye, but all the same. Aside from the numbered door, each house looked exactly like the next. Same door, same porch, even the same number of walking stones leading to the same number of steps. On the inside, the floor plans were exactly the same, two to three bedrooms, two bathrooms, a common area and a kitchen. He could walk in any house and know, unerringly, where each was located.

He certainly had to give props to the Elders. When he'd opened the pod door, he'd expected to be sitting in the middle of nowhere, possibly about to be plowed down by prehistoric looking beasts, and he couldn't have been more surprised. Yes sir. They'd seen to everything. Their concerns over not having all the necessary comforts vanquished upon entering their new homes. Indoor plumbing, lights, refrigerators; the homes were fully equipped. He'd been shocked to hell and back when he found out the town ran a system similar to what he'd designed for the bunker. The Elders had taken to modifying the design with a few minor improvements. *But of course*, Zack remembered thinking when they told him. *Yes sir*, he repeated to himself one more time. The Elders had taken care of everything. Not one detail had been overlooked. A nervous quiver threatened, but he straightened his spine and shrugged it away. Life was as good or good enough and he didn't want to rock the boat by thinking things over too much.

Sattya and two Svan, had been the welcoming committee. Zack and the others didn't know it then, but that little reception would be the one and only time an Elder would step foot in their town. And although the Svan went through great measures to not frighten anyone, they were daunting creatures none the less. Over the weeks he'd become accustomed to seeing them patrolling on the edge of the town and on occasion walking the streets at night. It was a bit of a mind fuck trying to grapple with the fact the very species responsible for wiping out almost the entire human race, now lived amongst them as their protectors. Eve had tried to explain by saying they had only been following orders. Did that make it ok? He didn't think so. Did that excuse work for the Nazi war criminals? Not in his book. Should it work for the Svan? No, not really, but at least for now they were more interested in protecting humans, than ripping them apart. Zack tried not to think about the morality of it all. Besides, what was he going to do? Wage war against a superior being? He thought not.

The medical facility was up ahead. He could see it now, towering over the treetops. Many discussions centered around this building and for various reasons, some more than others and one more than all. At fifteen stories, it was the tallest structure in town, the equipment was the most advanced anyone had ever seen. The facility was top notch, which made learning his job easy. These were topics covered repeatedly, exhaustively, but were not the *top* topic. Not the utmost topic, the one rousing people's curiosity, the one raising their anxiety levels. This subject matter had to do with what took place on the top three floors of the medical building. On these floors was where they came to give blood, they as in the humans. All day long, every day of the week, except the last Sunday of the month.

Each day of the week groups of people, ages five and up, came to the medical facility to donate. This part of their deal weighed heavy on his mind. He'd expected to give samples every couple of months, not every damn day. And after one-week Zack was floored by the discovery that every human on Paru was O negative. So the question of what the Elders were doing with the donations kept him awake, kept feeding that nervous feeling that something wasn't quite right in Paruville.

At the end of each week, on Sunday afternoon, the same two Svan would collect the samples. Zack being Zack had managed to befriend the collectors, Shaud and Jy, who he convinced to teach him to speak Svan. Zack always worked the weekend shifts, being he was the only non-religious doctor on staff. That the others chose to continue worshipping their gods baffled him, but who was he to question, to judge. Blind faith was something he'd been born without and would probably never understand, despite the numerous philosophical conversations he and Ed had on the subject of religion and in more particular, of the Almighty.

Zack stopped to chat with Jeremy, who worked part time at the facility. Since everything in Paruville was free, no one had to work, but the peculiar thing being, everyone wanted to work. Everyone wanted to be busy, to feel important, to feel needed, and to once again have a purpose in life. Part of the desire to work stemmed from the need to have a return to normality. For those who weren't part of the original bunker group, the test subjects as Zack referred to their group, coping with this new reality turned out to be more difficult than expected. He made a mental note to discuss this with Austin when he arrived, thinking perhaps Eve could work her magic on those who needed it the most.

Zack greeted Riri, the young nurse who usually assisted him in the deliveries. Once upon a time she'd been a pop music singer. She was a native of Brazil, in her mid-twenties, gorgeous, full of spunk and had a crush on Zack. The old Zack, the pre-Madison Zack, would have already had her in and out of his bed, but those days were well behind him. He was happy to have her on staff and that was as far as his feelings went. The patients liked her, which was a plus. When she worked the night shift, they were treated to her singing as she walked/performed her rounds. He guessed she missed the life. At least on Paru she didn't have to worry about paparazzi stalkers. But maybe she missed them as well. Zack came to a closed door and switched into doctor mode before knocking and entering the room. "Good morning Mrs. Chavez. Mr. Chavez. How are we feeling today?" he asked, using impeccable Spanish.

* * *

In the glass room on top of the jungle, Sattya sat alone at the table, his gaze directed out toward the ocean, his mind in a distant place. Matri entered and sat across from Sattya. She knew where he'd gone and why. The why being the reason for the rigidity in her posture. She waited in silence for his return. After a few minutes Sattya blinked and turned to Matri, his expression solemn.

"Eve has made her choice," he said.

Matri dipped her head down and then up in a slow nod. "And the captain?"

"He will follow Eve wherever she leads him."

"I think you underestimate him dear."

"While his human side is in control, I do not think there's risk he will surprise us."

"And of our word given to the humans?"

"Our word is to honor the Adita creed, no other promise or covenant can come before this. We must do the right thing for us Matri. The Elders demand it. Our people demand it. Our future is dependent on it."

"Are we doing the right thing?" she challenged. "What if we're wrong?"

"We aren't wrong. We must protect our way of life--"

"By all and any means necessary," she finished for him. "Yes, I am quite familiar with the Adita laws. I helped write them. But laws can be changed. Are we not more advanced? Are we so backward that we can't change antediluvian rules?"

"You know it's not that simple." He walked over to her, placing a hand on her shoulder. "What can I say that will ease your mind? Tell me and I will say it."

Matri laid her hand over his. "Say you will find another way." She turned in her chair and looked up at him. "Can you say that to me? If you can and you speak with truth, my mind will be at ease."

Sattya looked down into her face but said nothing for he could not say it in truth. Matri brushed his hand away, stood up, and walked over to the window. If by her beckoning, storm clouds thick and ominous formed on the horizon. Bolts of lightning crisscrossed the sky, electrifying the atmosphere.

"There's a storm coming Sattya. And this time I don't think the Elders will be able to control the outcome." Sattya reached for her hand, but she pulled away. "We should allow the council more time to debate the merits of such a tremendous endeavor as war."

"Wars can't be fought in comfort. They are not meant for the thoughts and meanderings of scholars as such that fill our council. If one is to wage war, then one must do so, and do so with passion and the commitment to dominate your enemy. Not the desire to win, no. Anyone can desire things. Humans desire things. Victory is not achieved by desires or wishes or whims. Sitting about in comfort, discussing the merits of war has no place in fighting a war. Wars are fought on the battle field. You cannot have one foot in and one out. You must commit both feet. You must drink the blood of your enemy to claim victory."

"War is not a brutish battle alone, fought by savages, as you make it sound," Matri argued.

"Ah, but you are wrong!" he exclaimed. "War is precisely brutal and those savages fighting are brutes in mind and body. But superb intelligence also guides the savage warrior, and the wisdoms they follow are not in the nature of those belonging to the meek and mild mannered. To those intellects who debate war while maintaining their own personal comfort. Warriors are brutally intelligent, not comfortably wise. Do you understand the difference?"

"I do not need a lesson on war nor on words from you. I understand quite well how wars are won."

"A war of words my dear is quite different than a war of power and brutality. Words can be debated, heatedly even while maintaining one's contented position, in the comfort of a chair or your lover's arms," he paused and Matri stiffened. "Don't bristle love. I know of your desires and do not hold blame. It was I who failed you. I hold no ill will against those who stepped in to do that which I have not. No dear, your desires of the flesh do not nibble away at my mind, they do not advise of caution, or warn of being wary."

"What of my thoughts causes you caution or otherwise to think you need to be wary?"

"Your loyalties love. Do they sway back and forth or are they steady and sure?"

Matri more than bristled at this comment, for it bothered her more than him admitting he didn't care that she found another's embrace preferable to his. Her loyalties had never been in question and certainly not by Sattya. "My loyalties do not sway in the least. I have always been loyal to the Adita creed and always will." Matri walked to the door and turned to face Sattya. "Be careful in your pursuits dear, for as comfort will, blindness can cripple the greatest of men." She left him alone with his thoughts.

Sattya crossed his arms and turned back to the windows. Storms were always brewing, wars were always being waged, and sacrifices were always required. This was part of life. Matri had been too long away from the battle. The thrill of victory long forgotten, but not for him, for him the sweet taste lingered on, the longing deep in his spirit. Soon it would be the Adita's time to rise, to conquer, to once again dominate the universes. In less than a fortnight the necessary steps would be taken, those actions that would guarantee their victory. Sattya glanced out to the horizon. The storm continued to brew, the clouds turning more sinister, the lightning's long tentacles stretched out across the sky. For a split second, a minuscule shred of doubt flitted by. He waved his hand in front of his face as if swatting at a pesky insect. Life was and always would be about endurance, about power struggles, about conquering one's enemy. He knew this. The Elders knew this. Soon Eve would know and understand the full implications of their edict. The wheels of this colossal machine had been set into motion long before the Elders had arrived at their decision and, even if he'd entertained the thought, he was powerless to stop the machine now.

Behind him Pala and two other Svan entered the room. Sattya turned to them and said, "It is time."

"Do you want them all?" Pala asked.

"Leave the good doctor and his daughter behind for now."

"As you wish." Pala nodded to Sattya and they left the room.

EXCERPT FROM LIGHT OF EVE (PART III)

June Sixteenth

Colin kissed Charlie goodbye, jumped off the porch and headed down the street toward his house. He turned, waved goodbye and she blew him a kiss. He almost went back to get the real thing, but he'd promised Zack a hot breakfast and kept walking. A look of disgust crossed his face thinking about his brother. Since moving to Paru, Zack had become domesticated and Colin had about all he could take. Zack as his brother was hard to live with at times, but Zack acting like his parent was downright excruciating almost all the time. At least the medical facility and the other doctors kept Zack busy. They offered a captive audience that his brother could bend and twist words with, which in turn allowed Colin peace for ten to twelve hours each day.

A strong breeze blew a few leaves down the street and onto the lawns. Colin stared at the leaves. When life was normal, he'd argue with his mom over whose turn it was to mow the lawn or rake the leaves. He'd give anything for a rake now and happily put it to use, but alas those things weren't needed on Paru. The Elders seemed to take care of everything. Tomorrow the leaves would be gone. Poof! Like a magic trick. Colin paused at the walkway to his house and glanced down the street towards the portal. He wondered, and not for the first time, what would happen if he dove into the murky center. The wind gusted again, this time accompanied by a rumble of thunder. He looked to the sky but saw no clouds.

"Must be out on the ocean," he said out loud, but not too loud. He didn't care what anyone else thought about Paru, he thought the place was creepy.

A large object flying high above cast a shadow over the ground, blocking out the sun for a moment. Colin shielded his eyes but couldn't find the culprit. He shrugged and went inside to make breakfast.

* * *

Across town, Zack handed Cathy Fox a bouncing baby girl. Gretchen Fox was the fifth girl delivered in the past week and fifty-second since they'd arrived on Paru. Zack wondered what the odds were of not having one boy after fifty-two deliveries? Three more babies were due at the end of the week, all to be girls. The facts defied reason, and after discussing with the other doctors, they'd decided to run tests. Which tests to run? They hadn't any idea. The question remained as to who they would even test; the children, the parents or the drinking water or maybe all three.

They could test every variable under the sun and still wouldn't find the answers they sought. Zack knew this. The others knew it. Answers weren't theirs to have, only questions and, by unspoken rule, it was best if they weren't too inquisitive. Zack followed several other self-imposed rules in the new world, one of those being always err on the side of caution when it came to the Adita. He'd never say outright that he didn't trust them, and rarely would he think it in those exact terms, but he always kept it in his back pocket. *Just like dear old dad, eh Zacky?*

Zack thought to argue with himself and stopped. He hated to admit it, but there had been times over the past few years when advice from the old bastard came in handy, probably saved his life a time or two. Zack smiled. Madison could have given Bobby Londergan a run for his money, that was for certain. A big wave of pain smashed into him thinking her name.

"Rule number one, don't think about her."

"Did you say something Doctor?"

Zack turned to greet Ri, one of the resident nurses. "No. I was... nothing, talking to myself. You do that when you get old or smoke too much dope or both."

"Well I don't know about the dope, but you are not old," Ri said, smiling and leaning forward.

Zack smiled at her efforts to entice him, and in another time or place, he would have already slept with her and most likely every other female working at the hospital. Those days were far removed from where he was now. Madison might be dead, but he felt her watching him and that was enough to keep him on the straight and narrow.

After giving instructions to Ri, he headed for the exit. Jenny would be dropping off his daughter in a couple of hours and, if Colin held true to his word, a hot breakfast would be waiting for him. A loud clap of thunder greeted him as he opened the hospital door. He looked for rain clouds, but the sky was clear. Let it rain, he thought. Today was going to be a good day and not even torrential rain could dampen his spirits. With the thought of possibly seeing his friend again, Zack hurried home.

* * *

Colin spooned another lump of the green leafy goop onto Zack's plate and crinkled his nose. Unlike his brother, Colin hadn't acquired a taste for the food offered on Paru. Being forced to become a vegetarian ranked at the top of his list of things he hated in Paru. They were only allowed to eat meat on the last day of the month. On the first 'day of meat', he'd been stoked thinking they were going to have thick juicy steaks. Not so. Not so. Not that the meat served tasted bad, but the flavor was more like fish and nowhere near beef.

"What are you so excited about this morning? Did you deliver another baby?" Colin asked, rolling his eyes.

"I'm not excited and I delivered three. You should try doing something constructive with your time. Something other than hanging out at Charlie's all day and night." Zack gave him a reproachful stare.

"And exactly what would that be?" Colin set the pan down hard enough to startle German and Josie who were snoozing under the table. "There's no school, no gym, no slopes. What the hell am I supposed to do here? Be your housewife? Your babysitter?"

Zack sat back from the table. "Wow. Aren't you acting like a spoiled little shit?"

"Save your self-righteous I'm better than everyone bullshit speech. I don't want to hear it. Again."

"You need to hear it. And you need to listen to it. You aren't special Colin. We're all in this together. Stop thinking about yourself all the god damned time."

"I don't need you telling me what to do. I'm nineteen not nine. I'm not your fucking little brother anymore."

"You act like your nine. And you'll always be my little twerp brother."

"You know what? Screw you." Colin threw the pan into the sink and stormed out, slamming the front door. German ran after him and stood at the door whining.

"Come here, boy." Zack held out a scrap of food, but the dog ignored him. He didn't like being a vegetarian either.

Zack picked at his food, having lost his appetite. Things shouldn't be like this between them, fighting all the time. Not that they hadn't fought before coming to Paru, but never like this and Zack didn't know what to do. Bringing the screaming bundles of joy into the world was the easy part of his new life, the part he did well. He wasn't equipped for the parenting part and if being honest, he'd say he sucked at it. Sometimes he felt Colin hated him. How in the hell was he going to raise his daughter when he couldn't control a nineteen-year-old?

Maybe Jenny could give him advice. The more he thought about this the better he felt. Jenny always offered good sound advice. She'd know how to handle Colin's temper tantrums. Feeling better about Colin, Zack took notice of German and Josie, both were sitting facing the door, ears perked straight and tall, turning in every direction. A 'holy shit' clap of thunder shook the house, startling him and the dogs. Josie ran for cover in the back bedroom, while German paced back and forth in front of the door.

"What's wrong with you?"

German ran to Zack, barked loud and sharp, and ran back to the door. He pawed at the knob and again barked. Zack walked over to the door and looked outside. He glanced up and down the street but saw nothing out of the ordinary. Meanwhile German continued to paw at the door, whining for Zack to open and let him out.

"Easy German, take it easy. There's nothing out there."

Zack's eyes came to rest on the portal. The murky inside shimmered in the sunlight, but something about that shimmer appeared off. He absently turned the knob, unlatching the door from the jam and giving German the opportunity he needed. German charged through the door knocking Zack off balance. Zack ran out on the porch after him but to no avail. The dog was halfway down the street, racing towards Charlie's house. Zack ran after him, an uneasy feeling settling in his stomach.

Up ahead on Charlie's porch German jumped and pawed at her front door like a rabid crazed beast. When neither Charlie nor Colin came to investigate, the unease in Zack's stomach hardened and pushed a rancid taste up into his throat. He swallowed hard to keep the lump down, to calm his nerves, which were about to assail his senses like a disturbed hornet's nest. German barked and jumped at the door again. He turned and snarled upon seeing Zack walking up the porch steps.

"Easy boy. It's just me." Zack stepped back to the bottom step. German advanced towards him, growling and drooling, eyes blazing and keen on him. Zack stood still, almost paralyzed thinking his dog might try to kill him. He risked a glance at German's face. The dog still bared his teeth, but he wasn't looking at Zack, his eyes were locked on something across the street. Zack took a chance and glanced over his shoulder. The street was empty. The street was quiet, too quiet. Zack turned all the way around, looked up and down the street, no longer worried about German pouncing on him. Bigger and badder things thrived on Paru. This last thought shocked him out of his trance and he bolted up the steps, yanking open the door.

"Charlie! Colin!" Zack ran through the house yelling their names, opening and closing doors like a madman. No one answered.

A Note from the author:

Thank you for reading Eve of Man. I hope you enjoyed it. I'm happy to announce, the third installation, Light of Eve, is now available on Amazon.

Best,
Anne Ferretti

Connect with me:
Friend at: https://www.facebook.com/pages/Anne-Ferretti/700972973254463
Follow at: http://www.pinterest.com/honeylulu13/the-harvest
Supporter of: http://bestfriends.org/Home.aspx